WHO KILLED WHAT'S-HER-NAME?

This Large Print Book carries the
Seal of Approval of N.A.V.H.

WHO KILLED WHAT'S-HER-NAME?

Elizabeth Daniels Squire

G.K. Hall & Co. • Thorndike, Maine

Published in 1999 by arrangement with
Luna Carne-Ross Literary Agency.

G.K. Hall Large Print Paperback Series.

The text of this Large Print edition is unabridged.
Other aspects of the book may vary from the original edition.

Set in 16 pt. Plantin by Rick Gundberg.

Printed in the United States on permanent paper.

Library of Congress Cataloging in Publication Data

Squire, Elizabeth Daniels.
   Who killed what's-her-name? / Elizabeth Daniels Squire.
LT-M   p. cm.
   ISBN 0-7838-8497-4 (lg. print : hc : alk. paper)
   1. Large type books. I. Title.
  [PS3569.Q43W48 1999]
   813′.54—dc21
                                                98-50793

ACKNOWLEDGMENTS:

A thousand thanks to all those who helped create this book — people who are responsible for what I did right but, if something is wrong, can blame Peaches Dann, who didn't remember exactly what happened. These people include:

— Topeka (formerly Asheville) Police Chief Gerald Beavers, Asheville Officer Luke Bigelow, and volunteer Lewright B. Mann of the Citizens Police Academy.

— Larry McDonald, Teresa Leonard, and the rest of the *News & Observer* crew, who showed me how newspaper library computers network.

— Robert E. Bohm of the Moultrie Tavern in Charleston, S.C., who suggested using Confederate belt plates as a plot device and put me onto Rick Plougher of the Museum of the Confederacy in Richmond. Rick, in turn, put me in touch with Steven Mullinax, author of *Confederate Buckles and Plates* (O'Donnell). Thanks to

Robert Bohm also for use of the Moultrie Tavern for some local color (and to Christoffer Don Hedberg for photographing it for me).

— Cleves Smith of Goldsboro, N.C., for agreeing to let me "lift" features of her unusual home to use as Mary's house herein.

— Ann Street Lautz of the Gibbes Museum of Art in Charleston, for information on miniature portraits — of which the museum has a magnificent collection.

— Larry Biggers of Charlotte, for advice on Pop's investment strategy (as well as some other advice I have found profitable over the years).

— Dean Justice, my locksmith neighbor, who told me what to do when my car ignition key wouldn't work (and gave me a plot turn); Walter Brank, for helping me rig up some decidedly non-code, potentially lethal (but fortunately fictional) electric circuitry; librarians at the Asheville-Buncombe Library system, for ongoing help; and the Rick Boyer Book Celebration & Encouragement Society, for how-to-find-out tips.

— Saravette Trotter, Rena James, and Katie Farquharson, for mnemonic tips.

— Melinda Metz, my editor at Berkley, and

Luna Carne-Ross, my agent, for valuable suggestions, mnemonic and otherwise.

— My writing group — P. D. Parris, Dershie McDevitt, Virginia Sampson, Florence Wallin, Geraldine Powell, and Margaret-Love Denman — for inspiration, suggestions, encouragement, and more mnemonic tips.

— Helen Hall Drew, my long-time friend and one-time roommate at Ashley Hall, for a few choicely outrageous examples of mnemonic mistakes, and a few tricks.

— Elizabeth Silver Cheshire, my cousin and favorite forgetting-expert, who is a whiz at chapter headings for the inner book in this novel, and who supplied some of its best ideas.

— My husband, Chick, for helping me to survive without a memory for forty-odd years, and my lyricist-son, Worth, for labeling Peaches "the absent-minded detective."

And if I've forgotten anybody, well . . . at least they'll know it's not on purpose!

CHAPTER
1

FRIDAY MORNING, MAY 24

When I began to write my book, *How to Survive Without a Memory*, it frankly never occurred to me to take that word "survive" literally, as in "stay alive." I didn't plan a chapter on memory and life and death.

I'm writing the book for my friends. I'm fifty-five. Some of them are older. Occasionally they miss appointments, forget names, lose their glasses, can't think of the right word. And then they panic. "Just relax," I tell them. "I was born without a memory. I know the tricks. So I am going to write a book." I was selling copies before the first chapter stared back at me from my computer.

I wrote in my head as I drove over to see my father. I was taking him a bunch of yellow roses from Cousin Mary — who'd rather weed than come herself. Her roses were early this year. May instead of June. They bloomed in a mason jar in a cardboard box on the floor of the passenger side and filled the car with fresh warm scent.

I hoped Pop would remember that Mary was his niece, his sister Nancy's daughter. My father is eighty-three and has the worst memory in the Western World. He remembers things that never happened, and sometimes he forgets who I am.

My book is not for severe cases like that. But it diverts me from his problems. I wrote down snatches on a pad by my side when I came to red lights. *A pencil is the first weapon against a bad memory*, I thought. So I wrote that down.

I thought about Ted, who wants to marry me. Ted with his great warm laugh. When he forgets a name, he just hoots at himself. *A sense of humor is the best comfort for a bad memory*. I wrote that down, too. So why didn't I marry Ted? Not yet.

I thought about my Aunt Nancy, because she was the true market for my book. She was just ten years older than me, sixty-five, much younger than my father. All her life she'd arrived places on time, put her fingers on the right fact fast, recognized every person she ever met by name instantly, and dressed like a model. She could even change daily from one color-coordinated purse to another and not lose her checkbook or her driver's license. She'd raised three children, humored an alcoholic husband, flourished in business, and never once forgot my birthday.

And then, after she retired as second-in-command of a big insurance company, Aunt

10

Nancy began to forget things. Nothing big by my standards. One day she came by to see my father on her way to a covered-dish supper at her church. Nancy in designer pants, with every blonde-dyed hair so carefully curled. She stashed an English trifle with gobs of whipped cream in Pop's refrigerator to stay cold while she chatted. It was one of my father's good days. And then she drove fifteen miles to the Short Branch Presbyterian Church with no trifle. I was there when she came back to get it, shaking. Furious. How could she do that? And she was the one who'd help run a company three months before.

Well, heck, I told myself, I had the answer to *her* problem. If she'd just calm down and swallow her pride enough to listen. *Swallow pride*. I wrote that down.

If you put something in a refrigerator and have to remember to take it with you when you leave, the trick is to put your car keys in the refrigerator, too. Works every time.

Of course, my father thought that Nancy's lapse was a great joke. Efficient Nancy Caught Short. "That's what you get," he told her, "for not bringing me a trifle, too. Doesn't your church teach you to visit the sick and feed the hungry?" He was still a great tease on his good days.

My father had been brilliant. Sometimes he still was. Brilliant and fun and cruel and wise and childlike. He'd made a fortune in the stock market. Now he was convinced he might not

11

have enough money to stay out of a nursing home, even though his accountant has promised him he has enough to *buy* a nursing home. Or a whole chain of nursing homes. So he held on tight to every dime. He wouldn't have lent a cent to me or Nancy or anybody else, not if the Mob had put out a contract on us for bad debts. But I thanked God my father had a genius for investments. He had the money to stay in his own house and hire people to stay with him around the clock. Suppose I'd had to take care of him myself, twenty-four hours a day? While he insisted on assassins and burglars. Sometimes he thought I was a burglar trying to kill him. I thanked God for the sitters, standing nearby, watching to see how they could help. They handled him with kindness and humor eight hours each. Eight hours was enough.

"Nursing homes smell like pee," he said. "They treat people like vegetables. They won't laugh at a good joke."

Pop held onto the arms of his wheelchair as if he'd fight every inch if we tried to take him to a nursing home. His hands were still strong, even if he looked so frail his clothes hung slack. His hands and his blue eyes could still grab.

Also his voice. "You'd like this joke, Peaches," he said. "For that silly book of yours." My bad memory bothers him. Especially my admitting it. He believes in saving face.

"There were two elderly friends sitting in the park," he said. "One said 'Dearie, I can confide in you because you know how it is to grow old and not to be able to remember. Now, I should know, but you won't mind if I ask: Was it you or your sister who died?' "

On Monday, after Nancy had left, he told that story and made us laugh: me and Elsie, our favorite sitter from the home health service with her cheerful red hair and a wide friendly mouth and bright blue eyes that can find what Pop loses.

But on Tuesday, Pop believed men with knives were on the roof, trying to get in to kill him. I had to talk him down to reality, or rather sing him down with old songs we both knew. Songs he sang to me when I was a child — songs his mother sang to him: Such as "Father, the Tempest Is Blowing" and "Frog Went A-Courtin' " and "My Darling Clementine." Some of them were songs I brought home and taught him, like "Yesterday Upon the Stair, I Saw a Man Who Wasn't There." Old songs, children's songs, funny songs — I guess they took him back to a safer time, and finally he forgot assassins or burglars or whatever on the roof and went to sleep.

So how, I wondered, was he going to be at ten in the morning on this Friday? I came in the back door to get a clue from Anna. No Anna in the kitchen. She must be in back cleaning the bedroom. My father calls Anna his housekeeper. She cleans, cooks, does what has to be done from nine to two, then leaves my father and the

13

sitter cold supper in the fridge. I walked through the dining room to the living room.

There Pop sat in his wheelchair, wearing his too-big plaid flannel shirt, back to me, facing the garden. Elsie, whose shift was seven to three, sat by his side — Elsie, in her no-nonsense man's shirt and jeans. I've never thought of redheads as self-effacing, but Elsie could half vanish when that was tactful, or keep my father amused for hours talking about himself.

Pop sat in the middle of the warm room my mother had arranged before she died. The rug of many colors glowed around him. And beyond him the rich flowered drapes were pulled back to show his million-dollar view: across the blooming garden and then the wide valley to tier after tier of green and blue mountains.

He heard me and jerked around. He'd shrunk. Each time I saw him I had that feeling. Wrinkles deeper, body frailer, but with eyes like lightning bolts.

"It's about time you got here. There's a dead woman out in the pond," my father said. He leaned forward in his wheelchair, eyes sharp, voice firm. Elsie just said "Hi."

I went over and kissed Pop on the forehead. "Mary sent you these yellow roses from her garden," I told him. "Smell how sweet they are. The old-fashioned kind."

"Of course," he said. "They always send flowers for dead people. You know that, Peaches. Mary sent roses when your mother

14

died. Here, Elsie, put these in a vase." He turned his head and looked out the double glass doors to the terrace, and beyond, to the sunny garden where my mother so often knelt, planting flowers. The fishpond was at the end of the garden, about six feet long and three feet wide, but kidney-shaped, shallow, full of fish and water lilies. "Now, please do something about the woman in the pond," he said. "The fish will eat her."

How did such terrible images come to haunt his mind? Fear of death, I thought. He wasn't ready. And yet some days he was his old self, full of jokes and horseplay and anger at the world. Laughing at Nancy, even when she didn't forget a trifle. She came by most days to check on him. "She always complains," he'd said, "because she married an ugly man, and then when she got used to him, he died and left her all alone. Horace was a damned ugly man," he'd said. "He wanted my money. But he died first. Always remember that you don't get money if you die first."

I hugged my father. I could feel his bones through his skin. I could also feel his determination like a pulse of energy. He pushed me away.

Pop's hair was was white and soft and thin like a baby's, but his face was focused, craggy, eyes piercing.

"The woman wants to pull us in the pond," he said. "I saw it on her face." His voice quavered, but stayed strong.

15

I sat down next to him in the small red velvet armchair that was my mother's favorite. I patted his hand. I changed the subject.

"Ted wants me to marry him," I said. "What do you think of that?" I wasn't sure what I thought of it myself. Me, fifty-five, widowed just a year; plus Ted, sixty-two, widower, no kids, except all the ones in his college classes. He'd been a newspaperman, now he taught journalism at the University of North Carolina in Asheville. But I'd invested my love in Roger, who had died so suddenly. I was still grieving.

Talking to my father on one of his bad days was like talking to myself. But sometimes the rhythm of words droning on was soothing to him. And talking to myself helped me. "I'm happy like I am," I said. That was a lie, but only a small lie. "My book keeps me busy." Also, I write funny poems, but I didn't mention those. Pop thinks poetry is a sign of weakness.

"Bring Ted here," my father said. "He'll have the sense to look in the pond."

That got to me. I shivered. Because, of course, that was the way to reassure him. To go see with my own eyes and report back. I stood up. I found that my body didn't want to go. This time, my father was so persistent that I felt myself pulled into his imagining, though I was sure it must *be* imagining. All based on that little goldfish pond.

He reached out and grabbed my arm, and held so tight he hurt me. "Go look in the pond," he commanded. "Go look, but be careful. She wants to pull you in."

I walked over to the glass doors, surprised that my heart beat so. If there was something in the pond, he must have seen it through the doors. He liked to roll his wheelchair over and look out at the garden. At the flowers that reminded him of my mother. There were roses on both sides of the long gravel path to the pond. He'd had that pond made for her, with odd-shaped rocks around the edge, and water lilies growing in it. Not the kind of pond to drown in.

I looked through the glass door, and I thought: *That must be a trick of light that makes me think I see something in the pond.* I wanted to think that. But the thing had too much substance. It could have had a woman's face, or was that water lilies massed into illusion? My heart was beating harder.

I opened the door and went out on the terrace. Slowly past the wicker porch furniture where no one ever sat since my mother died. Hearing my feet crunch on the walk in a normal way. The sun shone over the green mountains as if nothing could be wrong.

Something touched my leg, something alive, startling me. And then I looked down and saw it was only Silk, my mother's half-Siamese cat, who haunted the garden. He let out a desolate yowl. And rubbed himself against me, hair on end.

I began to run. Something was floating in the

pond. I ran between the flower beds on both sides of the gravel walk. Fear made my eyes sharper. I noticed a dandelion loose in my mother's flower bed among the white candytuft in front of the rosebushes. I saw a red bird dart across the pond.

I also began to see that the thing in the pond among the lilies had a human shape. Had arms that floated out from the body, pale hair that floated loose around the head. A blue print dress that clung with wetness. It was a woman, face down. I leaned over, grabbed an arm and pulled at her. The body fought me. By its dead weight. By the way it dangled. By the slipperiness of the wet skin. The dress caught on the rocks at the edge of the pond. She was cold. The arm I pulled, inhuman with cold. I was so cold I was shaking.

My father had been absolutely right. Except this woman couldn't pull me in the pond. She was long dead. I managed to roll her on her back on the gravel.

A dead leaf stuck to her left eye. It took me a moment to realize this wet thing, with streaming hair and a leaf over one eye, was my Aunt Nancy.

And there was something more, something my mind had trouble holding, something my eyes wanted to block out. This dead Nancy was wearing my dress. A dress just like the one I had on, with a print of flying butterflies, except that her dress was blue and mine was green. This poor dead Nancy was almost my twin — as if I had found my own body floating. The victim who discovered the deed.

CHAPTER
2

A FEW MINUTES LATER

"I was right. There *is* a body in the pond," my father crowed. I guess he could see how it was from my face as I ran in the door. "You thought I was a crazy old man!" He rolled his motorized wheelchair towards me. He smiled so his teeth gleamed. "Call the police. Call your Aunt Nancy."

"How can I help?" Elsie asked. She caught the door before it slipped shut behind me, and held it open for Silk, the cat, who immediately vanished behind the couch. Silk did that in times of stress. Elsie had gone dead-white, like someone had pointed a gun at her. But she was still trying to help.

"Sit down. Be quiet and write your alibi," my father told her. "We'll all be suspects. It's our pond. I'll be a suspect and you, Peaches, and Cousin Mary and Albert, and all of my damned nurses, even the substitutes, even if they weren't on this shift, and Dr. Spicewood because he came to see me yesterday, and . . ."

He turned to me and pointed a finger. "And you call the police."

All that before I had a chance to speak. Or maybe I didn't quite know how to tell him that the body floating in his pond, the body he seemed so pleased about, was his only sister.

Anna appeared from the back of the house with vacuum in hand, tall and awkward with kind eyes, now alarmed. "You'll be a suspect, too, Anna," Pop said. "But don't let it stop you from cleaning up the house. The police will be coming. If I say you're here because you're my housekeeper, the police will be more impressed if you're keeping house."

Anna, a no-nonsense country woman, was not about to be shut up like that. "What happened? Lord, I know it was something bad." She stood quite still near Pop. Red-haired Elsie, on the other side of Pop, had pulled a lined yellow pad out of a drawer in the table to write, as ordered. But her pretty tapered hands were holding the edge of the table, not writing. It was a time for holding on.

I went over and sat down by my father and took his hand in mine, tight. "A woman did drown in the fishpond, Pop, and — well, I think it's Aunt Nancy. I'm sure it's Aunt Nancy."

He didn't move or speak. I hoped he hadn't gone into complete shock. I prayed he wouldn't be thrown smack back into hallucination, with assassins on the roof to add to the real problem in the fishpond.

On the other side of him, Elsie gasped and reached out to touch his shoulder. Anna folded down on her knees next to me and put her arm around me. "Oh, Lord have mercy on us." Then she pulled back, and from the corner of my eye I saw her put her strong weathered hands over the bottom half of her long thin face as if to keep from screaming, shaking her head: No.

I thought: *Anna is used to trouble. She works because she's scared they'll lose the farm. Takes in family.* Her daughter's husband was in prison for getting drunk and shooting a friend. Her daughter, complete with three children, had come back to live on the farm. But Anna didn't let it faze her often or long. I was glad steady Anna was there.

"Call the police," my father repeated to me. At least he could speak and was rational. The phone sits on his favorite table, with a long cord for moving around from one place to another. He handed it to me.

I watched my white hand pick up the black phone from the table. The cold hand that had pulled my drowned aunt from a goldfish pond. Hard to believe. I heard my calm voice tell the woman on the line what had happened. I said: "Please come quick."

Pop listened with his eyes on my lips to catch every word. After I described Nancy, he bowed his head so that I could see his pale shining scalp through the thin soft hair. He raised his face and braced himself, holding tight to the arms of his chair. He pointed one gnarled finger first at me and then at the phone: "Call Mary. She needs to know her mother is dead."

I shook my head and tried to signal I couldn't. The policewoman was telling me to stay on the line. She had a caring voice. She began to ask me questions. Who was in the house? Was anybody hurt? Was it possible the killer was still on the place? Good grief, I hadn't thought of that. "Help is coming," she said, "but stay on the line."

Pop began to squirm. "Tell them you have to hang up to make a phone call," he commanded. He was the emperor in charge. O.K. I couldn't think of any role he could play that wouldn't be more painful. But I could have done without the emperor. "I have to tend to my father," I said. "If I hang up, you'll know what happened."

Pop broke into a broad grin. He reached over and grabbed the phone out of my hand and hung up with a loud click. "This is my house," he said. "Tend to me by dialing Mary."

On balance, Pop in a state, and maybe hallucinating, seemed worse than a policewoman annoyed. I dialed.

No answer. I looked over at Mary's roses on the table. Yellow roses. My mother's roses along the garden path were red. Red roses are a symbol of love, my Roger had told me. He gave me a bunch on our wedding day. In fact, I pricked myself on a thorn. Now the red roses in my father's garden seemed a symbol of blood and death. Don't be morbid, I told myself.

"Mary must be out," I said, and hung up.

"I hope," my father said, "that Mary has a good alibi." He shook his head like he was expecting doom. The little carved wood Chinese god of laughter on the bookshelf behind him seemed to dance on Pop's shaking white head. This was no time for laughter.

The phone rang. My father picked it up and said, "We can't talk now," and hung it up. I could have beaned him.

"The police want us to stay on the line. Suppose the killer is in this house?" I tried to appeal to his common sense. Ha.

"Call Albert in Charleston," he ordered. "He'll be at the shop. He needs to know his mother is dead." I dialed the number.

"Antiques and Lovelies," Albert answered just exactly like he always did. And I thought, as always: What an odd name for a shop. "Albert," I said, "this is Peaches. I have bad news." That was an understatement. I didn't know how to tell him. "Your mother is dead." The phone line numbed with silence.

Then: "But I just saw her." His voice was always tentative. Now it shook. "She looked well. What happened?"

I told him. He wanted details. And all the time I kept seeing her in my mind. "We don't know it's murder," I said. But for some reason, like my

24

father, I assumed in my gut that it was. I could see the body lying on the gravel where I'd pulled it. Ten o'clock in the morning. Cold. How long did it take for a dead person to get cold? The night had been chilly. That can happen in the mountains. Cold nights and warm days.

I could see the body on the gravel path, in complete detail, see it in my mind. How amazing. Shock helped me to remember. My own aunt, wearing one pearl earring on the ear near the brown oak leaf stuck on her left eye. Her right eye was open, unseeing, the lashes pointy from the water. There were bits of leaf stuck in her wet blond hair. Her black underwear showed through the wet blue-print dress. Like my dress. She would have been mortified at how she looked. One pocket was inside out, like an ear hanging out from her skirt. Her legs lolled apart and her white go-to-town shoes pointed in two different directions.

I told Albert the bare outlines of that.

Another picture came. Just as sharp. The body before I pulled it from the pond. Face down. But from the porch I'd seen a face. I shivered. Some almost visceral part of me had known the distant shape for what it was — a woman — and therefore seen a face in lily flowers. Some secret part of me had seen exactly what it expected to see. Not what was there. I was as bad as Pop.

What I really saw when I got to the pond was her body sprawled face down among the lilies, blond hair floating. And I saw a big bloody lump

25

on the back of the head. For the first time that registered. Somebody must have hit my Aunt Nancy over the head before she landed in that pond. If she fell backwards and hit her head, she wouldn't have landed in the pond face down. I shuddered, and saw the cat in my mind, hair on end, yowling. I said, "Silk saw whatever happened. Our only witness can't speak."

My father listened carefully to my every word, even about Silk, and there were tears in his eyes. Elsie, sitting near him, was totally still, listening too, as if in shock. Anna was still kneeling on the floor.

Albert made a choking noise. "My God," he said, "she was just here in Charleston. She came to see me yesterday. She must have gone back up there and then immediately . . ." His voice trailed off and then went up an octave, half hysterical. "Who would hurt my mother?"

"Think about it," I told him. "The police will probably ask us that."

"And I was here," he said, "just doing nothing, eating supper, watching a movie, sleeping. Not even knowing. And somebody killed her."

"You can't feel guilty for that," I said. "I was home doing nothing to prevent it, either. Writing my book. We aren't psychic. We can't feel guilty for that."

"I'll come now." I could hear him breathe hard. "I'll close the shop. I can drive it in five hours, maybe less."

"Close up properly," I said. "Don't rush." He

sounded so needy. But Albert was always in need. It was his nature. Now he had the tragedy to go with it. "We love you. When you get here, you'll want to be prepared to stay for the funeral, won't you?"

"Of course," he said. "I'm not thinking straight."

Usually Albert sounded like an elocution lesson. Very precise with a Southern inflection. He usually sounded reliable and slightly put-upon. Now his words meandered out with pauses.

"I'll get Ben . . . to mind the store. He's in Atlanta . . . but he can come back. Then I can stay as . . . long as I need to."

I didn't like Ben. He wore tinted reflecting glasses, as if he didn't want anybody to see into his eyes. But he was obviously handy. Not quite a partner. He didn't share Albert's fanatical love for antiques and other beautiful objects. He just thought they were good business. I was sure that was true.

"Good," I said. "Get Ben."

And Pop said: "Tell Albert he can stay here. It's quieter than at Mary's house with those damn children. And Nancy's house will be too empty." Then my father put his elbows on the table, leaned forward into his hands, and burst into noisy tears.

Elsie handed him a Kleenex. I finished my phone call, put my arm around my father, and thought about Albert. Poor Albert wouldn't

27

even get the consolation prize: money. Money was important to Albert, to buy treasures. His father, Horace Greeley Means, had been a gambler. My father was, too, in a way, on the stock market. But my father usually won.

Pop blew his nose loudly and said "Poor Nancy. She had a hard time." She did. Because Horace was a loser. What he lost was Nancy's money. And then he died. He was older than Nancy and loved his toddy. His liver gave out. All Nancy had left from a great career was enough to buy her small house, complete with mortgage. And a pension while she lived. There was lots of gossip after the big funeral for Horace, tears and gossip. Horace had been a charmer.

"If somebody killed Nancy for her money, they had to be crazy," my father said, trying to collect himself. Sometimes I think he reads my mind. "Maybe they killed her in a rage," he said. "After they stole her pocketbook and found out what was in it: about enough for one phone call, or a candy bar."

Pocketbook. Nancy always carried one. I hadn't seen one with the body. Was Nancy's pocketbook still in the pond? A white pocketbook — it would have matched her shoes. I could imagine the fish wondering at this strange white object, still invading their world.

My father stiffened. He wiped his eyes and said, "The police are here." Nothing wrong with his hearing. If he just wouldn't hallucinate. I could hear the police at the door. Elsie got up to open it. Anna was up from the floor now, perfectly still near the table, one bony hand clutched in the other, watching everything. I stayed at the table with my father, who had begun to tremble. I put my hand over his. Two men in blue were in the doorway.

"You see, I was right," he said. His laser eyes turned to mine. "I knew something terrible was going to happen. I just didn't know exactly what it was. And you said I lied." He glared at me. "Because you planned it. You killed your Aunt Nancy. And then you forgot."

CHAPTER
3

THAT AFTERNOON

Sirens echoed, one and then another, like a musical round. I went right to the door to meet the two policemen, and there behind them were a police car with blue lights flashing and an ambulance with red. An ambulance to give poor Nancy every chance to be still alive. I wished. But you're certainly not that cold when you're alive. I showed some of the officers the way to the fishpond. They looked like they knew what to do. Good. I sure didn't.

Then another siren, more men in blue. Several of them came back in the house with me. They took Pop and Elsie and Anna into other rooms. They questioned me at Pop's table, and I thought, *Boy, with me and Pop in the act, our stories are not going to match.* He would certainly tell them of burglars or assassins or some such. They might believe him. After all Pop *had* been the one to spot the body in the pond.

Afterwards I couldn't even remember exactly what I'd said. The policeman who talked to me had red hair. Flaming like Elsie's. I could at least remember his name because his buddies called him Red. Otherwise my mind was waffly with fear.

I wasn't much help to Red, except for details about finding poor dead Nancy.

He asked if we knew where she'd been just before I found her body in the pond. I could only tell him what Albert told me about seeing her in Charleston. If Nancy had told us what she intended to be doing the last couple of days, I hadn't paid attention. I hadn't even been aware she'd left for Charleston. She probably told Pop, and that was as effective as sending a letter to Santa Claus at the North Pole.

The next wave of police to arrive began to take pictures and dust for fingerprints.

They were methodical, I could remember that. The police photographer carefully took a picture from every corner of the room. This moment in Pop's house would be preserved. If I ever asked myself "Where did I leave my pocket-book the morning of Friday, May twenty-fourth," a picture would exist that showed exactly where.

I could hear Pop in the dining room, in a state, raising his voice about Mary. "We couldn't reach my niece to tell her her mother is dead. We have to reach her," he kept saying. "She may be in danger, too. I know you can find the girl. She wears red dresses." Red was the color of the day.

So they dispatched somebody to her house, and I heard them say they'd leave messages with the neighbors if she wasn't there and tell her to come to Pop's. That was what he demanded, our general ordering troops.

After a while Mary drove up, flustered and pale, complete with her two kids, all in primary colors. To find out what was wrong. The colors jarred. Pop had it right. Mary wouldn't own gray or brown or even white. Marcia, four, was sucking a lollipop and getting her yellow overalls sticky, and two-year-old Andy, in his mother's arms, was done up in bright blue. He was hiding his face against his mother's red shoulder.

There's a small bedroom off Pop's kitchen. When my mother and father moved to this part of Asheville and built this house, they were already looking forward to old age and the time when they might need someone in the house with them. So they built this room which was almost like a mini-apartment off a little hall by the back door. The police took Mary off to that little back room for formal questioning. I went with Anna to quiet the kids and give them each a peanut butter sandwich out in the kitchen.

God knows what the police asked Mary. She came back white and shaky, and said she didn't want to talk about it.

She ran to me and Pop and hugged us and said, "Oh God, I can't believe this."

By then Pop was sitting, in his favorite corner

with the bookshelves behind him. Somehow he'd talked them into letting us stay in his favorite spot after they searched and photographed and fingerprinted it. "I hope you have an alibi," he said to Mary. He had alibis on the brain.

Mary sat down beside him. She said she'd been home the night before, with the kids. With no husband to say that was true. She was in the middle of a divorce. And the kids went to bed early. "But would anyone really suspect *me?*"

I said, "It's their job to suspect everybody. It doesn't feel too good, does it?"

Pop changed the subject: "When you plan the funeral, Mary, tell friends and relatives to come back here. It's a larger house." He had that naughty-boy twinkle in his eye. I knew he had more in mind than what he said. Why did he want everybody at his house after the funeral?

Mary shut her eyes. Plainly, she didn't want to think about a funeral yet. But then she said, "You mean my house could use paint." And she swallowed and said, "You're right. And this house looks so lovely with all the fresh paint and antiques. My mother would have preferred to have people come back here. Thank you." But her voice was harsh. She pulled a tissue out of her red pocketbook and blew her nose. The kids had finished their sandwiches and come in to hold on to their mother's skirt. They'd picked up on the tension, whining and crying, and Andy had even managed to get the cat to scratch him.

Mary hugged me hard, then Pop, and said, "I need to get the kids home." Pop nodded. "You certainly do. They're out of control."

Mary glared at him, still acting the general in his wheelchair. Maybe influenced by the life of General Patton on the bookshelf behind him. Elsie was reading him that.

"Poor Mother," Mary said. "She would have hated this mess. She would have been nice to the kids if something happened to me or you." She said that directly to Pop, but he ignored it.

Then, thank goodness, Elsie appeared and said: "I'll take them out in the kitchen for a game of slapjack." That gave me a quiet minute to tell Mary what was on my mind. This wasn't a good moment, but I had to say it.

"There's something I'd like you to think about, Mary," I said. "It bothers me. You remember when you and I and your mother went to that wild sale at The Elegant Woman last week?"

"You have on the dress." Mary's voice faltered. She frowned. I suppose she couldn't imagine why I was bringing that up. "You have on that nice green butterfly print like the one my mother . . ."

"Like the one your mother bought in blue. We said what the heck, we both like it and the price is right and the colors are different."

"And so?" She watched me like I might be a little crazy to start talking about clothes.

"Peaches says your mother was killed in that

dress," Pop leaned forward. He remembered the damnedest things.

"Your mother had on the blue one when I found her," I explained. "All wet from the pond. The same dress. It gives me a spooky feeling, like it means something but I don't know what."

"Well, I know," my father shrugged. "If she was willing to buy a dress almost like someone else's just because it was on sale, she must have been as broke as she said she was."

What Pop said choked me up. Because Nancy was an original dresser. She had a flair. She enjoyed clothes. Remembering what she enjoyed made me suddenly sad.

Mary blew her nose again angrily. Even her nose was red to match her dress. "Mom liked to wear new clothes right away. I have to go. The kids need naps." And she hurried out to the kitchen, collected the kids over their loud protests, and left, slamming the front door. I pulled it open, followed her out, and stopped her on the steps in the sunshine. The weather was ready for a picnic, not death. Balmy. The kids ran down in the yard and began to pick daffodils. I put my hand on Mary's shoulder. "Pop doesn't mean to upset you. He just can't help it."

Mary's face twisted as if she might cry. I realized I had never seen her cry in her whole life except the time she fell off her bycicle and broke her arm when she was twelve years old.

"This is so awful," she said. "And there's something you don't know. I didn't want to tell

35

your father." She glanced at the kids, but they were having a friendly fight at the bottom of the stone steps, and not listening.

"Late Wednesday afternoon, I happened to drop by with the kids, and found Ma packing an overnight bag. She said, 'Wish me luck in Charleston,' and I said, 'Why?' And she said, 'Because I may have a confrontation.' And then when I asked what kind of a confrontation, she said, 'That has to be my business for now.' " Mary shut her eyes, took a large gulp of air, then opened her eyes and went on. "I didn't demand to know more. You didn't with Mother, some-how. Oh God, I wish I had."

She clutched the iron railing of the front stairs like it might be a lifeline. "I told the police what she said about a confrontation. I'll tell Albert. But I haven't told anybody else. So please, don't you tell, either. I figure people could start specu-lating. Can you think what your father would make of that?" She smiled as if it was a joke. "Marcia, don't hit your brother," she said auto-matically.

Then: "Oh, Peaches, I even find *myself* begin-ning to have wild thoughts. I wonder if that con-frontation that Mother talked about didn't have to do with Ben Arne. I know she didn't like him."

I didn't like him either. He was so smooth, he seemed sneaky.

"But then Ben wasn't Mother's business, was he?" Mary frowned like she was asking the question of herself rather than me. "So what could that 'confrontation' have been? Of course, she didn't like my father's brother Herman who lives in Charleston. Mother didn't think he took the right care of my grandma, now that she's ninety-five. But if Grandma wants to live with Herman, what could Mother do? And even if they had a fight in Charleston, why was Mother killed up here?"

I couldn't answer. Behind Mary in her bright shirt the yard was dotted with huge boulders, one in the center of the driveway loop, several out near the road. My mother had thought they lent a certain drama to the yard. They were rugged the way we were going to need to be rugged. Police cars were still parked in our driveway.

"Oh, Peaches," Mary said, "I've tried all my life to see the bright side of things, no matter what. I've tried to hope for the best. But this is just lousy, isn't it?" Then she ran down the steps, grabbed the children, jumped in her car and started to drive off before I could say a thing. A policeman stopped her at the end of the driveway and evidently asked her where she was going, then let her go on.

I went back inside. My father announced he wanted a nap. I was glad. I needed some quiet to digest what Mary had said. And I was hungry. Elsie wheeled Pop off, and I went out in the kitchen and had a late pick-up lunch at the kitchen table with Anna. I told her about the dress, which still nagged at my mind.

She put down her sandwich and nodded like she understood. "Are you a-thinkin' the killer was color blind?"

And I said: "What?" And then, "Yes. I see what you mean. You hit the nail on the head. I feel like maybe the killer really meant to kill me." And then I laughed. "I can see that's silly. I'm not rich. I'm not stealing anybody's man. I don't owe money to the Mob."

And Anna smiled and said, "Same with me."

Then the clock on the kitchen wall above the stove chimed two. The silly clock with the cat face and moving eyes that Mary had given my mother for a joke. Anna liked that clock and kept it wound. She kept all our clocks wound. Two o'clock already.

Albert arrived at three-thirty. I saw his white Toyota van swing into the driveway too fast. I happened to be looking out the glass panel at the side of the front door. A policeman stopped Albert before he got far into the circular driveway. Albert jumped out of his van by the holly halfway down the drive and talked to him.

Albert talked in that soulful way he has, all the time shaking his head as if to say: "No. It couldn't have happened. It didn't happen."

And I found myself thinking he wasn't acting like either one of himselves. Not like the Albert who pouts and feels sorry for himself, and hugs the hand with one deformed finger in his pocket like a dirty secret. And not like the other Albert

38

who gets so interested in what he's doing or finding out that he forgets to pout. That Albert can tell you wonderful facts that you'd never have guessed. Like the name of Robert E. Lee's second favorite horse.

I guess he was just stunned. All his movements seemed disjointed. His reactions were delayed. His whole face was gray. He looked worse than he did when his father died, but of course his *father* wasn't murdered. His father drank himself to death. Boy, talk about bad luck with parents. Fate singled him out. And Albert is the kind of person you wouldn't notice in a crowd. About medium height, smooth oval face, not bad-looking. Only his eyes catch attention. Soulful eyes like a poet, Roger used to say. "You write poems, Peaches, but Albert has the eyes for it."

The policeman walked Albert up to the front door. I just had time to give Albert a hug and notice how shaky he was. As soon as he was inside, the thin man with the mustache, the one who seemed to be in charge, took over, and whisked Albert off towards the kitchen. Mustache was so businesslike, even grim. Had he discovered some even worse horror than I knew?

I tried to concentrate on what I knew, not what I imagined. Not much. I couldn't remember any police names, except Red because of his hair, though I had them written down somewhere like it said I should in my book. I wished I could remember where I put the list. Never mind, they expected us to be in a daze.

After a while I might sort it out.

At practically the same moment that Albert went with Mustache, my father called, and when I hurried down the hall to his bedroom, he announced he wanted baked custard for supper. I guess the tension gave Pop a craving for something bland and sweet, like his mother used to make. And that was fine. When I'm nervous it calms me down to cook.

I didn't count on the bonus. From my father's big airy kitchen, I could hear every word Albert and Mustache said in the back bedroom. Perhaps Mustache thought he'd shut the door tight, but he hadn't. As I walked into the kitchen, Albert was saying, "My mother came over here a lot because my uncle was very demanding. You know how rich people are. And my uncle's daughter, my cousin Peaches, is spacey. You must have noticed that. If my uncle wanted something done right, he called my mother."

Stinker. If he was going to talk about me, I felt a license to listen. Not that I was surprised at what he said. Albert's problem is that he sees the worst in everybody, even in himself. I opened the refrigerator quietly and took out the eggs and milk. Silk came out of hiding. He came over and rubbed against my legs and meowed. I prayed they wouldn't hear the cat and notice the door wasn't shut. I found a little piece of chicken and gave him a treat.

Albert's voice has no overtones. It's flat. I've

always thought that was because he doesn't have a lot of self-confidence. Funny, because he has a super I.Q. Measured and certified. And he's handy. He can restore things like old clocks, even electric ones. He can find treasures. Old ladies like to be nice to him and show him what they have in the cellar.

But his flat voice can make him sound like he might be lying. I hoped the detective wouldn't hear it that way, even if Albert did call me spacey. We go back a long way, Albert and I. Though, of course, I'm much older. I was eighteen when he was three. Over the years, our families took vacations together, and he used to make me hold his hand when we walked down the beach together, so nobody would see his handicap. The top two joints of the little finger on his left hand are missing. Have been since birth. That bothers him a lot. And bathing suits don't have pockets.

"My mother was just down in Charleston yesterday," he said. "She has old school friends there. But I'm not sure who she stayed with. She stopped by my antique shop about eleven o'clock when I had a crush of customers. She was dressed up in her green silk dress with the stars on it, and the crystal earrings my father gave her, so she must have been meeting somebody for lunch. She said she'd be back when the store was quieter. But she didn't come back. I didn't know where to reach her. I should have tried harder." His voice cracked. "But I didn't

41

know anything was wrong until this morning when my cousin Peaches called just after I opened the store at ten. She said my mother was dead." His voice choked. "I thought she was still in Charleston. I don't understand."

I was listening so hard that the milk I was trying to scald almost boiled over. I lifted it off the burner just in time.

Then Mustache was asking Albert to tell him everything he did yesterday afternoon and evening, leading up to the time his mother must have been killed. He'd asked me that, too. Yes. Everybody was suspect.

I'd flubbed the what-is-your-alibi question. I'd spent the afternoon alone, working on my book, oblivious to everything else. I was working on the chapter called Hang It On: about pocket-books with shoulder straps, eyeglasses with idiot chains, car keys on bracelets, pens fastened by cords near to the phone so they can't be removed, and other objects kind enough to help remember themselves. I'd really gotten into the subject, talking about why, for me, a hang-on is better than one of those little find-it alarms you can get through mail-order catalogues. The alarm may go off when you clap your hands, and if it's attached to your car keys, for instance, it may save you from half an hour of frantic searching when you're already late. But on a bad day, doors are going to slam, objects are going to fall on the floor, and every single bang sets off the alarm. Each bang is a built-in automatic raspberry. I can live without that.

I'd told Red I stopped work on my book around six and put a frozen dinner in the oven. I don't cook much since Roger died. Then I tried to call Mary, but she was out. Same with Ted.

When I'd tried to reconstruct the afternoon and evening for Red, I said I had a feeling the phone rang and I'd talked briefly to somebody, but couldn't think who. I said when I'd stopped work I'd called my father, but that was no alibi because he wouldn't be sure what day I called. Then I ate supper and read a book and went to bed. All by myself. No witnesses.

Albert did better. He remembered details. Always has. All those details made his alibi sound great. He said he worked in the shop until five-thirty, selling a carved eagle to an elderly woman from Athens, Georgia, who wanted it shipped to her daughter in Utica, New York, for a wedding present. He said it was a rare carving by somebody-or-other Schimmel with the original paint, and he gave the date. The daughter's new husband was a curator in a folk art museum, so the mother had been pleased to death to find a present he would admire. Albert even gave Mustache the woman's name and address. Another customer came in, Albert said, looked around, especially at the antique miniature portraits, but didn't buy anything because she was horrified at the price. The one she liked cost $5,235.

I knew about the miniatures because Albert had sold my mother a portrait of a little girl who

43

reminded her of me. That was before he made a specialty of them. Later he was angry because he hadn't charged Ma enough. "What the heck," my father had said, "you made a profit." Then Albert wanted to buy it back after my mother died, at the same price she bought it for. But my father won't let go of anything that belonged to my mother. That's why he keeps Silk, even though the cat hisses at the mailman. I think Pop feels he's holding on to every little bit of my mother that remains. I can understand that. He wants to remember her and needs reminders. He'd rather remember *her* than the assassins on the roof.

Quietly, I beat the eggs into the scalded milk and listened to Albert tell about last night; about how he put the most valuable small antique items, like the rare Confederate belt buckles, in the safe, locked up the shop, drove home through a rainstorm and watched television news about a big local drug bust. Then he prepared himself some spaghetti with meat, tomato and mushroom sauce, ate half, put the other half in the refrigerator. It was still there, he said.

Even that part of his alibi was better than mine. I ate all of my frozen dinner, and threw the container in the trash. Then the garbage man came this morning.

"But the only real proof that I was at home in the evening," Albert said, "was that I called my neighbor Charles Murphy, who doesn't have cable television, and asked him if he'd like to come over and see *Dances With Wolves* on cable. He didn't answer so I left a message on his machine. But I watched." I half expected Albert to tell Mustache the plot. As a kid he'd go to a movie and then try to tell us the whole story, ad nauseum. My father made a rule that Albert wasn't allowed to tell movie plots in our house, except on his birthday.

Mustache was still working on Albert's schedule. "What did you do after the movie?"

Albert said he went over some of his accounts and then went to bed. In the morning he went to the shop early, stopping by McDonald's for a drive-in breakfast. He eats a fast-food breakfast every day. In the quiet time before the shop opened at ten, he said he worked on repairing a clock, a steeple clock with a painting of a pond and weeping willow on the glass front. He said he found the clock at an auction in Summerville the week before.

"Just at ten, as I was unlocking the shop door, my cousin Peaches called." Ah. Re-enter me. I listened extra sharp. He said I'd tried to be kind, but there's no way to make his mother's death anything but a shock. He told how I'd asked him to stay in his Uncle Harwood's house (that's Pop), but he would never do that. He knew he'd feel more comfortable at his mother's. So he'd spend one night with his sister, Mary, then as soon as the police had thoroughly searched his mother's house, he'd move there if his sister agreed, and he was sure she would. It would be like a last visit with his mother, to stay there with her things.

And speaking of her things, Mustache said, "What did she usually keep in her car? We found it parked in the driveway branch around by the kitchen. We found maps and an umbrella and a first-aid kit, and a can opener, and a box of cassette tapes for the player, and a box of tissues. Was there anything else she kept in her car?"

Silence. There was something else, but I couldn't think what it was. Albert could. "A flashlight."

"How large?" Mustache asked. His voice came alive, like he really cared about flashlights.

"A large heavy-duty black flashlight, about a foot and a half long," Albert said. "She was afraid the car might break down on a back road at night. But she never let that stop her. She often went to night meetings. I used to think that if she ever had a problem at night" — his voice broke but he went on — "that flashlight could be a weapon."

"She was a woman who took risks?"

"She was spunky." Albert sounded mad.

"The last time you saw her, did your mother act strangely in any way?" Mustache asked. I listened sharp at that.

There was a long silence. Finally Albert said, "I think she may have been upset about something, though she didn't say anything about it. She kept fingering her earrings. She does that

46

when she's upset." Yes. I could see her fingering her earrings the time her husband Horace wrecked the car on the way to Christmas dinner at our house. She had on pearl earrings that day and she nearly wore them out.

When I found her in the pond, she was not wearing the dress or the earrings that Albert had described. So, I thought, one thing I know about what happened to Aunt Nancy, between eleven in the morning and the time I found her the next day, was that for some reason she changed her clothes. And we know her flashlight vanished from her car, unless that happened earlier, and her pocketbook was stolen — I'd heard a policeman say they hadn't found it in the pond. I wondered if we'd ever know any more.

"One more question," I heard Mustache say. "When I interviewed your cousin, she said your mother had once or twice seemed to be dropping hints of some sort, she can't yet remember exactly what, but she thinks the little portrait you sold her mother was involved."

"Perhaps I can help," Albert said. "My mother and I were both upset that the little portrait seems to have disappeared from this house, and we couldn't get my cousin Peaches or her father interested in searching for it. That little portrait is much more valuable than you might think. I could sell it tomorrow for ten thousand dollars. But I can't think how that picture could have anything to do with my mother's death. If Peaches has some hunch about it, let's hope something will jog her memory soon. I regret to say her memory is not her strongest point. But she does have flashes when you least expect it. We can hope."

I wondered if there was anything besides my lousy memory, my lack of an alibi, the fact I found my aunt dead, and my father's crazy suspicion that I killed her and forgot it, that linked me to Aunt Nancy's death. I hoped to God there wasn't. I wondered what clue could be hiding in the back of my mind which might be coaxed into light. "It'll come to me," I said prayerfully. Now, *there* was a good name for a chapter in my book.

CHAPTER
4

LATER THAT AFTERNOON

Finally, the police were finished inside the house. Pop was calm. I was able to stay on the phone in the back guest bedroom long enough to reach Singapore and have a private conversation with my daughter, Eve. I sat in the pink-flowered chintz chair next to the pink princess phone. This was Eve's room when she visited her grandma and grandpa. The room my mother fixed for kids. Eve loved the cutouts of chickens and ducks and pigs on the quilts of the twin beds.

Eve is thirty now. She's in the import-export business in Singapore. I like to think of it as an international extension of the traditional North Carolina craft shop that Roger and I used to run. Eve used to help sometimes.

I told her what had happened to Nancy, but not to come home. "You can't really make things better," I said, "and we don't know what's happening here. The rest of us might even be in danger. I'd feel better with you out there safe." I was surprised at myself as soon as I said it. But I didn't take it back. I have always believed in following my hunches.

Eve just said, "I love you, Mom. I'll do what makes you feel best. But give Pop a great big hug for me." There's always been something special between Eve and Pop.

When I came back out to the living room, my father was still at his table, half dozing. Eve's message almost cheered him up, but not for long. "At least there's one member of this family with a first-rate mind," he said, "and she's not here to help." That woke him up.

I could have killed him (I should really stop using that expression!) for repeating again how he'd known there was a body all along but that I wouldn't believe him. Dorothy was the sitter who came on duty at three o'clock. The wide-eyed, small-voiced sitter who was sometimes shocked when my father said "damn" and "hell." I suspect he said it more often when she was there, out of sheer mischief. She was no help.

"Damn it to hell," he said, "they should have found the killer by now. He may be after me next. I have to solve this soon." Dorothy didn't divert him as Elsie would have. I asked her to get us some wine and cheese and crackers.

Fortunately the doorbell rang and Arabella from next door arrived for Pop's diversion. I welcomed her. Arabella Horton, the widow-lady with plucked eyebrows who owned five wigs for different moods and four horses which just happened to match four of her wigs. She went to Bryn Mawr years ago, and said she had a trained mind.

Did we know, she asked, that statistics showed that most victims knew their killers? Who did we think the police suspected most? She sat down next to Pop, and said she came over to offer condolences, which seemed to include questions. She agreed to stay and drink a glass of wine with Pop, who said he needed company.

She had on a black wig, maybe her idea of mourning, and green eye shadow to match her green eyes. I could never decide how old she was. Forty-five? Sixty-five with a face lift? "Nobody will kill *you*, Harwood," she said sweetly. "You're too tough. Have any other strange things happened in the last few days?"

He said no, except that Nancy told him to be double sure to keep his doors locked because people were stealing his things. Oh, dear, I hoped he wasn't back to the burglars on the roof.

Then the doorbell rang again. I opened the door, and there was Ted. I was so glad to see him. Ted in his ubiquitous turtleneck and moccasins. His blondish hair streaked with white falling this way and that, as if he's been out in a medium-sized wind. His sea-blue eyes fixed the whole room, seeming to take in every detail through those wire-rimmed glasses that sit a little low on his nose. At first glance you might think Ted is an absent-minded professor. Take another look at those eyes and forget the absent-minded. He has a thorough and comforting mind. He hugged me like he could almost make murder go away. He handed me the *Asheville Citizen-Times*, which none of us had remembered to bring in that morning. "You'll like this better than the next one," he said. Yes. The next one would tell about Nancy in the fishpond.

Ted had been a newspaper editor. Editor of the Greenville *Evening Watchman* before that paper shut down. His presses stopped and his wife died in the same month. Hard. They'd been married thirty years, two years longer than Roger and me. And then he had the offer to teach. That's how I met him. I was taking a writing course at UNCA to help me pull out of my own grief over Roger.

Ted and I met at a talk by Eudora Welty at the university. And we were friends right off. I liked the way his eyes twinkled at a good story, even when he was telling it himself, exaggerating just a little bit here and there for added drama. I liked the way he could finish my sentences without seeming pushy. I'd say, "I loved the mystery about Navahos by . . ." and then I'd hesitate over the name and he'd say, "Tony Hillerman," as if he were just agreeing that he liked the book, too.

Wherever Ted was, everything worked better. I swear clocks kept better time when he was around.

He said, "I'm so sorry. I just found out. I was out hiking." He hugged Pop too, and told Arabella he was glad she was there. Of course, he'd missed the worst of the excitement. To celebrate the post-police calm, Silk came out from hiding and rubbed against his legs and made little mewing noises.

Ted was one of the few men Silk liked. Silk had belonged to my mother and usually preferred women to men. He was definitely a sexist cat.

Pop pulled at Ted's hand. "Hey. Sit down here by me. You can help." Pop was flushed, like murder was a stimulant. Not happy, but on overdrive.

Ted sat. He said, "I'm ready to do anything I can."

My father nodded and raised his eyebrows, as if he and Ted were conspirators: "You'd better keep an eye on Peaches."

And Ted, God bless him, winked at me and said, "I think she needs some fresh air. I'll take her for a walk."

Yes. What I definitely needed was to get out of that house. Thank God the police were through with the back yard. I'd watched them through the window. They'd even brought in some firemen, and all of them had gone in a line across the yard so they couldn't miss one square inch. They'd even extended the search into the woods around the house.

Pop's road was a strange one, with houses not

too far apart, but backed up by woods. The shelf in the mountainside was wide enough for houses to the right and left of the road. But then the mountain dropped off, beyond Pop's garden for example. The mountain rose up sharply on the other side of the house.

We took the path through the woods that leads toward the trail where Arabella sometimes rides her horses. The woods smelled sweet, as always — in fact there was honeysuckle where enough sunshine filtered through the trees. Leaves brushed us as we passed through the trees hiding the far mountains. We walked quite a way without saying a word. Silk walked along beside us. Roger used to say Silk was the only cat he ever knew that liked to go for a walk like a dog.

We came to a big flat rock and sat down, and then I told Ted every single detail I could remember, everything that had happened from the time Pop said there was a dead woman in the pond. I could feel his orderly mind sorting it all out behind those absent-minded-professor glasses.

And then I said, "Nancy was not the type to get murdered. She was too well organized."

"She must have been the type in some way. There must have been a reason," he said. Ted wants the world to be an orderly place. Funny that he loves order and has hair that won't be ordered.

I told him about how Mary had said her mother expected a confrontation in Charleston,

54

that Mary said she had no idea what that meant, and how she told the police, but not Pop.

"And I told the police every single thing I could think of," I said, "even the fight Nancy had with Bill Havers over the church addition and where to put it, and the time she reported her neighbor for child abuse when the woman kicked her three-year-old to the ground and broke the child's arm. Can you imagine? So people might be mad at Nancy. But not enough to kill. Of course, her pocketbook has vanished. But why would a robber throw her in the fish-pond? And so the police think there's more to it than a robbery, and I agree, don't you?" I felt the cold solidity of the rock we sat on. Nothing else in my life was that solid.

"You told them the logical things," Ted said, fixing me with his blue eyes. "Now let go. Ramble. Brainstorm. You have your best thoughts when you ramble." God bless him for thinking that. I looked up into the green tops of the trees and made myself relax. I looked down at the earth.

A shiny black beetle was walking past my right foot. "Nancy hated bugs," I said, "especially ants. She had an exterminator come to her house once a month just to be sure. She hated to cook, except she liked to make fancy desserts. Roger loved her pecan pies. She had a wild sweet tooth. She usually had a chocolate bar in her purse. Cadbury's was her favorite. She hated disorder. She made lists. She would have hated to die in

55

such an odd way. She hated injustice. She belonged to Save the Children and the Civil Liberties Union and Common Cause." The beetle vanished under the edge of the rock we sat on. Ted was watching it, too — Ted, blotched with sunlight through the trees so that his hair was double-striped, once by its own wayward color, once by light.

"She must have gone too far in some direction." Ted stared hard at me as if I should know. "Everybody goes too far in some way."

I pulled one of the sparse blades of grass near the rock and chewed the end, considering. "She may have been too determined for everything to be done right. She may not have had enough pity for ordinary struggling bastards. Because she could manage fine and not let obstacles get in her way."

"What obstacles?" Ted reached down and squeezed my hand as if to say, "You're getting there." I felt warmer. I talked faster.

"Her husband, mostly. I remember my mother telling my Aunt Nancy she should leave Horace. Because once in a while he was so drunk he hit her. That shocked Ma. And Pop was shocked at the way the man lost money. Pop told Nancy she should never give him a dime beyond what he earned as a real estate salesman, which wasn't much. But Nancy said she married him for better or worse, and most of the time it was better. My mother said it looked to her like most of the time it was worse." I noticed a spider web between two tall weeds over near Ted, and thought : *Yes. That's it.* "It was like they were both caught together in some big spider web of life, but they pretended they weren't caught."

Ted frowned, and I said I didn't quite know what I meant by that, but anyway, Horace spent every cent they had. "Sometimes on fancy presents for her. One Valentine's Day he gave her a super-deluxe microwave oven, a black lace nightgown, a box of chocolates, and a dozen red roses — and a Cadillac."

"With her money?" He whistled. A bird somewhere off in the woods seemed to answer back.

"They had a joint bank account," I said. "Ma got mad sometimes. A joint account and he didn't put much in it. And yet sometimes he did. He'd sell a big house. He was a charmer. Especially when he'd been drinking. Which was any time between seven o'clock in the morning and when he went to sleep at night. He didn't get ugly often. But once in a while Nancy would show up with bruises. She always had an excuse. Then, just before he died, he began to act drunk in public, even stagger. Toward the end he wasn't well, I think. But he wouldn't go to a doctor. And I asked my cousin Mary if they couldn't get her father to go to AA. She shook her head so hard, an earring fell off. 'If you try to get between him and his bottle,' she said, 'he gets violent. I tried it. That time I had to go to the hospital with a nosebleed. My mother tried it now and then. No go.' "

"But your Aunt Nancy forgave him?" Ted scuffed his shoe in the dry dirt of the path.

"She always seemed to," I said, "but she was self-righteous with other people. I heard her talking once about firing a man. About how he asked for a second chance because whatever he had done wrong was when he was upset with a family problem. She said the company deserved employees who did not let their personal problems interfere with their work. No second chance." I picked up a dead stick and broke it in half.

"That bad?" He raised one eyebrow. "So maybe somebody she fired got even. Or maybe Nancy's husband did some awful thing. He killed the owner of a liquor store while trying to get in after hours, and she was paying blackmail. She tried to kill the blackmailer, but he killed her."

"In my father's fishpond? Now that's far-fetched, darlin'."

"We're just brainstorming," he said. "Maybe your cousin Mary had a deep festering grudge against her mother for letting her father give her a bloody nose. Maybe she killed her mother. With symbolism. In the drink."

I could hear another bird singing, but I couldn't see it. "But Mary is a sweetheart," I said. "She wears bright colors. She adopts stray cats. She has a wild sense of humor. Jokes posted around the house. That's what saves her. And she loves her own kids. She wouldn't put those kids in danger of losing her, not on a bet."

"So maybe it was your cousin Albert." Ted cocked his head. "Maybe his mother told him, 'Albert, you remind me of your father drunk.' He closed his shop, drove straight up from Charleston, killed his mother and drove straight back, just in time to open the shop as usual. Because — maybe his father gave him a bloody nose, too."

"Albert didn't have to come up here," I said. "He could have killed her in Charleston. She'd been on a visit. But he's not the type. All he thinks about is antiques. Now, if his mother had millions for buying treasures, he might be tempted. But she didn't. In fact he had a motive to keep his mother healthy. If Nancy outlived Pop, he might have left her money. She was younger. And she might have left half of that to Albert. Anyhow, why should it be a member of the family? Next you'll think it was me."

"What motive did you have?" he asked, and winked. But he didn't fool me. Ted is thorough. That's his main virtue and his main fault. Sometimes he wants to know so much about something that I get bored.

"It could be me," he said. "I might intend to marry you. I might be scared your father would leave his money to your Aunt Nancy instead of us."

"But you don't know if I'd marry you," I said. "I don't know, myself."

He made a wry face.

59

"Besides, you wouldn't kill for money," I said. "Neither would I. Because we're happy the way we are. We have enough to do what we want to do. And just as well. Pop may leave all his to the Anti-Crime League if they promise to save him from the burglars on the roof."

Silk jumped in Ted's lap and Ted began to rub behind his ears. The cat shut his eyes and purred in bliss. "Maybe one of the sitters was married to a man your Aunt Nancy fired. And then he killed himself. Threw himself into the Atlantic Ocean and drowned. The sitter wanted revenge." Ted was half-joking. Exaggerating to make me smile. And the strange thing was, it worked. Lightened the terrible.

"I don't like to think it was a sitter," I said. I knew as soon as I said it that it wasn't so. I'd much rather think it was a sitter than a member of the family, for goodness sake. I studied the thin grass at my feet. An ant was struggling through it. For him it was a forest. But he made good time down to the end of the rock. There was a crumpled paper down there. Some slob had littered, even here in the woods. And somehow, perhaps because it was half under the rock, the searchers had missed it — if they had searched this far. I reached down and picked it up. I smoothed it out, curious. There was foil and dark paper. A Cadbury's chocolate wrapper.

I jumped up. "Whoever killed Nancy came this way." Ted came over, took the paper gingerly, by one corner, and stared at it.

"The killer was hungry." My voice was shrill. "And he knew she kept a chocolate bar in her pocketbook. And he ate it. They haven't found her pocketbook. So maybe it *was* just a robbery, and the killer happened across the chocolate bar. But I don't believe that for a minute. I believe the killer, whoever it was, took this path, and he or she liked chocolate and was a slob."

Ted whistled. "Or perhaps," he said, "the killer was an amateur, so frightened by what he'd done that he dropped this paper and didn't know he'd dropped it. And yet he was clever," he said. "We haven't seen footprints on this path. And look, there's a ridge of rock he could have walked on and not left prints. He must have done that."

"He must have taken the flashlight from Nancy's car to see his way without leaving footprints. The flashlight is gone. So he was a clever amateur. Or she was. But scared enough to do a dumb thing like drop a clue." I could relate to that. But not to killing. "Let's hope," I said, "he'll do a lot more dumb things. When he has to lie, let's hope he'll forget his story and trip himself up."

And then suddenly right in the middle of my excitement at the clue, my anger at the killer, my hope we'd find him — or her — there came a silly little thought: "You know what?" I said. "My lousy memory has probably helped to keep me from a life of crime. Why, I could never stick to an untrue story well enough to get away with a thing."

And Ted burst into a big grin. "There you go. Even out of adversity comes another chapter for your book: The Advantages of a Bad Memory. Put that at the end to cheer your readers up.

"Come on," he added, "it's safe for you to come back to civilization. You've proved to me that you don't qualify as a suspect."

I carried the chocolate wrapper carefully by one corner. "We'd better get this right to the police," I said, "and tell them Nancy almost always had one of these candy bars in her pocketbook." And then I said, "We're not bad at this detective game, are we?"

But all we actually did at that point was give the crime its media nickname. The next day's paper had this headline: "Candy-Bar Killer Eludes Police." My Aunt Nancy, who had wanted more than anything else in the world to be dignified and correct, was reduced to being the woman who supplied the candy bar to the Candy-Bar Killer. I was sorry about that.

CHAPTER
5

FRIDAY EVENING, MAY 24

Arabella was gone and Pop was fretting when Ted and I got back from our walk. "You won't leave me alone in this house at night, will you, Peaches?" A lot of help I'd be if a killer returned. But what Pop wanted was moral support. For real physical needs he had Dorothy as sitter until eleven, and then Silva. At least there'd be three of us in the house.

I said I'd stay that Friday night, but on Saturday morning I needed to go home briefly because first thing in the morning the painter was coming to do the outside of my house. I'd had him reserved for several weeks, and in spite of our tragedy I wanted to go ahead and get him started. Life goes on. The funeral was set for eleven on Monday morning.

Ted kissed me good night and made me promise to be careful. He didn't want to leave. In fact, he asked Pop if he'd like him to spend the night too, but Pop said he slept too soundly to be a good chaperone, and he didn't want us two young things to misbehave. Really!

As it happened, I had some extra clothes and my portable computer at Pop's. In fact, I kept forgetting to take the computer home, where I like to use it during thunderstorms since it has a battery and doesn't have to be plugged in.

I put the computer at the front door so I'd trip over it on the way out in the morning and couldn't forget it. I have always found that's a sure-fire trick. I also put a note on the bathroom mirror, to remind me to go out the front door so the trick wouldn't be wasted.

I was exhausted. I crawled into one of the twin beds in the guest room next to Pop's room, and Silk came in and snuggled up next to me, so I didn't feel alone. I left a night light on, a small light nestled in a sea shell down by the baseboard. It made the shadows tall. My door was open, of course, to hear any unusual noises. I lay awake for a little while, hearing even the slightest creak of the house settling. Trying not to keep seeing Nancy in that pond. Then I was so tired I slept.

A bang woke me up. I jumped out of bed, ran towards my father's room and bumped head-on into Silva. We staggered to the light switch and turned on the hall light.

Silva looked this way and that, trembling. She's a funny, shy kid to begin with, and she was plainly scared silly. She rubbed her head where it had bumped mine. The two frown lines between her eyes were deep black. I know Silva is not really a kid because she has a grown son. But that bleached blond hair makes her look younger than she is. And less capable. "Come on," I said. "We need to search."

Pop seemed O.K. Still sound asleep. We ran and looked in each of the rooms near Pop's — the office, the front guest room where I'd slept, the back guest room. No one in sight. We even looked in the closets, which took nerve. We tried to keep quiet so Pop wouldn't wake up. Sometimes he sleeps the sleep of the deep. Sometimes he's jumpy all night.

We found nobody. Nothing. Until we looked more carefully in the living room and saw my portable computer lying on its side just inside the front door. Right where it would have fallen if the door knocked it over. "Someone started to come in this door!" I moved the computer, threw the door open and stared into the yard, silver in the moonlight. No one in sight. But the woods were close enough for quick escape, tree shadows black and threatening. I closed the door, and Silva and I ran to check in the back of the house, but the kitchen and back room were as empty as the bedrooms.

I called the police.

"But I don't understand how the computer got by the front door." Silva eyed my computer like an enemy. Like it walked there to scare us.

So I had to explain my almost foolproof

method of *putting a thing where you'll trip over it so you can't forget it.*

"But couldn't your portable fall over by itself?" Such hope in her voice.

"Of course not," I told her. "Besides, look how the rug is pushed back. Somebody opened the front door. Somebody tried to break into this house."

She hugged her thin shoulders and shivered. I figured I had to be brave for us both.

I examined the lock. No marks to suggest it had been forced. Could we have left it unlocked in all the excitement? I was positive I'd locked it myself. With my memory, who was going to believe that?

Now my father was calling, demanding to know what was going on. He was wide-awake. Agitated. "Who has a key to the front door?" I asked him.

"I told you there were burglars " he said. "I've heard them before. When I can't sleep. But these damned sitters are all deaf." He lay there in his bed, pouting.

"And the key?"

"Your mother has a key," he said. He was in bad shape. He'd forgotten Ma was dead. He said, "She never lends it to anyone since Albert lost his and we had the locks changed. She is very particular about that. Are you careful?" He pointed his finger first at me and then at Silva, as we stood by his bed.

"I use the back door," Silva said in her little

66

girl voice. "My key is in my pocket. And I was in the kitchen watching TV. So nobody could have come in the back way." She pulled her key out for him to see.

"I have a key to the front at home on my key board," I said. "Maybe somebody stole that. I'll look in the morning."

While Silva settled him down, I went and looked at my poor computer lying on its side, and prayed it wasn't hurt. But never mind — apparently it had saved us. Though we didn't know from what.

It wasn't pleasant to speculate who had tried to break *into* Pop's house the night after a murder just *outside*. I saw Nancy in my mind. In her twin-to-mine dress.

Finally I heard a police car drive up, and stop with a skid of tires.

Mustache was one of the two policemen who jumped out, hurried in, and searched the whole house, inside and out. He said he didn't believe the intruder got beyond my by-mistake alarm at the front door. With no body in the pond this time, I felt calm enough to study Mustache. He had shaggy hair and eyebrows, a straight firm mouth and intelligent eyes. A scar next to his right eye suggested a wild past. His neat blue uniform suggested an ordered present. He wanted to know all about why my computer was sitting in front of the door. So I explained, telling him that the trip-over memory-stimulant method was going to be in my book about *How to*

Survive Without a Memory. He broke into a smile and said, "Hey! I see. Now you can add a chapter about how a bad memory can be a good burglar alarm!"

Everybody wants to get into the act.

As he said goodbye, he tugged at his mustache and half grinned. "You know, my mother had tricks to remember things. She even had one she got from my grandmother that seemed kind of useless — a silly word to help remember the seven deadly sins: PWELGAS: Pride, Wrath, Envy, Lust, Gluttony, Avarice, Sloth." He looked around him like he expected to find those sins hidden under the couch in front of the fireplace, or under Pop's favorite table. "You know, that's been helpful to me," he said. "Behind every crime, I look for one of those sins." He smiled like I'd be sure to understand. "Sometimes I find them all."

I needed to remember PWELGAS.

CHAPTER
6

EARLY SATURDAY MORNING, MAY 25

When Mustache and friend finally left at around one in the morning, I couldn't sleep. Out the window, the full moon made the garden into a silvery shadowland. I was back in bed in the front guest room, under a light quilt my grandmother stitched together years ago out of the scraps of the clothes she'd made for me and my mother. Including my favorite red and blue plaid, and the dress with the big bow sash that I hated. Scraps from back before my father figured out how to get rich.

Lying there I couldn't see the fishpond, thank God, but I felt danger shining in the window with the moonlight, like the glint of a knife.

I lay awake, stroking Silk, trying to put the patches of the day into a pattern. No luck.

I did the old relaxing trick, tensing every muscle in my body one by one until I was like one big clenched fist, then relaxing every bit of me, beginning with my toes, ending with the top of my head. But I couldn't relax enough to sleep.

Something hovered in the back of my mind like a wild thing hidden in the bushes. Crouching so still that I could almost believe it wasn't there. I had a pencil and pad on the night table next to the bed. I can write fine in the dark, but in fact the moonlight turned the paper silver. I wrote down my feeling before the wild thing could slip off forever and pretend it hadn't been there. But what was it? Something to do with talking to the police? God knows I'd told everything I could think of to Red with his kindly country accent, right after I found Nancy, and then again to Mustache after the computer fell. They both seemed to think it was important that there was no pocketbook in the pond. So where on earth was Aunt Nancy's pocketbook, complete with appointment book, address book, credit cards, checkbook and scribble pad? The pocketbook which had almost certainly contained the Cadbury's chocolate bar, now removed and eaten. A mystery.

But the wild thing drifting in my mind didn't feel like police business. It felt like something I knew about somebody, something that was odd, but probably not plainly related to what happened. That's why I couldn't snag it. I tried again to sleep. I couldn't. The wild thing was like a mosquito buzzing just out of sight in the dark.

No point in lying there awake. I turned the light on and pulled out the first draft of Chapter I of my *How to Survive Without a Memory*. I keep a copy in my pocketbook in case my house burns down while I'm out. I could never remember it all if my words went up in smoke.

I re-read the chapter, hoping for help. I like to read what I've written. It calms my nerves.

Chapter I

How to Survive Without a Memory

This book is dedicated to my friends who are beginning to lose memory and getting upset about it. I have never had a memory to speak of, so I can share the tricks of how to survive without one. I have also gathered knacks for coping from others who are similarly afflicted. "If we can just remember what it is we can't remember," says my cousin Suzy, who has been particularly helpful.

Rule One of surviving is this: Figure out what your brain will do and use that to get around what your brain won't do. This is pleasanter than hitting your head against the wall in sheer frustration and much more useful than swearing.

A dramatic example of this is a woman who, for some medical reason [Note to myself: look up reason], was unable to remember words except when connected to music. But her musical memory was still good. I saw that on television, on a program about the brain.

I found out something a little like that when I

71

was a kid. I can remember rhymes. Don't ask me why, when I can't remember names or dates. I can recite poetry I learned years ago. I will never forget when Columbus discovered America because "In fourteen hundred ninety-two, Columbus sailed the ocean blue."

I have friends who can always remember a name or where they left their glasses. Yet they can hardly memorize poetry at all. So I guess every brain is different, and I have to go with the one I've got, even if I'd rather remember the names of the members of my book club than fourteen hundred ninety-two.

"I just discovered that if I repeat a thing over and over under my breath, I can remember it as long as I repeat it," a friend of mine told me. She's just beginning to have trouble with her memory. Gee, I thought everybody used that method. But evidently some people don't have to. For those in need it's a good trick — just repeat that phone number while you walk or glance from the phone book to the phone.

I can remember jokes. Don't ask me why. And it certainly isn't as handy as remembering my father's birthday. But I can remember a list of things by making up a ridiculous sentence with the items. Grocery list: salted eggs with onions and garlic are not good with maple syrup. Or I can make a silly sentence with the first letters of each thing on a list in the right order. Once in college I had to remember the planets in the order of their distance from the sun. My sentence was "My V8 Electric Mobile Jogs So Unevenly Now and Pluto. Or, in other words, Mercury, Venus, Earth, Mars, Jupiter, Saturn, Uranus, Neptune, and Pluto. I couldn't think of any word to key in Pluto, so I just left it dangling at the end. That was silly enough to work. I also had a sentence for the geological ages: "Old Oysters Slip Down My Pants Pocket." I can't remember the ages anymore, but the sentence still comes back to me.

You can imagine how surprised I was to discover there have been whole books on tricks like that. My husband, Roger, found me one called The Absent-Minded Professor's Memory Book, with long poems to help you remember long lists such as the Presidents of the United States or the Kings of England or the Books of the Old Testament, and short pithy sayings to help you to remember, for example, how to turn the clock for daylight savings: Spring forward. Fall back.

Silly sayings help lots of ways. I can hardly even spell my own name without looking it up in the phone book. But I can remember how to spell a word if there's even a mildly ridiculous rule connected with it. For years I couldn't spell presents. I often spelled it "presants." Then my friend Betty Grace said "Just remember you don't want any ants in your presents." Bingo. Likewise, I know the different numbers of s's in desert and dessert because there's s for sand in the middle of desert and ss for strawberry *shortcake in the middle of dessert. Unfortunately, the dictionary is full of words with no jokes. So God bless the person who taught computers to spell.*

My cousin Suzy remembers feelings. She may not know right off who a person is, but she remembers how she feels about them. Sometimes by following that thread of feeling and leading the person into a conversation, she can find clues to who they are. But more of that in the chapter on names.

One last trick that works for me and for some of my friends. I can remember things better if I don't have to. If I just relax, they may pop into my mind. If I start trying hard, there's no hope. My husband, Roger, and my daughter, Eve, both used to love crossword puzzles. I discovered I can supply words for other people's crossword puzzles off the top of my head, but if I start trying to do a puzzle myself, no words come.

So I've learned that if I can't remember something, one way to retrieve it is to start thinking about something else. For some reason Roger could never believe that.

That may be the problem here, I thought. I'm trying too hard. But if I let the wild thing get away — but I haven't. I've captured what-is-it in my notebook. Now I just have to find the shape.

I turned the light out, lay back and tried to make my mind blank. But I still couldn't sleep. I saw Aunt Nancy lying by the pond. I recalled the thump as my computer fell.

I turned the light back on and read the rest of my first chapter. At least, as I said, it calmed my nerves.

People with good memories think all these tricks are silly. Well, sure. A blind man walking along tapping with a stick would look silly to someone who didn't know why he did it. But what works, works.

What doesn't work doesn't, even if it "should." The Improve-Your-Memory books have tricks that fit the majority of minds. My cousin Suzy took a course in memory improvement and learned to remember names by associating them with something else. Trouble was that afterwards she could remember what she'd associated them with, but not necessarily the name. She'd introduce Mrs. Star as Mrs. Twinkle, Mr. Rich as Mr. Money. Luckily, she had a sense of humor and so did Mr. Meeker, who she introduced as Mr. Wimp. She didn't get in trouble like my other memory-course friend Katy, who introduced her boss's new associate as Mr. Heinie. His name was Butts.

Actually, Katy found out she was a rhyme person. She could name her cousin's girlfriend this way: "Susan Price has chosen someone nice."

The point is that if you are suddenly having more trouble than you used to when you try to remember, you probably have all sorts of hidden ways to recall that you haven't discovered yet because you haven't had to. As you read about the methods some of the rest of us have used, maybe you'll be inspired to try some of them and also find ways of your own.

You can get to know your mind as it is right now. Be kind to it. And make the most of what it has to offer. I notice some of my friends resent having to use tricks because they never had to before. But heck, a trick is better than a hole in the head.

If it takes you longer to remember, just keep in mind: It was the tortoise who won the race, not the hare.

End of chapter. So?

Then suddenly something popped into my mind. The what-is-it thing had to do with money. I couldn't think why. Nobody in the family but my father had real money, and he wouldn't let go of a dime.

I promised myself I'd talk to Ted about everything tomorrow. He has a great logical mind. But even so, he wants to marry me.

Roger appeared in my mind and bumped Ted out. Roger with his shock of brown hair that fell over his forehead, and that slow grin like a built-in double-take. I mustn't cry over Roger. I'd been blessed. When you aren't blessed anymore, it feels like a big empty hole. Somehow, it's a hole you have to honor for a while. Or I do.

Roger went so fast. We were laughing over one

of his outrageous jokes. Something to do with collecting some old-time pottery for our shop. Laughing until the tears rolled down our cheeks. And then I went out in the kitchen to get us both a Coke. I left him leaning back in his favorite rocking chair, shaking with laughter. When I came back, he was slumped forward. He was dead. They tell me it's the best way a person can go, without fear or pain. But he was only sixty-five, nearly ten years older than healthy-horse me. And it didn't seem fair. I wasn't ready.

I drifted off, thinking about Roger, who picked a right way to die. Even if I didn't like it. He was good at right ways. And as I drifted off, I remembered what Roger said about Aunt Nancy. Bingo. I was awake again. "In business she's a genius," Roger said, "but in personal relationships she makes the wrong choices and takes the wrong actions." He meant choosing her husband, of course. But why, come to think of it, did he say it in the plural? I had the what-is-it.

But what did I have?

CHAPTER
7

SATURDAY MORNING, MAY 25

I woke up early, considering that I didn't get to sleep until about two-thirty. Woke up at seven, to be exact, and couldn't get back to sleep. I threw on my clothes as if that would help me to do something useful. But what?

I went in the kitchen to have a cup of coffee with Elsie. The clock on the wall over the stove said 7:10. Elsie came on at seven o'clock, but she was often early in order to be sure not to be late.

She was sitting at the kitchen table reading the newspaper by the yellow glow of electric light, and eating scrambled eggs with ketchup, her favorite breakfast. The roasty smell of coffee filled the room. For a moment the scene seemed normal — Elsie, dressed as always in a man's shirt and jeans, red hair pulled back with an elastic band into a ponytail. But she was sick pale. "I hear you heard a bump in the night," she said, large-eyed and low-voiced. Behind her, out the kitchen window the world was gray with drizzle. "Silva told me the police came." Elsie shivered in one long motion from head to toe.

So O.K., we were only one day from a murder. And she was a possible suspect. But here she was, on the job. Dependable. Keeping up her strength with scrambled eggs.

Elsie was one of those people who give comfort. Even now she sat, as always, like a strong wind wouldn't blow her out of her chair. And yet she wasn't heavy — a tad plump, but with the curves in the right places. When her eyes were on me, I always felt she really saw me, including the hurts I hid down under. And I felt she saw without judgment.

I thought: We mustn't lose Elsie! Why, Elsie knew how to help my father not feel stupid when his brain didn't work quite right. If I forgot something when she was around, she quietly filled the gap.

She was Pop's favorite sitter, the one who could talk with him about anything from biographies of famous men, which was his hobby, to the stock-market quotations of the day. And she always laughed at his jokes. Yet she couldn't be more than thirty. I was so grateful that on this first morning after we found Nancy dead, the day after the bump in the night, Elsie was there.

I wished she weren't so deathly white, in contrast to her flaming red hair. All the angles in her face showed, as if she'd lost twenty pounds since the day before. I realized her eyes were pink. She'd been crying.

She stood up and handed me the newspaper, pointing to the headline about us. We were on the bottom of page one. Not in huge black type at the top of the front page, the way our story felt to me. That went to some big drug bust. They were welcome to it. Our story said the police had no real leads yet on the Candy-Bar Murder, except perhaps a candy wrapper found in the woods. The story described Aunt Nancy's vanished pocketbook, asking anyone who found it to call a police number right away.

While I read, Elsie brought me coffee, black and strong, and then sat back down and kept her eyes on me, as I re-read each line. She squirmed in her chair. She clenched her hands. I began to know that the trouble was more than our tragedy alone, or the police coming in the night. I put the paper down. "What's the matter?"

She swallowed, shut her eyes, opened them, and then spoke fast: "I'm not what you think I am." She sat right there in the familiar straight-back kitchen chair, at the familiar blond wood table near the window looking out over the rain-gray mountains. But her dependable calm face now clenched into wrinkles between her blue eyes. "My hair isn't really red. My last name isn't really Small. I'm dangerous."

I was amazed. Dangerous? "Elsie," I said, "how can that be? You are just the one we need at a bad time."

She rocked back and forth in her kitchen chair, squeezing her hands together on the table. "I'm hiding." She stopped and bit her lips together and then went on, slowly. "I've loved it here." She looked around as if the kitchen cabinets were friends. "This seems so far from my husband." She bit her lips again as if she wanted to keep her words inside, but then went on: "But you need to know he said he'd kill me if I left him. And I left him anyway. And he tried to kill me." She pulled a tissue out of the box on the table, wiped her eyes, and then continued. "That's part of his problem. He fails at things. If he was here last night, of course he knocked something over. He's like that. Oh God, why do I have to get mixed up with these people who have problems? I always do." She took a gulp of coffee, like maybe it was brandy, to kill the pain.

Silk jumped up in my lap. I stroked him and waited.

"He didn't quite kill me. He didn't stab me in the right place. He missed my heart. He's like that. So when I got out of the hospital, I dyed my hair and flew to a place where nobody knew me, and took a new kind of job. I shouldn't have come to work today. But I had to tell you myself."

I was so unnerved, I couldn't move. I just sat there with my china mug halfway to my mouth, and Silk purring in my lap. Behind Elsie, on the windowsill, was the clay rabbit with brown spots that Albert made in kindergarten and gave my mother. Anna used it for a paperweight. Out the window: first, lawn with garden chairs we never sat in anymore, then the white lilac that would bloom shortly.

"You've been our friend," I said to Elsie. Good grief, Pop would go wild if we lost Elsie. I'd miss her too. "Of course you had to tell us yourself." I didn't want her to be dangerous like she said. "But how do you know your husband has found you? How do you know he has anything to do with Nancy's death? That doesn't make sense." I didn't want it to make sense.

"Besides," I said, "you probably weren't even here at the time Nancy was killed."

"Oh God," she rocked back and forth in her chair. "Why did I have to double-shift and come at eleven that night? And her car was in the driveway when I got here, so maybe she was already dead. But the police aren't sure."

I interrupted. "But Dorothy was here before you, and says she heard funny sounds while she was listening to her TV program. A car, and then a kind of a crunch a little while before you came. Only, she figured the sound might be part of the TV show, until she thought about it later." Why did Dorothy have to be a television addict? I shuddered to think that life and death might have hung on whether Dorothy thought the sound of a car was background noise in her television show instead of a real car.

Elsie stopped rocking. "I hope to God that Harold doesn't have anything to do with the trouble here. But how can I know?" She blew her nose. "He said he'd find me wherever I went. And I believe it. And he's out loose. I couldn't prove he stabbed me. He did it from behind. I didn't see him. I couldn't prove it, so I couldn't get help. I ran away. I found a new kind of job. I used to teach high school. But he'd look for me in schools. Now, if I can't do this, what can I do?"

"Listen," I said, "you have to tell the police. But make them promise to keep your secret. Don't even tell me who you really are or where you're from. Certainly don't tell Pop your real name."

I got up, went around, put my arm around her shaky shoulders. "But you're the one in danger. Not us. Why would he kill my Aunt Nancy? She didn't look like you. Pop always said she looked like me, or vice versa. She wasn't even the one who was sheltering you. So I don't believe it was your husband who killed Nancy." That was my hunch. But was I foolish to follow my hunch? That Elsie was a friend we needed, more than a danger?

"He's crazy," Elsie said. "He might do anything. He might have killed your Aunt Nancy to frame me for it. He's so good at conning people. If he traced me here, God knows what he'd do. He's really crazy."

She blew her nose again, hard, as if she wished she could blow him away. "His first wife fell in a well and drowned when he was out visiting a friend. Or so he said. Nobody ever asked if maybe she got in that well just before he went out. That never occurred to me. Until after he tried to kill me. But you see, he likes water. And Nancy . . . ," She didn't have to finish that.

"Exactly what did he do to you?" I felt a rock at the pit of my stomach.

"When he stabbed me, he pushed me in a river. We lived near a river. I thought it was such a lovely place. I couldn't prove he did it. But I knew."

I thought about the chapter on hunches I intend to put in my book on surviving without a memory. Because now was an acid test. Could I trust my intuition? I'd sure had practice. If you can't remember things, you need to listen to and cultivate your intuition about who to trust, God knows. Because you have to trust the people who remember. And it's important to trust the right ones.

I'd even tried to write down how you tune into a true hunch. How you reach out with some deep layer of yourself to some deep layer of another person. For example, there was some deep calm at the center of Elsie, even while she was so upset. At some level she was at peace with herself. So I trusted her. But that sounded odd and maybe unreliable when you put it into words.

"You're looking at me," she said, "as if you're trying to decide if I've spilled mud on my soul."

And I was glad I could answer right back: "You haven't."

Because my strong hunch was that we ought to stick with Elsie. That she would stick with us. But if my father was having a lucid day, he had a right to help decide. He was the one who might be alone in the house with Elsie and whatever conditions came with her.

That's how the schedule worked. It was posted in the kitchen. Anna, the housekeeper, came from 9 A.M. to 2 P.M., cleaned, made lunch, and left dinner ready to reheat or eat cold. So Elsie, whose usual shift was from 7 A.M. to 3 P.M., overlapped with Anna, but not entirely. Dorothy usually came in from 3 P.M. to 11 P.M. And Silva, from 11 P.M. to 7 A.M., was almost always alone with my father. How sad that on Friday night, when poor Nancy was killed, Elsie also did the 11 P.M. to 7 A.M. shift — an easy one because my father often sleeps right through. Larry, our only male sitter, who came on Saturday and Sunday, was usually the one who substituted on week nights, but he couldn't that night.

As I pondered about that, the phone on the kitchen table rang. I picked it up: My house painter. I'd given him Pop's number for when he couldn't reach me at home. Elsie had knocked him right out of my mind. And he'd been due to start work at nine o'clock. But that's not why he called. Not because he arrived for work and I wasn't there. "I fell off a ladder and broke my leg," he said. One paint job on hold. Too bad, but just as well. I had to deal with Elsie and Pop.

My father's bell rang. He'd slept late. The kitchen clock said nine. I went in and kissed him good morning, watching to see how close he was to reality. "Yesterday," he said, "we found your Aunt Nancy dead." His voice was sad, amazed, but clear. He was having a good day. Elsie wheeled him into the living room in his red plaid bathrobe for breakfast at his favorite table. I waited until he finished his scrambled eggs with raspberry jelly. Not the combination I'd want. I seem to be the only one in the house with sense enough to eat my eggs plain. Elsie brought her knitting in and sat with us. Still pink of eye.

"Elsie is thinking about leaving us," I told him.

"You wouldn't dare!" he said. God in Plaid Bathrobe. "Why, Elsie, you are like a member of my family. I was even thinking of leaving you something in my will."

"Oh, for heaven's sake, Pop." He'd discovered he could say "will" and watch people jump to attention. He said it once to the electrician who came to fix the circuit that went dead, and then when I asked him if he really planned to put something in his will for the man, he looked quite hurt. "I only said I might."

Pop's doctor said it happened sometimes that with elderly people the sensor that makes us refrain from saying certain things we know we shouldn't say simply stops working. So when

Pop was bored or lonely, he told people he might leave them money. Elsie knew that.

"Elsie is in danger and she's afraid the danger may have spread to us. She wants to talk to you about it."

He listened to her story and then he shrugged. "Elsie, I like to have you here," he said. "I want you to stay. I'm sorry that happened to you."

"Look," I asked her, "why would your husband look for you in the mountains of North Carolina? You never had a connection with our mountains, did you? And the United States is a big country."

Also, I felt that Elsie had something in common with us. She'd withstood an attack. We hadn't been attacked directly, only through Nancy. I hoped. But we'd felt what happened like an attack.

"I don't know how he could have found me." She shut her eyes as if she wanted to shut the idea out. "I don't even write my mother except when I can get a friend to mail the letter from California or Mexico, or some faraway place."

"You're one of us," my father said, "even if Peaches won't let me leave you my money. Please stay. In fact, you can help me to find the killer. I intend to take charge of the investigation myself."

CHAPTER
8

MONDAY AFTERNOON, AFTER THE FUNERAL

"You must quote Mark Twain in your book," Arabella said. We were back from the funeral, and she was over from next door enjoying a dainty little chicken salad sandwich. We were all trying to cheer each other up. Besides, she had to drop her fact for the day. Literally. Into my hand. She gave it to me all written out on a slip of paper in her oversized handwriting: "I find that the further back I go, the better I remember things, whether they happened or not": Mark Twain.

She nodded her head in self-approval, and her roan wig slipped slightly. That was the wig that matched her largest horse. Perhaps she'd lost the black one. Wig, that is.

"Mark Twain knew how to relax about what he forgot," I said. "Good idea." I looked around at all the friends and relatives who'd come back to the house from the funeral. I should know their names, but even with the most familiar, sometimes when I *have* to remember them, my mind goes blank. When that happens, I keep them straight in my mind by using nicknames that go with their actions.

Cousin Mother Hen, in her black ruffles, instead of the usual pink, was big-breasted and protective like a hen. She was making us all feel good the way she often did: "Oh, Cousin Agnes, I haven't seen you since Cousin Mortimer died. You look so well. I just love that dress. I always enjoy family get-togethers like this so much."

Friends reminisced about Nancy: The man with the lawyerish dark suit and Yankee accent, who'd introduced himself as a fellow member with Nancy of Common Cause, had a voice that carried like ammonia. "I remember the time Nancy took on the County Council," he boasted to a mannish woman with white hair. "Nancy said we had to have a zoning ordinance in this county." Boy, zoning was so controversial that cousins eating sandwiches went stiff just to hear the word.

"This old farmer in overalls jumped up while she was speaking," Yankee Accent went on, "and shouted that nobody could tell him how to use his own property, and then dropped dead from a heart attack. And after the emergency people carried him off on a stretcher, Nancy went right on with her argument — picked it right up in the middle of a sentence."

The white-haired woman laughed. "That's like Nancy."

What a mixture of people had come to Pop's. Well, Asheville was like that, a mountain melting pot. With rich, retired people like Arabella who came from Atlanta, or Yankee Accent. And the folks who came to Asheville to work, like our sitters — from Elsie who was from God-knows-where, to Larry, most recently from California. And of course lots of Old Asheville types, like Pop's lawyer, Homer Sawyer. Homer had told me his grandfather was a character in Thomas Wolfe's *Look Homeward, Angel*, thinly disguised, of course. Homer was off in a corner talking to Albert, who looked badly, pale with circles under his eyes.

Lots of relatives had come from over the gap in Madison County. Bloody Madison. The nickname goes back to a massacre during the Civil War. About half the people over there were Union and the other half Confederate. Folks from Madison tend to be independent.

But our folks on Pop's side never missed a funeral or a wedding. They stood about, super-scrubbed in their church clothes, eating small cakes and sandwiches. Paying respects not just to Aunt Nancy, the sadly deceased, but to Pop, who was the oldest living member of his generation, and the richest. The living member they'd like to be like.

Pop, and Nancy too, did well in mission school, then worked their way through college. Meanwhile my grandma with the iron will made moonshine when she had to, to survive, and she cheered both Pop and Nancy on to success.

Grandma, with her snappy black eyes and bony grab-hold hands, was the one who had kept in touch. Took us with her to reunions and assorted weddings and funerals over in Madison, where outdoor tables were dish-to-dish with good food, and bearskins were nailed to the side of a barn.

My cousins from Madison knew guns, and not just for bears. I could actually remember the name of my Cousin Eltha with the sweet little-girl dimples, who was standing next to Mary and finishing a chocolate cupcake. Eltha had shot her husband dead. She was acquitted on grounds of self-defense. I admired the way she relaxed, as if nothing surprising had ever happened to her.

My Madison cousins knew religion. My second cousin Edward, over in the corner talking to Silva and looking like an older Albert with a suntan, was a lay preacher in the Church of God. My cousin Alice, next oldest to me in my generation, nodded her wispy gray-brown head and told me she knew beyond a doubt that my Aunt Nancy was safe in heaven.

I heard that with one ear, and with the other I heard my father asking loudly who had reason to kill Aunt Nancy.

My inner alarm began to ring flat-out. Pop was talking to Elsie, and for once she seemed unable to divert him.

He said, "I'm making a list of reasons

someone might want to kill Nancy, and I want everybody here to make a suggestion."

I ran over and said, "Pop, we have guests here who loved Aunt Nancy. This is not the time to make your list."

"You be quiet," he said, with his head cocked like an extra-wise eagle. "We have everybody together, and I'm sure that those who are not guilty will want to help. Besides, about half of these people are in line for me to leave them money, and I'm certainly not going to do that if they desert me at a time like this." He darted a glance around, like he was taking stock.

The old fraud! I could have choked him. He was enjoying being the center of attention, I could tell. He said "Think hard. We all know things we don't quite remember. Peaches here tells me that she's sure her aunt has told her things that will turn out to be clues if she can just remember." Did I tell him that?

But his I'll-leave-you-money trap didn't seem to work. Friends and relatives began to leave fast, like water draining from a bathtub. Take that, Pop!

Even Albert came over and told Pop that now that the service was over, he had to get back to the shop. He had a big customer coming in on Tuesday. "And in case you've lost track of time, that's tomorrow morning." I began to hope we could avoid Pop's inquisition.

Pop turned so red in the face, I was alarmed. He sat up so straight in his wheelchair he looked like he'd grown two inches and sat on a thumb-tack. "I know what day it is, thank you. And if my mother had been murdered, I'd want to help find the solution, even if I was a damned cripple."

I sucked in my breath. When I was a kid, my mother had a parrot, and if it got too noisy and annoyed Pop, she threw a cloth over the cage. I wanted to throw a cloth over Pop and wheel him out of the room. But he was my father, and this was his house, and I couldn't.

Albert said, "I'm not a cripple in my mind, and if you need a mind, I'll stay for now." He said it emphasizing "mind" as if contrasting his to Pop's. He showed his teeth like a dog snarling, walked stiffly around, and plunked himself in the chair one over from Pop's. Albert acted as if he couldn't stand to be too close because Pop smelled. Oh, brother!

Larry, our weekend sitter, came quickly and sat next to Albert in the circle of chairs around Pop's table. Larry the peacemaker, a born-again, reformed drug addict in a dark going-to-church suit. Larry had deep-set eyes under a sloping brow, and dark curly hair. Very intense eyes, like those of a saint in a picture a Catholic friend of mine had. Or like an angry convict I saw in the newspaper. Except for his eyes he was always calm. He'd explained how he was saving money to go to divinity school.

The police had asked me if his background with drugs didn't worry me. So, O.K., drugs and killings often go together. But when we took on

93

Larry, I went by my hunch again, and hadn't been sorry. Larry was absolutely dependable. He didn't even try to reform Pop, the way Dorothy would like to do. He said each person had to come to what he believed in his own way, and he'd like to be a good example, not a nag.

"I've always admired the way the members of your family get along together," he was saying to Pop and Albert, "but the strain of this situation must be hard for you all."

Only one of our Madison cousins stayed: Cousin Mother Hen. She was close enough kin to Pop so she might really have hopes he'd leave her money. But I didn't think she was the gold-digging type. The Yankee Accent man stayed too. Why on earth? He didn't know us well enough so that he owed us anything or could expect Pop to leave him any money. But we had both of Nancy's sides represented. Mother Hen for country roots and Yankee Accent for city determination.

Cousin Mother Hen was nervous. She couldn't keep her hands still. She wasn't making any of those nurturing remarks I kind of liked: Pop, you look well, or, Peaches, you have such a pretty neck. That was the most original she ever made. Imagine a neck being pretty.

While the others moved chairs around at my father's direction, I went in the office and got a lined yellow pad and a pencil. *A pencil is a girl's best friend*. Right? Even that wasn't going to be enough if our guinea pigs cut loose and all talked

94

at once. Didn't I wish! I found the tape recorder on the edge of the bookshelf, put a tape in it, and slipped it in my shoulder bag.

I went back to the living room and found the self-chosen nine still arranging chairs. I turned my back to them and acted like I was looking for something in the bookcase in back of my father's table. What I actually did was set the voice-activated tape recorder on the shelf between the Russian drinking horn and the carved redwood box from California, presents from traveling friends.

"You sit down," Pop said to me. "We're going to start now, and you have a big stake in this because you don't have an alibi." He banged on the table. I had to settle for a chair around toward the front door.

I made a diagram on my yellow pad. My father sat in his wheelchair in his usual place in front of the bookcase. Elsie was next to him, on the right, then Albert, still pouting after his run-in with Pop. Larry in his born-again church suit next. Ted, God bless him, settled into a small armchair pulled over from its usual place by the fireplace. I had Ted on one side of me and Yankee Accent on the other. Next to Y.A. came Mary, who had managed to tone her color scheme down to shades of blue for the funeral. Her hands were clenched into fists. Next in the circle came Dorothy, fingering the cross around her neck and looking too scared to say a word. She was the sitter actually on duty.

Next to Dorothy came Silva and then Cousin Mother Hen, completing the circle back to my father. Mother Hen with her broad mouth, snubbed nose and baby blue eyes, was usually as placid as a sleepy cat, and as warm and friendly as a puppy. Suddenly her name came to me: Gloria. I should remember that because it was what the angels said: *Gloria in excelcis Deo*. And most of the time she was sweet as an angel. Once in a while she had a temper tantrum. She was known for it. I'd never seen one of her tantrums, but Cousin Eltha had told Pop about one.

Pop beamed at us all and bowed his head at us graciously. "Nancy would appreciate your being here," he said. The Russian drinking horn pointed up behind him and seemed to come out of his head, like one of the devil's horns. Fifty percent devil. Was that Pop? No, forty-nine percent. That was enough.

"Now, our dear Nancy did have a habit of saying exactly what she thought. Nancy had a way of knowing things." Pop looked around at us, obviously hoping someone would wince. Nobody blinked. "So, maybe she found out something that somebody was afraid she'd tell. Something that some man or woman felt would ruin them." He raised his eyebrows and looked around the circle again hopefully.

"Any candidates?" Pop asked. Instant freeze.

Next to Pop, Cousin Mother-Hen Gloria sat rigid.

On his other side, Albert leaned over and

whispered something to Elsie, who was still drained pale. Mary was breathing harder than usual.

"Mary, what do you think?" Pop asked.

For once Mary was dead serious. "Charleston," she said. "Since Mother was just back from Charleston, there could be a connection with what killed her. My grandmother and Uncle Herman and Aunt Sue on my father's side live in Charleston, as most of you know, and of course my brother, Albert." She nodded at Albert. "But I was not in Charleston for several months before my mother died." I saw who she was: Mary the good example of coming clean. Almost every member of the group followed her example.

This is what it all boiled down to: Albert lived in Charleston and had his shop there; Silva had a daughter-in-law in Charleston; Elsie was a Navy brat whose family had lived in Charleston for five years while she was growing up; and I had been a boarder at Ashley Hall for two years, back when the school took boarders. The Yankee Accent man said he'd been down to the Spoleto music festival. He spoke up just like he was one of us.

All perfectly reasonable, at least, on the face of it.

My father yawned and pointed a finger at Yankee Accent. "Exactly who are you and why are you here?" I think we'd all been wondering.

"My name is John Q. Denton." Every head

turned toward him. Yankee Accent paused and straightened his tie. He stared us all down. "I retired here from Connecticut. I like to see justice done." I decided he had taught high-school civics, recycled his garbage without fail, and did not believe in life after death. He was that earnest. Maybe angry.

Silva nodded as if she thought justice was a great idea, and somehow long overdue. Pop blinked with surprise.

Accent's voice was accusing, even though his words weren't. "I was a member of both Common Cause and the Civil Liberties Union with your sister," he said to Pop. "I admired her. I was upset about her death. So naturally I wanted to hear what each of you had to say about the reason for it. And incidentally I'd like to ask the same question you asked me. I'd like to know the name and relationship to Nancy of everyone else in this group."

Immediately I knew by the chill that fell over us, that every person at the table thought he had a nerve taking over like that. And yet, I could see why he wanted to know.

"We've talked," I said. "I'm Peaches Dann, Nancy's niece."

Pop nodded and said he'd known Nancy the longest because he was the oldest one there. Then we went around the circle, beginning with Elsie, each person identifying himself, Mother Hen last of all. "I'm Gloria Larson," she said. "I'm a cousin to all the family members here."

She tried to smile her angel smile, but it wavered. One hand kept holding onto the other like the second hand might suddenly misbehave.

"Do you have a daughter who lived next door to Nancy?" Accent asked, very precise, as if he was a scientist being sure the experiment was set up right. He held his hands in front of him, fingertips together, balanced so the fingers tipped neither to the left nor to the right.

I felt a ripple go round the circle, not exactly fear, not exactly excitement. But we knew. The answer to that question was going to trap Gloria in something. We knew by the way her heart seemed to beat in her throat, by the way her eyes flew wider. She was one of us and he wasn't, so we were on her side. But he might be after something dark. In which case we were on his side.

"How do you happen to know that?" She glared at him like she'd caught him trespassing.

"You had a reason to be afraid of Nancy," he said in that piercing monotone voice. "You had a reason to be furious at her. I think you should tell the story yourself, not make me do it."

Gloria looked around at the rest of us. Perhaps she hoped we might rise up and throw him out. We sat fascinated. Pop smiled as if he couldn't wait for the next turn in the plot. Albert's eyes gleamed the way they did when he'd spotted a valuable antique. The lines between Silva's eyes went deep angry black. I thought: Why is Silva so on edge about all this? She was the late-night sitter. She hardly knew Nancy.

Gloria's voice went rough like a worn-out record turned too loud. "Nancy told you. She would. She meant to testify in my little granddaughter's custody hearing." The parts of her face twitched out of sync with each other.

Accent nodded. Formal as a judge. "She told me she was going to testify against a cousin's daughter who lived next door. She would testify that her neighbor abused the child, and recommend that the child be in the custody of the father." He paused and swept us with his eyes. "She told me she felt it was only fair to tell the cousin, who was the child's grandmother, exactly what she intended to do." He turned to Gloria. "It seemed to me that if only one cousin joined this interrogation group, that might be the one she told. You came to see what was said about you here, isn't that right?"

I sucked in my breath. Nancy was going to help take a child from her own third cousin, her second cousin Gloria's daughter. That made her a traitor in Madison County.

"I begged Nancy, I really begged her, not to come between our family and my grandchild," Gloria cried.

"Nothing stood in the way of my mother's sense of justice," Albert cried out. "Certainly not family loyalty." Was he accusing or was he bragging? I couldn't be sure.

Yankee Accent nodded: "Now that your cousin Nancy is dead, she can't testify," he said. The expression on his face hardly changed. He was like a cross between a robot and a judge. I was shivering.

I suddenly remembered that my mother said Gloria's daughter Stella was born just a little while after Gloria got married. A fact the family tried to hush up. But that had happened a long time ago. Could it matter now?

My round-faced, child-eyed, Mother-Hen Cousin Gloria sat up straight: "You don't understand. My Stella went through a bad time, but then she got help." She said it like that was a wonderful gift. Like she wanted to sing a hymn of thanks. She raised her face as if she was feeling the sun on it. She smiled. "I wanted to help Stella every way I could." She paused. Her eyes flashed. "Not go out and kill Nancy!" Then she burst into tears, pulled out a handkerchief, and held it over her sobbing mouth with both pink hands.

I noticed little bleached-blond Silva was quietly crying, too. She sat next to Gloria, but how could she know her? Because she did the late-night shift with my father, she never met visitors.

Pop said: "Gloria, I've always known that even though you're a good woman you'd lie or steal or kill for that child. I hope you didn't."

Larry said: "The greatest things a child can have are a mother's positive love and God's love." Was he going to start preaching? Probably only trying to inject a more positive tone.

Gloria bounced up and yelled at Pop. "You're

a nasty stingy senile old man who wants power. That's why you invited this terrible man here to accuse me." She stamped out, still sobbing.

My father said: "Thank you, dear," and raised both eyebrows. She slammed the front door.

"You upset her, Larry," Pop said. "And you, Silva, why are you crying? Please get me a glass of water. I'm thirsty." He looked like he needed the water poured over him. He was so upset he was red in the face. "You are all still suspects," he grated. "I don't even know yet what the rest of you are hiding." Things were getting out of hand.

Elsie stood up. "We ought to be grieving, not fighting." She turned to my father. "You have absolutely no proof that any of us had anything to do with the murder of your sister Nancy. You know she made a lot of people angry. Any strong woman would." My father raised his eyebrows in surprise, but he let her go on. His red face began to fade. "You can't rule out that the killer was after something she had, or someone in this family still has," Elsie said. "You can't rule out the possibility that she caught someone trying to break into this house and she was killed trying to stop him. All of us are innocent until proved guilty! And furthermore, someone tried to break into this house on Friday night, just one night after she was killed. That could be connected." She turned to my father again — but, with his head cocked to one side, he appeared to have dozed off, suddenly out of steam. She caught her breath and apologized to the rest of us. "I got carried away. But *he* doesn't realize how he hurts your feelings." She sat back down, trembling.

Silva came back with the glass of water and sat down in the seat next to Pop, where Gloria had been before. Her eyes were still red.

But now Pop was awake again. He drank the water. Elsie whispered something in his ear. "Be quiet, Elsie," he ordered. "I know what I'm doing. People want to help." He smiled his little-boy, please-help-me smile. "If each of you will tell me where you were when Nancy died, I'll be grateful."

At least that sounded logical. And I think our guests all felt emotionally wrung out. I sure did. If they told Pop what he asked, they could get away with leaving, gracefully.

I, of course, was home alone the evening Nancy died. I said so, as a good example. Albert told about inviting his neighbor over; Larry and Mary each told how they were home alone after nine that night, just like me. Yankee Accent said he was at a concert of the Asheville Symphony, and Elsie said she started her double-shift at eleven, with no alibi before that. Silva said she was home sick but couldn't prove it. Dorothy was home by herself because her husband was at a firefighters' meeting. Ted was alone with a good book.

"That's wonderful." My father smiled his ironical half-smile. "Most of us are first-rate suspects, even me. I was nearby when it happened.

103

And especially my poor cousin Gloria." He got a faraway look in his eye. "My sister Nancy didn't understand how protective people feel about their children. Nancy was not the protective type." He shrugged, like he'd given up trying to figure that out. "I thank you for your cooperation. Now, if you'll all go home, I'll go take a nap."

Larry and Elsie said they'd see us soon. Everybody left except Dorothy, who was on duty, and Albert, who kissed my father on the top of the head and said he knew they were both under a strain. He'd try to get his business on a good footing and get back soon to help Mary. Then he left to go back to Charleston.

I looked at my watch. We'd been talking about an hour and twenty-five minutes. The tape just covered.

"Time goes by so fast," I said.

Pop opened his eyes sleepily. "You're damned right. Yesterday I was ten years old. "As for you," he said to me, "I'm glad you're staying over."

I hadn't realized I was staying, but O.K.

"I don't want you to sleep." He began to tremble. I hoped he wouldn't go over the edge. "Keep a watch." He leaned forward and lowered his voice to a whisper. "Elsie is right. The killer will come again."

CHAPTER
9

TUESDAY AND WEDNESDAY,
MAY 28 AND 29

If a thing upsets me or pleases me a lot, silly details of it stick in my mind, sieve though it be. Like the fact that I was eating bread and butter pickles when I heard that World War II was over. Hooray. Like the fact that my father had on a red shirt with mustard spilled on the stomach the day my mother died.

So the details of my close escape stood from the gray of a discouraging Tuesday. Tuesday was the day Pop didn't want me to leave him at all. I think he'd just admitted to himself that his only sister was truly gone. The drama, the ritual were over. The fact remained. And then the police came over and asked more questions. They did not ask about the back closet. Why should they?

My confrontation with the closet had come first thing Tuesday morning. I'd spent the night at Pop's again because he'd asked me to. A nightmare woke me up in the morning. Some kind of chase in fog. It was the kind of day when I felt like putting on clean clothes might help protect me from God-knows-what.

I always keep a change of clothes in my father's back guest room closet in case some emergency should come up and I have to stay over. Otherwise, the closet is used to store off-season stuff, including some of my things since Pop has more space than I do. I stay in the front guest room, but my extra in-case-of-need clothes stay in the back.

This morning I opened the closet door and the blackness scared me. As if there were ghosts hiding behind the tight-packed clothes. Pull yourself together, I told myself. But the dark deep closet would be a perfect place for a killer to hide. The closet was jammed so full it was hard to find a thing. It was a thicket for a mad murderer to wait around in. Then pounce. "Get hold of your imagination, Peaches," I said out loud. And I looked at the digital clock by the bed. Somehow I felt the later it was, the less likely a killer would still be there from the night. I never said I was logical. The clock said 7:30. Still early.

My heart beat hard. I wanted more light. I reached to turn on the light, with its hanging chain, by feel. The chain hangs roughly in the middle of the closet near my father's winter coat. I pulled and the light came on. I pushed the clothes this way and that. A cheerful garment bag with roses on it, that my mother bought, had winter shirts in it. I knew that. My own green winter coat with the silver buttons was a friend. No ambush here. I laughed at myself.

I found a green skirt and a blue and green blouse that I like. I put them on and felt better. But not entirely right.

I looked in my father's room. He was still asleep, pale and gaunt against his white pillow in the big mahogany bed with the empty place where my mother used to sleep on the other side. A line came to me from a poem about loss: "Eventually, every bed is narrow." Wrong. Too wide.

I searched the house, just to be on the safe side. Nothing there but the antiques my mother collected over the years, all carefully dusted, the clutter of Pop's mementos. And Elsie in the kitchen making coffee. All normal.

Why did I feel so apprehensive? Well, if one unbelievable thing can happen, like murder in the garden, then what can you be sure of?

Friendship, I hoped. Elsie poured us both a cup of coffee and we sat and drank it in the silence that's O.K. with friends. A nice respite before the phone started ringing and Pop woke up.

At nine o'clock on Tuesday. Albert called from the shop in Charleston. He called to suggest that, considering the attempted break-in at Pop's house, this was the time to put any small valuables — like my father's collection of old silver dollars, and the Confederate belt buckle

Albert called a "plate," and the antique miniature portrait he sold Mom, and the best of the silver — into the safe-deposit box. Albert said he didn't have but a minute, he had an important client coming even before opening time, and I heard the bell on the door jangle as we talked. "But you can convince your father."

The break-in was on Friday. Delayed reaction. But Albert had a good idea. Now was the time. He'd tried before to get Pop to keep those things in a safe place.

Still, I figured nobody would have killed Aunt Nancy and then tried to break into the house again just for money, not when the trail was still so hot and the police were so itchy. For money, a thief would pick a safer place to rob, or a better time. But before he hung up Albert reminded me the little portrait was worth about $10,000, even though he'd sold it to Mom for a lot less because at the time he didn't know any better. I found the price hard to believe. I figured he liked to warn us because the fact that he sold valuable things made him feel important. Albert needed to feel important. Especially when things went wrong. Just like Mary needed bright colors. Just like Pop needed to feel in command, even though he was losing it. Just like I needed to feel useful, which was why I was writing my book.

Pop agreed to the safe-deposit-box idea, but we got distracted when the police arrived with more questions.

It was Wednesday morning before I took the

silver dollars out of the drawer of Pop's bedside table and began to look on the bookshelves for the portrait. Pop said he thought the buckle was already in the bank.

With all the little mementos Pop displayed on shelves, I could have looked right at the place where the tiny portrait sat and missed it. To find anything on those shelves, you had to look inch by inch. But even then, no picture appeared. Not next to the bronze medal the president of the Jefferson Standard Life Insurance Company gave Pop in celebration of his having been an early stockholder (and now such a large one). Not in back of the antique face mug that my Roger gave Pop for his seventieth birthday. Though that was valuable, too, because Roger, the collector, had found a real gem. Nor was that little portrait hidden behind the brightly colored nesting dolls that Arabella brought Pop back from her trip to Russia. I liked the way somebody had put the doll set in front of a book about travels through Czarist Russia. Next to biographies, preferably of financiers, or great leaders, Pop liked travel books best.

"You're not looking carefully enough," Pop called out. "Or you'd have found it by now. If you can't even find a picture worth ten thousand dollars, you can't look worth a damn." I went and sat down by him at the table.

"We must have put the little picture in a drawer," I said. "Or Mary's kids stuffed it in some strange place. Something like that. I can't

109

find it. But I'll keep searching."

"Call Mary," he said. "Maybe she moved it. Maybe Albert called her up yesterday afternoon and told her to put it in a safe place if we hadn't already done it. He says I can't be trusted. And Mary came by here yesterday afternoon."

"Now Pop," I began. But he was adamant. So I called Mary. She didn't answer.

"Call Albert!" Pop demanded. Oh Lord, it was going to be one of those days. But the easiest thing was to call and get it over with.

Albert was not pleased. "Listen," he said, "if Pop keeps valuable things just lying around, what does he expect? If that miniature is gone he got what he deserved." He was in a vile humor. "I certainly did *not* call and tell Mary to go over and hide that picture. You tell Pop he's a grown man, and he should take responsibility for himself."

I'd just as soon pull the tail of a lion. And by his age Pop's character is already formed. And I'm not the world's best looker. So I organized a search. I got wonderful help.

Larry was the daytime sitter on Wednesday because Elsie was at home sick. The strain had gotten to her. In his white suit, which he always wore like a uniform when he was on duty, he looked like the forces of good ready to do battle with the forces of loss and evil. Larry, who claimed he'd been a liar and a thief while he was on drugs. And now was in the Big Brother program helping a nine-year-old boy without a

110

father. What with those deep-set burning eyes, I could imagine Larry had the intensity to go over the edge and get in trouble. But I was sure my hunch was right to trust him now. He moved right. Slowly and surely. He never wasted a motion. At the end of his shift, he'd invariably collected all the lost pencils and pens into a handy jar. Or found some other extra, small way to be useful. I was glad he was there to help look.

And Ted, too. Just as we were about to begin our serious searching, Ted came in, not only windblown but perspiring and reporting a heat wave outside. He was ready to help, and so was Anna, who appeared behind the vacuum, and cut it off to say she couldn't remember dusting the portrait for some time.

Maybe, said Ted, it fell in back of something. It was small enough. Only about three inches high.

With a search crew so big, how could we miss?

Pop took charge. He darted around the house in his wheelchair saying, "Look carefully!" to Anna, who was searching under and in back of and in the cracks of every piece of furniture as she cleaned. "Don't miss any place," he warned Ted, who was looking on top of and in back of books. After all, the portrait could hide by lying flat on its back.

Larry and I did drawers and even medicine cabinets. I made myself look each place twice. So it took us a while. But finally I got to the back guest room.

I was surprised to find the bathroom door

shut. We just naturally leave it open. It's such a cheerful bathroom with the same pink and green and yellow color scheme as the room. In fact, I was so surprised, I knocked to see if one of my fellow searchers was using the facilities. In answer came a dreary yowl. I opened the door, and Silk got up off the duck rug and staggered out, meowing like it was the end of the world. He was upset, even frantic. He couldn't stay still in my arms. Ted came in and saw me standing consoling the cat, and he said, "What is it?"

"Someone shut Silk in the bathroom," I said. I felt confused. I knew that Silk's freaked-out state meant something more was wrong.

Pop rolled in, glared at me, and said, "Don't waste time patting the cat." But Ted went over behind the two chintz-covered chairs, and examined the windows, not touching, just looking, a frown between his eyes.

"Somebody shut the cat in the bathroom." Ted used his thinking-out-loud voice. "And nobody who was supposed to be in the house last night had any reason to do that. So it's possible the person who tried to break in before succeeded in breaking in last night and didn't want the cat in the way."

The hair on my arms stood on end. I tried to stay practical. "Silk would go to explore a strange noise," I said, rubbing behind his ears.

Ted leaned over in front of the middle window and examined the floor. "There's no sign of forced entry on the window frames," he said, "and the windows are all locked. But look, here just inside the middle window is dirt on the floor. Anna would never have let that stay there."

I looked. There was nothing as clear as a footprint. Just a small hunk of dirt.

My father took in the situation and bellowed for Anna. He was having an arrogant day, even for him. Anna and Larry both come running. Anna quivery nervous, Larry calm as always, eyes searching.

"There was no dirt on that floor yesterday," Anna said, indignant. She said she'd vacuumed well.

"Someone who came after the funeral could have left this window unlocked at the time," Ted said. His logic makes me feel so comfortable. "Then sneaked in later," he went on, "then locked the window and gone out the front door in the small hours of the morning. The front door locks itself." He turned to me. "Did you examine these windows before you went to bed last night — or the night before?"

I had to say no. Those windows are always locked. There was no reason to think they weren't still locked. Damn, I thought. It's hard to adjust to living under siege. Thank God we woke up alive.

"But if a thief came to this house after the funeral, why didn't he just stick valuable things in his pockets?" Pop asked. "You are jumping to conclusions about our friends, Ted." He sat back in his chair, head up challenging.

"Lord," said Anna, "one of those folks could have stuck ten thousand dollars' worth of picture in his pocket and then come back for the silver dollars another time. Most of those folks visit here now and then."

"So it must not have been a regular visitor," Larry said. He was frowning and looking around like we might be missing some clue. He looked as if he'd feel right at home with a magnifying glass in his hand. As if he was the Sherlock Holmes to put things to rights.

"We have no proof of anything except that someone shut the cat in the bathroom. What have we found in our search so far?" my father demanded.

It wasn't much.

Larry said he found the hammer and screwdriver we were looking for last week. Ted said that in searching behind all the books he'd found an unmailed letter, two pencils, the glasses I lost last month, and a spool of thread. I was delighted to locate the glasses. An extra pair helps. I'd found the sheet of stamps we'd needed the day before. I also found a packet of old photographs and put them aside to go through later.

Larry, being a conscientious type, had already gone back to the search as Ted and I told Pop our finds. Larry opened the door to the storage closet. Dark-haired Larry in nurse's white against the dark winter clothes. Larry who moved right. "Is there a light in here?" Larry asked, so bright in his white.

And I said, "Yes, about in the middle, there's a chain you pull." I almost went over and pulled it for him because my fingers know the exact spot. Right by Pop's coat. The old charcoal gray coat he's had forever. Larry stepped into the closet and reached for the chain, then screamed and went rigid. I ran forward, but Ted cried out, "Don't touch him! Go throw the main switch." But before I could do that, Larry fell backwards onto the floor. His own weight must have pulled him loose from the chain. Ted rushed over and pulled him out of the closet, out into the middle of the floor, and began pumping his chest and breathing into his mouth.

Pop cried out: "My God. Call the police."

And I saw that the floor was wet for some reason, and Larry's shoes, which stuck out beyond where Ted was working over him, were wet.

I ran to the pink phone by the guest room bed, and called 911 for help, though somehow I knew Ted didn't expect to save Larry. He was simply doing CPR in case there was any spark of life. I felt sick. I thought: *But why did this have to happen to Larry?* Everybody liked Larry. He even made peace between Pop and Albert. I heard Anna sobbing.

I also thought: The walls of this house don't make us safe. The locks on the doors and windows don't make us safe. Because someone had sneaked into the back room and shut Silk in the bathroom so he wouldn't make a fuss. Then somehow changed the light pull in the closet into an electrocution trap. All while I was asleep in the front guest room last night. Because I knew when the trap was put there. It was after I turned on the light yesterday morning at 7:30 and stayed alive. I could see the digital time, my green coat, the bag with the roses. And we were around the house all day. The trap had to be set in the night. And set so carefully. All while I slept.

And the trap was more devilish than just a hot wire. Someone had made double sure the power killed, by putting water on the floor. I went over to the closet and leaned down to look at the source of the water. A large cookie sheet, the old-fashioned kind with the turned-up edge, was sitting on the closet floor, with water sloshed out now, but some still in the shallow pan. The cookie sheet was in a spot where you wouldn't see it in the dark, and right where you'd stand to turn on the light. It wasn't a familiar household cookie sheet, but extra big, the institutional size. As if a school cafeteria had a tag sale, and the killer found it there and changed it from a source of joy into a source of death. I hoped Mustache would find the killer's fingerprints on it.

Ted continued to pump Larry's chest, to puff air into his mouth. But Larry was inert. Even his black curly hair seemed to have lost life. I caught a glimpse of his eyes and they were dull. His

116

body moved only with Ted's movements. I shivered.

I carefully pulled aside my father's coat and looked at the light chain. A wire was wound around the light pull. A hot wire, obviously. If I had turned on the light, I'd have been dead. And if Larry hadn't sprung the trap, it might have killed me later.

The idea of a deliberate trap, in a closet I used, scared me numb. It also made me mad. And double-mad for Larry, who had turned his life around to good kind person. Now, because he tried to help, he was dead. Somebody had killed twice. And the second time at least was a diabolical premeditated plan. I was furious.

I said "We'll get that son of a bitch."

Pop stared me down. "Not *son* of a bitch. Gloria did it. She was mad at Larry. She stalked out. Remember?"

But Gloria had been mad at *Pop,* not Larry. Pop was remembering like he wanted to remember. New Improved Memory. Should I have a chapter on that?

"Gloria fools people with those ruffles, and sometimes with sweet talk. She doesn't fool me," Pop said. "She'd kill for her daughter. She drowned Nancy. She has electrocuted that poor innocent boy. She'll kill again." Pop cocked his head. Exactly like he did when he said he heard burglars on the roof. At this terrible momet we had all we could manage, *without* burglars on the roof.

CHAPTER
10

A FEW MINUTES LATER

The police arrived right away. Mustache and back-up. They'd had practice getting to Pop's house. They rushed in and took our stories. Mustache frowning and pulling at his you-know-what.

Was there any reason I knew of that somebody might want to kill Larry? Drugs? But that was finished. "He was a fair, square person," I said, trying not to cry. "His trouble made him understand other people's trouble more. Even Pop's."

Strange that I began to cry over Larry, when I hadn't been able to do that for Nancy, even though I was the one who found her dead. The tears leaked down my face. I couldn't stop them.

"This is somebody crazy who killed him, isn't it?" I asked. I wanted that to be true.

"Maybe," said Mustache. "You say you kept clothes in the closet with the trap. Can you think of anybody who might have a reason to kill you and who knew about that?" I shook my head and felt numb again. Not unless I had seen or heard something that could put the finger on the killer but didn't realize it. Oh God, I thought, suppose there is something buried in my mind that would solve all this if I could just retrieve it. Suppose the killer thinks he's in a race against time to close my mouth before I can remember. My mother used to say, "It'll come to you." If it was going to come, why couldn't it hurry? There was, of course, the even more frightening possibility that whoever killed Nancy thought she was me. But that was ridiculous, wasn't it?

Mustache had to question us all again. He asked especially about the cookie sheet. I was no help, except to point out that it was obviously too big to fit in Pop's oven.

Finally, Mustache suggested that while his men went over the house, inch by inch, to be sure, for one thing that there were no more booby traps, Pop should spend the night some-place else.

Whereupon Pop announced he was going to Arabella's next door, and that Elsie would come, too. In fact, he personally called Arabella, and she said that was O.K. Elsie agreed, even though her shift was due to end at three. We left a note for Dorothy, who would arrive shortly.

Ted and I drove Pop and Elsie out onto the road, which perches halfway up a mountain, and then the short distance down to Arabella's, where we turned into her long driveway. The flat place in our mountainside gets extra-wide at her house and even leaves her room for a big split-rail riding ring which we drove past. But Pop's mind was still back on Cousin Gloria.

"These fools are searching our house instead of grabbing Gloria," he complained. Dry-eyed about Larry. Acting as if Larry's death was just a problem to solve. Using his burglars-on-the-roof voice. "They'll lose the scent. She did it and she'll get away." He kept repeating that with variations. There was no way I could calm him down except to say I'd follow Cousin Gloria to Madison County and talk to her right away.

Pop pulled the little tape recorder out of his pocket. "Take this. Make her confess," he said, as Ted rolled him in his folding wheelchair up to Arabella's bright red door. "You owe it to the family."

How could he be sharp enough to spot and bring the tape recorder, and be so off-the-wall at the same time? I wished I knew.

I could have pointed out to him that Gloria did not stomp out of his question-circle after the funeral because she was mad at poor Larry, like I heard him tell Mustache. She stomped out because she was mad at Pop himself. I could have pretended to go after her. In the shape he was in, he might not even remember the next day that he'd asked me to go. But he might remember. And, besides, in the state Gloria was in, if she knew any gossip at all about the family, she was likely to shout it out. That could be useful.

And I needed to do something, anything, to feel as if I was making up for Larry's being killed instead of me. Larry the peacemaker. Not to mention I would like to do something to find out who might have meant to kill me. Who might keep trying.

I didn't believe it was Gloria who set that trap. But I believed she knew more about Aunt Nancy than I did. Apparently, I hadn't known much. It was as if her surface was so polished that she deflected all my little intuition waves that tried to get past the polish and puzzle her out.

I looked at my watch. Three o'clock. "I'll drive over to Gloria's with you," Ted said. "But I won't come in. She'll say more to you alone because she knows you better."

On the way over we tried to sort out the day. "In one way," I said finally, "it was a terrible thing for Larry to die. But in another way, he was at peace with himself." I needed to comfort myself. "If Larry had a half second when he knew he was going to die, he would have expected to go straight to heaven," I said. "I'm glad of that."

Ted's car squealed around a curve and sent a chicken running. "I'm not sure where I'd go," he said, "so I'd better stay alive." I was for that.

There are parts of Madison County with roads through fields and woods, and along sheer-rock mountain sides, where nobody would be close enough to hear a scream. There have always been isolated parts of the county where any stranger after dark is considered to be up to no good and therefore fair game. Grandma told me that. In the state of mind I was in, I would not have liked us to drive through those parts. Especially if my interview took a long time and we came back after dusk.

So I was grateful that Gloria's house was right off the main road into Marshall, the pint-sized county seat. The house was on a mountainside overlooking the French Broad river. Steep rock at its back, road and river in front. Her driveway went into a cut in the rock, marked by a big sign: SECOND CHANCE DOLL HOSPITAL. An over-sized green mailbox suggested that some dolls arrived by parcel post. The steep driveway took us right up to a small yellow house with a peaked roof. Freshly painted, but obviously an old house. Close up, the paint was rough with earlier coats beneath. The rock-work foundation was weathered with moss growing in the cracks.

A Barbie doll, a baby doll, and a Civil-War–era costume doll were hand-in-hand in a row, painted on the front door. Dolls looked out the windows on each side of the door. They leaned against the sparkling clean window panes, face out, as if watching to see who came to see them.

On both sides of the door, beds of daffodils were sunshine yellow. If I had been a child bringing my doll to the hospital, I would have felt better even before the front door opened for me. The house matched Gloria's comfortable side. I did not feel better.

The other Gloria who stamped and yelled might not even let me in. I left Ted in the car and went over to knock. Pop's voice-activated tape recorder was in one of my pockets, my pencil and notebook in the other.

Gloria opened the door and pulled her head back like a snake about to strike. Her baby blue eyes narrowed. "Come in," she said in a rocky proud voice. "I have never turned anybody away from this door."

"I'd forgotten you ran a doll hospital," I said, as pleasantly as I could, stepping inside to the smell of furniture polish and glue and paint.

"When a car ran over my Stella's favorite doll, I started this hospital." She said it like the answer to a challenge. I could see past her, out a picture window at the back of the house, where a man in a black felt hat was loading a gun. A long gun. A rifle? Well, it couldn't be in my honor. He didn't know I was coming. Probably for target practice. Target practice was big here in the mountains.

"Then Stella's friends came to get their dolls fixed," Gloria said. "The hospital grew from there." She raised her voice like a television commercial. "I would do anything legal for my Stella. Not kill."

"I believe you," I said. She frowned, as if I puzzled her.

"The emergency room is in here," she said, leading me to a small room to the right, as if I'd come just to see the hospital. I figured she was giving us both decompression time. Good.

But the emergency room was not good. I saw a curly-headed Shirley Temple doll with one arm torn off. A bald Barbie doll. An antique-looking baby doll with the head separated from the body. One doll seemed half burned. Those dolls laid out on tables showed the variety of mutilations that could happen to the human body. In case I needed to be reminded.

"The dolls laying in boxes on the living-room table are the ones that are fixed. You'll see they're like new." She said that sharply, like she was daring me to say it wasn't so. She led me back out and shut the door on the emergency room.

The repaired dolls on the well-polished living-room table were clean, coifed, dressed to the nines. They looked as if they were laid out in coffins. Like Nancy after the undertaker painted her and fixed her hair.

Perhaps I looked as cold as I suddenly felt. "I was just about to have a cup of coffee," Gloria said. Still hostile, but less so than before. She led me into an old-fashioned white kitchen with a white enamel kitchen table, and waved me to sit down.

She banged pots as she took an already steaming kettle from an old white enamel electric stove and poured water into a battered coffee-pot. When did that table and stove date back to? The thirties? My mother still had a kitchen table like that when I was a small child. Somebody in Gloria's family must have known how to keep fixing that electric stove to make it last forever.

Nothing in Gloria's house seemed new except the phone book lying on the end of the kitchen table near a well-worn black phone. She gave me coffee in a white cup, then sugar in a flowered bowl, then milk from the milk carton. The hand of the doll surgeon trembled.

She sat down across from me.

"All right," she said, "what do you want?" Her blue eyes would have electrocuted me if they could, but she cradled her hot cup as if she needed its warmth. No ruffles to soften her today. She had on a man's shirt and blue jeans. She rested her elbows on the table as if it were an old friend trusted to hold her up. She sat in her chair as if it was an old friend too. I wanted to like her. She was into continuity. Into what the past could do for the present, and what the present could do for the past. But also into fits of rage where she slammed doors hard enough to break glass. And what else?

I said, "I need to know more about my Aunt Nancy. About what kind of person she really was." She sneered at the "really was."

"The only decent member of your branch of the family died. Your mama. And she wasn't our blood kin, she married in. Your daddy's mama made moonshine whiskey. You know that. My mother called her tough. She could shoot as good as a man. His papa drank himself to death and left her with two little kids, and without two dimes to rub together."

I nodded. That part of the story was family myth. Grandma who survived. Who could shoot a rattlesnake in the head across a field, plow, or make poundcake without a recipe.

"She made whiskey during the week and went to church on Sunday. She said God was on her side because she was a good woman. Oh, she was sure of that, all right. And she'd made up her mind your dad and Nancy were going to make it, no matter what she had to do — no matter what it took." Gloria's usually pink cheeks were bright red.

"You're saying it took too much?"

"I'm saying that's how Nancy got to be so hard. And how she knew that God was on her side, no matter what. Her mama said so." Gloria glared like she'd like to shoot me. *Bang!* A gun went off. I gasped and spilled my coffee.

Gloria smiled as she took her napkin and wiped it up, wiped it up like she was wiping me away. "A gun makes you nervous," she said. "Good. I didn't invite you here. That's my Herb shooting at cans out back. This is his house, where he does what he likes." I didn't know her husband, Herb. He never came to family reunions.

Gloria got up, took my arm, and pulled me

126

into the living room with its big plate-glass rear window. Beyond the window was the man with the gun, presumably Herb. He reached over and took a beer can off a nearby chair, took a long swig, then put the can back. Then, a distance away from him, a boy threw a tin can up in the air. The gun boomed again. The tin can zigged with the hit. At least he didn't waste his beer cans.

"That's my Billy," she said. "He's his papa's boy." Behind man and boy, the rock face of the mountain climbed almost straight up.

"Have a seat," Gloria said. "You might as well see what's making you nervous." I sat in a pink overstuffed chair on one side of a fireplace. She sat in a flowered chair on the other. The room was all bright pastel colors. On another day I would have said, "How cheerful."

We were not alone, even on our side of the glass. From where I sat, I couldn't see the faces of the dolls on the table. But rows of dolls in book cases on each side of the window stared at us with their painted or plastic eyes. They would never blink at a gunshot. I was sure I did.

"Sometimes I find dolls at flea markets and tag sales, and fix them just because I like to do it," Gloria said. "And I like to enjoy the others I fix for a few days before I mail them back." I was staring at a blond doll in a white pinafore. "That's a Madame Alexander," she said. "A dog chewed the hair off. People who care about dolls ought not to have dogs."

Ah. Another target for that anger. "How wonderful for people that you can save their dolls," I said. I needed her to relax. "I read somewhere that the Japanese believe that if a doll is loved enough it gets a soul. I had a doll I felt that way about."

She shrugged. She didn't want to think of me as human. Not today.

Bang! I winced. Out the window a can zigged, hit.

"About Nancy . . ."

"Nancy never cared about anybody but herself and her mother and that husband who pretended Nancy was the smart one. I liked him. He was fun. He used to laugh at Nancy like he didn't really mean harm. And she let him do it. But he had the last laugh." Gloria smiled, a demon smile. I could hardly believe it was on the face of the woman who usually went around spreading sweetness and fixing dolls. Her smile relished Nancy's pain. "You should have seen her when she found out he'd lost all her money."

Bang!

"People keep saying that Nancy had a way of knowing things that other people didn't want her to know," I said. "How could she do that?"

"Knowing made Nancy feel like she had power," Gloria growled. Still almost as red as the poppies on her chair. "I caught her listening at a door at a family reunion once. She could read weakness. She acted like she knew more than she really did, so you told her the rest. She

128

was a bitch. Speak no ill of the dead." She cocked her head to one side. " 'Cause Nancy isn't dead. Her evil is still here. You'll see."

Bang!

I wished I could leave. "She was usually kind to me." I watched Herb reload.

"Because she figured that was the best way to use you. And let you be a friend to Albert and Mary. I guess they needed friends. She wasn't much help to those kids. Too busy getting rich."

"My mother and Pop always cared about Nancy." Somehow I couldn't help defending her. But that might actually have been the best way to get Gloria to tell me the dirt.

The demon smile again, so strange among those spring flowers in the chair print. "Perhaps your father didn't dare to cross her."

"Pop?" I was surprised. "Pop would dare to do anything he took it in his mind to do. That's Pop."

"He wouldn't dare to hurt your mother. He needed your mother."

Bang!

I jumped. The gun was really getting to me. I wondered what Ted, out in the car, was making of the gunshot. He must know it was just prac-tice or he'd be running in to save me.

"Hurting my mother and daring are not related in my mind," I said. "You dare because you aren't afraid. You hurt someone because you're mean, or at least careless."

"And what would you say if I told you your

father was careless? How would you feel if I told you your father was the father of my Stella? And Nancy found it out? And blackmailed him?" She was shaking, out of control.

"Pop?" That hit me right between the eyes, totally surprised. I laughed. Nervous reaction. Stella was twenty-eight. That would mean Pop had an affair about the time he gave my mother the pearl ring for their thirtieth anniversary. "I wouldn't believe you," I said. Better perhaps to have shut up and listened. But the words jumped out.

Gloria laughed. Hysterical? "You'll never know whether to believe it or not, will you?"

"Are you suggesting that Pop could have killed Nancy and tried to kill me?" Now I was as angry as she was. "Just how do you think he had the strength to kill Nancy?"

"A man with enough money can arrange anything he wants to arrange. You know that." Her whole red face was a demon face. It glowed.

"But my mother is dead. So he didn't need to be blackmailed."

"To protect her memory."

"I don't believe it," I cried out. *My God*, I thought, *is that possible? Is Pop crazy?*

"I don't care if you believe it." She became cold calm. "All I want is for you always to be in doubt. To wonder if it's true. To know how it feels not to know. To understand how I've felt for the last three weeks. Since Nancy told me she reported Stella to the Social Services. Since

Nancy told me she was going to testify against my Stella at the custody hearing. And even now, with Nancy gone, I could lose the right to see my own grandchild. I can't stand to be in doubt. Not to know." She hugged her shoulders. Her color was fading, red to bright pink.

"But you haven't done anything," I said. "Even if Stella loses custody, certainly you . . ." I stopped. I could see by her eyes she *had* done something. And I could guess what it was. Just what she'd done to me. She had let fly her demon side at Stella's husband or at Social Services. Or both.

I was sorry for her. I was also furious. I jumped up and stood over her. "You should be ashamed of yourself," I hissed, "to try to deliberately make trouble. To deliberately upset me, without even telling me whether the hateful things you say are really true. Without taking responsibility." My elbow hit a baby doll, which fell to the floor and hit its voice box: "Ma-ma!"

I began to yell: "You want me to suspect my own father, without any evidence, because if you had evidence you'd use it to make trouble."

Bang!

She jumped up from her chair and slapped me. I heard the slap almost before I felt the heat of it. She had a nerve! I wanted to slap her back. But where would that lead? I turned on my heel and walked out, past all the sweet little dolls with the bows in their hair.

Ted was not in the car. I knew where he was.

Watching target practice. I honked the horn. He appeared, eyebrows raised in surprise, finger to his mouth, in the *shh* position.

I climbed in the car, cheek still smarting. Trembling with the slap I hadn't slapped back. He climbed in beside me.

"Are you upset with me?" he asked. "I was back far enough to be safe and out of sight. Honest," he said in that let's-be-reasonable tone of voice.

"I'm furious at Gloria." My voice shook.

"Her husband, or whoever, is scary, too." He started the car, and it lurched forward. "Let's get out of here. That man is drunk. How he manages to keep hitting the cans and not hit the kid, I don't know."

So Nancy was following a family tradition when she married a drunk? Thank God I hadn't. I was breathing hard. "When Gloria isn't in a rage, I like her." I made myself admit that. "When she *is* in a rage, I believe she could commit murder." I didn't tell him what Gloria said about Pop. I absolutely refused to believe it.

CHAPTER
11

I spent the night back at my own house while
Arabella looked after Pop and his sitter for the
night and the police went over Pop's house inch
by inch. As they'd pointed out, aside from clues,
there could be more booby traps. Maybe I should
have let Ted stay, but I didn't. I left all the lights
on at my house, which made me feel safer.

And I could see all my comforting favorite
things. I wandered from room to room and
touched them: the lamp in the living room that
was a carved face emerging from a block of
wood, the log-cabin-pattern quilt in greens and
browns with dots of red which stood for the
warm hearths. Roger and I had picked that as
our very favorite from so many quilts that passed
through the shop, and hung it like a tapestry near
the dinner table. My favorite platter, with a tree
and birds painted on it by Nels Arnold in nos-
talgic blue, was hung on the wall, like a picture.

A different kind of bird perched on each limb: bluejay, chickadee, cardinal, owl. The bluejay looked nervous. But the owl was reassuring. Stolid, like he could never be surprised. And that was my hope for the night. *Not* to be surprised.

I avoided looking at the black windows. With no house nearby, I'd never felt the need for curtains that closed before, except for the bedroom and bathroom. Now I remembered something Pop said after we found Nancy. First he asked, "I wonder why somebody killed her in the middle of the night?" And then he answered himself. "Because it was dark, that's why."

I couldn't sleep, even in my bedroom with the curtains drawn. To keep my mind busy and comfort my body, I lay in bed and leafed through some three-by-five index cards that had been lying on the bedside table. Notes on books I'd been reading, all about memory. Full of stuff I might find useful to know, from outrageous to technical to comforting. I picked up a card which told how a primitive tribe believed that eating a tribal chief would give the diner the chief's brain power. So if he had a great memory, well — Very interesting. But of course, I was not about to suggest cannibalism in *How to Survive Without a Memory*. I read my notes about how the brain works with neurons and axons and synapses and such. Heavy stuff. I was almost nodding off when I came to a card with a star on it. Something I might use to cheer up readers: Einstein couldn't remember his own telephone number. Even I can do that. At least, most of the time.

I chuckled, but I didn't manage to banish thoughts of Larry dead or what Gloria said about Pop, or the dark outside. Finally I threw my file cards down, and lay awake arguing with myself. Should I question Pop? I believed Gloria was lying. Suppose I asked Pop if he cheated on Ma and killed Nancy. That could drive him right over the edge, if he wasn't already over. I decided not to ask. Gloria was so mad, she'd like for Pop to go berserk. The worse, the better. So I wouldn't ask. But Gloria was so right. I hated not being absolutely, positively sure. I tossed and turned and was tempted to call Ted, and then didn't. Finally I slept. Then overslept in the morning, then woke up groggy when the phone rang.

It was Elsie calling to say it was ten o'clock, Pop was back in his own place and wanted me to come right away, if not sooner.

I had the presence of mind to say it might take a while. I brushed my teeth and began to gather my clothes.

I knew it was going to be a bad day when I couldn't find but one each of any suitable pair of shoes. And this after I'd had my favorite sandals right in my hand. On the shoe rack in my closet were a pair of red shoes with spiked heels, which I keep even though I'm too creaky to wear them much anymore. I can't bear to throw them away. There were two matching gold evening slippers.

A pair of high-topped hiking boots. But only one white sandal, one moccasin. Both of the tan sandals I like best had vanished. They were not even under the bed.

Well, there was no particular reason for this to be a good day. But why did the objects I needed have to get into the act?

So O.K. *Be calm.* I sure ought to follow the most important rule in my whole book. I made myself stop looking for the sandals, breathed deeply three times, and went downstairs barefoot to fortify myself with breakfast. I went in my little workroom just down the hall from the kitchen, and there was the rough draft of my chapter on Bad Days, sitting on a pile of papers next to the computer. A good omen. I brought my chapter back to the kitchen with me, pinching it tight so I couldn't forget it was in my hand, and put it on the table next to my bowl of puffed rice. I cut up my banana and then poured milk onto fruit and rice. I made instant coffee in my favorite mug Roger gave me, which says, "When life is a lemon, make lemonade." We'd painted the kitchen yellow in honor of that motto.

So, make lemonade. Maybe the chapter would soothe me if I read it while I ate. Or maybe what was happening to me would help me improve the chapter.

The title pleased me: Extreme Measures Day. Yes.

On a bad day, simplify things. In fact, the best thing to do may be to go back to bed. (Ha. Fat chance. I skimmed through that part.)

You can always tell a bad day because things vanish in your hand. (Now, that was more to the point.)

On a bad day, your brain can be so involved in coping with disaster that it forgets about your right arm with the hand at the end and the car keys in the hand. (Yes. For "car keys" read "shoes.") *The undirected hand begins to act as if it had never been introduced to your mind. This is not good. Then the next time your brain takes note of that arm, the hand is still there, but the car keys are not. Where are they?*

I skimmed through the list of maddening places keys could find to hide, like in a bowl with something else dropped on top, or between the couch cushions, under the cat.

The minute you realize that this is an extra bad day, be sure that the essentials are fastened to you. Key on bracelet or fastened to pocketbook or in designated pocket, or even pinned to your shirt. Essential pills at pill station. List fastened to a large clipboard. Oversized calendar on the hook where it lives. Ha. All that was ready to go. But where could I go without shoes at my age? Damn.

Tell a sympathetic friend, if available, that this is a bad day — you're going to do your best, but any help will be appreciated. Stay away from badgerers, if possible. Play soothing music if that helps. On an extra bad day there's one thing you absolutely must not lose above all others: your sense of humor. If you have a choice, stay around people who laugh a lot.

Fat chance of that. Pop would be having a bad

day of his own, after this second murder. But Ted would come over. That would help.

I went to the telephone to call Ted, and there were my sandals by the phone. I must have started to call earlier and been distracted. Ted didn't answer, but I thanked him in my heart for the shoes.

The phone rang. "Where the hell are you?" Pop asked. I said I was having a bad day and if he wanted me to be helpful to him, he'd better be helpful to me. Then I hung up.

I put on the sandals, found a clipboard to take for attaching any lists, draped myself with glasses, pocketbook, keys, and set forth. I was even labeled all over, like my Chapter V suggests — my name and phone number on every object I had with me, down to my watch. So if I put something down in some strange place in a moment of amnesia, I'd be more likely to get it back.

Later, in the Extreme-Measures-Day chapter, I'd written: *Be kind to yourself and enjoy whatever there is to enjoy.* I made myself look at the beautiful mountains, at the blues and greens of the near and far, at the wisps of fog that gave the name: Great Smokies.

And I was doing fine by the time I got to Pop's house. I picked up the clipboard from the car seat beside me, and several books I'd borrowed. Somehow as I walked towards Pop's back door, I shifted them against my chest in a way that yanked off the glasses hanging down my front. I

138

managed to grab my glasses before they fell to the ground. Then I saw that their gold-colored chain was broken. Damn. I held my glasses in my right hand and said to myself: Glasses. Glasses. Glasses. To keep them in mind as I went in the back door. For some reason I was thirsty. I'd stop on the way in for a drink of water.

Anna met me at the door: "Your father's bad to see you."

"Don't tell him I'm here yet," I whispered. "I just have to have a glass of water. Don't know why I'm dying of thirst."

I grabbed a glass from the cupboard over the dishwasher, dropped in ice from the ice-maker in the refrigerator. I put in lots. Gives me a feeling of luxury. Be kind to yourself on a bad day, right?

My father roared: "Hasn't she come yet, Anna?" I hurried over to the sink and turned on the water full to fill my glass quickly. What His Highness wanted, he wanted *right then*. I got one cold refreshing swallow before he roared again. "My God, where can she be?"

I went in the living room, to find him in his wheelchair by the table, shaking with impatience. Elsie sat there knitting near him. Outside the big glass window, the garden looked peaceful in the sunshine. Even the fishpond sparkled calmly in the sun. I concentrated on that calm.

He was holding out a long, off-white envelope,

hand shaking. "I want you to read this to me right now, Peaches."

I felt for my glasses, right where they always hang. Right below my bazoom. Damn. No glasses. I remembered the chain breaking and then my glasses in my hand, then nothing.

So why did he have to be in such a swivet? Why hadn't he even opened the letter? Elsie sat there, very sober, and said nothing to help. I would have expected that glint of humor in her eyes which sometimes greeted his wilder antics.

"I have to find my glasses," I explained.

"Oh, my God," he groaned, "I should have known it. I can't depend on you for anything."

I was busy looking through my pockets. I had on a handy skirt for that: two deep side pockets. But no glasses. "Why don't you get Elsie to read your letter?" I asked.

"This is no ordinary letter," he roared. "This is from your Aunt Nancy. Postmarked before we found her dead. Elsie did read me that much."

"Postmarked May twenty-second," Elsie added. "Before you found her."

That got my attention fast.

"This is serious," Pop said. "When Nancy wanted to tell me something, she called. When she wrote, it meant trouble, like the time she was insulted because I said Horace was an alcoholic. She wrote asking for an apology. I wrote her back that I never apologize."

He speared me with his eyes. "And I have a right for my own daughter to read me this letter, which may contain serious family business. Which could even explain why your Aunt Nancy was killed. And I have been waiting for you for over an hour." For my father to wait an hour to get his way was a milestone right there. No wonder his face was blotched red and white. And now I was as curious as he was. My heart galloped.

"If you can be calm while I look, I'll find my glasses sooner," I said. But that was a concept he could never digest.

"My God," he fumed, "you can't keep track of the simplest thing. You don't even try. I don't deserve an only child like that."

I kissed him on the top of the head. I didn't want him to have a heart attack. "Try to relax. I'll go look in the kitchen."

My glasses weren't on the kitchen table. That would have been too easy. Damn, I thought. This is what I did yesterday. Am I going to spend my whole life looking for things?

Anna began helping me. She looked all over the counters. I got down and searched the floor in case they'd fallen and slipped under the table or under the little overhang at the bottom of the refrigerator. But I hadn't heard them fall. I opened the left-hand door of the refrigerator to examine the ice machine. It looked like a full drawer of ice. The working part didn't show. No glasses on top of the ice cubes. And all the time I could hear my father calling suggestions. "See if you left them in the car. Did you go off like a fool and leave them at your house?" At least he didn't bring his wheelchair into the kitchen and get completely in the way.

So O.K., I mustn't panic. When I panic I can hold my glasses right in my hand and not see them.

I remembered what I had said in Chapter VII: *You have to re-create the scene.* I went back to the door and walked in, trying to remember exactly where I was when the chain broke, and then everything else that was happening. Anna saying, "Your father's bad to see you." If they'd fallen to the floor, wouldn't she have noticed? Besides, I'd looked on the floor. I tried to retrace my footsteps across the green- and blue-patterned floor as I walked over to the cupboard. I reached up with the non-glasses-holding hand and took out a water glass. I walked over to the refrigerator. I tried to feel my glasses as if they'd still been in my hand. I reached to open the refrigerator — with the same hand that would have held the glasses. I said, "Anna, this is the moment I must have put them down. But where?"

Then I remembered my own motto. "First look everywhere they could possibly be. Then, look everywhere they couldn't possibly be." Roger always used to laugh about that. "The funny thing is," he'd say, "it works."

Well, where hadn't I looked because they couldn't possibly be there?

My father came wheeling in with his wheelchair. "You've been hired by enemy agents," he said, "to drive me crazy." Great. He was going over the edge. Elsie had her hand on his shoulder. "Don't worry, she'll find them in a minute." He was holding on to her hand like he might drown.

Where hadn't I looked? I reached up and felt along the top of the refrigerator. That would be an almost logical place to put them while I got the ice. But no glasses. I looked carefully in the refrigerator. Behind the milk bottle? Next to the remains of a pie? Though I couldn't remember having that part of the refrigerator open. No glasses. So where was even more illogical? Hidden under the ice cubes? I told myself that as a joke. But just then the ice machine made one of those funny little mechanical sounds it makes when it's thinking of making ice cubes. And then I remembered. I'd moved them to the hand with the glass when I opened the freezer compartment door. Then moved the glass to my right hand to scoop up lots of ice. And after that my left hand must have let go of them on its own. Right into the ice drawer. When my father called and distracted me. And the ice machine made more ice on top! Elementary, my dear Watson! I scooped back the top cubes. An ear piece stuck up. The lenses, of course, were pretending to be ice. I pulled out one pair of well-chilled specs.

My father was about to declaim something else. "Pop," I shouted, "I have my glasses."

He settled back in his chair. "Well," he said,

"it's about time. I don't know what you do when I'm not around to help."

We went back to the table and opened the letter. My heart was beating hard. Inside the envelope was a newspaper clipping with a photo of a miniature portrait of a young woman with many ringlets, held in a man's large hand. The North Carolina Art Museum was going to have a show of antique miniature portraits, the story said, from June 10 to June 30. Portraits by such well known miniaturists as Charles Fraser (1782–1860), and Ann Hall (1792–1863), and Edward Greene Malbone (1777–1807) would be on loan from other museums.

Edward Greene Malbone was the one who did the miniature of the young girl my mother had bought because it looked a little like me.

The young girl in *our* tiny missing portrait had many curls on top of her head, and the narrow slanting shoulders that used to be considered elegant long ago. Ma said her eyes were dreamy like mine — eyebrows widely curved, mouth with my slightly lopsided hint of smile.

With the clipping was a handwritten note from Nancy. It reminded Pop that the little portrait Mom bought was by Malbone, and then said, "I'll be dropping by tomorrow night to talk to you about something concerning your picture, which may actually be of an ancestor of ours. Love, Nancy."

The signature sure looked like her bold handwriting. But exactly what did she want to talk to

144

my father about? I read the clipping more carefully, looking for some clue. "Before his death in Savannah at twenty-nine, Malbone was America's most outstanding miniaturist. He painted in major East Coast cities — Providence, Boston, New York, Philadelphia, Charleston. He spent time in England and was influenced by artists there. His most productive period was in Charleston." Which was, no doubt, how Albert had managed to pick up the little portrait there, without realizing at first exactly what he had. No wonder he was prodding Pop to keep track of his little gem.

"Some of the miniature portraits are on loan from Gibbes Museum in Charleston," the clipping said.

Could that possibly be related to Nancy's death? She did say the clipping had to do with why she was coming to see my father. And when she came to see him, someone killed her.

Some of the pictures would be on loan from Charleston. She went to Charleston. She told Mary she expected a confrontation. Then she came to see my father and was killed. Albert believed somebody had stolen the portrait. Was all that connected? Maybe this note would mean something to Albert.

The doorbell rang, then the door opened. Not Albert — he was still in Charleston. It was Ted. I was so glad to see his reassuring smile, I could have run over and thrown my arms around him. But my father was holding tight to my arm with that bony grip, and I was rooted in place. "You're a sight for sore eyes, Ted," I said. "I bet Pop will let you look at this letter because he admires your judgment." Encourage the old stinker to be trusting, I told myself. At least with Ted.

"Besides," Ted said, winking at me, "Peaches may marry me. You're going to help to persuade her."

I could see Pop struggling with himself. "What the hell," he said. "Ted, you might as well read it. And you did say you'd help me solve this mystery." He gave us that Julius Caesar glare.

"Then," he went on, "I want you to summon all the sitters and our damn lawyer who doesn't seem to be doing much to solve this crime, and Mary and Albert, and we'll question them all about the miniature portrait and find out what that can have to do with this crime."

He wanted to repeat his questions-in-a-circle act. Maybe he'd been watching Agatha Christie stuff on television again.

Ted was reading the letter for the second time. "A meeting might be interesting," he said to Pop, "but perhaps if you think about it, you'd prefer for us not to do that again."

"Perhaps you were right to begin with," I chimed in. "We want to keep this letter secret until we look into this quietly a little more."

"I know what I want!" my father shouted.

Ted put his arm around him. "Of course," he said. "But Peaches and I have promised to help you with solving this crime, and we can do it better without a meeting like that. We'll be your right-hand detectives."

"Peaches!" he shouted. "Peaches can't even remember her own name. How can she be a detective if she can't remember anything?"

"Listen," I said. "If you can't remember anything, you have to be a detective all day long. That's how I just found my glasses. First, I re-created the scene. Then I asked all the questions that made sense. Then I asked all the questions that didn't make sense. And then I found the solution."

"Wonderful," Ted said. "As a matter of fact, that sounds like exactly the way we should go about solving this crime. We'll use your method."

But Pop was still scornful. He fixed me with his eagle eye. "Peaches," he said patiently, "you write poetry. You even got some poetry prize from some North Carolina poetry group." Actually it was a special award for funny verse.

Pop's tone of voice said what he thought of poets and their ability to pick prize winners. If I'd gotten a poetry award from the Chamber of Commerce, he might have been impressed. "Poets," he said, "are not detectives. I saw that detective who was a poet on TV, the one called Adam Dalgliesh, but he was *made up* by an Englishwoman."

Ted ignored that. "We are a winning team," he said and he winked at me. "Peaches *has* to be a detective because she can't remember, and I had *practice* being a detective because I was a newspaper reporter."

"That's right!" I announced. Ted may have been half joking. But right at that moment I made up my mind I was going to show Pop. I was going to find the killer. Because, for one thing, just waiting around to see if the killer was trying to kill me made me very nervous. Mustache and his team were working hard, no doubt. But I read somewhere that the police never actually managed to solve most crimes. There are too many.

I turned to my father. But he had worn himself out getting upset. He leaned back into one corner of his wheelchair, eyes shut, snoring slightly like an ancient, innocent baby. Innocent. Ha.

Ted came over, put his arms around me, and kissed me. "You must want to crown the old bastard sometimes," he whispered. "But he does have spunk."

Pop opened one eye and said, "Damn right."

CHAPTER
12

LATE MORNING, MAY 30

Ted drove us up Elk Mountain Scenic Highway, beyond a point where hardtop turned to gravel, up and up and around one curve after another. "There's a wonderful lookout at the top of this road," he said. "A place called Buzzard Rock where I came when I visited Asheville years ago. There's a huge old tree and a view of a near ridge and a far ridge, and mountain tops beyond that. And the roadside on the way is banked with ferns, and the air smells good. We could use some mountaintop. And why shouldn't we study this tape of Pop's circle in a pretty place?"

I said, "Why not?" Actually, this was right in line with my bad day motto: Be kind to yourself.

At first there were houses on the up-the-mountain side of the road, and on the down side mostly a drop-off too steep for houses. Then, as we climbed, the houses were farther apart; then both sides of the road were wild until the mountain flattened enough for a white farmhouse with meadows and a pond and cows on the left. "We will revive ourselves while we brainstorm," Ted said. "I remember Buzzard Rock as one of the most beautiful spots in the world. And yet I haven't been back in years. Crazy."

We passed a car of young men parked with their windows rolled down, drinking beer from brown bottles. The radio blared country: *I've got friends in low places.* What a way to enjoy nature. Their car was right at the outside edge of the road. There was a sharp drop and no rail.

"Don't go too near the edge," I said to Ted. "I'm a sissy. A couple of years back, a man went over — on the Blue Ridge Parkway, I think it was — and they didn't find him or his car for about a week. By then he was dead. I get goose bumps," I said, "thinking about that. I reckon two murders make me jumpy. I mean, what if the killer wanted to force us off the road up here?" Damn my imagination. I felt queasy in the stomach.

"You just put your 'what-if' mind onto who could have killed Nancy and Larry, and I'll drive carefully," Ted said. We'd come to a high spot where the air smelled crisp and a big oak tree was silhouetted against ridges in the distance. Up the road from us a great thin wedge of rock stood on the side of the road, like a buzzard's wing. Hence the name. Ted turned off the road near the oak tree.

We got out and walked across a ledge of rock towards the edge. My stomach went into my

150

mouth at the thought of the drop to the valley, but as we got near the edge, I could see more rocks on the mountainside below. The drop was not that steep after all. Beer bottles and cans and broken glass lay among the rocks. "Somebody didn't care about your beautiful spot," I said sadly. Even the flat ledge had been written on with Day-Glo orange paint. To the right, big blocky letters said, "Mickey is Sexy." To the left: "Jesus Saves."

"If we sit in the car we'll see the view and miss the beer cans and the words of wisdom," Ted sighed.

We climbed back in the car and he reached over and took my hand. "I like showing you my favorite places, even when they're painted orange."

Then he seemed to be studying my face for some kind of clue. "They say this place is a lovers' lane at night, but we can use it for other inspiration if you'd rather." He leaned over and kissed me on the tip of the nose and said, "Bring out the tape recorder."

A bird was singing. "Roger asked me to marry him on a mountain overlook a little like this spot," I said. "Oh, Ted, I'm sorry I keep remembering what I ought to forget. Me of all people."

He patted my hand and sighed. "Never forget. Just let go. Just live now. Even if living right now is pretty damn hard."

And that darn bird went right on trilling. The far mountain ridges were lovely and mysterious.

And Ted was so kind it made my insides twist.

I took the tape recorder out of my pocketbook. Without diversion, I was going to cry. "O.K.," I said, "the first thing to do is to go back over this tape. Old business first." I pushed the play button.

Out came the frightened or angry or sad voices of Pop's circle of suspects. Good. They grabbed attention. Though they sounded out of place here on the top of the mountain. The buzzing of insects, the cawing of crows, mixed with the voices from Pop's living room.

I listened as hard as I could. Trying to keep my mind on what we needed to do and not on the conflict inside of me. Because I wanted to let go of the past, but I couldn't let go. I was glad the tape needed my whole attention to be sure I didn't miss a single bit of the talk. Not Cousin Mother Hen Gloria's tone of fury or the droop in Mary's voice or Yankee Accent's accusing monotone or, worst of all, Larry's voice. So unsuspecting that in two days he'd be dead. I swallowed hard.

There was more on that tape than I had actually heard when I was there in the flesh. Whispered asides from those who were sitting by the recorder. I knew Albert's voice even when he whispered. "Elsie, for God's sake, calm him down." He meant Pop, because he said it right after Gloria went berserk and left. When Pop was so excited. I stopped the tape. I replayed that part. I stopped it again. A car of kids drove by with music blaring: *Stand By Your Man.*

I said, "Albert asked that like you'd ask somebody he counted on, sure of himself like that."

"Of course," Ted said, "she did get your father calmed down by changing the subject. Elsie knows how to handle your father."

"But what's between Elsie and Albert?" I wanted to know. I wanted somebody to care enough about my loner cousin Albert so he could count upon them absolutely. To do good things together. But then, could they do evil things together? Please, God, no.

We started the tape again. *Keep at it.* That was the only way. We got to the part where Pop said Nancy did not understand how people feel about their children. And we found another little whisper. Not an on-purpose whisper like Albert's. This one was more like a sigh with indistinct words. Silva was whispering. After she moved into cousin Gloria's chair, she was sitting closest to the tape recorder. I pulled out my chart to check. Yep, the closest. I turned the volume on the tape as high as it would go in order to hear that whisper, and replayed it. The words still weren't quite clear. "Licksam"? We played it several times.

"Maybe it's 'Like Sam'," Ted said.

"Could this somehow refer to something Nancy did?" I asked. "But Silva is the nighttime sitter and hardly knew Nancy."

"That we know of. We need more information," Ted said, "even to set the scene." He moved his arm and inadvertently honked the horn. "Play a horn and set the scene. Tah da ta da ta da."

"You mean," I said, "let's think about the week or two or three before Nancy died. Let's make a list of all the happenings that could be related to the murders, and then a list of all the out-of-the-ordinary things that happened that seem entirely *unrelated*."

Ted grinned and nodded. "We'll follow the Peaches Patented Method." *Crunch.* His words were mixed with the sound of footsteps on gravel. "First we look into all the things that are possible." *Crunch.* "Then into the things that aren't." *Crunch crunch.*

I glanced in the rearview mirror. A tall, gangly man was coming up behind us. I didn't like that. Not in this deserted place. And Ted was frowning too, and watching him in the mirror. He rolled his window down as the man came to the side of the car.

"Hi," the man said. "This is a beautiful place, isn't it?"

"What are you doing up here on the mountain?" I didn't like his wheedly tone of voice, which gave me the nerve to be crude.

"It's beautiful," he said. "I like to drive here." I didn't believe him. His eyes were opaque. I wondered if we ought to roll the windows up. My lack of trust must have shown.

Gangly paused a minute as if he was taking

stock of us. He rubbed his jaw like it itched. Then he said, "O.K. I'm Dan Richards of the State Bureau of Investigation. I spotted your car coming this way and followed." He paused like he'd give us a chance to confess to ax murders. Of course we didn't. "I thought you might get out and search," he said, "because you didn't know we'd found Nancy Means's pocketbook." I felt myself gasp. "But you didn't search," he said, "and here you sit like you're waiting for somebody. Would you like to tell me why?"

By that time we were both out of the car, facing up to him. Ted said: "What the hell are you talking about? You found the pocketbook *here?*"

I said, "Maybe we like it here. Is that against the law?" There was something about the way he almost smiled and didn't quite look at us and had long eyelashes and restless hands, that made me hate him. It felt good to have somebody to hate. Behind him in the distance, the rock like a buzzard's wing was black as death.

"If you want us to answer questions, you'll have to tell us what's going on," Ted said, "and show us your identification."

He showed an ID, and then shrugged. "You'll hear what happened on the news when you get home," he said. "Some kids found Nancy Means's pocketbook when they were climbing on the rocks down there yesterday afternoon. The perpetrator must have thrown it off the

155

side of the mountain here." He said it like a challenge.

"Anything left in it?" Ted asked. Quick thinking.

Gangly backed up a step and frowned, but then he said, "Almost nothing. No money, no credit cards. Just one bill with her name. But we don't think this was theft. We think it was made to look like theft." He eyed us like we should know which. He said, "By the way, I wouldn't hang around here, especially after dark. It's been used for a drug drop."

Finally he left, saying he'd talk to us later. I felt depressed.

Ted got back in our car and sat still, frowning, head bent. "Why on earth did I bring you to this very place where somebody tossed your Aunt Nancy's pocketbook?" he groaned. His hair stuck out in spikes, like antennae waiting to receive the right thought. I climbed in my side of the car quietly. It'll come to him, I thought: There must be an answer.

He raised his head. His frown cleared. "The newspaper," he said. "That's how I happened to remember this place. There was an old copy of *The Citizen*, or at least a part of a copy, with a feature about this place." He nodded to himself. "About how tourists used to come to Buzzard's Rock back in the twenties before the parkway was built, and some people thought it had the best view in the mountains. I read the headline and the first paragraph or two, and I

156

remembered coming here. I thought Buzzard's Rock would give us a lift."

"Where was the newspaper?"

He frowned again. "At Pop's house, by the back door, on top of a pile to recycle. The picture of the rock caught my eye. I looked at the date, and wondered how I'd missed the story. And good Lord, that story was printed Thursday, May twenty-third, the day before you found the body!"

I shivered. "But what does that mean? Why that back date on top of the recycling pile?"

"There were two piles of papers. Maybe the other one had the later dates. But God knows. Nancy could have seen the story and come to see the rock like we did. I suppose it's possible she was hit on the head at the rock for some reason and then taken back and dumped in your pond."

"But she'd said she was coming to Pop's. And why would she have gone to a place with a beautiful view at night?" I looked out over the valley below us. Two houses on the near ridge were so tiny a human being would have been hard to see. Those houses would have been flecks of light at night. "The SBI man said this was a drug drop. I never saw any signs that made me suspect Nancy was on drugs, did you, Ted?"

He shook his head.

But now, because we had come to look at a view, SBI suspected us of goodness knows what. I felt sick.

"I'm sorry I brought us here." Ted slumped. Then he straightened up. "It won't do us any good to sit here wondering how seriously he suspects us. It will do us some good to get to work and prove who did throw that pocketbook here, and who killed twice."

We got out of the car and looked all around. The SBI had already searched and we didn't know what we were looking for. But there just might be some clue that we would recognize and they hadn't. No such luck.

We climbed back into the car and Ted offered me some pretzels from the glove compartment. I realized it was lunch time. Nourishment helps. "Cheer up, Chief Detective," he said. "Tell me, how should we set the scene?"

He was on the right track. Time to do that again. My battery charged. "For starters, we could look at Pop's calendar," I said. "And he has a guest book that unexpected guests some-times sign. Between those two we can recon-struct the time before Nancy and Larry died, the time when somebody was building up motive and working out means."

He kissed me on the tip of the nose again. "Good plan."

I was sorry to leave Buzzard Rock, even though the isolation had become a threat. Even though the rock had made us suspect. I was sorry the lovely place had been kidnapped by the beer-bottle throwers and the rock painters and the drug dealers. Maybe even a killer. As we sat

158

in the car, I'd been able to see what it must have been like before. I'd liked sharing that with Ted. Even on a bad day.

CHAPTER
13

WEDNESDAY AFTERNOON, MAY 30

Pop's great big calendar was not on its hooks near the kitchen phone. I came back to the living room to ask Elsie if she knew where it had got to. Ted had plunked himself in the chair next to Pop. "Sit down," Ted said to me. "We'll read the draft of your chapter on calendars before we start. That may help."

"I didn't give you that chapter!" I was amazed.

"It was sitting on your computer," he said. "I saw it when we went back by your house to get those records Pop wanted, so I brought it along. I want Pop to see that your methods really work." He had that tough twinkle in his eye. Was he teasing me or Pop? Or was he just trying to get us all to relax? We were pretty tense after two murders.

"She already made me get a calendar big enough to see a mile off," Pop said, "and now it's lost." He said it as if it was my fault.

Ted began to read from my manuscript:

A large calendar that displays a month of days at a time — with a square to write in for each day — is best for the absent-minded. (Elsie, who was standing behind Pop, winked and nodded.)

In the first place, calendars like that are harder to lose. (Pop laughed.) *Not impossible. And let me start by suggesting a few places to look for a misplaced two-and-a-half by three-foot calendar: Standing between chairs, it can hide effectively, or in a pile of newspapers, or standing against the wall behind something like a large chair, or lying flat on a table half-hidden by other papers, or out on the porch (in case you took it out there to check a date with someone who was just leaving), or up on the roof (in case there was also a high wind), and so it goes.*

Elsie got up. "I know," she said. "I had it on the office desk by the phone, writing in the directions on how to get to the podiatrist's office, and then our Chief Geographer here had me look up a city they mentioned on the TV news in the big atlas. The calendar must be under the big atlas." So. Pop was having one of his sharp, looking-things-up days. That could be useful.

Elsie brought us the calendar.

"Now, before we use this to set the scene of the weeks before the crimes," Ted said, "I am going to read one more part of this chapter, because it's about something we all do wrong, and it may cause us trouble as we try to set the scene. Even Peaches forgets and doesn't follow her own advice. So I'm going to read you an object lesson for the future while I have your attention."

He skipped past the part of the chapter about back-up positions. About having anyone who expects you at a meeting or appointment call and remind you the day before if possible. My dentist is very good about that. My daughter, Eve, used to be good about reminding me when I forgot to read my own calendar. She was a very pulled-together kid.

Ted looked straight at me as he began to read:

Main pitfall: cryptic notes written on the calendar in a hurry. Later you can't remember what they mean. Like MBFB 330 Very Important. Bring L. *Or* Thing in Hendersonville. *For the first kind of cryptic note, you pray for a moment of sudden enlightenment or a back-up position which causes Mary Bryant of the Fairview Book Club to call and remind you about the meeting at 3:30 and ask if you have the list of Cherokee poets you promised to compile. With luck, she'll call far enough ahead so you have time to compile the list, which, of course, you've completely forgotten.*

With No. 2–type notation, you may be forced to call several people you know in Hender-

sonville and ask what's going on over there that might concern you. Or if you don't know them well enough to admit your lousy memory, you could say, "Well, I'll see you soon," and with any luck they'll say, "Yes, at your cousin Reba's wedding." So then you know your cousin Reba's wedding was the thing you felt you couldn't possibly forget. You write on the calendar Brng Pres, *forgetting that you may forget what that means and try to take along the president of something.*

But of course, prevention is the best cure. Never assume you can remember what a cryptic note on the calendar means. If M *on* Wednesday *means that's the last possible day to make the mortgage payment, write* Mortgage *instead. Write clearly. The neck you save may be your own.*

I blushed. Ted was quite right. Especially when I'm distracted or in a hurry, I write notes I can't figure out later. "I will reform," I said. "Let's hope we can decipher all my code."

We lay the calendar out flat on the table. I had asked the sitters to write anything of importance in the blank squares for each day. So fortunately most of the notations on the calendar would not have been written by me.

We all sat at Pop's table with the calendar in front of me and the guest book in front of Ted, and Pop in his chair with his bright-eyed, leaning-forward, plot-thickens look. Elsie sat on the far side of Pop, knitting something green, ready to help if needed.

"Let's begin with Wednesday, May first," I said. "Begin with May Day. Why not?"

"Celebration," the calendar space by my finger said. I could remember what that was. "Mary and the kids came over and brought you a little basket with flowers the kids had picked," I said to Pop.

Ted said, "We have a cross reference. Marcia signed the guest book."

I smiled. "Yes, I remember. I was there. Marcia was so proud when Pop asked her to do it. Because she had just learned to print her name. Pretty smart at four years old."

Pop nodded. "They brought me a May basket because I'm too old to dance around the Maypole."

I'd just moved my finger to point at May 2 when the doorbell rang. I was annoyed. Some well-meaning visitor would come and make small talk and put off our calendar conference. Pop would never let me just tell whoever had come to see him that we were busy.

I motioned Elsie to sit still and went to the door myself, thinking maybe there was something tactful I could do to head the person off.

Albert stood in the doorway. Haggard as if he hadn't slept. Those poet's eyes were bloodshot. "But you're in Charleston!" I gasped.

"Oh, for God's sake," Albert said. "Don't act like Mary and try to be funny all the time." His breath smelled of alcohol.

But he walked steadily over to the table, kissed Pop, then sat down next to Elsie. Medium-drunk? "I'm too damn worried about what's going on up here to keep my mind on the shop. I broke a Tiffany vase." He shut his eyes, as if he could shut that out. "That's the last damn straw. I arranged for Ben to mind the shop. Now I'm here, and Mary's not home, and I forgot her door key." His voice was not slurred, but raspy with anger. That's how it was with Albert. When he wanted to cry, he got mad instead. Always had, since his father ran over his dog and maybe before that.

"If you're worried, you may want to help us," I said firmly. "We're going over the calendar to try to set the scene for what happened the weeks before we found your mother."

"Oh God," he said. "I'd like to do anything I can." He lit a cigarette with a trembling hand.

Elsie put her green knitting down and stood up. "Anna's off today, so I'll get us all some sandwiches. It's one-thirty, and even if we don't feel like eating, we ought to." Elsie, who'd seemed to be in cahoots with Albert on the tape of Pop's circle. Who'd obeyed when he whispered please to calm Pop down. Was there something between them? But what? Now she seemed perfectly calm and businesslike. In fact, I had the impression she was deliberately getting out of the way in case there was something private he wanted to tell us. Some particular reason he'd come back before he'd said he would. Some reason he was medium-drunk. But he began to explain before Elsie with her flaming hair could disappear into the kitchen.

His hand was still shaking. His face and the smoke were the same color. "I had a nightmare," he said. "Last night. And *she* came back all wet, and she said, 'You're too smart, Albert.' " He took a long pull on the cigarette and seemed to deliberately calm himself, as if he knew he might fall over the edge of some emotional precipice. He rested his elbow on the table to steady the hand with the cigarette. He kept his voice almost smooth with only a few jagged edges. He turned to Pop. "That may not seem like a nightmare to you, but that's exactly what she always said to me." He stopped, swallowed, and with an obvious great effort of will went on. "That I was too smart to be running a shop. She didn't understand. And it wasn't just that she thought I was too smart. She also thought I was a fool. I wish before she died we could have found some way . . ." He went over the precipice, and tears began to stream down his face.

I reached over next to Pop, took one of the tissues from the box near his elbow, and handed it to Albert.

"Mary told me she thought your mother was beginning to understand, to see that selling antiques took a lot of special smarts." I tried to comfort him. But he only cried harder, shaking all over. I felt uncomfortable, as if he was taking

166

off his clothes in public and his underwear was dirty. And yet I knew it was probably good for him to let go like that. Maybe he was crying for his whole life, now the tears were loose. It seemed like that.

"Albert," the Emperor said loudly, "we could all cry. But your mother, wherever she is, would prefer for us to straighten things out. Nancy was like that, wasn't she?"

The "wherever she is" part seemed to grab Albert. I remember, when he was a kid Aunt Nancy used to say, "Albert, be quiet!" like he was a small dog. So now he acted as if, wherever she was, he knew she'd be saying it still. He blew his nose. He swallowed again. He said: "I'll try to help."

"We're going over the calendar," I said again, "to set the scene before your mother died."

"So go on," he choked. "Please go on."

"Thursday, May second," I read, trying to keep my mind on the job. "Building Comm." That was in Elsie's clear handwriting. I remembered the occasion. "A member of the church building-drive committee came to ask Pop to make a handsome contribution toward the new parish house," I explained.

Pop squirmed and glowered at me. "You told me I'd look stingy if I didn't."

For May 3, the calendar read "FRZ Man." My handwriting. I said, "I remember." Say, I was doing great! "The man came to fill the freezer. I wasn't here when he came, but Anna told me all about it. Silk jumped out and hissed at him, but he just laughed, and Silk acted bent out of joint for the rest of the day." Then I got excited. "Silk gets upset at most men." I looked at Albert. He's had a number of scratches over the years. He was lucky today the cat was keeping out of sight.

He said, "Amen. A sexist cat. He even scratched the mayor when he tried to pet him."

Pop beamed. He was pleased the mayor came to see him in person to ask for election support. He even gave a donation, though probably not as big as the mayor hoped for.

"This may be a clue, right?" I turned to Albert. "Does this mean the killer is a man who knew that Silk could cause a fuss and, therefore, shut our cat in the bathroom when he set the electrical trap?"

And Albert nodded. "Yes. Of course!" He was beginning to lose himself in our process. I figured that was a good thing.

"Nothing is written on the fourth or fifth," I told our little circle. "Probably just routine drop-overs those days, like Nancy and Arabella next door."

"But on May sixth, the guest book has an entry," Ted told us: "John and Mary Lord on their honeymoon."

Pop raised his head in that peacock-pleased-with-himself bounce: "My cousin John Lord of Philadelphia, who is a Presbyterian minister, stopped by with his new wife. He said I was the member of the family he wanted her to meet most." Well, sure. Pop could be preposterous, but his friends and relatives loved to visit him. Maybe to find out what on earth he was going to say or do next.

No entry from May 7 to 9.

"Eltha Jones signed the guest book on Friday, May tenth," Ted said, "just exactly two weeks before Nancy was murdered." I shivered. Cousin Eltha had a way of dropping by to visit Pop when she came to shop in Asheville.

"Cousin Eltha," I said, "looks like an angel and killed her husband, and pleaded self-defense. So was there some way Eltha could have needed to defend herself from Nancy?"

Pop's eyes bulged with shock. "Eltha?" He shook his head hard. "That's ridiculous!"

The truth is, he's very taken with Eltha. God knows what he's promised to leave *her* in his will. "I dropped by just as she was leaving," I said. "And saw you holding hands." And then before he got a chance to tell me more about how I had the wrong idea, I said, "You gave me some literature from the *Watchtower* people." Now how on earth did I remember that? "You said you were popular that day. They'd come by to see you too.

"But none of these things, so far," I complained to the others, "seems either really suspicious or out of the ordinary."

"Unless the *Watchtower* people weren't really Jehovah's Witnesses but somebody casing the joint," Ted teased. "But casing it for what?"

169

"You mean," Pop nodded, "that nothing may be as it seems. I've found that out."

"Your cousin from Philadelphia could be a homicidal maniac who was getting the lay of the land." Ted sighed. "But I doubt it."

"Something out of the ordinary did happen the afternoon of May tenth." I put my finger on the entry: " 'Electrician one P.M.' Elsie's handwriting."

"The fuses blew and one whole circuit blew out every fuse we put in," Elsie said. "And we called you up to come over quick, Peaches."

"And the electrician said he'd come at one, though as I remember, he was late," I told Albert and Ted, who hadn't been there. "And then after he poked around, he said he had to re-do a section of wiring. You remember," I said to Elsie, "he said the house was built at the time aluminum was used for wiring and an overload can burn aluminum wiring out. But none of us knew of an overload."

"That was interesting," Pop said. He'd enjoyed watching the rewiring. Somehow he had inveigled the man into coming the next day, May 11, even though that was Saturday. "Arabella from next door came over," Pop said, "and we watched the man work. His name was Ellis King. We had to lock Silk up. He kept hissing at the King." Silk. Our only clue so far.

"That's the electrician you promised you'd remember in your will," I told him.

He smiled like a naughty boy. "It pleases people," he said.

"Electricians know how to rig hot wires," Ted said, "but I bet if a professional did it, the trap wouldn't have been so crude." I shivered. If an electrician did it, maybe he would have rigged a trap that succeeded in killing me. "Besides, he was an electrician that Mary knew and had used before."

"Sunday, May twelfth, was Mother's Day," Elsie said.

"M," the calendar said. My handwriting.

"I came up from Charleston to be with Mother and Mary," Albert said. His glare softened. "We dropped over here to pay a call."

"I was here. Very exciting," I said. "Silk ambushed you from behind a door. You thought that was funny, Pop," I accused. "Albert didn't laugh. I think that's why he gave you one of his lectures about keeping track of valuable things and keeping your coins in a safe-deposit box." I grinned at Albert, hoping to cheer him up a little. But it's true. Albert likes to lecture people he's mad at.

We still didn't know where the little portrait was. I changed the subject.

"Monday, May thirteenth, was Andy's birthday. Remember?" I asked Pop. "Mary brought him over to show you his birthday presents. Including a talking teddy bear," I said. "And Andy almost made off with a large quartz crystal that had belonged to Mother, except you

171

saw it bulging in his pocket." I'd never forget Pop's double-take when he saw what the kid almost snitched.

Pop grinned. The crystal was now on the bookshelf — in back of his left ear, to be exact, out of Andy's reach.

"On Tuesday, May fourteenth, your cousin Gloria from Madison County signed the guest book 'Gloria and Chocolate Cake,' " Ted told him. Pop said he couldn't remember about that, and Elsie said that nevertheless he loved the cake.

"And on the same day," I said, "your lawyer came. The calendar says 'Lwyr three-fifteen.' I believe that's the day he arranged some additions to your will. Some things you'd promised." Pop stared at me stonily. He knows I think he promises too much.

"Wednesday, May fifteenth. The calendar says 'Jameson,' " I announced. "That's Pop's broker, Herbert Jameson," I told Ted. "He likes to visit his most successful self-made client." I turned to the rest of our circle. "I remember that it was right after Herbert left that Nancy came by on her way to a covered-dish dinner and forgot and left her trifle in the refrigerator by mistake."

"And I told her," said Pop, "that it was her punishment for not also making a trifle for me."

Albert jumped up. "I can't take this," he grated. "All this silly going-over-the-calendar. Do you think a killer calls and makes an appointment or signs a guest book? Would he be such a fool?"

He strode over and stood in back of me and stared down at the calendar.

"Thursday, May sixteenth," he spit out: " 'Rev. Justice.' Now there's a cold-blooded killer! Not a damn thing on the seventeenth. You're wasting time."

"And on May eighteenth, just a note in the guest book," Ted said calmly. "It says: 'Marcia Davies from Philadelphia. You helped when I was lost in the mountains.' I suppose you think that's harmless. But how do we know who she really was?"

That seemed to calm Albert down. He plunked down next to me and dropped his head into his hands. "Oh God," he said, "I'm just in a bad state." He looked up at Pop. "I need a drink."

Pop took pity and asked Elsie to get Albert a bourbon on the rocks.

We had nearly finished the job. I felt we had to get it done. "On Monday, May twentieth," I said. "No notation on the calendar or in the guest book.

"And on Tuesday, May twenty-first, no calendar entry."

"But," Ted said, "Wednesday was busy. Wednesday, May twenty-second, was the day Nancy mailed her letter about the little portrait, post-marked Asheville." At least, if I didn't remember everything, I had Ted to do it for me. Each person is clever in his own way, right?

Albert said, "Thank God," because Elsie

handed him his drink. He took a long, grateful swig. I hoped he'd stay alert.

"On Wednesday, May twenty-second, Pop's calendar has something written on it in my handwriting," I said. "I can't tell what it means: BKL."

Silence round the table. Except Albert's ice popped. Pop frowned in thought. Elsie sat at attention. Ted massaged his ear lobe. Silence.

Then Albert said, "Well, BKL could be initials. Or each letter could stand for one word, the way the letters do in that example in your book." Still perfectly clear-headed.

Then I almost laughed because of what popped into mind. Those three letters were the initials of my roommate at Chapel Hill, Barbara Kennedy Lowell. Who did her homework and ate peanuts in bed. And what on earth could she have to do with our troubles? Barbara married a man from California who studied auras, and then we lost touch. I'd certainly remember if she'd called after all these years, now, wouldn't I? But memory was so much like a loose wire. Sometimes it worked. Sometimes it didn't.

BKL. I stared at the letters on the calendar. I was sure they were important. It *will* come to me, I told myself. But I'd read somewhere that after a bad shock you can forget things that happened just before.

"Wednesday is also the day when Mary says Nancy left for Charleston," I said.

That was just before the shock, all right.

"Charleston, where she told Mary she expected some kind of confrontation, but wouldn't say what," I added.

Albert had forgotten to hide his bad hand. He was twisting his two hands together on the table. "Oh, God," he said, "why couldn't Mary just demand to know why?"

"I asked the Mustache what they'd found out about Charleston," I said. "He said she'd been registered at the King Charles Hotel on Wednesday night."

"The twenty-second," Ted added.

"But," I said, "she had no reservation for the following night. And Mary talked to her Uncle Herman on her father's side, who lives in Charleston. Mary says he told her Nancy didn't call any of her relatives there, at least not that they'll admit. Mary says that's not at all like her mother. She says Nancy was worried about her mother-in-law — Horace's mother — who lived with Herman and his wife down there, and called every chance she got."

Albert said, "Yes, she worried," and took another long pull on his drink. "And my mother didn't call me that evening either, or even let me know she'd be in town. Which is very odd." Albert's bad hand was under the table again. He clenched and unclenched his good hand around the sweating glass of bourbon.

"So what did she do that night?" I asked. Nobody answered.

"All I know is that she came by the store on

Thursday." Albert's voice broke like a teen's. "She came by at eleven in the morning. And I suspected she might be upset because she kept fingering her earrings like she did when she was upset. Oh, God, why didn't I ask her what was wrong? She was dressed up in a fancy green dress, and crystal earrings, like she might be going out to lunch somewhere, and she said she'd come back when she wasn't busy, but she never did. I asked her where she was going, but she ducked that question. She was so independent. So good at ducking questions. And she never came back." His eyes were overflowing again, but he kept talking. "I was home all evening. Not worried because she was so independent. But I was there. And she never called back." He turned to me. "You were the one who called in the morning. Oh, damn, damn, damn!" He was shaking with fury. At fate, I guessed.

"About all we know," I said, "is that some time after she saw you, Albert, she changed her dress and earrings. She put on the dress that she bought at the sale with me, which looked like the dress I bought except for the color." I shivered.

Long, serious silence. Maybe the others were trying to see a pattern in all that, like I was. Maybe they just felt lousy thinking about it, like I did.

"And she was found dead with her pocketbook missing, and the flashlight gone from her car," Ted added. "Furthermore, we found a chocolate wrapper, from the kind of candy bar she usually carried in her pocketbook, out in the woods, and that makes it seem that the killer left the scene that way."

"And," I said, "her pocketbook was found thrown over the edge of Elk Mountain Scenic Highway just yesterday, with everything removed from it but one bill in a side pocket. Some kids found it on a path just down from the edge of the highway, and brought it to the police." Pop and Albert sat up straight.

Pop said, " 'Scenic Highway' be damned. It's a dirt road. And why the hell didn't you tell me about that sooner?"

So I explained we'd just found out ourselves and I'd waited to tell them at the right place on the calendar, to avoid a long discussion before we even started to set the scene. I said, "I was hoping it would jog your memory and imagination to do it that way." It jogged them all right — into being annoyed. And after we told Pop and Albert and Elsie everything we knew about the pocketbook, we talked for what seemed like three hours about the possibilities for how it got to Elk Mountain.

"Who steals my purse steals trash," Pop quoted. "I don't remember who said that, but it sure applied to Nancy. She never had two cents in her purse."

"She had credit cards," I pointed out. "And maybe there was something in that pocketbook that would tell us about her confrontation, what-

177

ever it was, in Charleston." We batted that idea around for fifteen minutes.

Final consensus: Someone needed to hide that pocketbook. Maybe hide what was in it. Reason unknown. We were all exhausted. Elsie went to get us coffee. And no matter how mad it made Pop, I was mighty glad we got most of the calendar cased before I told him about that purse.

We all had Elsie's good hot coffee to revive us, except for Albert who had another drink. I was worried about him. The last thing we needed was for Albert to crack up.

"We need to talk more about Nancy's letter to Pop," Ted said. "Elsie, could you get it to show Albert? Maybe it will mean more to him than it does to us."

Of course. Our job wasn't done. "She expected you to get that letter the day before the night she was murdered," Ted said to Pop. "She was an optimist. She expected you to get that letter overnight. And you might have, except the mail was slow."

Albert was reading the letter. Slowly after all that whiskey. His eyes didn't seem to focus too well.

"The letter said she was coming by to talk to Pop," I said. "About something to do with that little portrait Mom bought that reminded her of me. Any ideas about how that letter relates to the crimes?"

No answer. Albert, who might have made the best guess, hiccupped and shook his head.

178

"What else?" I asked. No answer. "We haven't found anything that could be even vaguely related to Larry's death. Oh, well. We can keep adding to our 'set-the-scene' list as we think of things," I said.

I noticed Pop was nodding: "We need to sleep on it, and besides you've made me late for my nap," he said. Elsie wheeled him off to his bedroom.

Albert announced he needed another drink and went over and poured one at the sideboard in the dining room. I could see him through the door. He was slowly pouring a double.

"So what do we do next?" I asked Ted. I was asking myself, too. "Of all the things on the tape of Pop's circle and on the calendar, what's most important to look into?" And even before Ted answered, I could hear the whisper on the tape again. I could hear Silva say, "Like Sam." Whatever that meant. I put my finger on the date when somebody rigged electric death. Silva was in the house on duty from 11 P.M. to 7 A.M. She had the opportunity.

"Why don't you talk to Silva?" Ted said. Great minds run on the same track. "You can easily arrange to be here when she comes on duty at eleven tonight and talk to her in a natural, unthreatening way. Find out what she meant when she said 'Like Sam,' during Pop's question-and-answer thing."

I sighed. I had to suspect the people I wanted to feel good about. Whoever. This was an equal opportunity crime. "But how could Silva be connected with the fact that Nancy was insensitive to the way people felt about their children? Because that's what Pop was saying when she whispered to herself." I remembered!

Ted nodded. "You have a good starting point."

"Good," I said. "I'll talk to her tonight. And why don't you talk to John Q. Denton with his Yankee accent? He must know about a whole side of Nancy's life that we don't know. And besides, no matter what he says, it's odd that he stayed for Pop's question group after the funeral."

Albert came lurching back with his super bourbon. He managed to phone Mary and announced she was home and he'd drive there. But when he'd finished his drink he almost fell over on the table, so Ted and I grabbed hold of him and steered him into Ted's car for safe transportation.

He felt feverish as well as uncoordinated. He reeked of alcohol. "I hope this isn't a trend," I told Ted, "but just a poison-letting, a way of getting the misery out of his system."

We laid him on the back seat of the car, where he lolled like a puppet after the show. But he still had a line. "I am an orphan," Albert mumbled. And then fell asleep.

CHAPTER
14

LATE THURSDAY NIGHT

I spent the night at Pop's again. My goldfish must be beginning to think I never came home except to feed them. The good thing about goldfish is that they don't care much, which is exactly the same as the bad thing about goldfish. They were really Roger's. He said that watching goldfish swim in an aquarium cleared his mind and made him think better. Now that he was gone I couldn't get rid of the goldfish any more than Pop could get rid of Silk. I was glad of that. Silk was my friend.

Silk was purring in my lap as I sat at Pop's table reading poetry. I do that to clear *my* mind. My favorite is Emily Dickinson. About ten o'clock I was reading *I Dwell in Possibility*. I didn't really need the book. I know it by heart. The book was a fence. I needed a little space by myself, between me and Dorothy, the sitter on duty. I needed, at least briefly, to relax my mind.

I thought about my friend Laura, back in school, who couldn't remember poetry at all and was pleased when someone told her that you can always recognize a poem by Emily Dickinson because the rhythm is like "The Yellow Rose of Texas." She needed that kind of trick in order to pass English. I had to try *not* to remember "The Yellow Rose of Texas" in order to enjoy Emily Dickinson. We're all so different!

Every person has a rhythm, I thought. What was the rhythm of the killer? Swift? Uneven? Full of surprises? He or she set up the electric trap just five days after Nancy's death. Slipped into the house (or tried to) twice in that many days. With the police still hot and heavy on the case. The killer had killed in two ways that seemed to be quite different, except that each involved water. Nancy was dumped into the pond. Water underfoot made the electricity that killed Larry more surely lethal.

I put down my book and went into the kitchen, where I smelled coffee. Dorothy was a coffee addict. Dorothy was also gentle and earnest and persistent, not swift, uneven, or full of surprises. Still, I might learn something helpful if I drew her out. She was sitting at the kitchen table, alternately sipping coffee and knitting a pink baby sweater. She looked like a plump, slightly anemic workaholic saint. Her dimpled hands were always busy.

She jumped up to pour me a cup of coffee.

"I can get it," I said. But Dorothy had it poured before I could get a cup.

"This is a hard time," she said, blue eyes soft-focus. "I'm praying for you."

"I appreciate that," I told her, lowering myself into the chair across from hers. "And I appreciate your keeping your eyes open for anything out of the ordinary that could be a clue to what happened."

She began to breathe a little harder. "I do notice things," she said, "but I don't like to speak against other people." She began to knit faster.

I sipped my coffee, hoping she'd go on and do it anyway.

No luck. "After all," I said, "this is an unusual situation. Two people we knew and cared about are dead." And then I thought: Maybe she didn't care about them. How did I know for sure? Maybe her pious words and the cross around her neck and her bumper sticker that said "God loves you and I'm trying" were all a front. Anyway, it was her husband who put on the bumper sticker. She'd told me that.

I felt like there were parts of Dorothy she kept hidden. Why? Just because she was ashamed of her fallibilities? Or for other reasons?

"Perhaps," she said, "you could talk to Silva. She's upset. I don't know why. But it might be related. Last night when she came in I could tell she'd been crying, and when I asked what I could do to help, she said she didn't want to talk." That was the only clue I got out of Dorothy.

When Silva arrived about fifteen minutes later, she did not look like she'd been crying. She looked angry to see me waiting up. She came in tentatively, as always, as if she wasn't sure she'd been invited, but the frown lines between her eyes were extra deep. She glanced at me, and then quickly away as if I were an eclipse of the sun and might burn her eyes. Strange combination: her where-can-I-hide manner, that bleached-blond hair, sticking out like an Afro, and those hostile brown eyes.

"Hi," I said. "Have some coffee."

Dorothy grabbed her big old knitting-bag purse and left in a hurry, as if she expected the house to blow up.

"Is it still raining?" I asked. Silva said no, it was just drizzling, and shook her head as if she wanted to get rid of any water sticking to her hair. Then she sat down in the seat Dorothy had left, and we drank coffee quietly for several minutes. I wasn't sure how to begin sounding her out. And, besides, I figured she needed a moment to settle in.

"What do you want?" Her voice was deep with resentment. But she pushed her bushy blond hair back from her thin face with both hands as if showing me she didn't have to hide.

"Silva," I said, "I appreciate how good you are with my father, but I need to ask everybody questions."

184

"You don't have to." She ducked her head but her voice stayed hostile. "The police have to ask questions. You *want* to ask."

"You remember when my father got everybody together after the funeral? I taped what we all said."

Silva started. Her hands flew down and clutched each other. Thin, knobby hands. "Without permission," she accused.

I got out my little cassette player and played her the section of the tape where she seemed to be saying: "Like Sam." I rewound that section of the tape and played it for her again. She leaned back, retreating as far as she could into her chair. Her eyes stayed furious, frown lines etched black.

"I need to know about Sam," I said.

She got up and poured herself another cup of black coffee, glancing up at that cat-face clock as if she hoped it would say her shift was ending, not beginning. She came back glowering, like she intended to throw the coffee in my face. Instead she threw words in my face.

"You'll find out anyway," she raged. "The police have probably found out already. My son was named Sam. Your wonderful Nancy did him dirt. That's how she was. Oh, I know, you think Nancy Means was such a fine woman." Silva got up and began to pace around. "But she took what she wanted. She let other people pay, and stayed proud of herself."

"Tell me about it."

"I suppose you're taping this?"

"No," I said. I pulled out a pad and pencil. "But because I have a lousy memory, I may take a few notes."

She was so wound up she accepted that and raged on, still pacing up and down, all her timidity burned off. "He was a beautiful boy. Here, I have a picture of him." She sat down again, grabbed her blue pocketbook off the end of the table, and pulled out a wallet with a picture under clear plastic of a boy about twenty with the wide, heavily lashed eyes and smooth oval face of a pretty girl. But his mouth was firm, lips pressed together. "His first job was as a driver and messenger for your Aunt Nancy's company. He drove Nancy places, to meetings and such like. He said that meant she could study her notes on the way, and besides she hated to drive. Or maybe she liked to have a handsome kid to drive her. A change from her husband. That woman seduced my son."

I was surprised. I was shocked, not because an older woman and a young man went to bed together, but because I thought Nancy was loyal and faithful to Horace, even if he was mostly soused. Goodbye illusion. I studied Silva's thin face. She might be lying.

"Tell me about it." That seemed a handy phrase.

"When he drove her they stopped in a motel for a little nookie along the way. He said she told her co-workers she was stopping to do research."

186

Silva's laugh was bitter. "Some research! But he fell for it. She was successful. She was good-looking in her way. Sam was impressed."

And maybe he thought it would help him to advance, I thought unkindly.

"So what do you think of that?" Silva asked, leaning towards me across the table.

My feelings were tangled: disillusion, sorrow, skepticism, and at the same time a lack of surprise. Horace *was* soused all the time. I ignored her question and said, "But that wasn't all that happened."

"No!" she exploded. But then she didn't seem to want to go on.

"What did Sam do that you're ashamed of?" I asked.

She got up and paced again. "He was so young," she said. "He had bad friends. He wanted to be like them. He used cocaine." She almost swallowed the last words, but I caught them. She turned defiantly towards me. "He stole from the company. Here and there, petty cash, even money from people's pocketbooks. Everybody liked him, so for a while he got away with it." She threw her head back defiantly, almost proudly. Then she shut her eyes and swallowed: "Your Aunt Nancy caught him.

"Your clever Nancy missed a hundred dollars that was in her pocketbook before they went to a motel together, and gone right after. That's what he told me." She spit her words: "Nancy was a bitch. Next time she put two hundred dollars in her pocketbook just to tempt him. She found it in his pocket. But she kept quiet and paid for a drug treatment program. He thought that was because she cared about him."

"But it wasn't?"

"No. She used him like a male whore. That bitch. Except you pay a whore. She made him return the money. She went on being nice to him because she was scared he'd tell about the nookie, that's what. She told him: 'My husband mustn't ever know about this.' "

"And then what happened?" I knew by the way she screwed up her face and let tears ooze down her cheeks that the worst was still to come. The black window behind the table mirrored the side of her face, complete with tears.

"He grew up," she said, hands clenched. "He stopped doing stupid things like taking cocaine or stealing from pocketbooks or letting a boss use him." She glared at me as she said "use."

"And you were proud of him for that."

That dissolved her. She cried for five minutes, elbows on table, head in hands. I could feel the table vibrate from her great sobs. Plainly, that boy was wildly important to her. I lowered my eyes and sipped my coffee, not knowing what to say.

"Sam got a better job," she gasped. "He met a really nice girl and they were married and had a little boy. And then he had an offer for a good job in a bank in Florida, except he had to be bonded. He figured Nancy was his friend. She'd kept her

188

mouth shut about his drug and money problems. She'd paid for his treatment," Silva choked. "He thought she'd be proud of him. He put her down for a reference."

She took a tissue from the box on the table and blew her nose hard. "But by then the bitch's husband had died." Silva took a deep breath and raised her voice. "So she wasn't scared of what he'd tell anymore. She wrote a letter that ruined my son. Your Aunt Nancy wrote that he was charming but couldn't be trusted. She wrote that he had a history of petty theft. She sent that to the people who meant to hire him."

Silva had turned a bad color, gray-green, as if she'd been poisoned. "He went and had it out with her, face to face. He wasn't a coward. He carried a hidden tape recorder with him. He told her that by not reporting his thefts she was a party to them. 'You can't hurt me,' she told him. 'I'm retired. My husband is dead. I don't care what you tell about me. I did one thing wrong and you exploited it to get away with theft. You blackmailed me not to tell. I'll warn anybody who tries to hire you.' That's the way she twisted it all in her mind."

I wondered how much Silva twisted in *her* mind. But the whole thing made me feel sick. And I'd been jealous of how well Nancy seemed to manage her life. How she remembered birthdays and color-coordinated her purse and shoes, and all that.

"My son had the tape, but he believed her

when she said she didn't care. He wouldn't use it. He couldn't get a good job." She cried out: "His wife left him. He killed himself. He drank cyanide. My beautiful son drank cyanide."

How horrible. Poor Silva. "And did you need to avenge him? Did you come here for that?" I tried to ask that gently, but the words were harsh.

She jumped up again. "I came here by coincidence. I didn't know your father was related to that woman. She had a different last name from your father's." She said that too fast. She avoided my eyes.

"Silva," I said, still trying to be gentle, "I don't believe that. You're smarter than that. You don't drift into things. You do them on purpose. Tell me the truth."

"You don't trust me!"

"You're scared," I said. "You're trembling."

"And you're just like that sanctimonious woman! That smug bitch. I would have enjoyed killing her, but I didn't do it. O.K., I did come here on purpose. I wanted her to know I was here, and squirm. But I never meant to kill her."

My heart beat faster. Was thin, shy little Silva a killer?

"So what happened?"

Silva lowered her voice, shut her eyes like she didn't want me to see in. "All I did was ask her for money for my son's wife. My poor April." She opened her eyes again wide. They were glittering with anger. "She has so much trouble. All by herself. Her kid has problems and needs help. She's not trained to work. She gets minimum wage. Your fancy aunt should have helped. I told her that."

"Wasn't that blackmail?"

"No!"

"When did you ask her?" I mustn't let sympathy keep me from finding the truth.

Silva's eyes opened even wider with panic. She put her hands over her mouth, as if she realized the full implications of what she'd told me. Then, pulling her hands away, she whispered: "About three days before she died. But there's no possible connection. I swear there's no connection."

"She didn't say she'd sue you for defamation of character or anything like that?" Knowing Nancy, that was likely.

Silva's face twisted into anger again. "Of course she did! But I knew she couldn't do it without telling the world exactly the things she didn't want anybody to know. And she was vain. You know she was vain."

Yes. That was true. And, because the whole conversation seemed to put Silva through a meat grinder, I believed her. I reminded myself Silva had no provable alibi for the night Nancy died. Was she home sick like she'd said? Or lying? She wouldn't hesitate to lie, I'd seen that firsthand. But I felt like I could tell when she did it.

She had been the sitter on duty, the sitter in Pop's house, the probable night when someone set an electric trap that killed Larry, and could have killed me. But I still believed her, even while I wondered if I was crazy.

"I'm truly sorry I had to ask you all this," I said. "But we're all in danger until we find out what happened."

She sat down and put her head in her hands. "Maybe."

"I won't tell what you've told me to anybody but one good and discreet friend who's helping me try to solve this," I said.

She raised her head and stared me straight in the eye. "Thank God and thank you."

I suddenly realized what Ted would have said if he'd been there. He would have said he hoped God would not be offended at the almost equal billing. Or something like that to break the grimness.

Silva and I were both crying.

I felt so badly I drove home to sleep in my own bed, even though the clock on the mantle said twelve forty-five. I didn't like going into an empty house, but I needed to be alone.

CHAPTER
15

FRIDAY, MAY 31

When I discovered that Friday was trying to be a Bad Day, I sat down to work at my computer for a while to calm myself. We were going to Larry's funeral. Kind Larry. Who died in a trap that may have been set for me. Which curdled my mind. But my computer is so logical it can work around curdle.

It can spell. Even without tricks. I was working on my chapter about ingenuity. Actually I put *enginuity*, but the computer lit that up and then fixed it. Wonderful.

INGENUITY

If there is one thing you have to develop if you have no memory, ingenuity is it.

So you forgot something essential, like where you put your door key when wolves were at your heels, or forgot the map to the treasure hunt, or your toothbrush before the out-of-town job inter-

view. There's nothing to gain by getting mad at yourself. In fact, you need all your think-power to figure out what to do instead of what you would have done if you'd remembered. That's ingenuity.

I skipped through to the part about arriving downtown with no money. That's where I'd left off.

One of the times you have to use the most ingenuity is when you have no money at all. Hopefully, it's not a permanent condition.

I stopped and shivered. A permanent condition of no money would require a whole *book* of ingenuity. Pop's life was almost like that when he was a kid. Not now.

Let's say you left your pocketbook or wallet at home, complete with money and plastic, and you have a long grocery list for the house guests who arrive in two hours. The quarters you keep in your pockets for emergencies are not enough by a long shot.
There are simple solutions. If you're near a branch of the bank where they know you, get a counter check. That's easy. If you're near a branch of the bank where they don't know you and you have no identification, get them to call the branch where they do know you, and get someone there to listen to your voice, and

194

vouch that you're you.

Also, it helps to get to know people in the smaller places where you shop, so in a pinch they'll let you sign a small IOU to be paid when you come back. That's preventive ingenuity.

Suddenly I thought: Suppose the killer has had the preventive ingenuity to make us all like him or her and allay our suspicions. And therefore the killer is the person I least suspect. But that would be Ted! I rushed back to the comfort of my writing.

That paragraph about preventive ingenuity was not colorful enough. I needed a good example. There was a girl I met in a writers' workshop, Marjorie-something, who told a funny story about discovering she had no money and no thyroid pills and no prescription with her when she had to make a speech. Without the thyroid pills she'd go to sleep at three o'clock. The speech was at three o'clock. I could remember the problem. I couldn't remember how she solved it. Well, heck, I'd call and ask her. But what was her name? It wasn't in my head, but it would be in my database. Wherever I go, I add to the database the people I meet. Ted's idea. He says when my book comes out I need to send a postcard announcing it to everyone I ever met. So I put them all in the database, ready to go when the time comes.

I found the database disk and slipped it into the slot in my computer. I clicked on my "People

List." Up came the Mustache file, the last one I put in. Complete with note to thank him for his help with my book. He hadn't told me much about what the police were up to, even though he was in charge of the case. Because we were all suspects. Which is why I'd kept some things from him. I never told him a lie. I just didn't volunteer. I wasn't comfortable about not telling. I also would not have been comfortable telling him about Silva or Elsie or the mean things Gloria said about Pop. Anyway, Mustache kept giving me memory devices, like "left loose, right tight," the way to turn a screw. So I'd let my guard down? I was grateful, but — speaking of "loose" — I prayed that soon I could thank him for catching the killer, and putting him "tight" under lock and key. I did not put that in my computer.

My computer's form for each person has a spot for name, business, address, city, state, zip, phone, organization, profession and, in case that's not enough, a place for notes.

To find Marjorie, or whatever her name was, I just had to choose "Select" and a blank form came up into which I could write anything I remembered. I wrote Marjorie under *name*. I clicked on *find* in another spot. A box came up on the screen. It said "No records match this request." Well, O.K. But I knew she was from the Hendersonville area. I erased the wrong name and typed in Hendersonville on the *city* line. Three names came up. None was a bit like

196

Marjorie. She must be from some smaller community near Hendersonville. Damn. She wasn't in business. I'd lost her phone number except in the database. I didn't know her street address. Yes I did, too. It was Cascade Heights. She'd told me that was funny because her well kept going dry. I typed Cascade Heights under *address*. I clicked on *find*. Up came Marilyn Coglin, 200 Cascade Heights, Horseshoe, N.C. Good. I made a note of her phone number. It was getting late. I had to grab some lunch and get dressed. I'd call her after the funeral. I closed down my computer.

As I put on a dark dress, I had the oddest feeling I was at the edge of some solution. Something to do with the computer. Because the computer extends me into what I can't remember. The computer is extra brain power with me as the pilot. Well, heck, I'm a good pilot. With the computer I can *use* being a good pilot, instead of drowning in the sea of the thoughts that get away. I must get busy on a chapter on computers. God's gift to the weak of memory. I drove over to Pop's, where we all were to assemble at one-thirty to go to the funeral together.

I still felt bad. Even when I came in the kitchen door and found Ted already there. Every object I looked at told me a sad story. Even the funny objects like the cat-face kitchen clock that Mary gave Ma. As the pendulum swung, the cat's big black eyes moved right, left, right, left. I walked in, looked at that silly clock, and told Ted: "That's how bad it is. We all have to keep looking in every direction every minute in order to stay alive."

He said, "Words of wisdom."

I looked out the kitchen window to see Albert and Mary just getting out of Albert's van. There on the kitchen windowsill was Albert's painted clay "rabbit" that he made in kindergarten with the long ears and catlike body and brown and yellow spots. Usually that rabbit was good for a chuckle. But suddenly I was telling Ted how Aunt Nancy talked about "Albert's rabbit" which was the only one in the world with spots like a leopard, and then laughed. And Albert was so upset he took his rabbit away from her, and gave it to Ma, who had tact. I was almost crying. I said, "Ma told Albert that anybody could make a rabbit just like any other, but it took real talent to make a new kind." I choked up. "Would you believe I look at that rabbit and feel deserted? Because I don't have my tactful mother anymore. Me, a woman of fifty-five. A mother myself."

"And a mother to Pop, half the time," he said. "Cheer up. If we can live to his age somebody will look after *us*." I don't know why we thought that was funny, but we both laughed.

We all went to the funeral in Pop's Cadillac with Pop sitting up by Ted. He'd asked Ted to drive. Nobody ever said Pop was not a male chauvinist. Mary and Albert and I were in the back seat.

We were crowded, but I think we'd felt the funeral was an occasion where we needed each other. We had to go and show Larry's mother how sorry we were about her son, even if it broke us up. Pop especially. I thought he was going to break into sobs when the preacher said Larry was God's gift to the sick.

Mustache was in the church. In a back pew. I suppose he was hoping some suspect would reveal himself. And Yankee Accent. He came up and spoke to Mary on the way out. Seemed delighted to see her. So maybe he came to Pop's after-funeral circle partly because our Mary attracted him. They sure were opposites. He was so serious, and dressed in gray like a poor man's lawyer.

Ted drove us home by way of the Blue Ridge Parkway. Plainly he still believed in soothing doses of mountain view.

So, O.K. I tried to fill my mind with the far mountains in the golden afternoon sun. The parkway wound along the edge of steep slopes. Below us, all we could see were the tops of trees and, off in the distance, winding mountainsides. Except for the cars we occasionally passed parked at overlooks, we could have been at the end of the world, not twenty minutes from Asheville.

One of the cars had a sticker on the back: "Johnson Ford, Hendersonville."

Hendersonville. That's where I first thought my friend Marilyn was from. Until my computer told me better — and also straightened me out on her first name.

"I just had the oddest thought," I said. "This morning I was trying to find a person in my database. And I did it by typing in the little bit of information I had that matched something in the computer. That little bit was enough to bring up all the rest of the stuff about that person.

"There ought to be a Computer of the World, and then we could find out all sorts of things we need to know. Things we had forgotten and things we never knew but that somebody knew and put in the computer."

"And people could also find out about you." Albert's voice rasped with anger. Anger to express his grief? "And the computer could be programmed wrong. I had a friend who lost his credit rating because a collection agency computer was programmed wrong. Do you think that's a joke?"

There was no time to answer. We came around a curve, and a man was standing right in the road waving his arm. A slight, black-haired man in khaki pants and a red-checked shirt. He waved his arm frantically, like a warning flag. Our brakes squealed as Ted swerved to miss him and a small tan van in the middle of the road behind him. We screeched and then slipped right to the edge of the grass by the road — a foot or two more and we'd have gone over the edge. My stomach was in my mouth. Ted backed up and parked. He looked pale himself. Pop said,

"My God, Ted. That's no way to drive."

But then the young arm-waver explained his van had broken down. He asked us to help push it onto the grass. Not Pop, of course, but the rest of us. And out we got and pushed in our formal funeral clothes. The van was heavy, as if it carried lead bricks. But it was dangerous to leave it in the road. We could see that.

Then our friend of the waving arms thanked us with too many words. He also said thank God we came along so soon. He said he broke down minutes before we arrived.

And I thought, life is like that. You're riding along, looking at the scenery, and suddenly just around a curve, whammo — there's danger. And you're not ready. And then life is out of kilter and everything around you could be dangerous. Because if you miss one trap, you could miss another.

The black-haired man kept swallowing and fidgeting. He said he was late to where he was going, and would we mind stopping at the nearest house to call for a tow truck.

Albert, who was looking in the small windows in the back of the man's van, asked, "Are you an antiques dealer?" I glanced in the back and saw a wooden angel, a weathervane in the shape of a cow, and other carvings stacked on top of primitive tables and chairs and chests. Also a portrait of a man in black looking very eighteenth-century.

"I'm just moving," he said quickly. Was there

something strange about his jumpiness? After two people I knew had been killed, I noticed strangeness more than I used to. There was a strong new category in the computer of my mind: "What doesn't fit?"

I saw Albert staring at the van's license number. Albert who remembers numbers.

We took off and Albert waited until the man and his tan van were out of sight around a curve before he said: "Good antique American folk art brings a lot of money. There are thieves who specialize in nothing else. There was something odd about that man. I wonder if he had stolen stuff."

That got Pop's attention. He turned as far around in his seat as he could to stare at Albert. "Have you been robbed?"

"Not me." Albert reared back like he'd been insulted. I could feel him stiffen on the back seat next to me. He was in the middle. "I don't take chances. There are some foreign collectors who will buy without asking questions. Which encourages thieves. It's a damn serious problem." Albert was so intense. "When it comes to really good pieces, I try to buy those that fit in my safe. I have a burglar alarm."

I knew that reminded me of something, but I couldn't quite think what. It was something besides our missing miniature, which I asked Albert about. "Could someone have slipped off with our little miniature portrait and sold it to an art fence?" I asked.

"You betcha," Albert said. "Easy."

"But isn't something as individual as that easy to trace?"

"Probably not if it's sold to a foreigner." He sounded furious. "Who's going to trace it to Tokyo or Buenos Aires or even to the home of a private collector here?"

And then he turned, first to me, and then to Mary sitting on his other side. "Hey! We might look into which of the people who visited Pop would know enough to know they could sell your antique art easy." Albert became an instant detective. "Maybe the way that picture disappeared is connected to the murders, through an art thief."

Sounded farfetched, but I remembered my rule. First look into the possible things, then the impossible things. And this was merely improbable.

"If we had a World Computer," I said, "we could put in the name of the artist: Edward something or other."

Ted said it: "Edward Greene Malbone."

"Yes, we'd put his name in, and up would come everything in the world connected with the man who painted our vanished portrait. Now, that might help."

Mary laughed. "If my aunt had wheels she might be a dump truck."

We dropped everybody off, and finally got Pop settled down. The funeral had upset him.

Ted convoyed me home. I realized I was

exhausted. And hot in my dark funeral dress.

We sat down on the back terrace to unwind with drinks. My glass of Chablis cooled my hand. I kicked off my shoes and touched the cold stones of the terrace with the soles of my feet. Now the sunlight was pale gold. The late-day chill felt good.

"I haven't had a chance to tell you about John Q. Denton," Ted said. He looked just right sitting there on my little terrace with the square-cut logs of the house behind him. "I tackled him while you had your sad session with Silva." I'd told Ted about that.

"Denton said he admired Nancy. He thought Nancy had a first-rate mind. He thought she was able to keep her feelings from getting in the way of her judgment." Ted grinned wryly. "Your cousin Gloria would not consider that a virtue."

"And besides," I said, "it wasn't true."

"He told me that, because he admired Nancy, he wanted to do anything he could to help catch her killer."

"My," I said, "how noble. Was he her lover, do you think? Or just an idealist who thought he'd found an ideal? Or is he bull-shitting us? And why is he so nice to Mary?" And I thought: I'm getting cynical.

Ted sipped his drink and shrugged. "He lives alone. Recently divorced. But he said he only knew Nancy from meetings of the Sierra Club and other public interest groups. Though, once they had coffee after a meeting and she told him she was due to testify in that custody case."

"Do you think he was hiding anything?"

"I couldn't tell. He told me again that he was at the symphony the night she was killed. I asked him where he was the evening of May twenty-eighth. You remember, that's the night when somebody created the electric trap."

I may forget birthdays, but I remembered that.

"Denton said he was home alone listening to music that night," Ted said. "I couldn't find out much more. He's traveled a lot. His home is full of art from all over the world, Thai grave rubbings and Russian icons and God knows what."

"Now, if we just had that World Computer, we might find out all sorts of added information about the man." I was joking.

Ted smiled. "You're smarter than you think you are," he said.

"Well, thanks. I could use being smarter than I think I am right now." I felt just like the clouds above us, all scattered out thin across the sky.

"I mean," Ted said, "there *is* such a thing as a World Computer, or at least something close to a World Computer. And I can get permission for us to use it."

"You're teasing me." I sat up straighter and my wicker chair creaked.

"No, I'm not." He stayed leaned back in his chair, one leg crossed over the other. But he grinned like the kid who won the prize.

"There was a time," he said, "when newspapers kept all their back stories and some of the materials that were used to write those stories in manila file folders and envelopes, so that a reporter could find those facts available when he needed them. It was called a morgue."

"Depressing name, but it would be appropriate for murder research." I slapped a mosquito. Mosquitoes are rare in the mountains but this one sure bit me.

"But now," Ted said, "the morgue is computerized and nobody calls it a morgue anymore. It's a newspaper library with world-wide resources."

"So" — I began to get excited — "you could call up any facts you wanted about the area the newspaper covered. Punch in a name, for example, and get the rest of what the computer knew about that person?"

"That is just the beginning." He sipped his drink and considered. "Newspaper computers form a network. You can put in a name and call up everything important that any newspaper in the network had ever reported about that person since that paper was computerized. And many large newspapers and some smaller ones are plugged in."

"Boy, that's what we need." In my mind I saw the map of the whole country dotted with bright spots for the cities. "We need a computer that fits the crime. A computer with Charleston and San Francisco where Larry came from, and all that in it."

"A newspaper library has more even than that." He gestured as if he was pointing to beyond the circle of mountains. "A newspaper library is also plugged in to newspapers in English in foreign parts and into all sorts of information databases from government statistics to Pentagon releases to business indexes." The late sun was turning his white hair golden, to fit his upbeat grin. His frosty glass gleamed.

"So this newspaper thing is a kind of a world community memory? That not only remembers a lot more than I would, or you would, but more than any person in the world could possibly store in his one brain?"

"Exactly," he said. "And backed by this super memory, all we need to know is what to ask. I'm sure you have lots of bits of fact in the back of your mind, left from the weeks before Nancy died and the days before Larry died, that might pull up useful information. When you sit down in front of the newspaper computer, I'll bet they'll come to you." His face shone with excitement. He raised his glass. "Here's to finding out," he said.

Then he frowned, and at the same moment the sun went behind a cloud. Eerie. "Don't mention this to anyone," he said. "In fact, work at seeming dumb. I suspect that may be the best way to stay alive. And we have to watch out."

Now, that was an advantage of a bad memory I didn't like to think about. Forgetfulness might help me seem so dumb that a wary murderer might not bother to bump me off. I'd have to work at forgetting even more than usual. But how many of my potential readers would be in a position to use that advantage? Not many, I hoped, for their sakes.

CHAPTER
16

SATURDAY, JUNE 1

Elsie was getting out of her ancient white Toyota in Pop's driveway when I stopped her. She looked even prettier than usual. Without much makeup and wearing jeans as always, but her skin glowed with health. She wore a soft green sweater that emphasized the glow, and gold loop earrings. "Can I talk to you a minute by yourself?" I asked.

She tensed, but she said, "Of course." A frown line came between her eyes for a moment, then vanished. "How can I help?" She stood waiting with her hand still on the handle of the car door.

"I won't tell Pop, but I think I'd feel better if I knew your real name myself," I said. I felt a little sneaky, because of course I was going to try out the names of all the sitters in the newspaper computer.

She froze, and the hand on the car door turned white with pressure. "I'd rather not tell anyone."

She lowered her voice until I could hardly hear. "It's nothing against you. But you know Harold might kill me if he found me."

"We may all be in danger," I said. "I need to know."

She hesitated a long time. We were like a movie with the motion stopped. Elsie as still as the green mountains behind her, eyes focused on the gravel driveway so I couldn't see into them. Then she said, "All right. It's Eleanor Bigger." She said it like a challenge, and yet she didn't raise her eyes.

Then she looked up at me, and there was dignity but also begging in her blue eyes. "But my life depends on him not finding me. I want to start a new life. Not be dogged by him forever."

"I do know that," I said, "and I'll be very careful." I meant it.

"I talked to Millie Davis at the newspaper library," Ted said. "Quite a gal. There's just one problem. She's so excited about what her library can do that when she first told me about it she forgot to tell me how much it costs."

"How much?" We were out for an early morning walk along the grassy edge of Beaver Lake, which is about halfway between Ted's house and mine. A breeze ruffled the water. The sun made it shine. "How much does it cost?" I said again.

He looked off at a plump man in red shorts jogging and puffing along the edge of the lake, then back at me. "Enough to matter. Millie is willing to give her time to the project because she's my friend and it interests her. But it will cost maybe twenty-five dollars just to ask one wide-ranging newspaper database like VuText to check out what stories there are about one name. Then if there are stories we want to pull up and read or print out, that will cost more. We have about ten names we want to check, and other questions."

"Pop has been talking about offering a twenty-five-thousand-dollar reward for information leading to the arrest of the killer." I picked up a pebble and skimmed it over the pond. "I was amazed. For him, that's a breakthrough. So maybe he'll underwrite our World Memory project. You're good with him, Ted. You tell him about it. And why not now?"

His blue eyes twinkled. Like the lake. "I thought you might suggest that."

We tramped back to Ted's car and drove on over to Pop's. Elsie was reading him the newspaper while he ate breakfast. Toast and bacon and eggs, with jam on the eggs, as always. One doctor had plumped for oatmeal. But Pop said oatmeal wasn't worth living for, and switched doctors.

"Elsie had to fix my breakfast," he said. "Anna's home sick. I think Elsie does the bacon better." Then he waved his hand at the newspaper: "They're crazy on Wall Street," he said. "And thank God for it. Because that's how I

211

make my money. By not being crazy when they are."

Sounded like this might be one of his good days.

"Elsie," Ted said, "I came all the way here to take some pictures, and I forgot to bring film. Would you run down to the drugstore and get me some?" He told her the kind he needed.

Pictures? I suddenly noticed he'd brought his camera from the car. I was about to ask "What pictures?" But of course what he wanted was to talk to Pop without Elsie there.

Elsie went without questions, but I suspect she figured why he sent her. Ted walked over to the window and watched her drive off, then came back.

"Pop," he said, "we have a great way to find out all the dirt about the people who could have killed your sister and Larry. They don't even need to know we know."

Pop lit up. He likes a little intrigue. "Good," he said. "These damn police hardly tell me a thing. If Nancy were here she'd be mad as hell that they're not making more progress. How do we learn more?"

"Recently," Ted said, "I got a newspaper friend to send my students some material about all the ways of gathering facts that a newspaper has today."

Pop faded. I could see he thought this was less exciting than he expected.

"A newspaper computer network can call up

212

murder stories from all over the country and from many other parts of the world. It can search for those where the method of murder was the same. It can print out any stories that seem relevant, and I can bring them back here for you to hear."

I could see Pop beginning to sense some adventure in that. He pursed his mouth like he was thinking of a good flavor.

"We can find any serious trouble that any one of our suspects has been in, in almost any part of this country, in Canada, and as far away as Tokyo. We can even find out if a suspect has gone into business or bought property or run for office."

Pop smiled. "And print that out for me?"

"I believe so," Ted said.

"When can we start?"

"The problem is that this kind of a search through computer networks costs money."

"I have never hesitated to spend money for a good cause," Pop said. I made myself keep a straight face. "How much?" he asked.

"A lot less than a twenty-five-thousand-dollar reward. Probably not more than a thousand dollars, depending on how many leads we find and how many different questions we have to answer."

Pop whistled, and hesitated. "You mean," he said, "the more you spend the more dirt we'll find." I could see him weighing that: cost versus reward. Finally he said: "Go to it."

Ted reached in his pocket and pulled out a paper for Pop to sign. Well. He *sure had* suspected that I'd say to ask Pop. And Ted was not born yesterday. The paper was all typed up and official-looking and said Pop would agree to reimburse the newspaper library for up to five thousand dollars.

Pop recoiled. "Don't you trust me?"

"Of course," Ted said, "but it's important for us all to remember what we decided to do in the same way. An agreement helps.

"And by the way," Ted added, "this is our secret. We mustn't tell."

Pop's eyes glowed with pleasure and he nodded. "Damned right," he said, "in fact, it's *my* secret because it's my money."

So in the late afternoon, Ted and I set out for the newspaper library, with Pop's agreement and our list of suspects' names.

Even Albert and Mary were in the dark about what we were going to do. We didn't tell another soul except Ted's friend Millie Davis, the newspaper librarian. She had agreed to let us come in at a slack time in the evening and she would be the one to help us call up what we wanted to know. No charge for her time, God bless her. Just for the commercial databases her library made available.

I'm not even going to say what newspaper we went to, because Millie was probably not supposed to let outsiders like us come in and use her information bank that way. But not only was she a friend of Ted's, he said, she was also intrigued at the idea of helping to catch a killer.

We drove through Asheville, past my favorite old buildings, mostly built in the 1920s — the Jackson building with gargoyle faces over the rain spouts; the pink-domed Baptist church designed by an architect who had hoped to start a trend in Asheville for cheerful vacation architecture. (Asheville loves tourists but doesn't go for trends.)

Ted and I drove through the Beaucatcher Cut, the road dynamited right through the bowl of mountain surrounding Asheville. We drove by the shopping centers just beyond, then off between the blue and green peaks on either side of the Interstate. Fast.

Ted is a skillful driver, but on a trip he drives about ten miles over the speed limit, and when he gets excited about what he's saying, he'll speed up a few more miles and not notice he's done it. I thought: That's why he always looks like the wind has been blowing through his hair, because he can't bear to do anything slowly.

We whizzed along, passing slowpokes like an old man in a pickup truck full of firewood, and I sat back and dreamed about that super-computer: Memory of the World. I felt wise just thinking about it. The computer full of extra memory power, where I could be pilot. Ted and I could be co-pilots. I wished I were next to the machine so I could hug it right then.

Ted was more practical. He said we'd better decide exactly how we were going to proceed: What questions we'd ask and in what order.

By the time we got to the newspaper, we'd decided to begin with the details of Nancy's death, then Larry's.

Because if we were dealing, not with a crazy relative or acquaintance, but with some real criminal or psychopathic serial killer, the chances were that the same pattern of killing had been repeated somewhere else. I realized we were humoring ourselves by starting that way. Because we didn't want the killer to be a friend or a relative.

So if crime comparison didn't ring a bell, next we'd put in the names of our home-grown suspects one by one and see what news the computer had about each one.

The pleasant middle-aged woman at the desk in the lobby of the newspaper building phoned up to Millie Davis, who came down and met us at the front door. Surprise. Millie was a swinger. About forty, I figured, and trying hard. I made sure my stomach was pulled in and hoped my lipstick wasn't smudged.

Millie the librarian wore a shortish red shirtwaist dress showing cleavage, and lots of bangly gold: bracelets, necklace, and earrings. She smiled at Ted like Christmas had arrived. She was polite to me. "I'm so sorry about your aunt and your friend," she said to me. "But I'm excited about what you're trying to do." She leaned towards Ted. What was *she* trying to do? "Follow me. Otherwise you'll get lost," she trilled. Then she led us through all sorts of corridors and twists and turns.

At last we went through an informal room of desks with computer terminals, mostly empty since it was now nine-thirty at night, and into a long room with a row of gray-green file cabinets down one side, a long bookcase parallel to it, and several more desks with terminals. Millie took us around a corner and into her private lair with a wall of pictures, another wall of assorted file boxes, a large desk, and three chairs.

She flipped into a chair in front of her terminal and waved towards chairs on each side of her. "Sit down," she said, crossing her legs so her skirt rode up. "I can call up whatever kind of information you want, and let you see how this works."

We told her our idea of how to search, beginning with the elements of each crime, looking for a pattern in crimes across the country.

She nodded, bobbing her gold earrings, and pushed a button. Light-colored words and numbers began to appear on the dark computer screen. An automatic "log-on," she explained, that began moving her into the most promising database.

"Wonderful," Ted said. "You're great at saving time, Millie."

"Nobody I'd rather please." She smiled. She even had dimples. And dimples on her knees, yet.

217

"We could begin in VuText," she said to Ted, as if maybe I didn't understand those things. I told myself I didn't mind. I did mind.

"Why VuText?" I asked.

"More newspapers are stored on VuText or DataTimes than any other databases." Now she turned to me, like Ted knew it all but I needed to learn. "A few papers like *The New York Times*, *Christian Science Monitor*, and the *Deseret News* in Salt Lake City are found only on a database called Nexus. We may not need that. It's more expensive." I wrote that down.

"How far back do the stories go?" Ted wanted to know. He was relaxed and casual. "Would a crime committed, say, ten years ago be in the computer?"

"I have a present for you." Millie absolutely glowed at him. She rooted out a chart and a map of the United States. "This chart," she said, "tells what databases each newspaper's stories can be called up from and when that newspaper went online."

"Online," I could see, meant "joined the system."

"*The Washington Post* had computerized records all the way back to 1977," she told us. I wrote that down. It could be helpful. Dorothy, our earnest three o'clock to eleven o'clock sitter, grew up in Washington. "*The New York Times* goes back further," our bangly hostess said.

"But then again you'd have to be in a pretty important story to get in *The New York Times*,"

Ted said. "They aren't big on routine police news."

Millie had her tapered hand on his shoulder. Very chummy. I tried not to show I was annoyed. "Lots of papers were online by 1985," Millie said, "from the *San Francisco Chronicle* to *The Charlotte Observer.*"

Good! Poor Larry had lived briefly in Charlotte.

"But lots of papers," Ted remarked, "have just recently gone online." He was studying the chart.

"You have to hope," Millie said, stroking her blond hair into place, "that if what you want appeared only in the *Baltimore Sun*, it was reported after September 1, 1990, when the *Sun* went online. On the other hand, if the story you want was in the *St. Petersburg Times*, you could call it up from as far back as 1986." I kept writing down dates.

Now Ted was studying the map of the United States titled "Newspapers Online." It showed that our World Memory was strongest in the Northeast, Southwest, and Far West. This memory still had blank spots, even in the United States: Montana, North Dakota, South Dakota, Nebraska, Iowa, Wisconsin. We had to hope none of our suspects had been there. Mississippi, Alabama, and Tennessee might be more of a problem, being nearer by. So, O.K., the World Memory was like my memory. It had holes in it. But with what was there, maybe we could get around what wasn't. I was used to that.

"I could call up all murders on this database," Millie told Ted, "but I would get literally thousands of listings. The more specific facts I include, the fewer and more exact listings I'll get."

"Nancy was hit over the head," I said, trying not to sound neglected. Millie typed in *murder* and *head*.

"And thrown into a pond." She typed in *pond* and then *or pool*.

"This is based on Boolean logic, as you know," she said to Ted. "Which," she added, turning to me, "is a mathematical procedure. You can combine the key terms like *head* and *murder* with this word or that word. If you don't know whether you're looking for John Perry or Jasper Perry, you can tell the computer to call up either one combined with your other key terms. In this case we can't be sure whether a story would call a body of water a pond or a pool."

The screen said there were 35 stories that used the words *murder, head, pond,* or *pool.* We skimmed through what Millie called "briefs" on these stories, which included the name of the newspaper, date, section, and the first sentence of the story.

"Thank God," Ted said "that newspaper reporters are taught to write a lead, putting 'who, what, when, where, and why' in the first sentence if possible."

So we could learn from the "briefs" that a man

in Texas had shot his brother in the head and weighted down his body in a pond with a big rock. A drunk teenager in Kansas named Billy Pool knocked his friend's head against a wall and killed him. The computer, Millie explained, couldn't tell the difference between a pond-type pool and a game of pool or, in this case, Billy Pool. Even worse, the computer turned up a story about a homeless man in San Francisco who was found hit over the head, then stabbed and left in a pool of blood. And so it went.

A few briefs seemed promising enough so that we asked Millie to call up the whole story: The president of the League of Women Voters in a small town in Texas was found bashed over the head and dead next to a swimming pool. Trouble was, they'd arrested a suspect: her estranged husband who had announced to five friends that he was going to kill her. The murder weapon was his gun. So why didn't he shoot her instead of hitting her over the head with it? Anyway, we couldn't find a pattern.

"Of course," Millie said, "the word *murder* may not appear in the story. If no one has been charged yet, the story may say shooting or stabbing, or some other specific word for killing, instead of murder. Some papers add a word like 'murder' at the bottom of the story to key it into a category. Some don't."

I could see this "world memory" had to be approached with ingenuity just like my own memory did. Oh, well.

We tried again and asked the computer to bring up *police* or *sheriff* with the other key words. After all, murders that had the same pattern as Nancy's might be in either country or city. That way we could pull up a story that didn't use the word "murder," from a paper that didn't key its stories by a murder category. Lots of lurid stories. I made up my mind never to turn my back on anybody, it seemed so easy to get ambushed from behind. But we didn't find a pattern that matched what happened to Aunt Nancy.

It was midnight and we'd come up with zilch.

"Let's don't start looking for a pattern for Larry's death, now," I said. "Let's look up one story that we know will work. We need something to take back to show Pop. And I need to feel we've accomplished something."

"O.K. What's the story?" Millie poised, ready.

"I want to find out everything possible about Elsie — no, *Eleanor* Bigger. She's from Minneapolis." I looked at the list of papers. "And this is great because the *Minneapolis Star-Tribune* has been online since January, 1986. Eleanor would be in the police news in the last year or so, but we can maybe find out something about her even before that." I felt a little disloyal to poor Elsie, but we needed to know all we could about every suspect.

"O.K.," Millie said, "let's call up the police news first. Then we can try for more kinds of information."

She typed *Eleanor Bigger, Minneapolis, police.* We all leaned forward, waiting. The terminal told us there were no stories on that subject.

"Perhaps the word 'police' wasn't in the story," Millie said. She tried again without that word. No luck. So then I suggested she try just plain *Elsie Bigger.* A story did come up but it was in the *Albany Times-Union and News.* It was about an Elsie Bigger who bought a house on the corner of Main and Pine for half a million dollars. A property transfer. I said that didn't sound like our Elsie.

"Damn," I said to Ted, "Elsie lied. She gave me a false name." I was tired and depressed. "Me and my big ideas about a World Memory. It can't help unless we can find out what to ask. But she must be in that computer if she was stabbed in Minneapolis."

Millie sat back. "Boy," she said to Ted, "this gal, Elsie-Eleanor, has a past but no history."

"Don't give up," Ted said firmly. "An alias often bears some relation to the real name. The alias may keep the same initials. I covered a murder story once about a nurse who smothered deformed babies. She worked in a hospital in Montana as Leola Morris Gentian, and then at a hospital in Texas as Lila Montague Green. She had a silver-backed hairbrush with her initials on it. She said her godmother gave it to her when she was a child."

Millie frowned at that. "I don't know any way to check initials in the computer unless the ini-

223

tials appear as such in the story." I thought: another blank wall.

"Sometimes people who want to hide ring some other change on their name." Ted seemed absolutely determined to stay hopeful. "I had a friend named Mortimer North who wrote a pornographic potboiler under the name Mortimer South. Maybe Elsie has changed her name in a way like that."

"Elsie is not such a common name," I said. "Why don't we just try all the Elsies in stories from the Minneapolis paper, and see if there is a last name somehow related to Bigger. If that doesn't work we'll try the Eleanors."

Millie pulled up the Elsie stories from Minneapolis. Two hundred and five.

"Elsie said her trouble with her husband was last year," I said. "I think I may actually know the day because it was Mary's birthday and I found Elsie in the kitchen crying and she said it was the anniversary of the worst day of her life." But then I couldn't remember the date of Mary's birthday.

Ted, God bless him, remembered her party was on the first Saturday in June. Mary had invited Ted to come with me to a birthday brunch at her house. Then we'd taken the cake over to cut at Pop's so he could take part.

"Great!" Millie was enthusiastic. "The best way to pin down a story is to know the name of the person the story is about and the date. Let's try again." She punched in Elsie and the date.

Bingo. A story about Elsie Little of Long Road. The headline said "Estranged Wife Accused of Shooting Broad Street Stockbroker." I read the story in shock. In June a year ago, she had shot her husband with an unregistered gun when he came to see her. Elsie was not just afraid of her husband as she'd told me — she was a fugitive from justice. Another story said the husband was off the critical list. Luckily or unluckily, he had lived. So she had left a wounded lion. Elsie hadn't actively lied except about her name, but by not telling me all that, she had deliberately kept me from the truth. The Elsie I had trusted. The Elsie that Pop truly loved.

But wait. "We could have the wrong Elsie." There was a prayer in my voice.

"Now that we have a name, we can call up all the stories about this Elsie back to 1986," Millie said. She called them up and started printing them out.

I read them as they emerged from the printer. Elsie Little got a speeding ticket in April, 1989. The story said she was a teacher at Central High School. Our Elsie said she was a teacher. Damn.

This Elsie's mother died in 1990 and Elsie was the sole heir to the estate. Our Elsie's lifestyle didn't suggest she'd inherited much money. A good sign.

"No marriage so far," I said.

Millie explained that lots of newspapers put

wills and estates into the permanent data bank, but not marriages or deaths, or even births, unless those are newsworthy.

"An odd priority," I said. But we didn't need the marriage report unless we wanted the maiden name. We could probably do without that.

The next story killed my last doubts. Elsie Little was our Elsie. On March second a year ago, Elsie was stabbed and thrown into a river. That was the story she had told me.

So much for my being absolutely sure that I could trust Elsie. So much for intuition. My head ached.

Ted waited until we got in the car to tease me about Millie. "Well," he said, "how do you like my girlfriend?"

I tried not to bristle. I had no right to feel Ted shouldn't have a girlfriend. But I felt that way.

He began to laugh. "Millie treats all men that way," he said. "It's kind of nice. But it doesn't mean a thing."

I reached over and took his hand. "I can't tell you how great it is to have a friend like you."

I knew he would have liked me to say more than that. Somehow I couldn't.

CHAPTER
17

MIDDAY, SUNDAY, JUNE 2

Millie had agreed not to reveal anything we found out — to let us handle it. She was merely the catalyst.

And on the way home Ted and I agreed that I would talk to Elsie before we told anything to the police. I was half-sure we'd be crazy to hold back. And yet I couldn't entirely ignore my hunch that we should go to Elsie first, especially when Ted felt the same way.

By the time Ted and I got back to my house, my kitchen clock said 4:30 A.M. By the time we had a cup of coffee and unwound, the hands said 5:30. He went home. I locked up tight and slept fitfully. The sun woke me up at ten of twelve.

Pop hadn't called to find out what had happened yet, but then we hadn't told him when we were going to the newspaper. By one-thirty I was dressed, fed, and ready to go talk to Elsie. I took my time. By about ten after two Anna would be gone for the day and Pop would probably be taking an afternoon nap. I would find Elsie alone.

I slipped Pop's front door key in my change purse so I could enter the house quietly and make sure that Pop was asleep. I parked on the road just down from his house, where the car was out of sight. I wasn't sure why I was doing that, except that Elsie was now unfortunately a strong suspect. If she was using Pop's nap time to do anything suspicious, I wanted to come upon her when she didn't expect it.

Albert's car was in the drive. Damn. Maybe Pop wasn't napping after all. I unlocked the front door to a silent house. I tiptoed into Pop's room to make sure he was asleep. He lay on his side, eyes shut, breathing deeply, his favorite crocheted white blanket rising and falling gently. The portrait of my mother in her garden — the portrait that hung to the right of the bed — smiled down on him like a guardian angel.

I shut his door and walked quietly out into the living room again. Silence. The oriental rugs swallowed any hint of sound. I went on through the dining room to the kitchen door, which was open.

Albert and Elsie were standing in the middle of the kitchen, kissing. His back was to me. Her arms rested lightly around his neck. Her eyes were closed. I felt a sharp pang of hurt. Because this was one of those "you-are-a miracle" kisses. I remembered how it was the first few times

Roger kissed me. How I couldn't believe that someone as wonderful as Roger loved me. How I felt as if I were drunk and totally alert and alive all at once. And I could feel, by his central stillness, that Roger had felt the same way.

Roger who noticed what I did right, not what I did wrong. Who said: "Peaches, you're kind, you're clever, and you have a sense of humor, and I love the way you make every person you meet feel good about himself." I was warmer all over remembering that. And sick that maybe Albert was going to lose something that life-giving. God knows Albert, with his great self-consciousness about his short-changed hand, truly needed somebody as nurturing as Elsie. Or at least as nurturing as Elsie had appeared to be. And Elsie the fugitive needed that miracle, too. I could feel their need and their joy in the way they held the kiss, in the way they melted together without pressure. They both wore blue jeans and white shirts. As if they were one person with variations. But with the passion that took two.

Damn. I backed silently out of sight. Let them feel rapture a while longer. I couldn't bear to interrupt. And when I did interrupt, I might destroy what they had forever.

Damn, damn, damn. Albert had been so shy of girls, I'd wondered if he was gay. Occasionally I'd wondered if his partner, Ben, was really a lover. But I hadn't felt warmth in that relationship. Their voices when they spoke to each other were businesslike. If they were lovers, it was without joy. And Albert needed joy like a desert needs water. I remembered him as a child hugging that big collie he loved so much. After his father backed out of the garage and ran over the collie and broke its back, Albert would never have another pet.

I wanted him to have Elsie to love. I wanted Elsie to be what I'd thought she was before she lied. Then I wanted her to be loved by someone who wouldn't hurt her — at least by somebody who wouldn't stab her, for goodness sake.

Albert was speaking: "I have to go now, but I'll call. You be careful."

I heard her voice, but it was a murmur I couldn't make out. Then the back door closed.

I remembered how, when I was young, I relived my happiness after Roger kissed me. After he said good night and left, I experienced it over again in my mind. I could give her five minutes to savor her happiness, five minutes or until she came into the living room, whichever came first.

I sat down at Pop's table. I remembered my mother sitting there and laughing at Pop with love in her eyes. He'd take being laughed at from her. It was what he needed. Love is medicine as well as joy, if it turns out right.

I heard a small gasp. "How long have you been here?" Elsie asked.

"Not long," I said, "and I'm thirsty. Let's have a Coca Cola."

I was a coward. I was putting this off.

I sat down at the kitchen table and sipped my drink. I traced the grain of the wood tabletop with my finger. Elsie sat down too, warily. She must have sensed something was wrong.

"Elsie," I said, still tracing the loop in the grain, "you haven't told me the truth. I know that your real name is Elsie Little and that you are wanted for shooting your husband." The sun shone through the window as if I hadn't said that. I made myself look at her.

Her eyes challenged me. "Who told you that?"

"A detective," I said. "Not the police. Someone who is helping me." After all, Millie was a kind of detective in the larger sense of the word.

I gave Elsie details from the newspaper story. Her eyes went dull. I could feel the happiness drain out of her like blood from a wound.

"I told you all you needed to know about me, all you needed to know that I might be in danger, to know I could put you in danger." She sat straight, eyes turning to fire-blue. "I felt I had a right to keep secret the part I was most ashamed of." She began to crush one hand in the other, in her lap. "You're saying I don't have that right."

"Not when two people have been killed." I shook my head. "I'd trust you more now if you'd told me what happened. Can't you see that?"

A flush spread over her face. "I suppose you'd think I was lying if I said I shot him in self-defense?"

"Tell me about it."

"A friend of mine at work lent me a gun. He taught phys ed. He was worried about me after I was stabbed from behind. And like I said, I couldn't prove it was Harold. I knew. But there was no way I could get some judge to say he couldn't come to the little apartment I'd taken. I felt helpless. And Harold wouldn't have obeyed a stay-away order like that anyway."

She got up and began to pace, back and forth across the very spot where she'd been so lost in kissing Albert. "Harold came to see me and he said I'd have to come back to him or he'd kill me. He was crazy to think I might come back. He was just plain crazy. I backed to where I had the gun in a drawer in the kitchen, a tiny little kitchen, not like this. So small he could corner me. But I felt safer near the gun. And then he put his arms around me too tight and said, 'I could choke you as quick as a wink' and laughed." She massaged her neck with those smooth hands.

"And I laughed and said, 'Have a drink first.'" She swallowed. "I suppose in a way I led him on. But I was so scared, and I knew he was crazy. And when I told him the whiskey was in the cupboard by the refrigerator, he leaned down to get it and I got the gun. I'd left it loaded. I was that scared. When he saw that gun he began to yell, and he threw the whiskey in my face, and he began to charge me, and I shot him." She stopped right in the spot where she and Albert had stood together. I wondered if she was aware of that.

"I lost my head," she whispered. "Maybe somehow there is something else I could have done. I didn't know what."

"I wish you'd told me." I shivered. I could understand why she hadn't.

"And how could I prove it was self-defense?" she demanded, blue fire burning. "How?

"I took all my savings out of the bank and rented a car, and got this far before I called my friend who lent me the gun, and asked him to call the police from a pay phone and report the body."

"Where is the gun?"

"I still have it. I'm still scared. And I'm not sure I know how to get rid of a gun that I shot a man with. At least he didn't die. I called my friend again and found that out. But if somebody found that gun in a trash bin or buried somewhere, there might be some way to trace it. At least, I don't know that there isn't." Her voice trailed off. She sat back down and put her head in her hands. "What do you want me to do?"

I believed what she said. I felt awful for her. "Is Albert important to you?" I asked.

She raised her head "So you saw us."

"Yes."

"I think he's as lonely as I am," she said. "Yes. I love him. But I don't know what to do." She shut her eyes and rocked back and forth in her chair, hands clutched on the wooden tabletop.

"Have you told him what happened?"

"Not yet. I wanted to be happy for just a little

233

while before I ruined it."

"You must tell him the whole story," I said. "He has a right to know it if he loves you, or if he's headed that way."

She flushed again. "And then what will I do?" She was asking herself as much as me, I figured.

I thought about Albert's bliss. I had never seen him that happy in his whole life. That ready to float up off the floor and take off like an eagle into the clouds. At least in spirit. Albert who often glowered and felt put upon. God give him love.

"I leave it up to you two to decide what to do," I said. I'm out of my mind to keep quiet about all this, I thought. But I remembered the joy of loving a man who was also a friend. I couldn't help giving them that chance.

CHAPTER
18

MONDAY EVENING, JUNE 3

Ted and I found ourselves back in the newspaper library Monday evening. We meant to complete our look into the World Memory. There were holes in it, sure. Some of those we could plug.

Ted had gone by the *Asheville Citizen-Times* on Monday morning and looked for local stories. The *Citizen-Times* wasn't online yet, so the stories were clippings in manila file folders. He got copies of the local news about anybody who'd been attached in any way to Pop's household at the time of the murders or the weeks before the murders: Cousin Gloria's involvement with the Folk Art Museum, a handful of weddings and funerals, and Anna's son-in-law's arrest, trial, and sentencing after he got drunk and shot a friend. (They had been arguing because the friend spilled beer in the son-in-law's lap — what a needless death!)

Ted even copied the clipping about Pop and

Mom's wedding anniversary reception some years before. I enjoyed reading that again. Over 100 people came to offer congratulations. I remembered how proud my mother was. And how she cried when Pop gave her a big diamond ring. Pop does have his rare moments of wild generosity. And Nancy gave her and Pop a trip to Hawaii. One of Nancy's extravagant presents. Back when she could afford it.

The most surprising clipping Ted found was a small item about Dorothy, our pious three-to-eleven sitter. Now that was unusual. Two years ago virtuous Dorothy got caught speeding. I figured she must have been late to church.

Ted had been thorough. I was sure he didn't truly expect that the drunken foolishness of Pop's housekeeper's son-in-law, for example, would explain my Aunt Nancy's murder, or Larry's, but we were leaving no stone unturned. Nothing he found seemed immediately helpful, but I figured that as we kept gathering information, something was bound to click.

Just one other surprise from Ted's visit to the newspaper files. He found out that John Q. Denton had checked out all the same stories Ted did, the day before, and also all the stories about Ted or me. Yep. Yankee Accent turned up everywhere. He must have been disappointed. About all there was on me was the story of how I'd sold the store to Roger's partner, John Sherman, after Roger died. Sad, but John called me back to work around Christmas and at other peak times. And there were stories about courses Ted taught at the university. What did Denton expect? Ax murders? Still, his delving made me nervous.

Anyway, he didn't have Millie to help him. I forgave her for the way she hugged Ted when we showed up at her online newspaper library Monday evening. Millie the librarian welcomed us dressed in an electric green pants suit that clung. Of course. She seemed as excited about our search as we were.

No luck at first. We'd decided to start with the name of the miniature portrait artist that Nancy had sent Pop the clipping about: Edward Greene Malbone. The artist was hardly a suspect, since he died in 1803. But in her letter, Nancy said that she wanted to talk about our little portrait, and was coming to do that on the night when, in fact, she was killed. Was there any connection? We wondered about that.

Malbone's name brought up a story about an art exhibit of American works on loan in London. We also found the very story Nancy had clipped and sent us, and a couple of others about art exhibitions. Nothing out of the ordinary. But then, we didn't know what we might be looking for. There must be something more about the artist and his work, more than was in the original clipping, that would ring a bell.

"For an artist, you might try magazines," Millie suggested, and she plugged us into the Nexus database which could scan about one hundred and fifty magazines, everything from *The Saturday Evening Post* to *Interior Design* to *International Defense Review* to *Skin Diver*. Not that we expected much from *Skin Diver*. No underwater portrait exhibits so far.

Nothing productive. Phooey.

So we went from the beautiful to the ugly: electrical deaths where police or sheriffs were called in. We could not find a killing that seemed at all like Larry's. These deaths were mostly labeled as suicides or accidents. I sat on the edge of my straight chair, watched the white words march across the dark computer screen on Millie's desk, and got more and more impatient.

"If somebody is killing with electricity, he must be doing it in Montana or Wyoming or Tennessee, or some one of those other states where no newspaper is plugged into the universal memory yet," Ted said.

"Maybe the killer is a newspaper librarian who knows where he can kill without getting posted in a database," I said. I carefully used *he*.

Millie raised her head from the screen and gave me an odd look. She didn't appreciate my crack. Maybe she had no sense of humor. Ted would never go for a girl with no humor, cleavage or not. The fluorescent light in the ceiling gave a little blink as if winking at me. There was a bulletin-board on the wall, covered with snapshots of smiling friends. I felt like at least they enjoyed a joke.

We tried suspects. Sitters first: Dorothy and

Silva and poor Larry. We'd done Elsie. Surprise! First, Dorothy's divorce in 1988 in the *Atlanta Constitution*. She was divorced from a racing car driver nicknamed Lightning! Prim little Dorothy! The story mentioned they'd been married in his car, with the racing crew for attendants, and great fanfare, back in 1985. They'd both worn T-shirts that said, "Winning counts, not how you play the game." So our Dorothy had a different life before she was born again. Either that or she was a fraud.

Next we tried Larry. His drug arrest in the fall of 1985 showed up in the *Los Angeles Daily News* and the *Los Angeles Times*. He was on cocaine. But we knew about that. He'd told us.

The Miami Herald and the *Miami News* both told how Silva's son, Sam, drank cyanide in his morning coffee. Horrible. He'd left a note asking his family to forgive him, but the handwriting was not true to form. At first his mother said it was a forgery. But an expert ruled that it was his handwriting, shaky from stress. Finally his death was ruled a suicide. The story fit what our late-night bleached-blond sitter Silva had told me.

"Boy," I said, "this is depressing. Do you have any stories about winning the lottery or building churches or child prodigies or other upbeat stuff?"

Ted said sure, but we didn't have time for diversions.

So on to family: Albert. We tried his name and

we drew a blank. Good. Like the Asheville paper, the Charleston *News & Courier* wasn't online yet. That meant that Albert would probably have had to do something important enough to get in *The State* in Columbia, or important enough to be picked up by a national news service, before he'd be in the network. He hadn't.

"Let's try Albert's partner. Let's try Ben the Arrogant," I said. "Let's try somebody we don't like. The bad news about him won't seem so bad!"

We called up Ben Arne. Another surprise. One of the three stories listed about Ben was in the *Toronto Star* in October, 1987. So. A world traveler. We began by reading all of that story. He was in an accident. Not too remarkable, except that he'd sideswiped a Member of Parliament.

The other stories about Ben were more electrifying (pardon the expression). Both were about an arrest for speeding following a fender-bender — one in the *San Francisco Chronicle* and one in the *San Francisco Examiner*. Ben had been arrested last April 12 on James Street. He had a passenger. And the passenger was Mary Sernan. What?

My cousin Mary had been in San Francisco with arrogant Ben Arne? It must have been the time right after Andrew said he wanted a divorce, when she went out to visit her best friend from high school who was married to a mail-order millionaire out there. We'd been so glad for her to have that diversion, when she was

240

so depressed. But what on earth was she doing with Ben Arne? And if it was all so innocent, why hadn't she mentioned it when she came home?

Ben was arrested for speeding at 9:05 P.M. on April 12. Mary's name was in the story because the police searched the car and found marijuana cigarettes in her pocketbook: two recently put-out stubs crushed inside a tissue. I wrote that down. "Oh, damn," I said. "This is not what I wanted to find."

And Ted said, "Did you expect to like what you found?"

So, of course, we punched in Mary's name. No news except the marijuana story. And that probably would not have been newsworthy, Ted said, except that she struggled with the policeman when he asked for her purse. So resisting arrest was part of the charge. No follow-up story. Odd. Were the charges dropped?

The clock said 12:30.

"If you think of something else you want to check out, call me," Millie said, beaming at Ted.

I was depressed, tired, and fresh out of ideas. But others would come to us as we tried to figure what happened to Aunt Nancy and to Larry. I was sure of that. New facts would crop up. If our crime had been committed by the boyfriend of a sitter, for example, and he'd committed a crime somewhere else that showed his weak character, how would we find out if we didn't know his name? Only if his existence suddenly came to our attention. Right?

I hoped new facts would crop up. I didn't like the ones I had.

"If it's something small you want checked out, I can do it for you. You don't need to come all the way down here," Millie said. So, all right, she ogled Ted. That was just her way. And besides, Ted was worth ogling. He had on a blue shirt that brought out the piercing blue of his eyes. She had good taste.

We took copies of all the stories we had found related to suspects, and put them in the folder with the more innocuous stories Ted had found in the *Citizen-Times*, like the one about Dorothy's speeding ticket.

"Let's not tell Pop about Mary until I have a chance to talk to her and hear her side of the story," I said. And Ted agreed.

We could tell him about Dorothy marrying and then divorcing the racing driver. In a T-shirt, yet. Pop would love that.

CHAPTER
19

TUESDAY MORNING, JUNE 4

The next morning Mary called *me* before I could call her. The phone on the end of the kitchen table rang just as I was having my first coffee in my yellow kitchen, being lazy, watching a chickadee splash in the birdbath out the window in the sunshine. The clock over the stove said eleven. But then, I'd gone to bed at four-thirty. Mary sang, "Peaches, can you do me a favor?"

And since the next thing I had to do was talk to her, I said, "Absolutely."

"You don't even know what it is yet," she giggled. "This is my day!" In my mind I could see her smiling her white-teeth smile into the phone in her kitchen. Right next to the plaque on the wall which said: "Dinner will be served at the sound of the smoke alarm."

"You know that nice John Denton who was a friend of mother's?" she trilled. Ah, yes — Yankee Accent. Who got to the newspaper files before Ted did. "Well, he called me up and said he could see how hard all this was for me, and he'd like to cheer me up, and maybe I'd like to go to a horse show this afternoon. There's a show of miniature horses out at the agricultural arena and he invited me to take the children to see that. He's the nicest man."

"So what do you need from me?" I felt disoriented. This was not the way a suspect ought to act. If Lizzy Borden took an ax and gave her mother forty whacks, Lizzy wouldn't be so gushy afterwards, would she? This also wasn't the way the recently bereaved ought to act. But I told myself a lonely woman in the middle of a divorce just might.

Mary gushed on, "I want to get something new to wear. And there's a sale at Dillard's. Could you come over and watch the children while I go to the sale? You can bring your computer and work while they play in the yard. I wouldn't ask you, but Alma, the one I trade baby-sitting with, has got some kind of virus. You're so sweet to offer."

Well, that's what I got for telling Mary that if there was anything I could do to help her or the kids, I was available.

Besides, I'd have a nice informal chance to question Mary, and who knows what the kids might volunteer?

"I have to take Pop to the doctor for a checkup at three-thirty," I said. "If you can be back by two-thirty at the latest, I would enjoy being with the kids." Actually Pop's appointment wasn't until four, but that meant getting to Pop's by three-thirty. And I wanted time to talk to Mary.

"I'll be right over," I told her. I had thrown on an old pair of shorts and a T-shirt when I got up. The weather was hot for Asheville. One of those unseasonably sticky days. I had intended to work in the garden a little. Relax and give a few good ideas a chance to pop into my mind before I talked to Mary. Forget that.

I threw some going-to-the-doctor clothes in the back of the car. The sooner I got to her house, the sooner she'd be back from the sale.

One thing about Mary's house, no one would ever mistake it for any other. On one side of the stone front steps sat a cement lion with one paw raised. The kids (or was it Mary?) had tied an oversized red silk scarf around the lion's neck. He reminded me of a long-haired poet at a poetry reading. The lion's scarf matched the house, which was red with white trim and only slightly in need of a coat of paint. As I understood it, one of the arguments that finally led to Mary's divorce was about what color to paint the house, though there must have been a deeper reason behind that. Andrew was for gray. She was for anything else. Now the very ownership of the house was in limbo until the divorce was settled.

I walked past the red-scarfed lion up the steps and rat-tat-tatted the shining brass door knocker on the red door. Mary loved to polish brass. Amazing to me. When my daughter, Eve, was little, I avoided owning all objects that required extra work, like polishing. Still do. Life is too short for all the things I *want* to do. But if Mary wants to polish, the result *is* cheerful. Next to the door knocker was a small neatly lettered sign: "Beware: Attack Kitty Inside." Attack Kitty was the name of Mary's mild little cat. It would have been a better name for Pop's Silk. Silk growled at men. Attack Kitty never growled at all.

Mary opened the door as soon as I knocked, and held her hand up like a traffic cop: "Stop. I have a funny for your book." Mary can never wait to tell a joke. She'd finish one before she left a burning house, to be sure you didn't miss the point.

"This girl saw her mother in the grocery store tapping first her head and then her chest and then her belly button and then her crotch." Mary demonstrated. "The girl was real embarrassed and she said, 'Mother, why on earth are you walking around tapping yourself like that?' " Mary stood tall for the punch line. "And the mother said, 'Why I'm just doing this to remember my grocery list: A head of lettuce, breast of chicken, navel oranges, and Fantastik.' "

We both laughed and I said, "Why that's almost like the way the ancient Greeks remembered their speeches. Only instead of using parts of their bodies to remember them by, they used parts of their houses." She went blank. History is not her thing. "I mean," I said, "that they'd associate the first paragraph with the front door and the second paragraph with the front hall, and so on."

"Crazy," she said, and told me to leave my stuff in the bedroom, just to the left of the front door. "Right where you might put paragraph three."

She pulled me through the living room and into the kitchen, where the kids were sitting at the kitchen table eating sandwiches. Peanut butter again. I could smell it. Behind Andy's head I read a new plaque on the wall: "Eat, drink and be merry, for tomorrow we diet." "Albert just gave me that," she said.

I smiled, but Mary's nonstop humor was depressing me. All her life Mary collected jokes while her mother was a workaholic, her father drank, and Albert got lost in enthusiasms. So now she still collected "funnies" while we wondered who killed her mother, while we wondered if someone had tried to kill me.

I remembered one she told a while back: "Apart from that, Mrs. Lincoln, how did you like the play?" It was one of a genre called sick jokes. In my present mood, all her jokes struck me as sick. Even the way she dressed those kids got to me: Andy's red, white, and blue sailor suit, with "Hi!" embroidered on the pocket, and Marcia's sky-blue T-shirt that said "Laugh and The World Laughs With You" struck me as too much.

Nothing depressed the kids. "We're going to see little horses," Marcia announced with a bounce. "Little like us." Andy was jumping up and down in his chair and munching his sandwich at the same time. Attack Kitty, an orange tiger, sat on the counter and watched and purred.

I clapped my hands and said, "Hoorah for little horses!" What good would it do if we all wept?

And I told myself Mary and Albert had always had to work at finding some joy in life. Albert so busy: collecting and labeling moths, hiking, riding horseback (as a kid he chose the sports you could do alone), collecting arrowheads, fixing clocks, and now, collecting and finding good homes for antiques. And Mary with her china animals, bright colors, and jokes.

Mary was, well, kind of gallant, kind of whistling in the dark, wasn't she? Wearing that "Smile" T-shirt. I hoped to God there wasn't a dark side to Mary or Albert that I hadn't wanted to see.

Mary drove off. As soon as the kids finished eating, they ran out in the fenced back yard and began to ride round and round on tricycles, like a bright two-kid parade. Attack Kitty sat on the arm of a rustic wood Adirondack chair in the middle of their circle and went to sleep. Since the kids were safe and happy inside that fence, I wandered around inside the house. What can a house tell?

The living room said the past lived on and

Mary liked animals and glitter. Half the furniture had belonged to Nancy before she moved into a smaller house, including the mahogany coffee table, the antique drop-leaf table at one end of the couch, the cut-crystal lamps. Mixed with that elegance were small porcelain birds on the mantlepiece, two china poodles on the edge of a bookcase, a china donkey ashtray on a lamp table. Everybody knew that Mary liked china animals for her birthday. The china frog door-stop was from me. Why china animals?

Was the glitter for good cheer? All that shining brass: lamps, candlesticks, ashtrays. And so many mirrors, including a gold-leaf-framed mirror that had belonged to Nancy and now hung over Mary's fireplace. I saw myself reflected front, back, and sideways. I wrote myself a note to get my hair cut. It was just on the edge of looking shaggy. Millie the newspaper librarian would never look shaggy.

I glanced out the window to check the kids, set up my portable computer on the dining room table, and went to work. After a while the kids came in for a drink.

I mixed frozen lemonade, poured it in three glasses with Mickey Mouse on them, sat down at the kitchen table with the kids, and asked them if they liked to go on trips. If the subject was trips, maybe they'd mention Mama's. They said they never went on trips. Except to the grocery store and Pop's. They used to go to Ammah's house, but now Mama was mad with Ammah. Ammah was their father's mother. Marcia said she'd like to go to China. I knew she had a book about a little boy with a pigtail in ancient China. Andy said he'd like to go on a trip with Daddy.

"Does Mama like trips?" I asked. Marcia said Mama couldn't go on trips anymore because they stayed with Ammah when she did. And Mama wouldn't let them stay with Ammah right now. Both kids began to fidget.

I said "Mama went to California, didn't she?"

Both kids fidgeted more. Marcia said, "She didn't take us." Then they ran outdoors again to play, like they wanted to escape. Dead end.

So O.K., Mary had to be my source. Mary should be home soon. I figured I'd get dressed and be ready to talk to her until the very moment I had to leave for Pop's house.

I hurried into the front bedroom, hurried past a tall mahogany chest of drawers with a hat stand in the shape of a pig's head on top. The pig stand wore the straw hat that Mary gardened in. The china pig's eyes stared into the bathroom where I'd left my going-to-the-doctor clothes, hanging on a ceramic hook shaped exactly like a goose's head. China pets won't die or go away. Was that it?

I took a shower and started to put on my underwear. Problem. I had panties, bra, and pantyhose. No slip. Which would have been O.K., except I'd brought a summery see-through blouse.

I put on bra and panties and decided Mary

wouldn't mind lending me a slip. We are both size 12. I looked in her drawers to case the underwear situation. The small top drawers contained scarves and jewelry showing through. Seemed like Mary meant to leave the jewelry hidden by the scarves, but over time she'd pull things out in a hurry and forget to keep the jewelry out of sight. Nothing too valuable, but things she wouldn't like to have stolen, like her grandmother's pearl earrings.

I found the slips in the fourth drawer down. Beneath those silky underthings I could feel the stiffness of paper. I pulled out a white slip that seemed substantial enough to go under a see-through blouse and lacy enough to be elegant. Under the slip was an opened letter. Would I have read it if I hadn't seen my father's name next to the adjective *stingy?* Yes. But maybe not as fast.

The letter said: "You've got to help me, Mary. There's no reason my stingy uncle can't lend me $50,000. I have this once-in-a-lifetime chance to buy a collection of Colonial dueling pistols. It's only the idea of lending the money that upsets him. Maybe you can talk him round that. I can sell these and make a profit, I know.

"He won't appreciate the real value of these beauties. But maybe he'll like the idea of making some money on the loan.

"Mary, you know I have always been clever about finding beautiful things in out-of-the-way places, about buying them from people who didn't appreciate their true value and selling them to those who do. I cannot bear to lose these antique pistols. Please help me."

All that was typed, and then below he had written in pencil: "I could KILL the old man for being so damn stingy!" Lucky he hadn't said that about his mother. That kind of chance remark sounds incriminating after murder.

And below *that* was a second P.S., also in pencil, and harder to read, as if he'd dashed it off at top speed. I was figuring it out when I heard a car stop in front. Mary. But I had to be sure what the note said: "Mary: Don't pick a fight with Ma. I know how mad it makes you when she sides with Andrew in this divorce thing. It's her bending-over-backwards-to-be-fair complex. I know you could choke her but she can't help it." So Mary's constant smile hid rage at her mother?

I heard the car door slam. I quickly put letter and slip back like I found them and shut the drawer. I went back into the bathroom and combed my hair.

Mary said, "Hi. Hey, those are the bikini panties I gave you. They don't look bad." She'd meant them as a joke. But hey, I try to keep in shape. I explained about a slip. The slip would lead naturally to the letter.

She pulled out the very slip I had selected myself, carelessly, not as if she was trying to hide the letter. In fact I must have left the letter in a fold of the slip. As she pulled out the slip, the letter fluttered after and fell on the floor.

"Mother gave this slip to me," she said, stroking the lace. "Back when she thought she had lots of money." I knew that was the nearest she'd come to mentioning that her father gambled it all away. She handed me the slip and I put it on, and stuck my arms into the sleeves of my blouse. She picked up the letter from Albert. "This is from my brother," she said, almost absently, "asking me to help persuade your father to lend him fifty thousand dollars to buy some special-opportunity antiques. But that will never happen. How sad my mother didn't have the money to lend him."

I must have looked startled. I misbuttoned my blouse, then fixed it right. I couldn't imagine Aunt Nancy lending Albert money. She was always saying she hoped he didn't go broke collecting antiques that didn't sell. Laughing at some of his stock, like some "antique" 1920s Kewpie dolls. "My God," she'd said, "I played with toys like that."

Mary put the letter on top of the bureau next to the pig hat stand. She went over to the bed and switched into the shorts and T-shirt she'd left lying there.

She said, "Ma was just beginning to understand Albert, I think. To see that running a shop like he does is not a waste of his talents. She was beginning to understand he's an expert, with a reputation for stocking remarkable things in his shop, not just a fool to go into a business that means snooping in attics. And then, before they

253

really had time to be friends, she was killed. Well, they did begin to be friends. That's something." She had tears in her eyes as she came back towards me. I was still standing by the bureau.

I reached over and picked up the letter. She didn't stop me, but she frowned. I read it over while she watched. I read aloud the P.S. *"Mary: Don't pick a fight with Ma. . . . It's her bending-over-backwards-to-be-fair complex. I know you could choke her but she can't help it."*

"You were angry with your mother?"

"Oh sure," she said. Nonchalant? Or pretending to be? "Off and on for years. Like Albert said, we all got mad at her bending-over-backwards act, because what it meant was that if we had a fight with somebody, she was likely to be in their corner." She shook her head from side to side. "It was weird. In the first grade Ellen Moore challenged me to a fist fight and all the kids who walked home our way said I had to fight or be a coward, and I was terrified but I fought. My mother made me apologize to Ellen Moore." She reached out for the letter. I handed it back, and she put it in the drawer.

We walked out into the living room. To the company of the china animals, to the blinking mirrors. "In the middle of your divorce," I said, "when your mother took Andrew's side, that must have made you furious."

Her face went ugly. Ugly reflected in the gold-framed mirror by the front door. "I was upset, but if you're suggesting I killed my mother,

Peaches, you can just get out of this house." She took hold of the shiny brass handle of the front door as if she was going to open it. "Right now." The corners of her mouth turned down. Flip side of smile.

I stood firm by the bookcase next to the door. Full of big flat children's picture books. "I am not suggesting anything," I said. "I'm asking.

"And, Mary," I said, as evenly as I could, "I have to ask you about something that may disturb you even more. I don't know a tactful way. How did you happen to be arrested in California last April twelfth in the company of Ben Arne?"

"That is none of your business." She went stiff all over. She was still holding the doorknob, but she didn't turn it.

"The police probably know it," I said. "It must be on their computer network."

"If they do," she choked, "that's between me and them." She was shaking.

So they'd questioned her about it.

"Mary," I said, "I promised Pop I'd find out all I could about what went on that could have led up to the two murders. And frankly I feel like I may be a target. I want to know when to duck."

"Quack quack," she said, joking even in her rage.

"You may think it's funny for people to get killed," I said, as evenly as I could. "But, frankly, I don't. So I intend to find out about everything out-of-the-ordinary in the relationships and happenings around here in the weeks before your mother was killed. I would think you could help."

"California is hardly around here," she trembled harder, like she might either throw something at me or cry. Cry? Not Mary.

"You never told any of us that you saw Ben in California or showed that you knew him more than casually," I said, "or that you were arrested."

"I damn well didn't," she exploded. "And if you can't figure out why, you're feeble-minded." She strode over to the blue leather couch and plunked herself down. Nancy had that couch in her study, back when her house was big enough for a study and a living room. I followed Mary over and sat on the other end of the couch.

"If you don't want me to mention this to Pop, you'd better tell me what your relationship with Ben is and why it's secret." I knew I had to be firm.

She changed completely. Her eyes went from blue fire to imploring water. Her shoulders went from military to weeping willow. "You don't know what it's like," she said, "to feel like no man could ever want you. Because the one you counted on walked out. To feel you must be so unattractive that the man who said he loved you can't bear anymore to have you around. To feel heavy all over. And awkward." She picked up a small cast-iron monkey from the table by the couch. Anger made her face wrinkle like a monkey's. "I felt like that, and then an attractive man

256

asked me to go out with him. Why would I say no?" she cried. "And why would I tell any of you?" She put the monkey down with a thump. "You don't like Ben. The one time he came to visit your father, Uncle Harwood said Ben acted like he was figuring out the selling price of all the pictures on the walls. Like he was pricing all the rugs in his head and auctioning off the furniture. And you told me you thought he seemed sleazy."

I'd forgotten that, but it *was* what I thought. I also did know what it felt like to be awkward and lonesome. I had a terrible case of that in my teens.

"So you went out to California to meet Ben? And said you were visiting a friend?"

"No. I did not."

"I have proof you did."

We sat there glaring at each other, daring each other to back down.

"You can call my friend Lara. She'll tell you I was with her."

"But around nine o'clock on the evening of April twelfth" — I remembered because the twelfth was my wedding anniversary — "you were in a car with Ben in San Francisco, and you were arrested for possessing marijuana and resisting arrest. And he was arrested for driving while impaired."

"You snoop." Her face of rage was so out of place above the smile face on her T-shirt that I thought to myself: Is Mary cracking up?

"I intend to be a snoop," I said, "until I find

257

out what led to your mother's death, and Larry's death. I intend to stay right here until you tell me what happened in California."

I guess she believed that, because she calmed down and began to explain. "You see, I met Ben in the airport just after I arrived. Lara was going to meet me but she got mixed up about what time my plane arrived, or maybe I told her wrong. I was looking for a phone to call her, and there was Ben. You don't believe that, do you?"

"I might," I said. "Keep talking. What happened next?"

"He said he was out on a buying trip. He was so pleased to see me. He asked me to have dinner with him the next night. And I said yes. Is that so bad? I told Lara I'd bumped into an old boyfriend and I wanted to spend the evening with him alone. She thought that was exciting. I guess I kind of implied he was a married man or something and I didn't want to talk about it. Well, I felt intimidated. I knew what you all thought of Ben. And I wanted a secret. Something just for me." She hugged herself.

I wasn't sure if I believed her or not. "So you went out and drank and smoked pot."

"I had a good time," she roared. She jumped up, a kitten turned into lion. "I was damn sick of behaving and smiling and being a mom twenty-four hours a day, all by myself. Don't you see?"

"Yes. I see that." I stood up too.

"And Ben wanted to celebrate," she explained

more calmly. "Please understand. He said his trip had gone so well. He'd found some lovely stuff for the shop. So we had champagne, maybe a lot. And then we sat in the car and looked out over the Bay and smoked a little pot. But Ben likes to drive fast, and a cop stopped us, and he asked if he could search our car. I guess he could smell the grass. And Ben said, 'Go ahead. Search.' He thought I'd thrown those stubs out the window, instead of hiding them in my pocketbook. I admit we were both a little high. And then I panicked when I thought they were going to arrest us." Her eyebrows went up, her voice became surprised. "I thought what my mother would say. What you would all say. And how being arrested could hurt me in the divorce. And I don't know what I did, but they called it resisting arrest."

I decided she wasn't making this up. She'd have made herself sound smarter if she made it up.

"But you're wrong about Ben," she said. "He had this really marvelous lawyer out there who talked them into dropping the charges."

I guessed this was all possible. It could all be made up, too, except for the part about telling her friend she was going out with an old flame. Mary would know I could check that. Possibly the police had already checked it. If Mary and Ben were in conspiracy together, what could it be? And if they were, wouldn't they have been more careful?

The kids burst into the room and ran over and hugged Mary. Andy looked up at his mother and smiled. He came just midway up her thigh, small for two and a half. "Mom," he said, "don't go away."

CHAPTER
20

LATER TUESDAY AFTERNOON, JUNE 4

"I think I need a younger doctor," Pop said, adjusting himself into a more comfortable position in the front seat of the car. "Dr. Spicewood is too thorough." Pop hates checkups. "At least my eager-beaver doctor didn't forbid me to take a drink." The doctor wouldn't have bothered. Pop is going to take a drink if he wants one, no matter what.

I turned the key to start the car. Absolutely nothing happened, not even a something-is-wrong noise. I tried again. Zilch.

"I hope to God you haven't broken the car, Peaches," Pop said with alarm. "I need a drink right now to make up for that checkup. We need to get out of this damn maze."

We were in the open concrete parking garage in back of the doctor's building, a spiral of parking spaces. But I'd parked in the handicapped place near the entrance to the building, even though my car didn't have the right license plate. I'd figured anybody who saw Pop try to walk very far would forgive me.

I wiggled the key in the ignition and tried to start again. Nothing. I didn't want to leave Pop in the car alone while I went in and called for help. Suppose his mind did one of its scramble acts and he tried to get out of the car? He'd been pretty alert lately, but suppose he got out and fell down?

I jiggled the key hard and tried once more. The car started with a purr. I said a little prayer of thanks.

When I left Pop's house later, my car started right up as if there had never been any trouble. It didn't fool me.

I called my favorite mechanic. I was in luck. Somebody had called in sick and couldn't bring his car in the next morning. So Jeff Stewart said I could bring mine in at eleven o'clock. Jeff is one of those mechanical geniuses you happen upon if God is on your side. He could fix almost anything, and since his shop was in what amounted to his back yard, he didn't even charge a lot. He also sold tombstones in his front yard. Never mind.

That will take care of the car, I said to myself. One problem off my mind.

The other immediate problem was Mary. I needed to talk over with Ted her account of what happened in California. I needed to bounce it around a little. Ted was out.

So now what? I wandered in to my computer and sat down. My feet voted for a little time to work on my book. I pulled up the chapter on names. Boy, do I have trouble with names!

Chapter IV

The Nameless Crunch

"I'll never forget what's-his-name." *Was that a line from a song? The punch line of a joke? The whence escapes me. But the words sure paint the picture. What to do?*

I have found modern memory systems like that of Harry Lorayne, that help. Basically, Lorayne tells how to make any name or number into a funny image. For instance, he said you could remember Zimmerman by changing it to simmer-man and make a mental picture of a man cooking. That's simplified. He had a whole memory system. I recommend it to people who are not as far gone as me. But I am so talented that in a pinch I might call Mr. Zimmerman Mr. Cook. And if I don't see a person for a while, I can even forget the funny image. And I can forget to even use the system.

How come?

I found that out when I took my dachshund, Woof, to be obedience-trained. (I got Woof from a weaver who had another pup named Warp.) "Speak loudly and clearly and be sure you have the dog's complete attention," the trainer said.

263

He had a voice that would raise the dead.

"To train a dog," he trumpeted, "you have to know what a dog's mind is like: A dog can't think about but one thing at a time."

And suddenly I understood. I'm like that. Especially when I'm uptight. I can't think of but one thing at once. If I'm thinking about what kind of a person it is that I'm meeting, I'm not thinking about any system for remembering the name. It won't all fit. I have a dog's mind.

Fortunately I am very fond of dogs. That softened the blow. If you have a dog's mind, remember the dog is man's best friend. But, as a result, seeing a funny picture with a name can be a big help sometimes, but sometimes not.

So I have backup systems to help with all three major degrees of name blanks.

If you've had practice not remembering, you've known all three.

In a first-degree *blank, you remember nothing at all but the person obviously knows you — may break into a big grin and come hurrying toward you. Or worse yet, ask about family members by their names. Gulp.*

In a second-degree *blank, you know the face but haven't a clue as to where you saw that person before. Most embarrassing when the person seems to know you well. Like Familiar Face who recently ran up to me and said, "I'm having some friends to dinner Saturday, and there's one I want you to meet so I hope you can come." But where?*

In some ways, the third-degree blank *is the most annoying. You remember everything except the name. I've had to field several classic third degrees in the last few weeks.*

Take White-Hair-and-Freckles: I bumped into him at Pritchard Park by the Wachovia bank. I knew that's where he banked. I knew he had three grandchildren and liked to play chess, was a chocoholic, collected stamps, and used to be a good customer in our shop. He once lent me ten dollars when I found myself downtown with no checkbook. He went to my church. He seemed overjoyed to see me. I couldn't remember his name.

"I know you're collecting money for the Community Ministries," he said. "Call me tonight, and I'll tell you how much I can pledge."

Or there was the equally nameless friend more recently, also a former customer at the craft shop. "Get in touch with me when your book is out," she said. "I want to give copies to all my friends for Christmas." Oh boy.

So what tricks can save you in the Nameless Crunch?

In every case, whatever degree, try simple things first.

You can hand the would-be contributor a paper and a pencil (if by the grace of God you remembered to have them with you) and you say, "Would you write down your telephone number." You can ask Books-For-Christmas to write down her address. Nine times out of ten a person will put her name with her phone number or address. Of course, she may wonder why you're too dumb to use the phone book. But her feelings won't be hurt that you forgot her name.

You can ask Dinner-on-Saturday to write down directions to her house. But people don't tend to put their names down with directions. Odd.

Let's say you have a good feeling about Dinner-on-Saturday, but basically she's Degree Two, face only. If she writes directions and omits her name, you could get to the dinner party, but be unable to identify the hostess. That would be bizarre.

Fear not. You can always try more serious detective work. Any small memory may help as a starting point, no matter how extraneous.

"How have you been?" you ask cheerily. Keep her talking. She may drop a hint.

"Oh, I've been fine, but my dog got hit by a car and broke her leg." You commiserate and suddenly one small clue floats into your mind: There is something funny about her dog. The breed? No. The name? Yes! The dog has no spots on him and is named Spot. Wait! This woman's name rhymes with her dog's name. Yes.

But here comes somebody who's going to expect to be introduced to her. Think fast: Aott, Bott, Cott, Dott? The name comes: Mott. "So

266

what's new with the other members of the Mott family?" you say. With luck, more clues: "My daughter Amelia is interning in Oncology at Johns Hopkins, and Larry Junior is working on a construction crew in Dallas during his summer vacation." Bingo. You are talking to Mrs. Larry Mott. If you introduce her like that, she may laugh and say don't be so formal. Never mind. She won't have her feelings hurt because you forgot her name.

Chapter IV was O.K. as far as it went. I had to add something about the database, for example, about how to find anybody with one bare fact. What luck for me that I started a name and address database when I was helping Roger in the craft store. Extra Memory Neatly Canned.

I tucked my chapter into my unconscious mind to let it grow. I called Ted again. He was about to go out to an evening class. We made a date for lunch the next day. He said he'd pick me up at my mechanic's, take me to my house, and make a cheese omelet if I'd make a salad. Then we'd brainstorm. Good bargain.

At eleven o'clock Wednesday morning I took my car to Jeff Stewart's auto repair shop. Jeff's only disadvantage was his popularity. When I arrived, he was talking to one man about the problems in his car's inner workings. Another was waiting near the three-bay garage where Jeff does his work.

"Hi," Number Two said. "How are you

today?" Good grief, he knew me. A first-degree case. No bells rang about the name or the face or the history. He leaned casually on the hood of one of the cars that Jeff always has parked around his place, and smiled. All right, I told myself. Opportunity knocks. Here's your chance. Improvise. Do something that will be right for Chapter IV.

He had on a red plaid shirt and clean, fairly new jeans. Since this was 11:05 on a weekday morning, he was not likely to be a doctor or a lawyer. He was also not likely to be one of the hard-core unemployed, unless, of course, his wife or mother bought him new clothes. He was sun-tanned. Outdoor work?

"I haven't seen you lately," I said, matching his friendly manner. "What have you been up to?" That's usually a good ploy.

"Not much except working," he drawled. An uncooperative type. But he had the air of knowing me quite well. Big lazy smile.

"What's the problem with your car?" I asked. Some people will open up more if they talk about a pet car or a pet dog or something, than if they talk about themselves.

"Brakes," he sighed. "Thelma rides the brakes. They're so worn they're squeaking. In Madison County you have to count on brakes."

He was from mountainous Madison like all of Pop's folks. I should have known that from his accent. Good grief, I was probably related to him.

"How's Thelma?" I asked. Her name was the only clue so far.

"Just fine," he nodded. "Now that her cousin Art has started work here as a mechanic, she gets me to bring her car here. Art's a wizard on brakes, and most everything else in a car."

So Jeff had a new mechanic, and I had a double mystery. Who was Art?

I decided to take a chance. "I don't think I know Art."

"Yes, you do," he said. "He's Gloria Larson's first cousin." In other words, Mother Hen. I remember her last name because she doesn't look like the type to steal, at least not often, and Larson is just short of *larceny*.

"You know *her*, don't you?" he asked like he knew the answer.

I sure did. Her and her doll hospital and her wild temper and her husband who liked to shoot empty beer cans.

"Art's the one who's such a bear hunter," Thelma's husband said.

Good grief. The new mechanic was not only Gloria's cousin, but the very one who shot all those bears and fastened the skins to the side of the big barn on the farm where we met for family get-togethers in Madison County. Did I want him to work on my car? Stop being paranoid, I told myself. How could I be enough of a threat to Cousin Gloria to make her persuade her cousin Art to sabotage my car. Ridiculous. Thelma's husband sure didn't look like he smelled any

269

danger. He leaned back against the hood of the old car and chewed a blade of grass.

And then a light dawned. Thelma's husband wasn't sure who I was. He just knew he'd seen me around at family get-togethers. If he'd been sure who I was he wouldn't have brought up Cousin Gloria and then said, "You know her, don't you?"

It was time to come clean.

"I'm Peaches Dann," I said, "Harwood Smith's daughter. I know we've met. Was it at family get-togethers?"

He looked relieved and thunderstruck. "You're Nancy Means's niece! I was so sorry to hear of your Aunt Nancy's death. I'm Reed Johnson. My Thelma is Gloria's cousin, just like you are. I go with Thelma to her family reunions sometimes. I knew I knew you from some place." He smiled and nodded to himself. "Nancy was a grand lady." He expanded as if her grandness had become part of him. "I like to know unusual people like her. I like to see what a person can do by hard work." He deflated. "She was a great loss."

He frowned, fidgeted, leaned towards me. "I saw Cousin Gloria yesterday." His eyes shone, as if that was exciting. "We were both making a trip to the dump. I been re-roofing the chicken coop. She cleaned out her barn. She told me a man from the State Bureau of Investigation asked her a lot of questions about the whole family." He paused and looked hopeful, as if he wanted me to comment on that. I didn't.

"She said she thought that SBI man believed a family member killed Nancy and then killed that other man to cover up." He paused and leaned closer, eyes hungry. I waited.

"Now, I don't believe that, do you?" He said that politely, even sadly, but his eyes were full of eager speculation, as if he was asking himself: Is this Peaches Dann an aunt-killer? Or not?

Obviously, he hoped I was. He liked meeting unusual people. Nancy thrilled him because she started on a farm and became the vice president of an insurance company. But if I was the cold-blooded killer of my own aunt, I was even more unusual, more of a thrill to meet than my Aunt Nancy. Thanks a lot. I was glad Ted would be there shortly to pick me up. Or so I thought.

Jeff came over wiping black grease off his arms with a cloth and said there was a call for me in the office. It was Ted, sounding sheepish. "I've been arrested for speeding," he said, as if he dared me to say "I told you so." "And I guess I need your memory book myself. I don't know how I managed to leave my wallet with my driver's license in my other pants. This is going to take me a good long while."

"Fear not, I'll manage and see you later," I said. "I'm used to handling emergencies that result from lack of memory. In fact it's always nice to have one that's not my fault. I'll get a ride or walk over to the Weaverville Diner, and if my car's not ready by the time I finish lunch, I'll get a ride over to Pop's and borrow his."

Jeff patted my car and said he'd at least look and see what was wrong with my starter pretty quick. Then I got a ride with Thelma's husband. No point in wasting his admiration, even if it was for me as the nearest at-hand member of his wife's family who might have committed two murders. He admired me so much, he managed to think of every possible connection on the way to the diner. His second cousin used to sell my mother manure for her roses. My cousin Albert bought the belt plate and buttons his Union great-grandpa took off a Confederate colonel he shot through the head at Shiloh. Bought them from his mother. She'd sold the pistol years before. His nephew sold real estate in Asheville, so if I ever wanted to get rid of my house and buy a condominium, just let him know. If I happened to want a cat, Thelma's big striped tiger just had kittens, and three weren't spoken for yet. Absolutely beautiful kittens from a family of good mousers.

By the time we got to the diner, I was exhausted just from listening. I went inside to enjoy a little quiet. Instead, who did I find but Cousin Gloria! She was sitting at one of the little tables, all done up like one of her dolls, her pink face leaning close to the childlike face of Silva. Close to the bleached-blond sitter who believed her son had killed himself because of my Aunt Nancy. When they saw me they started and pulled apart.

CHAPTER
21

LATER WEDNESDAY, JUNE 5

Cousin Gloria in ruffled pink and bleached-blond Silva had been whispering about what? About how sorry they were for each other? About how mad they both had been with Nancy? They looked so startled to see me that I began to imagine something worse. Some conspiracy. I walked over to the small table where they sat and said, "Hi," and Silva was polite or guilty enough to say, "Won't you join us?" She pulled over a chrome chair from one of the larger tables. Gloria radiated rage.

Nothing ventured, nothing learned. I said thanks. And while I waited for my chicken-salad sandwich I told Gloria I'd enjoyed getting a ride from her cousin Reed Johnson. "I take it he's from the side of the family that were Union in the Civil War." She nodded stiffly. As if the war was about to start again, between her and me.

We'd been split here in the mountains, and

compared to those Union-Rebel massacres, two murders were nothing — except they were *our right-now* murders. I decided not to say that.

Gloria gave her noodle soup her entire attention. Silva ate the rest of her sandwich in a few gulps and they both said they had to leave. I sure made them nervous.

I finished my sandwich and walked to the Frozen Yogurt shop in the shopping center a quarter mile away. I bought a cone. No point in calling about my car too soon. I had to give Jeff time to check the starter. In the distance I saw a man who looked a little like Albert hurry into a discount store.

Trust Albert, I thought, to find every antique in every family attic and buy it quick. He said there were antique thieves around about. They probably stole Pop's little portrait. Why did he get so upset about that? I figured Albert's crime was to know what a thing was worth when the longtime owner didn't. He probably paid peanuts for Reed Johnson's Confederate belt buckle. And never felt a pang of guilt.

I finished my cone and called Jeff from a phone booth. He said he had to order a new starter. "But you can drive your car till it comes," he added. The gist was that if I pressed the key firmly into the ignition, even tapped it in with a hammer, if necessary, I was not likely to have the same trouble again right away. That didn't make sense to me. But he was the mechanic. Tried and true. "I didn't have time to check anything else," he said. "But that was your only problem, right?"

Right. In fact the car had had a thorough checkup just before Nancy died.

I figured the fifteen-minute walk to the car shop would do me good. As I trudged past the new town houses toward the turnoff to the shop, I passed a white Ford in a driveway. The license plate said "Handicapped Veteran." I felt a little jolt of "this could be important." What? Why? It had to do with Larry. Yes. I remembered that Larry had a brother in the Veterans Hospital in Oteen, on the outskirts of Asheville. Larry used to tell me how his brother was a Vietnam veteran with recurring bone infections. I'd never talked to him. Why not do that?

It was just possible that because I was so sure that Larry had been killed by mistake in a trap meant for me, I'd missed something important. I mustn't give myself airs. It was, after all, possible that Nancy was killed by mistake in some plot to kill Larry. That he was the kingpin of the killings. The premier victim. I didn't believe that, but if it was true it would get all my favorite suspects off the list, including me. I stopped in a gas station phone booth and called the hospital to be sure the brother was still there. Yes.

I picked up my car, which started with no problem, and decided to drive to the hospital by way of the Blue Ridge Parkway. About as fast as going through the city, and Ted was right — we needed some beauty to help balance murders.

As I drove out the drive of the car shop, past the tombstone with two entwined hearts etched on the front, and onto the main road, an old dark blue Ford started to follow me. I told myself he'd just stopped by the side of the road to check a map or something and started up by chance about the time I drove out, but the longer he stayed in back of me, the more nervous I got. If he was really following me, he wouldn't be so obvious about it. Let me admit it. I was getting paranoid.

When I reached the entrance to the Parkway, he was still there. He won't turn in, I hoped. Then I'll know how silly I am. But he did turn in after me.

If I speeded up, if I could lose him far enough behind around those sharp curves so I could turn off when I got to Town Mountain Road, then he wouldn't know which way I'd gone. That would give me a three-way chance to fool him, since Webb Cove Road took off right after Town Mountain branched off the Parkway. I might get arrested for speeding. That would be a laugh. Me and Ted arrested on the same day. That would keep me from saying, "I told you so."

Nobody much on the Parkway except a few cars at the overlook point. I figured that was a break. Then I noticed the little warning light that means the car is running low on gas. I'd forgotten to get gas. I'd have enough for a few miles. No service stations on the Parkway. No anything on the Blue Ridge Parkway except over-looks of deep valleys and neighboring mountains. So beautiful that I couldn't help noticing the vibrant washed blues and greens. It must have rained here. Yes. The road was black-wet.

I probably had enough gas to get to a gas station. If I avoided diversions. I'd be safe in a public place like a gas station. I passed one tan pickup with an old lady driving. Good. Something between me and the blue car that seemed to be following me.

I pulled beyond that truck and swung around those curves so fast I could feel the car wanting not to swing back quick enough, but I kept it under control, whooshing past blurred banks of wild flowers on my right and far views on the left where the mountain dropped off. Then I came to a curve that was a little sharper than I had expected. I braked hard to keep from going too near the edge.

Something inside the car gave. It all happened so fast. Suddenly the car was in the air, heading straight into space, while the road curved back around. No crunch of fence. It was one of those spots where the grassy bank on the edge of the road gave way to sky.

And I was driving on sky. I almost laughed. I didn't believe it. But the pit of my stomach did. The car seemed to fly forever, and I thought of Ted with some policeman, and Eve in Hong Kong, and how I'd never be able to tell them goodbye. And it came to me that Pop would cry and then take a certain pride in having better sense than ever to have gotten himself killed like I did.

I was shooting out through the air over a drop that went down, down, down. Then I was falling, the car rolling in the air. Some white object crashed around inside the car, somehow, by the grace of God, not hitting me but once. I prayed for a treetop to fall into, something to break the fall. The car was rolling over in air, but my seat belt was holding me snug. Leaves seemed to be around me but no branches stopped the fall. Then there was a crunch, a thud and further twist. The car hit and settled with a final lurch. The windshield had disintegrated. At least it was safety glass. I hurt like you wouldn't believe. But I was alive.

And I thought: Gloria. She arranged this.

And then I thought: Maybe not. But *some* killer arranged it. Nancy and then Larry flew through my mind. Nancy in the pond. Larry pulling that damn electric cord. And why me halfway down a mountainside? And who would ever find me?

CHAPTER
22

TIME: ENDLESS

I was lying at an odd half-sideways angle, feeling dizzy. My legs hurt like hell but I couldn't move enough to see why. My head ached. I could smell gasoline. I thought, Dear God, please don't let the car start burning.

My head was near the smashed side-window of the car. I realized I was lucky not to have glass in my face. The car seemed to have rolled against a boulder or something which kept it from lying flat on its side, so my window was several feet above the ground. My back was against the seat, but that was tilted sideways. I couldn't move my legs, but I could move my arms. I was glad of that. My nose itched. I scratched my nose.

A story floated into my mind. That newspaper story a few years back, about the man who went off the side of the mountain and was found several days later after he had died of exposure and from the gasoline that soaked his body. And then with joy I remembered the warning light. I had almost no gas. I'd forgotten to buy gas. Thank God. Thank God.

But here I was. Trapped. I tried to remember why nobody found the poor soaked-in-gas man.

There had been no guardrail where he went over. That was it. There was no damage to the side of the road to alert anybody that a car had gone over the side. Oh, God. Me too. No guardrail. My head hurt so much, my mind didn't work very well. But I had to remember. There was more. The man's car fell so the tops of trees hid it. So he died before they found him. Out the broken window I could see a tree root snaking on the ground. I must be near a tree. In fact the top of the car might be against the trunk of a tree. That could be what prevented the car from rolling further. Perhaps a tree had saved me from death in a crash, and now it would hide me to die slowly under its leafy branches. I hated the tree.

Ted will keep looking, I told myself. He won't give up until he finds me. But Ted had no reason to think I might be on this side of town. And how long would it be before anybody even realized I was missing?

I remembered the horn. I throbbed with relief. Someone would hear and come help me! Why didn't the soaked-in-gas man blow his horn for help? I pushed the horn hard. Nothing. The crash had done it in. My legs ached, I felt completely helpless. Tears rolled down my cheeks. I tried to think of something hopeful. Well, if they found my body, they'd know who I was — or, at least, who I'd *been*. I had those damned name tapes all over everything I owned in case I left something somewhere. I always felt that if I said to do it in my book I ought to do it myself, even if it was a suggestion from a friend. Even if I hadn't done it before. I wasn't wearing a sweater or anything else I'd be apt to lose that would have a name tape in it. But after I left my watch at a friend's swimming pool, I'd put an adhesive label on the back of my watch. I was marked. I began to sob. And then to laugh at myself. As if my name tape mattered now. They'd find my driver's license in my pocketbook and the car registration in the glove compartment of the car. One well-identified pulled-together corpse. Ha ha ha.

You stop that, I told myself. Pray and think. Get out of here.

I looked at my fancy twenty-four-hour watch: 1435, which translates to 2:35 in the afternoon. A wave of faintness came over me. Suppose I passed out and then came to? Would I even know how much time had passed? I set the alarm on my watch for the time I went over the edge: 1435. In twenty-four hours it would tell me twenty-four hours had passed. I shivered. But somebody had to find me before that.

I mustn't give up. I wasn't screaming, because I figured nobody could hear my scream. But suppose I was wrong? Suppose I died in hearing distance of somebody who could have heard me if I'd yelled? "Help!" I called out over and over. No answer, till my throat began to hurt. If I fainted, at least I wouldn't feel the pain in my head. But I had to stay conscious and figure out a way to escape.

There had also been a story about a woman whose car went over the side of the mountain. I'd heard about it on television. A lame woman. She got help. I flushed with hope. She used her ingenuity. She fastened the batteries of her wheelchair to her CB radio and called for help. I didn't have a CB radio. I didn't have a wheelchair. But there had to be something. I'd written a whole damn chapter on ingenuity. If you have no memory, you have to be inventive, right? But nothing in that chapter could help me now. A lot of silly stuff for emergencies that didn't even count. Like what to do if you forget your comb and your toothbrush. I'd been so pleased with that. How you clean your teeth with a washcloth and salt. How you comb your hair with your fingers, and if you can use some part of your body to make up for what you forgot, that's great because it's very difficult to forget a part of your body. Ha ha ha. How could I use a part of my body to help myself now? I couldn't think of a way. I didn't even have the use of my legs. The car was crumpled in a way that trapped them. I wished I could forget *them*.

All I could see out the window was straggly grass and the tree root and a few rocks. I must be on a narrow shelf of the mountainside.

So why did I write such drivel instead of the stuff that could help me now? Like what do people already know about ingenuity: Like use a newspaper for an umbrella or a plastic bag for a raincoat if you've forgotten your umbrella. I thought how nice it would be to get caught in the rain. If it rained I wouldn't even feel it. The car covered me. I couldn't even stick out my tongue and catch a raindrop. I was beginning to get thirsty. I wished I hadn't thought of that.

Why had I written such useless stuff? Like two great facilitators of ingenuity were a pocket knife and lots of quarters. Maybe a pocket knife could have helped somehow, though God knows how. A pocket knife was great for slitting a trash bag into a raincoat, but no damn good for getting me untwisted from a two-ton car. I didn't need to know how to improvise if I forgot my umbrella. I needed to know how to remove the crushing weight of a car from around me with no tools, not even a can opener. How to send a surefire telepathic message with a map to the police department and Triple A. A card in my pocketbook said AAA would send a wrecker to rescue me anywhere. Ha ha ha. The only good thing in my life was a view of a few sprigs of grass. Green is for life, but green leaves might kill me by hiding the car. I prayed.

I must have passed out and come to a while later. I tried screaming again. My throat got hoarse faster. I began to be powder-dry thirsty.

Ingenuity. It did seem to be my only hope. But not the penny-ante kind in my book. So O.K., I had quarters in both pockets of my skirt, like my book suggested. So I could make phone calls quick if I forgot how to get where I was going or needed other help. Just absolutely great. A marvelous help. Except there was no phone booth on the side of my tree. I could count on that. And I couldn't get to it if there was, could I? The faintness swirled closer. I must have passed out again. When I came to, my watch said 1545. Almost four o'clock.

The nearest I had to a drink was a broken china coffee cup which shouldn't have been in the car anyway. That was the white thing that had zinged and crashed around the car while I was falling. I was lucky it hadn't beaned me harder. If I'd needed to dig myself out of a cave-in, the shards might have helped scrape dirt away — not much but some. They'd hardly make a scratch on the twisted car.

I'm going to die here, I thought. I summoned Roger in my mind. At least the thought of Roger hugging me would be a comfort. Wherever Roger was, I'd be going there. What came into my mind instead was Ted.

Ted, who had to rush everywhere he went, and then could sit so still listening that you felt recharged by his presence. I ached for his presence. Ted with his firm patient mouth that could twist into a wisecrack. Amused by the world and dead-serious at the same time. With those snapping eyes that seemed to be just one step ahead, anticipating what I was saying. And yet never bored. Ted with those broad shoulders. I wanted to put my head against his shoulder and cry.

Ted will find me, I told myself again. Then I must have passed out.

When I came to again it was still half-light, but my watch said 0625. Early morning. I heard a noise, a movement in the dead leaves near the car. Not enough to be a person, but something. I pulled myself awake. Whatever it was went away.

Somebody was glad I was here. That came to me with a rush. Somebody had tampered with my brakes so they'd go if I put my foot down hard. Somebody wanted me not to be found. By God, I was going to fool them. I'd read somewhere that strong emotion seemed to be one element in sending a telepathic message. I worked at sending Ted a picture of the turn in the road where I went over. The strong emotion came with the turf. I held that picture until it went black.

I came to again when my watch alarm went off. Twenty-four hours. Nobody had found me in twenty-four hours. My mouth was wooden with dryness. My mother appeared. "It takes time," she said. That had been one of her favorite expressions.

My leg had begun to throb. The right leg. The left didn't hurt as much.

I heard that rustling sound again. "Come

here," I said. Partly to see if my voice still worked. It did. Then a small wiggly hound dog appeared near the window of the car. "Good dog," I said. If I could catch hold of the dog, I could send a message by him. I wasn't sure how yet. But, by God, I'd find a way.

But he was shy. He stayed just out of reach. I wished I had a dog biscuit or a piece of meat to lure him close, something with a smell he'd want to investigate. I picked up a broken shard of the coffee cup and cut the end of my longest finger. A drop of blood welled up when I squeezed the finger. I poked it out the window as far as I could. The dog came nearer and sniffed. He was tall enough so that his head was just on a level with my hand. I pulled my hand back closer to me. The little dog followed. I mustn't scare him until I was sure I could snag his collar — if he had one. I pulled my hand closer. Some noise in the woods diverted him and he ran off. I shut my eyes and saw black circles. I opened them and called, "Here, puppy." He came meandering back. He came close and licked my finger. In a kindly way. As if he wanted to help a hurt. I had two fingers through his collar quick. He growled and tugged. "Good dog," I said again.

He tussled with me, pulling at his collar. I was afraid he'd slip his head out. Or I'd lose my grip. "Good dog." I said. "Sit." To my surprise he obeyed. Somebody had been training this little dog. He regarded me with large, questioning brown eyes. I couldn't just hold him there forever. How could I send a message? What did I have that would fasten to his collar? A scrap of paper from my purse with a message? But that would slip out of his collar as he ran through the woods. My car keys? God knew I wasn't going to drive anywhere in my poor car. But the keys would be difficult to fasten to the collar. My watch. It had my name on the back! I held the dog's collar tight with my left hand, and with the other struggled to take off my watch. I had to turn at an angle that increased the pain in my head. I kept fighting off the blackness. I had to get that watch on the dog before I fainted again. I looped it through his worn leather collar. He must have inherited that collar from another dog. A dog family heirloom. Please, I prayed, don't let that collar pick this moment to wear out. I managed to get the little tongue of the buckle through the hole in the watch strap. Then the dog jerked his head and almost pulled it out. Not quite. Finally I had the watch buckled to the dog. But who would know it was a cry for help? A desperate come-quick cry for help. I cut my finger again and smeared blood on the face of the watch. Then everything went black.

Then Mary was standing there. Mary in one of her red T-shirts. "Greed," she said. "Envy and greed." Her T-shirt said PWELGAS. She was only six years old. I said, "You should be thirty-five." She vanished.

A bird was singing. I don't want to die, I thought. I want to hear the birds singing. I'm not ready. Then my mother appeared again. She was wearing a green silk dress that she used to wear to church, and she was smiling. She had some wonderful message to give me. Something that would remake my life. "BKL, BKL, BKL," she said, and then she said, "You're still alive!" in a man's voice. She said it in the voice that belonged to Thelma's husband.

CHAPTER
23

THAT EVENING AND EARLY
NEXT MORNING

"Thank God," said the same man's voice. And I thought: Right now I haven't got much to thank God for. And then I knew I did. Because that wasn't Thelma's husband's voice. It was Ted's. Not alike. Except in a dream. And then, there in front of me, was Ted's face in the twilight. His body seemed attached to his face at an odd angle. He was leaning towards me in the half darkness. "Hello," I said. My voice was a frog croak. I waited for him to vanish. He persisted. I croaked, "Are you real?"

"Thank God I am," he said. Tears ran down his cheeks. I decided to believe him.

I said, "Brakes. Brakes failed," and blacked out. Then there were noises and pains and especially a sawing noise, and lights moving around.

The next thing I remember clearly was a hospital bed. I loved it. It had smooth sheets. I could move in it, not that I felt like moving much. All of me hurt, though not as badly as before by a long shot. I opened my eyes. A nurse was staring into them. She shined a tiny flashlight into one eye, then the other. Then she had the grace to leave. I was in a white room, a one-bed room. Not intensive care. A good sign.

Ted said, "You're awake!" He was on a chair by the bed. He took my hand and beamed. He has nice firm fingers.

"You found me! I knew you wouldn't give up until you found me." My voice was still hoarse, but better. My eyes went to a glass of water on the bedside table. Ted put an angle straw in it and raised it to my lips. Delicious!

"I found you," he said, "with the help of one hound dog, one old farmer, his eight-year-old son, the Park Service, the highway patrol, the Asheville police, five fire departments, some Boy Scouts, and a lot of good luck." The crinkles around his eyes said he was pleased with himself. The firm way he held my hand said he was glad and relieved.

"How?" I asked. "Don't make me talk yet. Just tell me how you found me."

But he shook his head. "First we need to do what we can to help find the skunk who tried to kill you."

Then he left me. He came right back with Mustache.

"Somebody definitely tampered with your brakes," Mustache sounded angry. "Somebody left them ready to go the first time you jammed your foot down hard. But that's all we know. Please tell me what happened." Talk about instant action. I'd been conscious two minutes. But, then, I just missed being the third murder in a row, hadn't I? The killer gambled that my brakes would go when I needed them most, when I put my foot down extra hard, preferably in a fatal spot. He almost won. Or she almost won. I shuddered.

I told about the ignition trouble, about taking my car to Jeff. Turned out Ted had told the police about that. But they hadn't known about the new mechanic who was Cousin Gloria's cousin. I told about deciding to go talk to Larry's brother, and how nobody knew I was going to do it. Mustache wrote all that down. (Ha, I thought. Just like it says in my book.)

"Do you always keep your car in your garage at night?" he asked.

"Yes. But the garage door is always open."

"Have you heard any noises from the direction of the garage at night?" Good grief, that question meant he thought anybody could have come by at night and doctored my car. Of course they could! A killer has so many sneaky ways to kill. I felt cold.

I tried to be businesslike: "No. I haven't heard a thing, but I'm a talented sleeper." I wanted him to know how bad it was. "A Chinese gong next to my bed might or might not wake me up. I sleep through thunderstorms."

Then I remembered the blue car I thought was

following me, and told him about that.

He wrote everything down and thanked me, so serious he didn't even stop to tell me one of his grandmother's memory tricks. He said he'd get right to work checking out Jeff. "But Jeff didn't do it," I called as Mustache went out the door. "Jeff's not the type." The last thing I needed to lose was my great mechanic.

A gray-haired nurse with a large black watch came in and took my temperature. She shined a small light in my eyes. I told her the other nurse already did that. She nodded wisely and said nothing. Seemed like that took three hours. Finally she smiled, said, "Doing good," and left.

Ted said, "Thank goodness."

"So how did you find me?"

"I kept calling you on the phone to give you a chance to say, 'I told you so,' because you did tell me I'd get stopped for speeding at the worst possible moment. When you weren't home by eleven at night, I was worried. I called Pop's. You weren't there. Dorothy said you hadn't been there all afternoon. Nobody knew where you were." He shook his head and grinned. The corners of his eyes crinkled in that way that makes you know he's going to laugh with you, not at you. "Fine help you are. Going off and not telling anybody where, when there's a murderer loose."

"My partner had been arrested for speeding. Police plot. And I was impatient to talk to Larry's brother."

He ignored that. "So I called Jeff and woke him up, and he said he didn't know where you went, but you'd been talking to a Reed Johnson from Madison County at the car shop, so I called Johnson and woke him up, which seemed to please him. He said when he was a kid he always wanted to be a detective, and he wished he could help in any way. But as it turned out, he couldn't. Then, I've got to tell you, I was getting frantic. At eleven-thirty I called the police. Then I went over and broke in and searched your house. That telephone book you couldn't find was on top of the refrigerator, by the way."

"Thank you," I croaked. He gave me another drink of water.

"I drove around town wondering what to do, and then I went by the TV station at six and collared one of the people going to work early and talked the early newscaster into reporting a bulletin that you were missing. That took some fast talking. I don't think he would have done it for me so soon after you disappeared except a member of his family had been murdered, it turns out. He bent the rules for me."

"Ted," I said, "you could talk a candidate into saying he's for raising taxes."

"Then I twisted the arms of all the radio station folks. The police chief helped me. He wouldn't ordinarily have called you a missing person that quick, either."

"But you talked him into it."

"I persuaded him you are not the type of

woman who would go off for long without telling somebody where you went. Especially when two people have been killed.

"When nobody had seen you by afternoon, I was sick. I was down at the police station when the old farmer called in. That was about three-thirty. He said he had a little farm down the mountain from the parkway. His grandson found your watch on his dog's collar. First the kid thought it must be some kind of a joke. Then he saw the blood on the crystal. He thought it was mud and started to wash it off, but when it was wet it was redder, and he thought it might be blood. So he took it to his grandfather."

"Who'd heard about the missing woman on the radio," I said.

"Yes, in fact, he had. And the name on the watch matched yours. But we still didn't know where you were, except that it must be within the range of where a hound would wander. A hound will go a long way after a rabbit. And the blood on the watch scared me silly.

"So we got all the volunteers we could find to help with the search, which is where the members of several nearby volunteer fire departments, like Haw Creek, and the Boy Scouts came in."

"I am very grateful," I said. I realized my voice was doing better. And then I remembered my mother's voice saying, "BKL, BKL, BKL."

I tried to pull myself up on my pillow to talk better. Ouch. I could talk lying down. Ted brought me a second pillow from the closet and put it under my head just right. He kissed me on the tip of the nose. The BKL at the edge of my mind almost got away. "What's on your mind?" he asked.

Oh, yes. "I had a dream," I told him. "My mother told me something wonderful that would change my life. I think it had to do with the killer. I think it was something that could make me safe. And what she said was 'BKL.'"

He sat down and took my hand again. "That was on Pop's calendar on May twenty-second in your handwriting. I remember because you obviously wrote it there such a short time before Nancy was killed. It must be important. But what does it mean? Did your dream hint at that?"

"I don't know." I felt so frustrated. I wrote BKL, so I should be able to figure out what it meant. The answer seemed just around the corner out of sight.

"There must be something I can do to jog my memory. But what?" I was so impatient I was hot.

"Relax," he said. "Your best thoughts come when you relax. That's what it says in Chapter Eight!"

"But what can I find out lying here? When do I get out of this place? What did the doctor tell you? Did you see him?"

"He said you have a slight concussion. He'll have to keep you still a while. Don't groan like that. It could be a lot worse. None of the worst things that can happen have. Your brain isn't swelling. You came in suffering from shock and bad bruises too. But other than that, he said you seem to be in surprisingly good shape. You're a testimonial to seat belts."

I sighed, started to toss, then stopped quick with a wince. Oh, my head! "We could go over our notes here," I said. "Maybe if we went over all of our notes, something would jog my mind. Forget that word *jog*. Anyway, I can *almost* remember."

Out in the corridor I heard one of those wheeled carts go by, clanking. I tried to relax. "My cousin Kate on my mother's side couldn't come to Nancy's funeral because she's eighty-three and in bad health."

Ted had his how-on-earth-does-this-fit-in? expression. Leaning back in his chair, eyebrows raised just a little, eyes alert.

"Last year, though, she came to visit and she told me something that I haven't fitted into my book yet. I don't know where to put it. She said, 'I used to have a fine memory, but now I have to have the key before I can remember anything.' At first I wasn't sure what she meant, so I got her to explain.

"She told me: 'Someone has to mention something that brings back a trip I once took, for example, before I remember it. Then it all comes back. Or I have to see something that reminds me strongly of a thing or person. Then a lost memory lights up.' "

He nodded. "Yes. That's happened to me."

"I think Cousin Kate has come to mind because BKL is a key to something. Maybe something about a murder suspect. That we need to know."

Ted kept saying "Yes." Encouraging my thought to come. But my thoughts were slow-motion.

"Sleep on it," Ted said. "You look exhausted. Your body needs sleep to heal." And sure enough, my eyelids were so heavy that he slowly blacked out.

Ted came back the next morning with a vase of apple blossoms. "To inspire us." He removed the remains of my breakfast from my bed table and put the flowers there. They smelled like spring. Then he sat down in the chair by the bed and got down to business. "You said you'd had a friend whose initials were B.K.L. but she moved to California. Any further thoughts about that?"

"She wasn't the murdering type." I almost wished she was. "She was a fellow poet. The serious kind."

It's a long chance, but we could ask Millie and the World Memory about that date and those initials, I started to say. But then I remembered that the World Memory can't deal with initials, unless of course they appeared in a story just like that: as initials. That didn't seem likely.

"It'll come to you," Ted said. "We'll find the key. Something will happen that will remind you

297

strongly of BKL, whatever it is, and unlock the memory."

"Let's hope it happens quick," I said.

"Yes. Preferably before you get out of here and wander around where there may be another trap."

He was right. I was impatient to get home. And yet I knew that when I got there, I might be in even more danger.

CHAPTER
24

HOME FROM THE HOSPITAL, NOON

Ted stood by the refrigerator in my lemon-yellow kitchen, watching me break eggs into a cup. In one hand he had the milk I was going to need in a minute; the other hand had hold of the refrigerator door. I sat at the table with a pillow at my back and my legs up on one of the split-wood chairs pampering my body.

He'd stopped still when I told him that Mary took a course in auto repair.

"Mary, the smile girl? Under a car?"

"It was a hands-on course," I told him, "sponsored by a women's group. The idea was that women were naive and fair game when it came to mechanics, and they ought to know how a car was put together. And the amazing thing," I said, "is that she reminded me of that course herself when she came to see me this morning. She and the kids brought me those yellow roses on the windowsill."

He whistled and frowned. "So maybe she was afraid you'd remember that she knew how brakes work. Maybe she wanted to be sure to mention that course to you first and act innocent. After all, she already knows you think there might be something fishy about her trip to San Francisco." He ran his fingers through his hair as if he were trying to smooth it down, to make the hair make sense, even if Mary wouldn't. No use. His hair had a mind of its own.

"Of course, what's really suspicious is that she never told anybody she met Ben out there," I said. "Not until we found out from the World Memory reporting their incident."

He set the milk on the table next to me and sat down in the chair where Roger used to sit, facing out the window.

He whistled softly to himself. "Wait a minute. I've just had a thought. Your friend, the one with the initials B.K.L. You said she went to California and you lost touch. Was she a friend of Mary's, too? Could there be some connection between Mary and Ben and B.K.L.?"

"But what? And why?"

I felt my body stiffen. Resisting the idea of Mary as a suspect. Even while I was busy trying to track her down. Mary who used to sit in my lap while I read her *The Wizard of Oz.*

An egg stared up like a large accusing yellow eye. I'd broken the egg into the last saucerless white teacup that had belonged to my grandma from Madison County. "Stick by family,"

Grandma always said, fixing me with those sharp black eyes of hers.

I dumped the staring egg into a bowl with the others. The egg had proved itself in the teacup: not rotten. So each of us had to prove ourselves, including Mary. Damn.

I added about two tablespoons of milk to the eggs, and beat it all together in one of traditional potter Neolia Cole's bowls, a wonderful bowl covered with small bright round splotches of red and yellow and blue and other colors. The happy colors of trust. I handed the bowl to Ted and he took it over to the stove.

"That bowl was from the craft shop I ran with Roger," I said. "I thought we ought not to use beautiful handmade bowls in the kitchen, but he insisted that bowls are for enjoying, not for leaving on the shelves. He said Neolia Cole agreed, and she'd been making bowls in Lee County for over seventy years." I needed to change the subject from Mary. I needed a breather.

"I would have liked Roger," Ted said. "I do like him, just from what you say. I like knowing about the people who helped you be you."

"That's Grandma's black frying pan you're putting the butter in," I told him. "She wanted me to have that pan because I like to cook. But it sure is nice that you're cooking now. I do still ache."

He poured the eggs into the hot pan. I could hear the butter sizzle. "Would you believe that bowl has a message on the bottom?" I asked him. He turned the empty bowl over and read it while he waited for the omelet to get firm enough to add the cheese.

He read the date on the bowl out loud: " 'January 1, 1976,' " and then " 'It's snowing and the wind is blowing.' " He puzzled out Neolia Cole's scrawl. " 'And the year is brand new. Start again.' "

He put the bowl down and went back to the omelet. He added the cheese, folded the omelet over while the cheese melted and then divided it onto two plates.

"Neolia writes the first thing that pops into her head," I said. "But sometimes, when I use one of her pieces, I feel like the words are just for me. That's not bad advice," I said, "to start again."

Ted put both omelet plates on the kitchen table with the small bowls of salad from the fridge. He raised both eyebrows. "Why? What do you mean: start again?"

I explained, between bites: "When a thing gets so complicated I can't see all of it in my mind at once, I find it helps to make a list. Like if I'm packing and check the list, I notice if I've forgotten shoes. And if things get really complicated, it helps just to pick the essence of each thing and list that."

Ted let his fork rest on his plate, sat perfectly still, and looked me straight in the eyes as if he were trying to see inside my head.

"I mean," I said, "it's like the time Roger and I

had to decide which of six houses to buy, and they all had a lot of things right about them and a lot of things wrong about them. So we listed the essential thing that attracted us most about each one, and the essential thing that put us off most. That helped us decide."

"Poetic logic," he said. "Your very best."

"We have a list of suspects, right? Each one had the opportunity and maybe the motive and maybe the expertise to kill poor Nancy and Larry, and try to kill me."

"So what is the essence?" he asked.

"A man or woman doesn't kill just because of motive and opportunity," I said. "Or the streets would run with blood. The essence of murder is weakness. Some weakness in a person who may be otherwise strong."

Understanding jumped in his eyes. "Yes. Exactly." He pulled a pencil and pad out of his pocket. "I'll be the scribe. Do you want to start our list with Mary?"

"We can," I said, "because we've just been talking about her. But that doesn't mean she's the prime suspect. We need to write down every suspect's weakness before we pick number one."

Ted wrote "Mary Sernan" on the first line. "No alibi," I said. "Not for Nancy's murder or what I'll call electric-trap time. And she said her mother was meddling in her divorce, even siding with Andrew. But that wouldn't seem enough to kill for." I hoped to God it wasn't.

"So," he said, "we get to your essence of

303

murder, Peaches: Mary's weakness. What is it?"

"Maybe loneliness," I said. "Maybe even despair. Maybe that's why she has all those china animals and jokes all over her house. Why she always has to smile. If she cracks, she'll fall apart. She'd be easy prey for a charming bastard. And that's how Albert's partner, Ben, seems to me: a charming bastard. With a Rolex watch and too much brilliantine and aftershave." I felt like crying. Is that any way to solve a crime? Ted handed me a Kleenex. I must be over the edge.

"O.K.," I said, forcing myself to be tougher. "Albert next. He appears to have been in Charleston the critical nights. The police found the recording of Albert calling his neighbor and asking him to come over on the night of his mother's death. Mustache told me that. It was still on the neighbor's answering machine. The machine recorded the date and time of each call. Eight P.M. for that one. Just two hours before the probable time of Nancy's murder. It takes about four hours to drive up from Charleston. Of course he could have called the neighbor long distance, but if he wasn't home, he ran the risk the neighbor would come right over and find that out. We know Albert was working in his shop both the day before and the day after the electric trap. Same with my brake failure. Mustache says the police checked that out. His alibi is better than Mary's. But not ironclad."

"So Albert probably didn't kill his mother. But," said Ted, "by a superhuman effort Albert could have driven up after work one day, prepared the electric trap or sabotaged your brakes, and driven back down to Charleston in time to get to work."

"Yes," I said, "and since Albert can fix anything, he should be able to unfix anything." A piece of my lettuce was roughly the shape of an automobile, a green curly automobile.

I shivered again. "But why would Albert try to kill me? I think Albert is fond of me. I really do. And he hardly knew Larry. And would he kill his own mother? I can't imagine Albert killing in cold blood. And we know that at least the electric and brake traps had to be planned ahead."

"And now for your essence," he said: "Weaknesses?"

"Yes."

"Just *yes?*"

"He never accepted his deformed hand. It's not that obvious or debilitating, really. The top two sections of his little finger missing on his left hand. I had a friend at Carolina with no hand who did fine — he's a successful lawyer now with a wife and three children. But Albert feels like his hand is a curse, I think. And he's angry because he thought it was his mother and father's fault. His father was drunk and pushed his mother so hard that she fell partway down the stairs. That was a few months before Albert was born. God knows why she told Albert that story. He blames his finger on that. But somehow he also blames himself for being imperfect. I think that's why he gambles."

Ted sat straight and raised his eyebrows. "He gambles?"

"Oh, not like getting mixed up with the Mafia," I said. "But all his life he's taken chances. Like the time he set out for Charleston with his windshield wipers not working, and Aunt Nancy said the weather report was a forty percent chance of rain, and he said he'd take those odds since he needed to get back. Or the time when he was six and had his allowance raised to one dollar, and he bet his allowance against the money in my pocketbook that one raindrop would get to the bottom of the window before another, and it did. He had an annoying way of winning. Not always, of course. But I knew from way back, somehow, that it wasn't the money he needed to win."

"Then what?"

"I'm not sure. After he won my money he took me to a movie with it. He gambles with fate. If he wins, the Fates love him; if he loses, he's no good. And it's so important for him to win that you take his small bets and pray that he will win. When he can't get someone to bet, he drives too fast, which is a kind of a bet with the highway patrol that they won't catch him. And with his radar detector and all, mostly they don't. Which means to him that the Fates love him. I think."

Ted grinned. "The best people drive fast. But I never will again." I doubted that.

Ted was massaging his earlobe, looking thoughtful. His plate was empty. I passed him bread and butter. He shook his head no. Focused on Albert. "And if Albert's need to gamble grew from raindrops to horse races," he said, "if it got out of hand, would you know? Or would he have the equivalent of a radar detector to hide his habit?"

"Yes. He'd hide it if he could. He hides what he's ashamed of." I thought how carefully he kept that hand hidden in his pocket, even when we were just family alone. From the time he was a little kid. He wanted big pockets when he went to nursery school.

"But suppose he lost money, even owed money, what good would it do to kill his mother? Her pension died with her. All he'd get is a heaping dose of feeling no good." Ted took our plates to the sink and came back with a package of chocolate chip cookies.

"Other weakness?"

"A grudge against the world," I said. "Not always. Sometimes he's sweet and helpful. He can understand people with problems. When I broke my arm shortly after Roger died, he came up for the weekend and drove me around to do errands. His grudge is against his father, I think. But his father died and left him with no target. So maybe his weakness is no target."

"So who next?" Ted held his pencil poised. "Your explosive cousin?" He wrote "Gloria Larson" in his notebook. Then, glancing at his notes, he said: "No alibi for probable time of the first crime."

"Would you believe I was so upset when I questioned her that I forgot to ask where she was at the time the electric trap was probably set? And she hasn't been speaking to me worth a darn since," I told him. "So I don't know about an alibi for that. But we do know a cousin of hers was working in the place where I had my car fixed."

He underlined that in his notes.

"As for Gloria's motive," I said, "what could make a super-mother like Gloria more upset than the fact that Nancy was about to stand up and testify against her Stella? God knows Nancy didn't understand Gloria's kind of tiger mother-love." I took a cookie and thought about Stella when she was little. "Gloria's kid always had the prettiest dress at any family get-together. One had rows and rows of ruffled lace. And the kid played the piano. She must have had lessons. She was like a little princess. And always had a doll dressed up like a princess. Maybe when you're a princess it's hard to grow up. And Nancy reported Stella to Social Services for child abuse. In my family, telling on your own folks to outsiders is unthinkable. And God knows I've seen Gloria's temper."

"And that is Gloria's special weakness?" Ted asked.

"Temper, and being a tiger mother. Double-header — and yet. . . ."

"Any other family members?" Ted asked. He offered me another chocolate chip cookie, but sorting suspects was beginning to kill my appetite.

"God knows we have relatives all over, but I can't think of motives to make them suspects. My mother's folks have moved away from here. Aunt Lula is in a nursing home near Greensboro where her daughter lives. Her son, Bob, is in the foreign service. In Sri Lanka right now, I think. Of course we ought to consider Pop on general principles."

I stopped. "Ted, there's something I haven't told you. I didn't believe it and I couldn't bear to repeat it." I hesitated. I hated to repeat it now. "Gloria said Aunt Nancy was blackmailing Pop because he was the father of Gloria's daughter. She said Pop must have hired a killer." Ted didn't even blink. "And then she said maybe Pop was the father and maybe he wasn't — she just wanted me to be in doubt and know what that felt like!"

Ted burst out laughing. "Boy, that woman is a Jekyll and Hyde. I don't believe it either." I was relieved that he agreed. "Next weakness," he said.

"There's Cousin Eltha on Pop's side, who killed her husband in self-defense. You remember her from the funeral. A real looker. Pop likes to hold her hand. She's the only known killer in the family. But I've never heard that killing is habit-forming, except for psychopaths."

Ted winked. "If you like, I'll go question her on general principles, and hold her hand."

"I would *not* like," I admitted. "Let's try sitters. Silva seems like the best bet as a suspect. And I saw her thick as thieves in the Weaverville diner with Gloria."

"She looks like a suspect," Ted said. "With that bleached hair and that rabbit frown."

"Silva knew Nancy before she came here. You remember that awful story about her son."

Ted wrote in her name under Gloria's.

"She says she was at home sick when Nancy was killed," I said. "But she was on duty as sitter in Pop's house, with every opportunity to fiddle with the electricity at the time we think that happened. And yet I don't think she did it, even though she believes Nancy seduced her son and caused his death. Even though I know she was angry. She came here to ask for help. To try a little blackmail. I think that's all." Out the window two chickadees were fighting over the birdbath. Maybe I don't like to admit to myself how vindictive people can be.

"She had a strong motive," Ted said.

I sighed. "Nancy wore blinkers. So she was cruel. She didn't know how much she hurt other people. She had no talent for connections." I thought of her bundling off the kids to the babysitter from the time they were in baskets, ignoring her husband's drinking, ignoring whatever reason there was behind it. Taking quick comfort where she could find it, if what Silva said was true. I readjusted the pillow behind my back. My bruises were still a nuisance.

"Nancy took after her grandpa the revivalist, my grandma said."

"How on earth?"

"I can remember Grandma just as plain," I said, "shelling peas and saying 'Oh, he was a one. He could move you with words till you cried, but he couldn't *see* you. He couldn't even see *himself*.' I think I remember her exact words because she said that with such feeling, and I didn't understand what she meant. Now I do. Nancy's weakness was like his: Not seeing. Then judging."

"And what was Silva's weakness?" Ted asked. Right. I was meandering.

"Pent-up rage," I said. "She asked Nancy for money for her son's wife and sick child and Nancy said no. Silva told me that wasn't blackmail. But suppose Nancy took it as blackmail and threatened to call the police? Suppose something like that happened? I can see Silva boiling into a killing rage. And yet I still don't think she did it. Did you ever see her feed the birds? Or how kind she is to Silk? And of course Pop. Silva is not the type to kill." I wished people would be good or bad, not all mixed up together.

"Then there's Elsie," I said. "No alibi before she came on duty as sitter at eleven P.M., the night Nancy was probably killed around ten. Said she was home alone asleep the night of the electric trap. Seemingly no motive. But she lied to me — about her name, for instance — and she didn't tell me that she shot her husband, even if it was in self-defense." I sighed. I liked Elsie. Albert evidently loved Elsie. Pop loved Elsie.

"So do we believe her?" Ted frowned. "Do you believe her when she says her ex-husband might have recovered from his wound, traced her here, and killed Nancy? When she says he could have done it out of mistaken identity or to frame Elsie — is that too farfetched?"

I answered with a question. "But then who killed Larry? Who killed Larry and tried to kill me?"

"Yes — why would Elsie's husband have a reason to do that?" Ted demanded, as if I were hiding the answer. We were both getting annoyed at the lack of answers.

"And when did this great romance blossom between Elsie and Albert?" I demanded. "So, sure, they saw each other when he came to see Pop, but never — as far as I know — alone. Except for that one time when I found them kissing. Elsie says the feeling between her and Albert grew without either of them really realizing it, and then just suddenly exploded the night I found them," I said. "That's possible. But if Albert is a suspect . . ." The thought petered out.

"Are you suggesting that Albert and Elsie were in some kind of conspiracy to kill your Aunt Nancy and cover it up?" Ted asked.

"No. That's too farfetched."

"So what is Elsie's essential weakness?"

"Either she's a very talented actress and a psychopathic liar, or else the only real weakness I can think of is that she got mixed up with the wrong man. She's too compassionate."

"Which leaves Ben," he said. "Your favorite suspect, right?"

"Yes. I don't like Ben. He's cold. I think he cares more about things than people. Why did he and Mary hide the fact they met in California? There's something sneaky about Ben.

"And besides, since I like or love all of our other suspects, at least most of the time, I would be pleased to make Ben suspect number one. Albert told me he was in Atlanta when Nancy was killed. As far as I know, Ben hasn't been in Asheville in two months. God knows what his motive could be in any of this, but I have the feeling he has some sort of a hold on Albert. Maybe Nancy found out and confronted him with it. Maybe he thinks I've seen something that incriminates him. Maybe he thought Larry did."

"Albert doesn't seem to like him much," Ted said. "He talks about Ben in a monotone." He put a question mark next to Ben's name on the list.

"Pop says his lawyer, Homer Sawyer, is a suspect." I sighed. "But that's because Homer came by the house the week before Nancy died to put a couple of bequests that Pop had promised people in his will. I managed to make Pop do that. The bequests were small: one hundred dollars to the man who fixed the electricity after all the fuses blew, a thousand to Anna. I was trying to impress on Pop that he can't keep promising to leave people money and then not do it. I got Homer to give him a little talk about how that kind of promise was not a good idea."

"So Pop resented it and wanted Homer to be guilty?"

"Yes, but Homer was home with his wife and two kids when Nancy died. Pop had made the police check that out. That's a dead end.

"But, heck," I added, "maybe somebody expecting a big bequest thought Nancy was me and wanted me out of the way. We had on look-alike dresses. Maybe I have been the target all along. Of course, they'd have to kill off Eve when she came home to my funeral, to be sure a chunk of Pop's money went to them. At least my funeral would remove *me* from the suspect list. Or maybe whoever tried to kill me didn't even know I have a daughter. Singapore's a long way off. Out of sight, out of mind. They'd probably figure Pop, at his age, wouldn't be around too long."

I thought about that sly look on Pop's face when I told him he mustn't promise to leave people money: the narrowed eyes, the small smile. The old skunk. "God knows what lengths Pop has gone to, to tell people he'd put them in his will. God knows what hopes he's raised."

Ted put his hand over mine. "So be very

314

careful," he said. "Don't take chances. We don't know for sure why someone tried to kill you. But we know for sure that someone did."

I shuddered. "So we have to find him before he succeeds." My back felt unprotected. My eyes went to Neolia Cole's many-colored bowl still sitting on the counter. Still the color of trust. Who could I trust?

"We have our list of weakness, and still I can't spot suspect number one. Maybe this isn't the right angle," I said. "Maybe weakness is not the key. Maybe some silly little piece of the puzzle that doesn't fit is the key. Like that BKL on Pop's calendar and in my dream. Which could be the initials of my old college friend Barbara Kennedy Lowell in California, and yet I can't believe I'd have forgotten that she called. The last time I heard, she was in Pasadena. I don't even know if she's still there."

And then I had an idea. "Why don't we call information and find out if she's there? Her husband's name was something funny: Pole. Yes, because her name was Barbara and that made her almost like a barber pole. And he wore striped neckties like the stripes on an old-fashioned barber pole. And his nickname was Tad. Tad Pole." I was pleased with myself. Then I sighed. "People are not listed under nicknames."

"But their nicknames are often derived from their names," Ted said. He picked up the phone and asked information for the number of a T.

Pole in Pasadena. "Yes, that could be Thaddeus Pole," he said and winked at me.

I was excited. "Why don't I just call my old friend Barbara and talk about old times and see if she's seen Mary lately or anything like that."

So that's what I did, and I was through to Barbara's husband in nothing flat. Seemed too easy. He remembered meeting me at their wedding thirty years before. I said I felt sorry that Barbara and I had gotten out of touch. Then he said he had bad news. Barbara was in the hospital with cancer. She wasn't expected to live long. Wasn't even in shape to take telephone calls, though she was still conscious. I sent her my love. I was glad I'd called in time to do that.

And then in an odd way, the shock cleared my head. "You know what? One reason I haven't been able to remember what BKL means is because I had a preconceived idea. Initials. Like Barbara Kennedy Lowell. And the preconceived idea may be wrong. Let me see the calendar."

Ted pulled out the May page from the calendar. We kept it with our notes. We both leaned over to study it, and bumped heads. Talk about shocks to clear the head.

"Two heads," he said, "are not always better than one."

CHAPTER
25

EARLY AFTERNOON, SAME DAY

"Look at May sixteenth, Ted," I said, touching my finger to the square on Pop's calendar page for that day. "It says 'FRZ Man.' That's my handwriting, and I remember the man who stocks the freezer called and said he'd be coming out to do that. If FRZ means freezer, then BKL could be short for a word. Not initials at all, but — " Bingo! It came to me. "BKL," I cried out, like it was an old friend. "Buckle! That's what I wrote down when Albert called and told me to be sure the Confederate belt buckle that Ma bought was in the safe-deposit box.

"Albert called it a belt plate, but to me anything in the middle of the front of a belt is a buckle," I said. "He said there was a ring of thieves stealing Confederate stuff. Because the price is getting crazy. How on earth did I forget that?"

Ted laughed. "So now even thieves specialize."

"That all sounded so unlikely I'm not sure I believed it," I said, "but Albert should know. He says one buckle or plate sold in Baltimore for twenty thousand dollars. He says ours is now worth about ten thousand dollars. Imagine. I think Ma bought it from him for about one thousand, and she did it to help him out."

"And where is this Confederate BKL buckle, which I am going to call a plate?" Ted asked. "I gather plate is the accurate name?" Ted the reporter.

"Yes," I said, "and I supposed I should be proper and accurate too. Anyway, it's in Pop's safe-deposit box, I think. But," I added, "I have to admit that when I took the coins to the bank, I was in a hurry and forgot to check what was already in the box."

"You've been distracted," Ted said. "What does the plate look like?" Well, of course, if Ted was going to help look for it, he needed to know.

The thing hadn't really made much impression on me. "Small," I said. "Maybe three inches long, maybe two inches wide. Oval. With big initials on it: CS. And some stars. Brass, I think, but not polished. Historic, of course, but otherwise it wouldn't catch your eye." I felt slightly unloyal to the Confederacy to describe it like that. But I had to be honest.

"Do you feel well enough to go look in the safe-deposit box right now?" Ted asked. "God knows what this plate could have to do with somebody trying to kill you, but we better check it out."

Actually I still ached all over like crazy, but I figured I might as well keep my mind busy with something else. So I was ready. Off we went to the Wachovia branch bank.

"Walk Ovah Ya," Ted said and chuckled. "When I was a kid, I used to think it was pronounced Watch Ovah Ya, and that's why my dad had an account there. Not so."

But Pansy Pullman, the branch manager, acted like it was Watch Ovah Ya and even put a chair in the small room full of silver-fronted safe-deposit boxes so I could look carefully through Pop's big box while sitting down.

I needed to sit down. I'd been so surprised when I signed in. As soon as Pansy left, I groaned. "Dern my one-track mind! You know what else I didn't see when I put those coins in the bank? The name above mine on the sign-in card: Nancy Means."

Well, that, by itself, wasn't unusual. Nancy had Pop's O.K. to go in his box, just like I did. "But I was out of my mind," I said, "not to notice the date and time on the card: May twenty-second, three-thirty P.M."

Ted whistled softly: "The afternoon of the day before she died!"

I began to look through the box. Not just for the Conferderate plate, but also for any clue about Nancy. Pop's coins in a leather case were on top. Next, the velvet and satin cases of my mother's jewelry.

"Of course Nancy could have just borrowed some of Ma's jewelry," I said. "That was O.K. with Pop and me. But Albert didn't describe her wearing any."

I opened the velvet cases and looked to see if anything was missing: There was the Victorian seed pearl necklace that belonged to my mother's mother, a pair of old-fashioned deep-cut diamond earrings Ma had inherited from a great aunt. Technically that jewelry was mine now. Pop had announced I could wear it on special occasions, which in fact I forgot to do. But he said that I was too absent-minded to keep it around the house. Suited me. I didn't have to rent a box of my own. And I was glad for Nancy to enjoy it.

"All the jewelry is here," I said, "even the sapphire earrings that Nancy liked best."

"Maybe she was returning something to the box, or doing an errand for Pop," Ted said. Maybe if you ask him he'll remember."

But I had a nagging feeling there was some other reason why Nancy went in that box.

We found Pop's black-covered passport, left from the trips he'd taken to look at possible investments. We found all sorts of insurance policies with fancy scrolled writing on top, the deed to his house, and such.

We did not find any trace of Nancy's last visit. We did not find the $10,000 Confederate belt plate. Not anywhere.

"Albert will say 'I told you so,' and be

furious," I told Ted as I rearranged the papers so they'd fit back in the box. "Albert wanted to buy the plate back from Pop for what my mother paid for it. But Pop wouldn't sell at any price because he said my mother liked that buckle. I mean plate. Then Albert said well, at least it was still in the family. Family is important to Albert. More than to Mary."

"But if someone stole that plate . . ." Ted paused.

And I said, ". . . And since we searched the house the day Larry was electrocuted, and didn't see it, maybe someone did. Just like we didn't find the little portrait."

And he said, "Wouldn't a thief just get out of town and stay out of sight? Would he commit murder?"

"So, O.K.," I said, "we'll go home and call Albert. If people are stealing plates, Albert knows more about what's going on than we do. So let's go call him."

But Ted held onto my arm as if to say wait. "I bet Pansy will let you use her phone. And maybe home won't be the place we want to go next."

Pansy said no problem and took us into her small office with the pictures of her kids on her desk and waved me to sit in her chair. Then she was called off to attend to something else.

I took out my phone charge card, and charged a call to Charleston. Albert didn't answer his phone. He should have been in the shop. Perhaps it was a dull day and he put the "Closed" sign on the shop door and went out for a late sandwich. My happily returned watch said 1415. Late, but possible.

I fingered the three pens lined up together on the edge of Pansy's desk. "There's a man named Reed Johnson in Madison County," I told Ted, "the man I met at the car shop who gave me a ride to the diner."

Ted's eyebrows did their *So?* wiggle.

"Albert bought a Confederate belt plate from his mother." How nice of that to pop right into my mind. "A belt plate that could be traced right back to the colonel who died wearing it. Reed Johnson told me about that, along with a bunch of stuff about how our families knew each other. He thought I might want a kitten from his cat, I think. I have a hunch we ought to call Mr. Johnson. Pansy won't mind one more call." I knew it was a ridiculous long shot. Even that he'd be home. But he answered on the third ring.

He congratulated me on being rescued. "These mountain curves can be a mortal danger," he said. "After so much tragedy, one more thing would be too much. Do you suspect foul play?" His voice rose with hope. I was glad that the police hadn't released the fact that my brakes were tampered with. He would have talked about that for half an hour. Funny, because in my experience mountain men don't talk a lot until they know you well. Sometimes not then. But Reed Johnson sure made up for all the rest.

Finally I steered him around to the belt plate.

But, no, he said, Cousin Albert hadn't told him anything about any ring stealing belt plates, but there was a funny coincidence. The man who'd bought his mother's plate from Albert had wanted to talk to him about everything he'd heard about how his granddaddy found it, even where on the battlefield. The man kept at it until he got Reed Johnson's name from Albert and actually made a trip to see him. Nice fellow. From California, but he had children he visited on the East Coast. And on and on. I realized Reed Johnson might talk forever and offer me another kitten.

"Well, thanks a million," I said.

Reed said his mother even knew the Confederate colonel's name. His grandpa had learned it somehow. She even knew what regiment he was with, and the man from California had a wonderful visit and she fed him some of her black walnut poundcake.

I said "Well, thanks a million."

"But it all had a sad ending," he said. "He wrote me to say that belt plate had been stolen from him. Now that might be related to your ring of thieves you were talking about."

Well, the upshot was that Pansy gave me a glass of water to take with my pain pills and then we got in Ted's car and drove over to Madison County to talk to Reed Johnson. First on Route 19-23, then along smaller and curvier roads. Finally we were on a narrow mountain road that wound so much my head swam. I shut my eyes and was glad Ted was driving.

Turned out Reed was a collector. It was a wonder he'd ever parted with anything, even a belt plate. In his front yard were six whirligigs, the kind that go round and round when the wind blows and make a small figure take action. A man chopped wood, a boy pedaled a bicycle, a woman in a sunbonnet waved, and so it went, all in primary colors. He met us at the door and ushered us proudly into his small bungalow where the coffee table housed assorted birds' eggs under glass. One wall displayed old iron work: hinges and stakes and horseshoes and even an old set of ice tongs. Another wall was all old photographs. A cabinet filled with long, shiny guns stood against the third wall. At one end of an old green couch was a small lamp table with no lamp but a clutter of small iron pieces and a hammer and a box of nails. Looked like more of his collection waiting to be mounted.

In a recliner chair sat an ancient woman under a crocheted afghan of many colors. "This is my Mama," Reed said. "Thelma is at work." Mama nodded without expression and took no further part in our talk, didn't even move or focus her eyes.

A cat brushed against my legs. Ah, yes.

"Now you'd like to know about our belt plate," Reed said. "Somehow my great-grandpa discovered the name of the man he took it from right on the battlefield. Colonel Delancey Robertson.

"Now, the guy who bought this plate, he was a collector," Reed said. "He had all sorts of great stuff. He had a collapsible candlestick that he said belonged to a cousin of Robert E. Lee. When I heard all that stuff was stolen, I could have cried."

"Did he write you all the details?" Ted asked. "Like, how the thief got to his collection? Weren't his doors locked? Didn't he have a burglar alarm?"

"Somebody got round that man's security system. Somebody who knew a lot about that kind of thing, the police told him. Somebody took about fifty thousand dollars' worth of stuff."

"When?" I said. "When did it happen?"

"Not too long ago."

"But what month? What day?"

He shook his head as if to say he didn't know. He turned to his mother still inert on the recliner. "Was it in April, Ma?" No reaction. "I think it was in April, maybe about a month before your Aunt Nancy died. Because he wrote me about that plate in an envelope with a stamp on it I really liked. With a picture of a bald eagle. That eagle reminded me of Willie P. Wallen, my first cousin once-removed who was just celebrating his fiftieth wedding anniversary. Now, his anniversary is April sixteenth. That man from California wrote me like I was a friend. Said to tell Ma hello. Said he hoped nobody ever stole my collections. I collect stamps, too, as well as eggs and old iron stuff. But I've not had trouble with thieves."

"You collect stamps?" Ted asked.

"Why, yes, since I was a kid." He hesitated. "But why do you want to know about somebody stealing plates?"

We told him we thought it was possible there was a connection between our plate being missing and the two deaths. That pleased him so much that he grinned like a jack-o'-lantern, a lit jack-o'-lantern.

But Ted's mind was still on stamps. "Do you put those stamps right into a scrapbook, or do you keep the letters for a while until you get time to mount the stamps?"

"Why, I keep those letters for a while." I saw the light dawn on Reed Johnson's face just as I, too, saw what Ted was up to.

"Why, you want to see that letter! Why, I must still have the thing!" He ran into a room off the small living room and came back in nothing flat with an old shoebox full of letters and cards, all higgledy-piggledy. He put the box on the birds'- egg coffee table and began to sort through it.

"I think it was a yellow envelope, wasn't it, Ma?" No reaction.

"Here it is!" He whipped out a creamy envelope, heavy paper like a wedding invitation, pointed one stubby finger at the bald eagle stamp, and opened his mouth to tell me all about it, no doubt.

"What does the letter say?" I was getting impatient. Reed started reading:

"I know you and your dear mother will understand better than most just how I feel. My collection of Civil War memorabilia has been stolen, your wonderful belt plate and buttons included. Someone the police said knew enough to disarm the burglar alarm broke in and took everything.

"The police place the loss at around $50,000, but you and I know that the value to a collector is much more than the money that would be needed to replace his collection. Your belt plate was the thing I valued most. Fortunately the collection was insured. If you should hear of another family with Civil War memorabilia they'd be willing to sell, I'd love to meet them.

"All best to you and Thelma, and to your dear mama.

"Tony Jamison"

No date for the theft. Ted noted the postmark was April eighteenth. I wrote down the San Francisco address.

"He said my collection of birds' eggs might be valuable, but he wasn't interested in birds' eggs, was he, Mama?"

The eggs were rather pretty, nestling in their cotton nests under glass. One was quite large and a lovely speckled blue. But we didn't have time for eggs. We managed to get away without the guided tour. Or a kitten.

I was exhausted by the time we got home. I lay down on my bed, and Ted brought me a glass of sherry. He tried San Francisco information on the bedside phone. Unlisted number.

"Call Millie," I said, sipping the warmth of the sherry. "The World Memory can cough up the story of the crime in nothing flat, since this time we have the right name and the subject of what happened. Millie would do anything to help you. She said so."

Ted winked at me. "You have no cause to be jealous," he said, "but it really raises my morale when you are."

Never mind. Ted certainly was nice to Millie on the phone: Told her how wonderful she was to help. Millie called us back so fast I could hardly believe it.

Ted said a glad hello and then began to frown, an excited frown, eyes alert. He grabbed the pen out of his shirt pocket and wrote down notes on the pad by the phone. "You're wonderful, Millie," he said again. Then he thanked her profusely and said, "Yes, I'd really appreciate it if you'd check that."

He put the phone on the cradle thoughtfully. "Whoever stole that stuff," he said, "broke into an apartment with a sophisticated burglar alarm the night of Friday, April eleventh — and that's the night before Ben and Mary had dinner together in San Francisco." He whistled. I sighed.

328

"And furthermore," Ted said, "Millie is doing a rundown on any other Confederate belt-plate thefts." Thank God Millie had a crush on Ted. Besides, I didn't mind the way she crossed her legs in miniskirts as long as she and Ted were in separate rooms.

"If someone killed for fifty thousand dollars, it was someone who didn't value life." That thought depressed me, though you hear of druggies who kill for twenty or thirty dollars.

Soon the phone rang again. Ted picked it up. He nodded at me to say yes, it was Millie. He furrowed his brow, very serious, and kept saying "Yes," and taking notes. When he hung up I could see before he said a word, by his furrowed brow and pursed lips, that we'd hit serious pay dirt. "Albert is right. There have been a lot of thefts, including one in Denver. Seems to me I heard Ben went there. You better try again to call Albert."

"No," I said, "I think we had better go to Charleston and feel things out. Suppose Ben is blackmailing Albert? Something like that. Albert couldn't tell us. Let's just get the lay of the land. Then we can tell the police if all this appears to be more than coincidence." I prayed Albert was not mixed up in whatever it was. Albert who had always looked to me for help. I was quite sure Albert would not kill for fifty thousand dollars.

CHAPTER
26

IMMEDIATELY AFTERWARD

Well, of course, right at that moment the phone on the bedside table rang. It was Dorothy. She said Pop was hysterical. He believed the house was under siege by men with knives. "You're the one who can talk him out of it," Dorothy said. "And he's trying to get out of his wheelchair and fight. I keep praying he won't fall and hurt himself." Poor little Dorothy was the sitter Pop could buffalo most. I looked at my watch: 1800, which I translated into six o'clock. Competent Anna would have left supper fixed and gone for the day.

"Call next door and get Arabella Horton to come over until I can get there," I said. "Pop likes her, and she may be able to calm him down. I'll be there in fifteen minutes." I filled Ted in. Somehow we had to deal with Pop on the way to Charleston.

Luckily, my overnight bag lives on my closet shelf with a nightgown and a change of underwear in it, in case I have to go over to Pop's on short notice. I grabbed it, then stopped for a second to comb my hair, then hurried out to Ted's car. Ted drove us to Pop's. "Thank God for Arabella," I said. "Why, most of the time Pop actually cheers her up. That's what she says. I am always amazed that a woman who seems to be so widely traveled and widely read needs five wigs, four horses, and Pop to cheer her up."

At Pop's we found Arabella sitting by his side, holding his hand. "This is the Fairy Queen," he said. "She says she can keep me safe. You can tell she's the Fairy Queen because she's blond. Otherwise she looks like my next-door neighbor Arabella Horton in her riding jeans. Except for horses and what's in books, Arabella doesn't know her ass from a hole in the wall."

Arabella ignored that. Obviously Pop was having one of his mad-with-the-world-and-everybody-in-it days. Except the Fairy Queen. I remembered the book of fairy stories my mother used to read me and the fairy queen *was* blond in the pictures. Arabella wore a Dolly Parton bouffant. I hadn't seen her in that wig before. I would have expected it to scare the horses.

I managed to get her to come into Pop's office with me for a minute, on the pretext that we'd be sure every door and window was locked. I asked her how bad things seemed to be with Pop and explained that Ted and I had to go to Charleston.

Dorothy simply didn't know how to handle

Pop, she said. "She was about to convince him I wasn't the Fairy Queen who could keep him safe. He was about to have hysterics again. So I sent her out to the kitchen to answer the phone on the first ring. When he's in this state the phone can get him going." Arabella patted her Dolly Parton hair. "Old age is a bitch.

"But I can stay here with him," she said. "I've got to tell you, these killings have made me nervous. I want to see them solved as much as you do." She hugged herself and shivered. "I'll just have to call John Denton. He was coming over to watch a movie with me on TV."

Yankee Accent again. He was on close terms like that with Arabella? And also going out with Mary? For a semi-robot, he sure got around.

I gave her Dr. Spicewood's number from my little carry-out address book, and then remembered it was already programmed among the numbers on Pop's push-button phone. I told her Mary was on a push-button too, in case she needed help. But Mary was a last resort because she'd have to bring the two children.

I said we'd have a very short visit with Pop and maybe call Albert just to say hello and get the lay of the land. "I'm telling you things I'm not going to tell anybody else," I said. "We are not going to tell Albert we're going to Charleston. We suspect his partner, Ben Arne, and want to catch them unawares. We wouldn't want Mary to know where we were, either. Only you will know." I wondered if I ought to be trusting her with all those secrets. But I had to trust somebody in case of an emergency. Arabella could look pretty dippy, but she didn't seem to be a blabbermouth.

She hugged me, smelling of Chanel No. 5 and horse, and she said, "You can count on me."

We went back out to find Ted and Pop playing checkers. I hoped all the company had made Pop forget the imaginary men with knives. He had such sudden ups and downs, ins and outs of reality.

Arabella plunked down beside Pop and watched the game. I dialed Albert. He should be just getting home from the shop. In fact, the phone had to ring six times because he was unlocking the door on the first ring, or so he said when he picked up. I said we just wondered how he was doing, and Pop wanted to say Hi. Pop, of course, told Albert that he was playing checkers and didn't want to talk to anybody. Then he handed the phone back to me.

"So your father's having a bad day?" Albert asked me. And I said, "To put it mildly."

Then I told Albert how I'd just met a friend of his, Reed Johnson, and he said, "Oh, yes, the man who sold me the Confederate plate. A sad story. That plate was stolen from the man who bought it from me." And suddenly I wanted to ask him if he trusted Ben. But I hesitated. "How is your grandma down there?" I asked.

She wanted him to come over and visit her more, Albert said. But it was hard because Ben was away so much. Ah. An opening. "Is he off somewhere now?"

And Albert said no, but that Ben was leaving for Albuquerque in the morning. As soon as he came by the shop and picked up a couple of pieces for a collector out there.

"Ben's leaving early?"

"He wants to be out of here by ten-thirty," Albert said. "He has to do some errands and catch a plane." I repeated that out loud so Ted would hear it and know we needed to get started. Then Albert and I chatted a little further about such earthshaking subjects as the weather, and he asked if we had any further leads on the killer. I said no, except we hoped the police could figure out who had tampered with my brakes. Albert told me to be careful.

Pop was just lifting his red checker to jump over a string of Ted's black men. "Check!" he cried. "Now let's have another game." Ted winked at me. Sometimes I think a wink is the favorite word in Ted's vocabulary!

I explained we had to go. We had errands to do but we'd be back soon.

The clock on the mantle said nine-thirty. Fortunately Pop seemed too confused to realize you can't do many errands at nine-thirty at night. If we took four hours to drive to Charleston, we'd get there by one-thirty. I wasn't in any condition to take on the question of Ben without some sleep in a bed. I could sleep in the car while Ted drove, but that wasn't going to do any good for

334

the ache all over, so we might as well brainstorm in the car and sleep when we got to Charleston.

I sat back down for a three-minute visit with Pop, and that's when Arabella began to tell me about cathedrals.

Pop said, "Divert me, Fairy Queen. That's what a lonely old man needs."

Lonely? Hah! Pop had more friends than I could count.

"Tell me one of your interesting facts," he said. "Something the most or the least or to gasp at."

Arabella considered that. She said, "Oh, yes," and turned to me. "Peaches, you're a writer." That was an interesting fact? But then she went on: "So you and Harwood might be interested to know that Victor Hugo wrote what's believed to be the shortest letter in the world to his publisher after *Les Miserables* came out. There was nothing in it but a question mark and his signature."

"He wanted a financial statement," Pop said. "What's unusual about that? That's a silly fact."

She smiled and patted his hand. Her hands were half as big as his, and twice as pink. "You know, I did come across something that might be useful to Peaches." She turned to me, very pleased with herself. "Did you know that cathedrals in the Middle Ages were crammed full of memory aids?"

Now that surprised me. I was in a hurry to leave, but I couldn't leave until I heard about that.

"I came across it last night in a *History of Private Life* I'm reading," she said. "Ordinary people didn't have books in the Middle Ages, since the first printed book appeared much later. And even after that, you had to be rich as Pop to buy one." Pop inclined his head graciously as if that were a compliment.

"So the cathedrals were filled with pictures and carvings to remind people of stories from the Bible and the lives of the saints, symbols that people knew. For example, a phoenix meant the Resurrection. What do you think of that?"

"Not much." Pop shrugged. "I have pictures and things that bring back stories right in this house, and it's not the Middle Ages, and I could read until my damn eyes got so bad. I have those three monkeys that Nancy gave me: See no evil with the damn paws over the eyes, hear no evil, speak no evil. Nancy gave me those after Horace got drunk at Thanksgiving dinner and called me a sanctimonious son of a bitch just because I told Horace he'd had enough."

Arabella smiled, like he'd said something witty, and turned to me. "So a cathedral was designed to be covered with memory joggers, Peaches. What do you think of that?"

I said Wow, that was amazing, but logical with no printed books around in those days.

I was facing the bookcase in back of Pop. Yes. He could sure read. Or at least be read to. Financial statements and biographies. That's what Pop liked. And he sure did have memory joggers.

336

In front of *Churchill: A Life,* was the face jug that Roger gave Pop for good luck after his stock went down in 1987. Of course the stock went back up again. In front of *Ghengis Khan,* the horseshoe that Grandma from Madison County had kept since she was a child, also for good luck. In front of *Franklin and Eleanor,* those see-no-evil, hear-no-evil, speak-no-evil monkeys.

In front of *Adolf Hitler* stood that picture of my mother and Mary on Easter morning, admiring that cake I made with the Easter Bunny on it. The first fruit of that course I took on how to decorate cakes.

And then suddenly I had my almost-remember feeling. Something at the edge of my mind. Something serious. But I couldn't catch it.

I said: "If we were lucky, one of the objects in this house would be the key to whatever memory we need, to know who killed Aunt Nancy."

"That," said Pop, "is the most ridiculous thing I ever heard. I still think she was killed by a passing tramp."

Yes, and there were imaginary men with knives on the roof. But I wished he could be right about the tramp.

CHAPTER
27

LATER, ON THE WAY
TO CHARLESTON

The headlights shining on the road in front of us punctuated the dark. The moon was totally blacked out by clouds. Ted, of course, was driving. Some singer on the radio was wailing about the man she'd lost. Lost. Discomfort began in the center of me and spread out. So what bothered me about the word *lost?* And then I saw a picture of my overnight bag sitting right inside my front door. It was still there. That's as far as I'd gotten with it. It was not even as far as Pop's front door. I told Ted. "I'll just have to manage without it." I was annoyed.

"Don't be silly," he said. "We go five minutes from your house anyway. We can spare ten minutes." I thought God bless Ted for being so laid back.

My house is nowhere near a street light. In the dark, it seemed larger than in the daytime. A black hulk. We stopped in the driveway. The car lights brightened the inside of the garage. No one lurking there.

"I thought I left a light on inside the house," I said. Black night made my own familiar place mysterious. Even threatening. "I'm sure I left a light."

Ted took a small penlight out of the glove compartment. I thought of Aunt Nancy's heavy black flashlight that had vanished. At least Ted's was not large enough to be a weapon. Nobody could grab it and kill us with it. Which was a good bet for what had happened to Aunt Nancy. We hurried to the front door and I reached in my pocketbook for my keys. They were not fastened to the key ring on the inside of the pocketbook. Was it going to be one of those nights when I forgot to follow my own rules? Dumb. The keys were not in the depths of my pocketbook among the loose change, the two pens, and the small spiral notebook, the pocket knife, and the extra dime-store glasses I put there after the ice-maker debacle.

"I've lost my keys," I groaned. "But the backup keys are around in the rock garden in a special hollow rock I bought from a magazine ad. The rock is right at the base of the rosebush."

But it wasn't. We looked all over the rock garden with Ted's little penlight. A pinpoint in the dark. The shadows of the plant stems moved in the light. My own house seemed to glower at us, full of blackness. I wished I could be sure I *hadn't* left a light turned on. Then it wouldn't worry me. Finally we gave up on my rock. I hoped the killer hadn't read the same magazine and found my "rock." No. The magazine didn't tell I hid it by the rosebush. Time was passing.

"Never mind," I said, "we'll take the ladder from the garage, and break in the window on top of the side porch."

"You mean break a window in your own house? And then go off and leave the window unsecured?"

"O.K.," I said. "It's not smart. I could live without the overnight bag. But if we went off in such a mad rush that I didn't even follow my own rules about suitcase or keys, or leave the light on, like I always do, then God knows what else I did. Did you check to see the stove was off when we left?"

No. He hadn't. Neither had I. "I just have a hunch it's important for us to check out the house." I wished the house wasn't so forbodingly dark. I wished we had a bigger flashlight.

"All right, I'll go and look around inside," Ted said. "You shouldn't be climbing ladders." But I insisted I had to come. "It's my house we're breaking into, and I'm the one who left the bag and lost the key."

"That doesn't matter," he said.

"Yes, it does matter. If you forget things, you have to make a rule to do the things that make up for the trouble it caused. To make up for the trouble yourself."

He laughed. "I know you're sorry you forgot,

340

and, believe me, you'll be more trouble if you get another concussion."

That made me mad. "I will not fall off the ladder. And, listen, I don't believe for one minute that being sorry all over the place helps much. Being sorry gets old and bores people. I am not a bore. I'm coming with you to break in."

I did let him carry the ladder — with my aches, I gave in there. Ted set it against the side of the porch. Then he put his arms around me and kissed me, first on the tip of the nose and then on the mouth. He wore a nice spicy kind of after-shave. I had to struggle to stay mad. In fact, I gave up and thought how much nicer it would be to stand there for hours and kiss Ted rather than to go into that dark house. But this was not the time.

"Take care," he said. Then he stood back and held the ladder for me. I could have cried. He understood. He really understood that if you goof you have to be the one to ungoof, in order to feel O.K. I can't say that climbing the ladder did much for my aches, but it helped my spirit. He came up after me. We walked over to the bath-room window. The screen came off easily. Then I tried to raise the window from the outside, just in case, by happy chance, I'd forgotten to lock it. Why couldn't I forget the right things? The window wouldn't budge for me or for Ted either. Then I took off my shoe and broke the glass with the heel. The tinkle sounded loud in my ears. We knocked out the loose jagged pieces. I reached inside to unlock the window, and a voice boomed: "Stand still and don't move." I was so startled I whirled around and a flashlight shone in my eyes, one of those big powerful ones like Aunt Nancy's.

Whoever it was stood at the top of the ladder, judging by the height of the blinding light. The light began to move across the porch towards us.

Ted boomed back "Who are you? What are you doing here?" Very loud and clear as if he owned the place. That was the right attitude. He got an answer.

"Police. We're keeping an eye on this house. Who are you?"

I said "Thank God. I'm Peaches Dann. I live here. I left my key somewhere. We lost it, so we're breaking in." And then that sounded strange, so I explained further. "I think I left a light on in the house, and it's off. Will you help us look around inside?" Well, of course, the officer had to look us over and even check identification. Fortunately Ted had his wallet in his pocket. Flashlight was not one of the men I knew. But when he was sure we were us, he broke in with us. We turned on every light, and all of us searched the house. We couldn't find anything suspicious. Nobody was lurking in a dark corner. I'd been getting paranoid, I thought. My suitcase sat to one side of the front door where I suppose I thought I couldn't miss it. I underestimated my own talent. I needed to leave it right in front of the door, so I couldn't get out without it. At least the stove was not on. I hadn't left the water running. Things could have been worse.

We were standing inside the front door, about to leave, when I heard a siren. Oh, brother, all this commotion because I didn't anchor my key onto myself. And where could it be? I'd used it to lock the door when we left.

Flashlight said, "I radioed in that someone was breaking into this house."

The siren produced Mustache. He pounded on the front door, and we let him in out of the dark. He was, after all, in charge of our case. "Too bad," he said when he saw us. "I hoped the killer was breaking in."

"To set some new and more fiendish trap?" I shivered. And I'd been so pig-headed I was going to go off and leave the window open. Not that the killer had been deterred by locks.

Mustache wandered in and looked around for himself. He never seemed to hurry. Then: "We've had a new development," he told me. We were all in my living room. Things had calmed down enough so I remembered my aches. I sat down in the big armchair, also remembering I should be polite. I asked them all to sit down. Mustache did. Flashlight said he'd make one more check outside.

Mustache sat in the ladderback rocking chair by the fireplace, one of the chairs that Woody makes by hand over in Spruce Pine. Roger's favorite. Mustache had that portentous look on his face like a chicken about to lay an egg. "We have a new development," he repeated. "Someone in New York City tried to charge over a thousand dollars' worth of clothes to your Aunt Nancy's credit card."

"Wonderful!" I said. "Nobody in my family has been to New York recently. Does that let us all off the hook?"

"We've interviewed this woman," he said. "And she claims she found your Aunt Nancy's pocketbook in the parking lot of the Asheville airport. Can you think of a reason it would be there?"

I shook my head. "But you-all found the pocketbook on Elk Mountain Scenic Highway this week." I was thrown off base.

"The woman who used the card is named Florence Ells." He paused and waited for reaction. I'd never heard of Florence Ells, and judging by how quiet Ted was, he hadn't either. Ted was sitting on a stool on the other side of the fireplace from Mustache.

"Her mother lives on Beaverdam Road, not too far from Elk Mountain Scenic Highway." Mustache began to rock in the Woody chair. I figured he appreciated nice things. "Florence had come home from New York to see her mother, who is old and sick. She said her mother paid for the ticket. The daughter is evidently one of those people who manages to stay down and out, and doesn't care if you know it. But for some reason she prefers to be down and out in

New York City." Amazement made his words say *Why?*

He paused again, and looked first at Ted, then at me. But I didn't have a thing to add, and evidently Ted didn't either. Mustache went on: "Miss Ells said she found the pocketbook in the airport parking lot, and I guess advertising pays."

"Advertising?" Ted turned and stared at him. "How advertising?"

Mustache grinned. I could see he liked to amaze Ted, just like he liked to surprise me with nuggets for my book. Maybe he thought if we were amazed we'd tell more.

"Miss Ells said the wind blew a piece of newspaper past her feet. And on that newspaper was a picture of Buzzard's Rock. And she remembered the Buzzard's Rock lookout point was not far from the house where she was going. She said she figured a lookout point would be a good place to throw a pocketbook off the mountainside into kingdom come. So she took the credit cards, and then on the way to her mother's she threw the empty pocketbook off the side of the mountain."

"And we went there because of the same story! Boy," Ted said, "talk about the power of the press!" I could see that Ted the journalism teacher was pleased with that.

"And because it was dark, she didn't know the pocketbook only fell on the rocks just below!" I saw those rocks with their broken bottles in my mind. "How amazing no one had turned that pocketbook in sooner."

"It is," he said. "She told me she saw on the television that your Aunt Nancy had been killed and her pocketbook was missing. Then she was scared to tell us how she took it. She was afraid she'd bring suspicion on herself. But somehow, when she got back to New York after visiting her mother, she thought she could get away with using one of those credit cards in a small shop in New York City. She was wrong."

"And you believe what she told you?" I asked.

"She has no motive that we can find," Mustache said. "We've asked her to stay with her mother where we can reach her for a while. The mother seems delighted for every minute she can know where this Florence is."

I debated whether to point out that Ben traveled a lot. Spent a lot of time in airports. That's where Mary met him in San Francisco, right? Why didn't I tell Mustache that? Or even tell him we were going to Charleston? Maybe I felt like that would make Mustache more suspicious of Albert. I wanted to know how Albert fit into all this, myself, before I told the police. Besides, they should know their business. What was it Grandma said? "Don't teach your grandma how to suck eggs." She meant don't tell an expert how to do his business. Exactly.

When I was a little kid I always wondered why on earth Grandma knew how to suck eggs.

Conference over, I set about collecting myself.

If I forgot my suitcase again that would be the absolute end! I glanced around the living room. Was there anything else I could have forgotten? There was a cigarette butt in an ashtray. Good grief, could someone have come in the house and left that there? I have never smoked, and Ted has given it up. Oh, come on, Dummy, I told myself. Don't panic. It was Mustache. He was smoking. Remember? But my nerves were on edge. Sensitive to what did not fit. I even noticed a book that stuck too far out of the bookcase. A big one: *The Cambridge Biographical Dictionary*. Left from Roger's crossword puzzle days. I went over and pulled it out. A strange kind of red cylinder was behind it. In fact there were two of them. How odd. My heart speeded up. Too small to be a bomb? I hoped. And then I laughed. They were rolls of quarters, in those wrappers the bank supplies. Left from our shop days. I remembered the night I put them behind the book. We'd been talking about how we should have some money somewhere around the house in case of a sudden emergency. For some reason the quarters were on hand. A roll of quarters actually contains ten dollars. They add up. So we hid two rolls behind the book. Out of sight, out of mind. Even though that book must have stuck out slightly for five years, I'd never noticed it until I was afraid that something was out of kilter in my house. I pulled the rolls out. They didn't explode.

"What on earth are those doing there?" Ted asked.

And I explained. "The only good thing about losing money," I said, "is that if you find it years later it's a nice surprise. Like a gift from the gods." I felt that finding the quarters was good luck. I started to slip them in my pocketbook with my extra dime store glasses and my pocket knife. My pocketbook immediately weighed a ton. Think again. I hit one of the packages hard on the edge of the bookcase. That's how you crack them open. I put half of the quarters in one front skirt pocket, and was about to put the other half in the other pocket. I noticed that pocket number two bulged more than it should have. I stuck my hand in and felt. My keys! I never put them there, so I hadn't looked. I'd broken another rule: First look where you expect a thing to be and then where you *don't* expect it to be. I promised myself to reform. I fastened the keys in my pocketbook and then put the other half of the quarters in the second pocket. I was obeying that rule in spades. My book said, "Keep *plenty* of quarters handy in pockets in case of the need for emergency phone calls due to memory lapses."

Easy, because I had on my foreign correspondent's skirt. I'd bought it years before from the Banana Republic travel-clothes company, when Roger and I took a trip to South America. It was that kind of color and texture where you could go through a mud slide and nobody would ever notice. Comfortable, too! And best of all, it was covered with big pockets.

I put the second roll of quarters back behind

the book, for another nice surprise some day. Ted had grabbed my bag. I had my pocketbook. We were ready.

Finally we managed to set out for Charleston. Ted drove in silence. Something was bothering him. "I hope you're doing the right thing, trying to protect Albert in case he's in trouble," Ted said finally. "I don't think he seems like a killer, any more than you do. But suppose we're wrong?"

I had no answer. "Do you think we're wrong?"

He merely drove on through the night, considering that, I figured. Drove toward the airport, to be exact. We were going to pass it. We could go and look where Mustache said that woman claimed she found the pocketbook. But I was sure Mustache and his friends would have searched thoroughly. And it was late, and I ached. We did not search the airport. We drove on by. I almost dozed off, but Ted was wide-awake.

"I was amazed, back when I was covering murder trials," Ted said, "at how often the man or the woman who got convicted of murder looked out of kilter or weird. But not always. There was that woman who was convicted of poisoning her new husband and several other people. She looked like a middle-aged angel. And they say Ted Bundy was a charmer. He killed a lot of women before he was caught."

I shuddered, and thought "Please God, don't let me be wrong. At least not fatally wrong." And meanwhile we hurtled towards Charleston.

"I'm only going ten miles over the speed limit," Ted said. I think he had noticed my eyes on the speedometer. "And ten miles over the limit," he said, "is almost legal."

CHAPTER
28

DRIVING TO CHARLESTON

Ted kept his foot on the gas. "If we keep going as fast as we can," he said, "we'll get to Charleston in time for some sleep."

God knows I needed it. I felt like somebody was driving nails into me. I'd taken pain pills before I left my house, but they weren't up to the job. To sit up in a confined position in a moving car just days after driving off a mountain was no help at all.

The sky was still black as we approached Charleston. We drove to the end of I-26 and onto Meeting Street, heading toward the historic district, past lovely old houses with long side porches and gardens. I could only half-see them in the dark, but they were etched on my mind from my long-ago days at Ashley Hall. "You'd think living in a lovely place like this would bring out the best in somebody," I yawned. "Are there rotten apples in Paradise?"

Ted was still wide-awake. "The Boston strangler wasn't softened by lovely old Boston."

"No. He must have walked by with blinkers made of hate." I half woke up as we continued down Market Street. Back when I was a boarder at Ashley Hall, I loved the mystery of the old houses. They had walled gardens. Shutters covered the windows near the street as if wonderful secret things happened inside. But now I could imagine a warped killer hiding behind those shutters, not ready to look out on a blooming garden when daylight came, but in on his own ugly greed or lust for revenge.

We parked in the entryway in front of the King Charles Hotel, and Ted went in to register us and get our room keys. We could just stay until noon, the clerk told him. A convention was coming in. Never mind. At least we could get some sleep. We drove down into the garage under the building and took the elevator to our adjoining rooms. Ted said he'd place a wake-up call. He kissed me good night and said, "Sleep tight." That's exactly what Roger used to say. I was so tired I thought I was going to cry. I went into the bathroom, made a face at the tired old prune in the wall mirror, took two pain pills, took off my skirt and blouse, lay down on the bed, and fell asleep.

A dream woke me up with the help of morning rain and thunder, a nightmare. It was about my wedding in a big cathedral with red and green windows. Drums were rolling and trumpets blew

352

a fanfare. Everybody I knew was there, waiting: I saw Pop and Mary and Mustache, and rows of people I knew were all my relatives and friends. The minister stood at the front with his prayer book, waiting. Roger was there in a tuxedo to give me away, with a big smile. I had on a white lace dress with a long, long train. But I was in panic, and looking everywhere, tripping over the train. Because, through sheer carelessness, I'd lost the groom. I woke up with a scared stomach.

I joined Ted for breakfast in the small, cheerful hotel dining room. The rain streaked down the windows and occasional thunder boomed, almost like drums. Ted and I shared the *News & Courier*, which had a complete roundup on the work of rebuilding the city after Hurricane Hugo.

I wanted to reach over and smooth down Ted's cowlick. To tell the truth, I wanted to act like a small child and sit in his lap and feel safe and feel him breathing and rub my cheek against his cheek and. . . . But I was getting out of the small-child department.

Albert would be opening the shop soon. I had to keep my mind on that. We had agreed to be there as he opened the door. I settled for holding Ted's hand as we walked down to the car in the cave under the hotel. "I believe," I said, "that we are going to find out today who killed poor Larry and Aunt Nancy and tried to kill me."

He held my hand tight as we walked across the

shadowy garage. "The first rule," he said, "is that it's better to be a live coward than a dead hero. Dead heroes tell no tales." An especially loud clap of thunder punctuated his words.

We were early getting to the neighborhood where Albert hung his "Antiques and Lovelies" shingle. A wonderfully quaint neighborhood. The street was cobbled. We parked around the corner from the shop. Ted raised his big navy blue umbrella, and we walked along under it together, almost snug, and looked in the windows of other shops. There was a lull in the thunder and lightning even if the rain still poured down. I liked the shop full of all sorts of statues of pigs. One wearing a chef's hat, one with a wreath around its neck, one in a suit with vest, the kind of suit a human might have worn in the late 1800's. Fun. But we were not here for fun. In the next shop window a display of antique weapons seemed more appropriate to my mood. How would I protect myself if Ben should realize I thought he was the killer? And if, in fact, he was?

Act dumb — Ted was the one who'd told me that. The way I felt, that would be easy.

Albert's van pulled into the alley alongside his shop at just ten o'clock. A punctual type. He dashed through the rain, unlocked the door, and went in without seeming to notice us down in front of a window full of old clocks and chairs and quilts. "My grandma had a quilt like that," I'd just been telling Ted. I pointed out a huge many-pieced star in graduated colors. "I don't know who has it now. Nothing is permanent, is it?" I shivered and realized my feet were wet. I wanted us to be a little bit permanent, namely alive.

Albert came back out to get something from his van, leaning into the wind as always. Fighting an umbrella that wanted to be a kite. He saw us. "Good morning," he called cheerfully. "Surprise, surprise."

Then he froze in the middle of the sidewalk. The umbrella almost took off and carried him with it. "You're not coming with bad news?"

We hurried over, and I said, "No, good news. We're still in good health." Since I was aching, that was half a lie — but never mind.

He waved us inside as he retrieved an antique bird cage from the back of the van. I was always amazed at what became valuable if it was old enough. "Come in from the rain," he said. "What are you doing here in Charleston?"

"We've been under too much stress," Ted said. "We needed to get away and relax."

Albert looked from one of us to the other, so close under our umbrella, and I could see what was in his mind. That we were lovers. So, O.K. fine. I reached over and took Ted's hand again. He squeezed mine.

"Come on through to the back and have a cup of coffee," Albert said. "I've hooked up the bell that rings every time the door opens." He hurried us past the case of antique jewelry, mostly costume, which always fascinated me, past a shelf full of antique toys, past some ancient books about Charleston, and of course past the clocks he'd found and restored: I was always amazed at the variety of things that Albert knew about and collected. He hurried us under a Confederate sword, hung over the doorway to the back, and invited us to sit down in two metal folding chairs drawn up to a card table in the middle of the back shop. All around us were shelves of small antiques, from a clock with one broken steeple to a stone angel marked "sold." The ceiling light was dim, but a small lamp like a little spotlight sat on a work table in one corner.

He poured water into an electric coffee maker that stood on a shelf between a Victorian flowered teapot and an ancient doll baby, and put a filter with coffee into the top of the pot. "Ben is going to drop by shortly." He punched a switch on the pot which turned on a small red light. "It's amazing how well you look, Peaches, after that awful accident. Mary told me. I have always thought you were indestructible. Every man should have one indestructible cousin." His poet's eyes twinkled. He threw me a kiss. It was the first time I'd seen him in one of his rare good humors since Nancy died.

I sat down at the metal card table with my feet on a mellow old Bokhara rug, an odd combination of furniture and carpet.

"So, tell me more about the ring of people who are stealing Confederate belt plates," I said.

"Not just plates." He produced three assorted cups and saucers. "Anything from the Civil War. The Civil War is *in*."

"And so what is happening?"

"All I know," he said, pulling out a bowl of sugar- and creamer-envelopes, "is that there was a warning in one of the antiques magazines that there seemed to be some kind of a ring stealing Civil War memorabilia. That's really all I know." Or wanted to talk about, I thought.

At that moment the shop bell rang. Albert hurried to see who had arrived. He came back with Ben, who seemed out of place in this back room. Ben who always looked almost like the president of a bank.

Except he went too far in every way. As he came in with Albert, his aftershave extended around him like a cloud. His shoes were so polished, they looked ceramic. His suit was so dark, he could have moonlighted as an undertaker; he was shaved until his face shone like Albert's lusterware; his shirt was neon-white. He carried an oversized leather briefcase. "Good morning." He smiled, teeth flashing. Albert had told me Ben had his dentist paint them with something called "Rembrandt" to improve the color.

Albert introduced Ted to Ben. I'd met the man before. Why did I bother to dislike him so? "It's lovely to see you," he said to Ted and me. "I'm afraid I can't stay long. I am very fortunate to have a chance to bid on a collection of antique toys in Albuquerque. It's a private collection.

And I'm going to deliver some American primitive art to another collector."

I have to admit I was impressed by the interesting variety of deals he seemed to pull off. Ben unfolded another chair from against a wall and sat down with a flourish.

"You travel a lot," I said. "I seem to remember you were in Atlanta when Albert's mother died and had to rush back to take care of the shop."

His smile was half sneer. "And I was in New York just before your sitter was electrocuted, and in Dallas just before your car ran off the mountain." His hostile eyes said: *Don't try to be subtle with me.* He stood up. "I'm afraid I can't linger. I have a plane to catch."

It was Albert who became shaky, as if Ben's rudeness was a threat to him. His hands trembled as he gave Ben a flat wrapped package which he put in his briefcase. Ben bowed to us and left. Bowed. How European. I'd heard he was from Louisiana.

Albert gave us each our coffee. I was not quite sure what to say. We drank in silence. Then Ted asked, "Why does Ben have such a chip on his shoulder?"

Even if Albert wanted to answer, which I doubted, he didn't have much of a chance. We had just finished our coffee when the doorbell rang again. Albert went to the front of the shop. We followed him, ready to leave. There stood a three-hundred-pound woman who said she was looking for Kewpie dolls. And behind her came a thin, almost haggard man with a nose like a vulture, who wandered around looking at price tags. Customers.

I said we were going to enjoy the sights of Charleston and could we get together with Albert at five when the shop closed. We weren't going to learn much with customers in and out. Albert said great, he'd see us later.

So off we went under Ted's umbrella. I felt at loose ends, not sure what to do next. Wishing the rain would stop. Or at least that the thunder and lightning hadn't started up again.

We sauntered past the pigs. I specially liked the one in the three-piece suit. We climbed into the car and Ted said he figured we might as well drive along the Battery and enjoy the lovely old mansions that overlooked the water while we sorted out our thoughts.

"A gal I knew at Ashley Hall always writes me chatty notes on her Christmas cards." I told Ted. "Last year she mentioned a good informal restaurant she'd found when she came back to visit Charleston. It's called the Moultrie Tavern, and it's full of all sorts of Civil War memorabilia. Let's go there and have lunch and see what we see."

"Always combine business with pleasure," Ted advised. We stopped at an antique shop and asked how to get there. Then off we went.

But we'd hardly gone a couple of blocks when Ted said, "Somebody is following us who is not good at it. He's driving a blue car." I turned and looked. I might have missed the car about a block behind us, but where we turned, the car turned too. We drove slowly past the tavern, an old brick building down near the waterfront. Then Ted drove back around away from the water. The car still followed. Ted found a place to park in a street of shops. We wove our way on foot back to the tavern, with its gold-lettered sign and a Confederate flag on one side of the double front door and the free-standing figure of a drummer boy on the other. The blue car was not in sight. I couldn't spot anyone following us. We went inside.

The Moultrie Tavern was stuffed full of all sorts of bits and pieces found at the site of the Yankee attack on Fort Sumter. All labeled. Old bottles were on the windowsills. Around the walls were glass cases with buttons, fragments of glass bottles, even a rusted pistol, and photographs of Confederate soldiers.

The waiter who came to take our order was young, a college kid perhaps. He gave us big menus complete with a picture of General William Moultrie, a delegate to the Continental Congress in 1775. Say, this tavern commemorated two wars. It was named for a Revolutionary War hero "as was customary in the 1800's," the menu said, but was "typical of establishments here in Charleston in 1862." So, O.K. I ordered Confederate Bean Soup with sausage and a Blockade salad. Ted ordered a Foot Soldier's Sandwich with beef and cheese.

Before our waiter left, we asked him who collected the Civil War artifacts in the cases. He immediately brought over an intense young man who turned out to be the owner, introduced as a real Civil War buff. Did he know much about Confederate belt plates?

Oh, yes. He seemed pleased that I asked. He brought us a big black book with a gold title down the spine: *Plates and Buckles of the American Military — 1795–1874.* He sat down in the empty chair next to me and eagerly explained there were many kinds of flat brass fasteners called plates: plates for sword belts, shoulder and cross belts, cartridge-box belts, and even for cartridge boxes.

Then he left us the book to study, and I found a picture of a "waist belt plate" a little like the one Albert sold Ma. I showed it to Ted. The same small oval with a hook on the back, and two large initials on the front: C S. Small stars surrounded the C S.

"Some of the other kinds are more fun to look at," I told Ted as we turned to Union plates with eagles on them. Confederate plates with stars, palm trees, and even state seals. Louisiana's had a pelican. "Those shiny brasses must have made the soldiers look snappy."

"And sometimes killed them," Ted told me. "It says here they went out of style because they made such good targets for enemy riflemen."

Now there was a horrible thought. We found a whole series of pictures of plates with bullet holes. How often, I wondered, do we dress ourselves up as targets and not even know it?

Our lunch came and I gave the book back to our host. We didn't want to get soup or salad on *Plates and Buckles*. "Have you heard of any belt plate thefts?" I asked him. No, he hadn't. So where was this leading us?

I ate my soup, which was filling enough for any soldier, and was about to attack the salad when Ted grabbed my arm. "Don't look out the window," he said. Of course he meant there was something worth looking *at* out the window, but, surprised as I was, I made myself sit still. "That friend of Nancy's, that John Denton, is out there. I'm going to catch up with him and find out what on earth he's up to. You stay here." Well, thanks a heap.

Ted came back towing John Q. Denton, who did not even seem to mind. "Sit down," Ted said in a heavy whisper, as if he had a rifle to Denton's back. Denton sat. "Now, why are you here?" Ted demanded.

Old Yankee Accent didn't lose his cool. He was still deliberate and logical as a robot. "I'm following you because you're acting strangely."

"What!" Ted and I both said at once. I think we meant "How?" or "Why you?"

"You broke into your own house," he said to me. "I heard it on the police-band radio. So I drove over and saw you two take off, speeding all the way. I had trouble following you," he complained to Ted.

"Are you trying to play detective, for God's sake?" Ted asked.

Yankee Accent squared his shoulders. "I have a right as much as you do," he said. He was as intense as Ralph Nader. Then he softened slightly. "I've made some interesting discoveries."

Was he offering to trade? I knew I should encourage him.

"I broke into my house because I forgot my suitcase," I explained. "And then lost the door key, and then I thought I'd left the light on." Farfetched, but he seemed to accept it. The waiter came over, and Yankee Accent ordered coffee, as if he was a casual visitor.

As soon as the waiter was gone he turned back to me: "And after you broke into your house, why did you come speeding off to Charleston?" This man could have worked for the Grand Inquisition.

"I was driving and I always speed," Ted broke in. "I have a speeding ticket to prove it. But I'm going to reform to please Peaches."

Yankee Accent pursed his lips and frowned. He was not amused.

I said, "We came down here hoping to find clues because we weren't getting anywhere at home. We might be able to help each other." Ted was nodding.

"We may know one thing you don't," I said.

"Very well," he said. "You give me a new fact.

363

I'll give you a new fact."

So I gave him the fact about the belt plate. Told him it appeared to have been stolen in California a little while before the time Nancy was killed. That Albert said it was worth thousands of dollars. Then I sent him over to ask our host to show him the picture of the other Confederate plate like the one that was stolen from Pop. I did not tell Yankee Accent about the Ben connection. I still didn't entirely trust him.

"What will you trade us for that information?" Ted asked when he came back.

Y.A. smiled coyly: Now that was certainly a contrast to his Marine haircut and button-down collar. "I have been able to tell the police something they didn't know!" So he was human enough to want to brag.

He lowered his voice and leaned forward. "Somebody let Arabella Horton's horses loose the night your Aunt Nancy was killed."

Now that did surprise me. "And she tried to hide that?" Arabella, who was presumably keeping an eye on Pop at that very moment, was not what she seemed?

"No." Yankee Accent confided. "She didn't try to hide it. She didn't think it was important. Some kid in the neighborhood let them out twice before as a prank. She said he was mad that she wouldn't let him ride her horses. She figured it was the same thing."

"But she didn't tell anybody. That's strange."

He regarded me like I was silly. Even with

scorn. "The horses were all nearby in the morning. She had them back where they belonged several hours before she heard about Nancy. And she was so shocked about Nancy she forgot about the horses." He bristled with self-satisfaction.

"So how did you find out?" Ted asked.

"I went by to see her. She's lonely. She showed me her horses, and she told me about the bad kid who'd let them out before. I asked for the dates." He was becoming positively chummy. I decided he was lonely just like Arabella.

"But maybe it *was* the kid!" I said.

He beamed with self-congratulation. "The kid was away in Florida with his family at a family wedding! His mother told me that. I told her I was looking for people who might have heard something that night. I told her I was a friend of Nancy's." He looked so pleased with himself, I thought he might explode. "I found that out about the kid just a short while before I heard you were breaking into your house, and followed you down here."

People from other tables were beginning to stare at us. I realized we'd been raising our voices. I lowered mine.

"So what does this mean?" I asked. But I knew what it must mean before he said it. If the killer let the horses loose, and if he did it because he needed to borrow one, then he or she had come to Pop's without a car, had come with Nancy, perhaps, and not wanted to drive away in her car. But this only made the picture more confusing.

"Who lived far enough," I asked, "so that they needed a horse to get them safely home, but near enough so that the horse could find its way back to Arabella's by the morning?" I asked myself if it could be Mary. She was a ten-minute drive away from Arabella's. So was Nancy's house, but Nancy hardly rode away on a horse when she was lying in the pond dead.

"I don't know horse logistics or even horse habits," I said.

Whereupon Yankee Accent said he had been intending to look for the nearest U. S. Agricultural Extension agent, or some other animal expert. He was ready to charge off. Evidently he figured we checked out O.K., though he made us promise to call him in the evening at the Hampton Inn, where he said he was going to stay.

I was glad to get rid of him. The horse bit might be a help. But I sensed he was erratic. I believed we'd learn more without Yankee Accent at our heels.

Even with all that excitement, I'd finished my lunch. "We can go see Nancy's Charleston relations," I suggested. "Mustache says they claim they didn't even know Nancy was in Charleston. They're really Horace's family. But since we have the time, we can check them out for ourselves. They didn't get along with Nancy worth two cents."

Our host now considered us fellow Civil War

buffs and he let me use the phone. Nobody answered. Albert's grandmother was in such bad health that I was surprised she was out. Maybe she was at the doctor's.

So then we had the bright idea of going to the Gibbes Museum and checking out the miniature paintings. Sure enough, their collection was so large that even with some on loan we found a whole room full of the tiny jewellike portraits in glass cases: wonderful tiny replicas of gentlemen with lace at their necks, ladies in bonnets, charming children. Some of them dated back to the eighteenth century. Some much later. One young man wore his Civil War uniform complete with belt plate. But the plate was so tiny I would have needed a magnifying glass to see the design. One portrait of a young woman appeared to have been painted in the 1920's. Some of the tiny pictures were mounted in intricate frames, some in plain gold frames. Immediately I understood how we'd undervalued ours. Ma hadn't. She'd kept it in a special display stand on her bedside table. But after she was gone it somehow drifted to the edge of a bookshelf. Who moved it? Not me. I wasn't sure when it vanished.

"Maybe we should talk to the curator," I said. I couldn't see exactly how that would help our detection, but it might. "First I'll go to the ladies room. I haven't fixed my lipstick since lunch."

I instinctively reached for my pocketbook, where my lipstick lives.

But my pocketbook was not hanging over my

shoulder. Oh, brother. I'd lost it.

Ted said I might have left it in the car. We searched there. Even under the seats. No luck. We found a pay phone and called the Moultrie Tavern. It wasn't there. The last time I could remember having my pocketbook was in Albert's shop.

I groaned. "I know what's wrong. The moon is full. When the moon is full I write poetry and get more absent-minded." But this was a lousy time to be absent-minded.

"We'd better go back to the shop and get it," Ted said. "You wouldn't want Albert to sell it for an antique."

I pictured that shop so crammed full of everything in the world. And God knows where I left my pocketbook, maybe some place that Albert might not notice but a customer might. I certainly didn't want my pocketbook, complete with my house key, to be stolen.

Ted looked at his watch: "Three-thirty," he said.

And then I had a bright idea, or so I thought. "Maybe," I said, "we're better off going back to see Albert right now, even aside from finding my pocketbook. I mean, just by arriving here this morning when he didn't expect us, we've thrown Albert off base in his relationship with that creep Ben. Did you see how agitated Albert was when Ben got upset?"

By five o'clock, when we're due back at the shop, Albert'll be all pulled together. He's not dumb. But if we drop in a little early, when he doesn't expect us, Albert may do something that could give us a hint of what's going on, maybe even a clue of what kind of hold that man has over him. Because I still think Ben is suspect number one. I wonder if Ben knows how to ride a horse?"

CHAPTER
29

LATE THAT AFTERNOON

We found Albert alone. He hurried toward us from the back room as soon as we opened the door to the shop and the bell on the door jangled. He'd changed since morning. He'd become Somebody-Done-Me-Wrong Albert with the sad eyes and pouting mouth.

"Albert, I left my pocketbook," I said crisply. You had to be firm with Albert when he was in that mood.

He started. "You mean it's been here all along?" He glared at me like I'd tricked him. He looked like he'd like to grab the Civil War sword off the wall and run us out of the shop at sword point. But why?

"I'll just look around," I said, heading for the back room. He came along with me, hovering. Ted came, too. In fact, Ted's sharp eyes spotted my pocketbook quick. There it sat on a shelf between a pair of brass andirons with a "sold" sticker on them and a pair of black iron hand-cuffs, of all things, lying on a section of white paper towel. Handcuffs were a kind of antique I certainly never thought about. But why not?

My pocketbook is a kind of earth-red color, designed to go with everything, and it had vanished in the shadows between brass and white, but not from Ted.

Albert smiled like he was going to forgive us. "Well," he said, "you're all set for now. I'll see you at five o'clock." I thought: He really wants us out of here now.

Before we could say a word, the commotion started: the doorbell, and then soprano shrieks and a low bass rumble. We ran to the front, and there was the three-hundred-pound Kewpie-doll woman and a policeman. "That's it, over the door," she was screaming to the policeman. "I know it's my father's. There's a nick in the blade. My great-grandfather carried that sword in the Battle of Shiloh. And it's mine when my father dies. Mine. I may not have anything else, but that's going to be mine."

Albert stayed perfectly calm. "She will have to be quiet," he said to the policeman, "or I can't explain."

"I don't want him to explain," the woman shouted. "I want him arrested. I went to my father's house to check. The sword's gone. It's all I have." I could believe the last bit. Her tent dress was picked polyester knit. Her shoes were scuffed.

The policeman managed to quiet her down by saying he wouldn't arrest Albert, no matter what, unless she shut up. He put it more tactfully than that, but not much. He was large, too — large and short of breath and red in the face, like either his collar was too tight or he had a short temper.

I was standing in back of Albert, holding my breath. Was whatever had gone bad unraveling? Was my Aunt Nancy's death related somehow to the Civil War? My plunge over the mountainside due to a sword nicked at the Battle of Shiloh? Past, present, even future, all so intertwined?

Albert didn't act like he was alarmed. He didn't even tremble as he had when Ben got mad. In a perfectly calm voice, he began to tell the policeman that his partner had bought the sword in person, from an elderly Charleston aristocrat. That he had papers with the provenance. My heart beat hard. So had Ben lied to Albert? Forged false papers?

While Albert explained, I quietly slipped into the back room. Ted would witness any more ruckus in front. I began to examine every object in the room, beginning with those on the shelves — a strange assortment, from the small stone angel to a big mailing tube which must have had posters or a picture rolled up inside, to a small bottle of pills marked NoDoz, to a roll of paper towels on one end of a shelf. For dusting, perhaps? Albert was meticulous.

Albert had acted upset when we arrived and

headed for that room unannounced. Why? Could it somehow be related to Kewpie Doll and her accusation? I had the strangest feeling that it was. But how would I even know what was suspicious in that room full of unrelated objects? Each with its own story of the past. There was only one story I knew part of. My mother had almost bought that Oriental rug under the table from Albert — or, no, its twin. This one had a hole in a corner. Pop had said the rug Mom liked was too expensive and, while Pop waited to see if Albert would come down on the price, my mother had died.

I noticed the Oriental rug was wrinkled. Earlier, it had been lying flat.

Albert came into the back room with the policeman, eyeing me like I was a traitor to witness his accusers. He went through the top drawer of the green metal file cabinet in the dim corner and came up with a piece of paper that he waved like a flag. "Here," he said coldly, "is the bill of sale!"

Kewpie Doll, right at the policeman's heels, reached over and grabbed it. She gasped, "Oh, no!" She sat down in one of the folding chairs. "He sold it! The old bastard! He promised it to me, and he sold it! That's his signature. I'd know it anywhere with that big bold writing." And she burst into tears. "He only cares about himself," she sobbed. "Not my children. Not tradition. Not family glory." I hoped the folding chair would hold her up.

So this circus wasn't going to get us anywhere.

I was glad for Albert. Sorry for Kewpie Doll. Disappointed for me. I felt like I deserved to find just one strong clue as to who it was that tried to kill me. And succeeded with Nancy, and maybe killed poor Larry by mistake.

Albert, the policeman, and Kewpie Doll went into the front of the shop. Which is to say that the policeman took Kewpie Doll by the arm, helped her stand up, and towed her along, still sniffling. I heard the door shut behind them, or so I thought, but then I heard the rumble of the policeman's voice still talking to Albert. Ted winked at me, sidled over to the file cabinet, adjusted his wire-rim glasses, and began to examine the bill of sale.

I looked around me. The most suspicious thing I could find in the back room was the wrinkle in the rug. It had definitely been flat on our first visit. And the feet of the folding chairs and the card table should have held it flat. I tried to ignore the wrinkle. This was no time to explore it, with Albert in the next room. If that wrinkle meant anything, it could mean that Albert was dangerous. Mild Albert?

My eyes fell on a picture of a gold-haloed saint in a gold-leaf frame, sitting on the shelf by a small steeple clock. And I thought, Why, in a way, Albert's shop is like a cathedral. Where every picture or carving is designed to bring to mind a story. The way the sword was family glory to poor Kewpie Doll. And so she mourned it. Every object had been a memory jogger to someone for something he wanted to remember, or to forget. I felt like crying, which seemed ridiculous. And then the oddest picture floated into my head.

It was Albert's clay rabbit, with the spots like a leopard, that he made in kindergarten. Which sits on the windowsill in Pop's kitchen, and made Elsie laugh. It had its story. I began to shiver. Oh, my God, it was a self-portrait. Suppose I knew Albert's hurting rabbit side, so I hid from his danger, from his leopard spots.

I heard the door to the shop shut. The policeman was gone. Another jingle. Someone else entered the shop. I found myself thinking of the Swiss Army knife in my pocketbook, the one on hand for slitting trash bags into raincoats, and opening cans at picnics in a pinch. The nearest thing I had to a defensive weapon. Maybe I ought to have it totally handy, just in case. A high-pitched woman's voice asked about teaspoons, and I heard Albert say, "Over here."

I remembered my rule. A thing is harder to lose if it's part of your body. I wanted the knife hidden on my body, almost like a part of it, in some place that a killer would not expect. I took a piece of Albert's string and made a loop through the small loop on the end of the knife. I tied it with a slipknot so that a good yank would pull the knife free. I hung the knife around my neck and under my blouse. Not that I really suspected Albert.

But Albert could ride horseback. As a kid he

loved the sports you could do alone. Suppose he came to Pop's with Nancy? And left his own car at her house, ten minutes away? And rode one of Arabella's horses back to his car? I had no proof. I swung to the other extreme. Thank God I had no proof.

But I had to try to find it. A wrinkle in a rug is a small thing, but it drew me because it shouldn't be there. I heard the voices in front ramble on. As quickly as I could, I moved the chairs and card table far enough back to fold up one side of the rug. Ted hurried over to help, glancing nervously toward the front room. The floor beneath the rug was slightly uneven. I poked at it this way and that, and by gosh I got a couple of boards to lift off, like the top of a box. In the dim recess underneath we could see an assortment of small objects, some square, some oval, and I knew with a rush of blood to my ears and a sick lurch in my stomach that one of them was the little portrait Pop lost.

I knelt beside the cache in the floor and picked up the small oval portrait. The face that was supposed to look a little bit like mine stared back at me. Ted whispered, "Good God." Two other miniature portraits and a number of antique "plates" lay in the box in the floor. One plate had stars on it, so exactly like Pop's that I was sure it was the same one.

My mind jumped to conclusions so hard, it felt like a blow. Albert stole those things. Albert had that bottle of NoDoz pills. Albert could have killed his mother for finding this secret, just as I had found it. He could have killed her at night and been back in the store five hours away in Charleston when I called in the morning. All he had to do was go a night without sleep. He must have done that. Must have phoned his neighbor long distance. To leave that message on the answering machine. I felt staggered.

More pictures flew to my mind: Albert driving up from Charleston at night, Albert in my dark garage with a flashlight, tampering with my brakes. Albert in the closet in Pop's back room, with a flashlight again, hot-wiring the trap that killed Larry. I shuddered. Albert who could fix clocks, and what else? The room around me felt hot with danger. Ted felt it too. His hands flew as he helped me put the rug back, as fast as we could even before we heard the teaspoon woman leave. Without speaking, we each knew that we agreed. We needed to know more before we confronted Albert. Mild Albert! If he was the killer, he was probably armed.

God knows how we got that table and rug back in place as fast as we did. I was still moving the last chair back when Albert came through the door to the back. I tried to act nonchalant, as if I were just rearranging the furniture to look better. Albert's eyes went straight to the floor, and back to me.

"Well, you certainly showed that Confederate-sword woman how wrong she was," I said. Ted came and stood so close in back of me I could feel his warmth. I could feel from the hesitation in his breathing that he thought what I thought — there was a chance Albert knew what we'd found, but an equal chance we could bluff our way.

Albert looked from my face to Ted's. He glanced again at the floor where the rug was now flat. He turned dead white.

"You found it, didn't you?" he said straight out. "The hiding hole." He squeezed his eyes shut and shook his head "no," as if he could make us dematerialize from his shop. Then he opened his eyes, swallowed, and said, "I'm almost glad. I've been worried sick about that stuff. And what if the police found it? They'd think I had a motive."

Relief rushed through me. Albert was going to explain. This wasn't what it looked like, I told myself. Albert wouldn't kill just for money. Why, when he was a little kid he sometimes saved his allowance to take me to the movies. I knew I was right. I congratulated myself.

"Yes," I said. "Exactly. So why in God's name did you hide Pop's Confederate belt plate and his little portrait and that other stuff under the floor, of all places, as if you were a thief?" I wanted him to have an innocent reason so bad, I was trembling.

"I won't lie to you, Cousin Peaches. I am an accessory to theft." He said it like a challenge, but his voice was hoarse. With shame and fear? He lowered those poet's eyes and stared at the floor.

"And I'm trapped. I don't know what to do. And the police would think I killed to hide that. But you know me well enough to know I would never kill my mother on purpose. You believe me, don't you?" He raised his eyes to mine.

I was confused, but I thought I believed him.

"Sometimes I hated my mother, but I also loved her. You know that." With one hand he loosened the open collar of his shirt, as if it was too tight.

Yes, I did know that.

"Listen," he said, in a rush, "Ben does the books now, and about six months ago he showed me how we were beginning to do well. The shop was making a good profit. Before that we'd just scraped by. I was so happy." He smiled, as if he could bring that back. His eyes begged. "I wanted to feel like there was *something* I could be good at."

Well, I could understand that.

"And then I found the secret spot where Ben was hiding things. When I took him by to visit Pop, he even stole the belt plate and the little portrait. I was sick, Peaches. I didn't know what to do. A business like ours would be ruined if people didn't trust us. Especially here in Charleston. They still believe in honor.

"But Ben told me he was a kleptomaniac. It was a sickness. He did it when he was under strain. I was trying to figure out what on earth to do, when someone killed my mother. Then I didn't dare tell anyone. I was frozen." He shivered like he meant frozen from real cold. "I didn't want to call attention to myself or to Ben. For God's sake, he's not a killer. Only a kleptomaniac."

"But before your mother died, she found out," I said. It was a guess. But spying out would be like Nancy. Albert's gasp showed I was right. Good old self-righteous Nancy. She must have had a fit. And scared Ben, if he knew.

Albert began to tremble. "You don't know how bad it was. I loved Ma. She was difficult. You know that. But she was the one who I could count on growing up. When I needed my father, he was always drunk. You remember. When she found those stolen things, I couldn't bear for her to think what she thought."

The clocks picked that moment to begin to chime. Clocks all over the shop that Albert found and fixed. Some with a deep chime, some with a friendly tinkle. Each striking five times, in counterpoint.

A trembly smile twitched his mouth: "I'm a useful person. I find beautiful things and I save them. My mother didn't appreciate that. Your father didn't appreciate that. He didn't even take care of that little portrait or the belt plate I sold your mother, Peaches."

"What happened with *your* mother, Albert?"

He cast his eyes around the room, as if he was looking for a way to escape. I kept my eyes hard on him, waiting.

His voice broke, but he went on. "I actually

had the little portrait out on the table in the back. I did. Studying that lovely thing. Trying to figure how to get it back to Pop without his knowing. Then *she* barged into the shop. I came to the front when I heard the bell. I knew I had to keep her out of the back.

"But she reads my face." His voice rose with anger, as if she was still around to do it. " 'What are you hiding?' she said. Not 'Hello,' or 'How are you, dear,' but 'What are you hiding?' She was psychic in the wrong ways, Peaches. When I was a child, she used to say, 'I can always tell when you're lying. You get that look on your face.' And I swear that look would come for her. As if it were a dog and she could call it. My mother had a killer instinct. Sometimes I got that look when I was telling the truth and couldn't prove it. Because she waited for it. She wanted it. My God, she needed somebody to get mad at."

"Albert," I said firmly. "Stick to the story. Tell us what happened."

"She walked straight into this back room. She stood here, right where you're sitting, Peaches. I walked faster than she did and managed to stand in front of the portrait. But that just told her where to look. 'Your Uncle Harwood owns that!' she yelled at me. 'By God, you stole it! I thought you had.' And then she got that steely calm way I hate, and then went on: 'You've had that look on your face off and on for two months. I knew you were up to something. You got tha look when Peaches said she didn't know where the portrait was.' "

And why hadn't I noticed any special look? Until a few days ago, I hadn't even realized the portrait was that important. Ted was standing by me, perfectly silent. Figuring, I guessed, that Albert was my cousin. That I knew how to handle him.

"She'd never trusted me," Albert cried. Tears came to his eyes. "She thought I was going to be like my father and tell lies. So she set out to prove I stole the portrait. My own mother."

"Is that why she went into Pop's safe deposit box?" I asked. I had to keep Albert on track. "She went to check if it was there?"

"Of course. She searched the box because you said the portrait and that belt plate might be there. She said that was the last place left to look. She made up her mind I stole the picture because it wasn't in the box. Without any proof." He clenched his hands together. His voice shook.

" 'I'm going to fix the frame,' I told her, 'to surprise Uncle Harwood.' But I could feel that look turning my face to wood.

"She was already in one of her fits. 'You are coming with me now, to take this back to Harwood and apologize. There is nothing wrong with this frame. What do you think I am? A fool?

" 'I won't be the mother of a thief,' she yelled at me. 'But this time you can return the picture ᵃnd apologize. Unless you want me to go to the police. If you were as damn smart as you think you are, you wouldn't lie and steal. You've always lied.' And then she brought up the way I used to steal money from my father's pockets. Well, why not, for God's sake? He'd've just lost it at the race track. And yes, I did lie about that. But I used that money to buy my first clock I fixed." He looked around him at the ticking clocks. "I used it to do something useful. Why couldn't she ever see the good side of me? Why couldn't we have been friends? Now it's too late. She's gone." Tears began to stream down his face.

"Albert, you snap out of this," I commanded. "You have to pull yourself together. We have to figure out what to do now. Don't you see that the only way to prove you didn't kill your mother is to find out who did it? And not just to save yourself. There are people who count on you." I was thinking of Elsie. Of Albert and Elsie kissing. "Mary does," I said. "And am I wrong about Elsie?"

Albert crossed his arms, hugging himself. His eyes went sharp and then flat with the worst look of despair I'd ever seen on his face. My goodness, I wondered what had gone wrong there. But the tears dried up.

He nodded in a dispirited way. His eyes swept the room again, as if he was looking for a clue to his mother's killer. "I've been thinking about that. I have, Peaches." His voice lost strength. "Someone my mother cornered killed my mother." His voice grew stronger. "You know she cornered people. That's why my father drank. So he wouldn't be able to do what she'd tried to corner him into doing. I'm sure of that." His voice broke, like it did when he was a teen. "But whoever killed my mother, it was my fault because I couldn't do what she asked me to do."

I was annoyed. Albert was going to get even more maudlin. He was always at his worst when he was sorry for himself. But I took my cue from Ted, who just stood quietly and listened. Right. No telling what Albert might spill. It might all be lies, like his mother said. But I didn't think so. I was sure Albert preferred telling the truth. And he was telling us a lot of the truth. But not the whole truth. That was my gut hunch.

"My mother grabbed the little portrait and she said, 'This ought to be in our family.' " Albert was rambling again. "She said, 'The long neck and the eyes with that silly twinkle are so much like your cousin Peaches. Peaches never lies. And God knows she has a handicap. She's scatterbrained as they come.' That's what she thought of you, Peaches. She said, 'Now, you close up this shop and come back to Asheville with me and apologize to your uncle!' She acted like I was six years old. That's what she thought of me. 'You get in my car this minute,' she said. 'You come with me right now, or I go to the police!'

"So I said I'd go, but I wouldn't go in her car. I couldn't stand a lecture all the way to Asheville.

I said I'd go in convoy." He swallowed a sob. "And if I hadn't said that — if I'd just gone with her — she might still be alive." He stopped, struggling with tears.

"Why?" I asked.

"You see, I went as far as the rest area in Skyland. Then I had to go in and pee. Even my mother couldn't prevent that. I'd told her I'd meet her at your father's house if we got separated, and then we did, and I lost my nerve. I went back to Charleston, Peaches. I couldn't bear the confrontation. What could I say to make it better? I could accuse Ben. But I need Ben. He makes this business work.

"But, oh God, I should have gone. If I'd just gone along with what she wanted, she might not have been killed." Now he sounded so upset, I was inclined to think he was telling the truth.

"Did Ben have any way to know you'd gone off with your mother or why?"

Albert flushed. "We were yelling, I guess. The windows in the back room were open. That wasn't very smart."

"What do you know about Ben?" I asked. "Did you know he was in San Francisco at the time of a big theft of Confederate artifacts there? Did you know he met Mary there? And she kept it a secret. Why are you so sure Ben is just a kleptomaniac? And, by the way, is the back window open now? Could someone hear us now?"

Albert turned white. He closed a barred

window at the back of the room. "I'm not street-wise enough to be a crook," he said bitterly. "My mother was right."

With that, the bell at the front door rang. Albert ran to the front to intercept whoever it was.

Ted whispered, "Do you believe him?"

"Partly," I whispered back. "On and off. Like a loose wire."

"He's not being logical." Ted said.

No. "He's either protecting Ben or Mary or himself." I said. "But he's not functioning right."

He nodded. "Why on earth did he keep the evidence here!"

Suddenly the black flashlight came into my mind. The one that vanished from Nancy's car. That Mustache said could have been the murder weapon.

My eyes went straight to that mailing tube, lying on the shelf next to a Victorian glass paperweight. A shudder passed through me. The flashlight would just exactly fit inside. Talk about keeping the evidence here. I had to check. Albert was still talking to someone out front. I hurried to the shelf. I wiggled the end off the mailing tube. I poked my finger inside. No flashlight. Just some paper coiled inside. I was so relieved I could have cried. And then alarmed. I couldn't get the damn cap back on the tube. I heard the shop door close. And here came Albert's footsteps. I pushed the tube back on the shelf quick and hoped he wouldn't notice the top wasn't on.

Albert came back carrying a paper bag. He set it on the shelf near his elbow. "Who was that in the shop?" I asked.

"Ben," he said. He swallowed. "His flight was canceled due to the weather. He's going in the morning." I felt a jolt of alarm. Ben was the one who made my skin crawl. And why hadn't he let Albert know sooner? That was odd.

"Did you tell him we were here?"

"Yes. He's going by his house. He'll be back. If you want to, you can ask him about San Francisco. I know he can explain." He said that so calmly. But I was quite sure that with Ben back we were out of our depth. And my Albert hunch did a flip-flop. Albert was lying.

Albert glanced around. We made him nervous. He didn't trust us. His eyes stopped at the mailing tube with the cap off.

He turned toward the shelf in back of him and I heard a rustle as he reached into the paper bag he'd brought. When he turned back toward us, he was holding a gun. Not a pretty little antique gun, but a black businesslike pistol. Pointed at us. "I keep this in the cash register," he said. "You're so clever, Cousin Peaches. I was afraid I might need it. You're looking for my mother's flashlight, aren't you? It would just fit in that tube. But it's not there. I'm not that dumb. It's in the bottom of the Ashley River. You're just like me. You're not as clever as you think you are. And you don't believe me. I can't take a chance on that.

"I didn't kill my mother on purpose. It was a mistake." His voice went up as if he was still surprised. "I got so mad when she cornered me, I went out of control. But who would believe that?"

"And when Ben comes back and you accuse him of killing my mother, he'll be mad. Because he doesn't know I killed my mother. And if anyone finds out I did it, I will have ruined his business. And to tell you the truth, I'm a little bit afraid of Ben, myself."

CHAPTER
30

IMMEDIATELY AFTERWARD

So staying alive might depend on Cold-Snake Ben. On somehow persuading him it was in his own interest not to let Albert kill us. What a job.

Albert the Collector was now collecting murders. There he stood, surrounded by his things. In back of his head on the shelf were wooden candlesticks, sticking up almost like he had devil horns. On a level with his left hand was what looked like a red velvet Victorian bell-pull, neatly coiled like a snake. And the clocks ticked.

"You tried to kill me," I said to Albert. "I've been your friend all these years, and you tried to kill me."

He didn't answer. He turned to Ted. "All right," he said. "Sit down in that nearest chair. Hurry up — sit! You thought you could trap me, didn't you? You both thought that." He was more than nervous now. His eyes were wild, his nostrils distended like a horse trapped in a fire.

"And you," he said to me, "take this twine and tie him up, one hand to each side of the chair, one leg to each chair leg." Albert's eyes might be wild but his voice was cold and sure. He threw me a ball of the string they used for packages. Automatically, I caught it.

But I said "No. If you want to tie us up, *you* do it."

"If you don't do exactly what I say, I am going to shoot you both." He waved the gun. He seemed right on the edge. Ready to shoot. I began to tie Ted's hands. I felt so dumb. I couldn't think how to get my knife out and open it. I couldn't think how to use my only weapon against a gun. I thought how wonderful Ted's hands were. Strong and sure, and so mobile when he talked, so reassuring when he held my hand in his. And I was taking the power from his hands. Tying him up. And I loved him. I thought, Dear God, yes, I do. And he'd be better off tied up than shot. But not much.

"Come on," Albert barked, "round and round the wrists. Use plenty of string. Tighter than that! Come on. If that ball runs out, I have more. I'm watching."

When I had Ted tied so tight I could have cried, Albert threw me scissors and told me to cut the string and tie the loose end of the ball of string to the leg of the empty chair near Ted. Under his gun, of course I did it. Then he picked up the pair of black iron handcuffs from the helf. "These may be antiques," he said, "but they still work. Sit down. No, wait. Move that chair closer to Ted, where I can aim at you both together. Now sit." I hoped his attention would wander, if only for a minute, so I could slip the knife out. I never got the chance.

I sat down in the chair, so near Ted I could touch him. My arm against his arm. Thanking God he was still warm because he was still alive.

"Now, put your wrists together," Albert snapped, sticking the gun hard into my neck. He was trembling, like he might go berserk at any moment. I put my hands together in my lap. He snapped the black iron handcuffs on my wrists. They were cold and tight. He was breathing hard. "I've never killed anybody on purpose." His voice cracked. "Never in my life. And you're going to force me to do it." Tears ran down below his eyes, but he kept his gun pointed at us. He was shaking all over, like a washing machine just slightly off kilter.

I hoped he'd remember that if he shot us, the sound of the shot might bring help. I don't know guns, but the one by his hand didn't seem to have a silencer. I prayed he wouldn't think of the quiet ways of killing people, like strangulation. "The victims were found strangled with a red Victorian bell cord" — I could see it in the press. See it on the World Memory screen. I prayed that Albert could not read my mind.

He picked up the ball of string with one end tied to the chair leg, circled round and round me, binding my two legs to the chair without putting down the gun. Without taking his eyes off me for a second. When I was so tight to the chair I couldn't kick, he wound the string round and round the top of me. He obviously bought the stuff wholesale. I was tightly anchored to my chair, top and bottom. Tears were still seeping down Albert's face, as he put the gun down long enough to knot the string.

I was not sorry for him. I was furious at myself. Me and my intuition that Albert was not a killer. More fool me. "Albert," I repeated, "I have been your friend. This is not the way you treat a friend."

In answer to that, he took sticky strapping tape and wound it round Ted on top of the string. Albert is thorough. Always has been, damn it. He did the same to me. By the time he got to me, there wasn't much tape left on the roll. He didn't get another roll. I suppose he figured I wasn't as strong as Ted. Never mind, I could hardly wriggle.

Then he turned and went to the file cabinet. I turned my head to Ted. Maybe I hoped he could nod his head in a special way to show how we'd overpower Albert. Us with our string and tape. I hoped he'd come up with a miracle, since I couldn't think of one. Ted sat tense and rigid in the chair, not relaxed and alert like he is when he has a plan of action. He winked at me, and I knew what he meant: *Don't give up.* That's all we had going for us, not to give up. Fortunately, that's one thing I'm good at.

Albert took something out of the green file cabinet: a fifth of Jack Daniel's whiskey. He set it on the little worktable, came over and inspected us to be sure we were immobilized, then picked up a CLOSED sign that was hanging on a hook, and disappeared into the front of the shop.

He came back shortly with a crystal water tumbler — an antique, no doubt. He sat down at the card table facing us, lay the gun near his right hand, and opened the bottle of whiskey. He poured the tumbler full and took a long swig and then another. He sighed. He looked me in the eyes. He drank more whiskey.

"I really love you, Cousin Peaches," he said sadly. Thanks a heap. "I get jealous sometimes," he said, "because whenever you need anything, somebody helps you out. Because you have this I-know-you're-going-to-be-wonderful look that people fall for. But I couldn't kill you on purpose. I set traps you might fall into — or might not. You *are* my friend. I'll miss you a lot."

This was Albert at his very worst. Lying to himself. Sorry for himself. Once I would have gone out of my way to laugh him out of that kind of stuff. But the down-side of Albert wasn't funny anymore. It had taken him beyond the point of no return.

"So you drove up to Pop's at night and rigged the closet light to kill me if I pulled the chain. Because you know I keep clothes in that closet. And to make the trap double-sure, you put water in that cookie tray where I'd step in it. To kill me

393

quick. You are so thoughtful."

"I came across that tray in my basement," he said. "With stuff I got at a sale, which wasn't quite good enough for the shop. The leftovers. I made a good trap. I did think about that. So if Fate intended you to die, you'd die quick. I didn't want to hurt you."

I wanted to say "You bastard!" That wouldn't help.

"I was afraid for you to stay alive. Uncle Harwood said there was something you could almost remember that would solve Nancy's murder. That's the trouble. I can't trust you, Peaches. Sometimes you remember."

I couldn't remember what it was that Pop thought I could almost remember. But it didn't matter now.

"But you must have had your mother's key," Ted said. The voice of reason. "Why did you climb in the window when you came to fix that electric trap?"

"To confuse the police," Albert said. "And it worked. Although it really upset that damn cat. Then I threw away my shoes in two different dumpsters in Charleston in case I left footprints. I'm not dumb."

Not as dumb as me, I thought. To get into this fix.

Much as I hated the man, part of me wished Ben would hurry and come. At least I knew the rule Ben worked by: self-interest. If we could persuade Ben it was in his self-interest not to allow Albert to kill us, we might stand a chance. In his present state, Albert seemed totally unpredictable. Off the wall. Predictable is better.

Albert refilled his whiskey glass and took a large swallow. I prayed he'd drink enough quickly to pass out. If his hand wasn't near the gun, maybe we could yell loud enough so someone would hear us.

"I don't expect you to understand how hard it's going to be for me to have to kill you." Albert said that like even the whiskey wasn't helping. Like he deserved better.

"Cheer up," I said. "You've had the strength of character to try it twice."

"And it did take guts." He took another long pull of whiskey and half smiled. "I knew that if I made a loud noise in your garage in the middle of the night you'd call the police. And it took me a while to get your brakes just right. Not weak enough to go immediately, just enough to go when you jammed your foot down hard in an emergency." His voice slurred slightly on "emergency."

"And Fate came close to getting you that time. Your brakes could have gone in some easy spot. Maybe in traffic when the guy in front of you panic-stopped. And all you'd get is damage to your silly old car." He took another swallow. "But you went over the mountain!" He grinned. Drunk.

Hurry, I thought. Pass out quick. We haven't got all night. Because maybe Farfetched Hope

No. 1 was that Ben would persuade him not to kill us. But Farfetched Hope No. 2 might work better: If Albert passed out, we yelled like crazy and maybe attracted a passer-by. If any.

"You might have died," Albert said very slowly and precisely, "if you hadn't tried one of your silly tricks. My mother used to say 'Peaches has no pride about her silly tricks.' But it worked. Fate saved you with that dog." He took another swallow of whiskey. Good boy.

"And, oh, Christ, now I have no choice. It's my life or yours and Ted's, Peaches. All my life I've been a goddamned victim."

As he raised the bottle to pour more whiskey, I heard a key in the lock of the outer door, then the doorbell jangle hit my nerves like a blow. Ted and I both turned our heads. That must be Ben.

CHAPTER
31

A FEW MINUTES LATER

"For God's sake, Albert," Ben gasped, "what on earth is happening here?" He stared at us as if we should have been ashamed of ourselves, sitting there all tied up. He stared at Albert as if he thought Albert had lost his mind.

"They know everything," Albert said, backing away from Ben. "And what they don't know they suspect. Like how you steal back stuff, and how we sell it. They're going to ruin us."

The skunk. Was he going to let Ben think that's all we knew? And was it possible that Ben really did not even suspect that Albert killed his own mother?

"So what do you think you're going to do about what they know?" Ben asked Albert. He had that tone of voice my third-grade teacher used when the new kid in class wet his pants. Ben raised his eyebrows and pursed his mouth, as if he was sure Albert was going to

397

make the wrong choice.

"I will have to kill them," Albert said. He was still playing martyr.

Ben laughed. He leaned against the door frame as if he didn't want to come closer to us or to Albert. "You're going to commit a crime you could get death for? Don't be silly. You always take things far too seriously, Albert." Ben shook his head as if he was amazed we could be such a joke. "We'll pack up everything valuable in the vans, and we'll take off," he said to Albert. "I know somebody who will hide me, for a price, until things calm down. The police will find these two in a few days."

"You think it's so simple!" Albert blazed. "You got me into this, and now you want to run. To run forever." He looked around that room, like he couldn't bear to leave. Eyes lingering on each thing, especially the clocks. "I only meant to steal the little portrait and the buckle from my Uncle Harwood. And that was his fault. Because my aunt and uncle bought those so cheap. Before I knew what they were worth. And I offered to buy them back. And he wouldn't sell. The old bastard owed me those. And he never would have even noticed they were gone if my mother hadn't interfered." Albert sounded tired. He leaned on the table with his head in his hands, his face in shadow. Because Albert knew it was already too late to avoid murder. He'd killed twice. He said Fate killed Larry. Tell that to a jury!

"And is it *my* fault that I saw the opportunity to steal from other buyers who told us all about their collections?" Ben asked. "You were willing to go along. And to sell to foreign collectors through a rather good fence I know. My dear friend, that's what has finally made this business a success. We are doing very well, you and I. And I'm discreet. You evidently are not." But he didn't know the half of it.

"He killed his mother because she found it out," I blurted. "And that's not all. He killed Larry, when he tried to kill me." Albert's hands trembled so on the gun. I thought he was going to pull the trigger.

"Don't shoot, you fool," Ben cried. He walked over and took the whiskey bottle away from Albert, put the top on, and stowed it back in the file cabinet. For gosh sakes, why didn't he take the gun?

Albert began to shake all over. "My mother was going to make me tell Uncle Harwood I stole his things. My own mother. And God knows he can't keep his mouth shut. They'd have found out the rest. We'd have been ruined." He glanced at Ben as if he wanted approval. As if Ben might say "Of course. I understand." Ben's eyebrows stayed up. He said nothing.

"And even at the last minute I tried to warn her." Albert turned to me as if I was going to say, "That makes it all right."

"She was always that way. Not on my side," he said despairingly, "but I tried to warn her, anyway. After we left my car at her house and went in her car and parked in his driveway. Even after I knew how I could use her flashlight if I had to. But I hoped not to. I really did try." Albert's eyes begged me to believe him.

" 'I want to show you something,' I told my mother. I got out my side of the car with the flashlight in my bad hand, out of sight.

" 'Look at the lights of that big pretentious house with one old miser living in it,' I said. 'He could have lent me the money I needed when the business was doing badly. You know that. He drives me wild. He ought to drive you wild. But instead you want him to ruin me. Because he's crazy. And he will. You know that.'

" 'He likes all the lights on, so no one can hide in the house,' was all she said. 'And that's his business.' "

Ben was hardly listening. He shrugged. "Albert, I don't care about all this shit," Ben said. "I care about saving my ass. And if you're smart, you will too. We'll get out of this place fast, taking the valuable small stuff." He glanced around with dollar signs in his eyes. "You owe me most of it for being such a damn fool. But you can have some, too. I have a place to hide until this cools down. You'll have to find your own. I have to get some junk out of my van."

Ben vanished out the door. Albert ran to the file cabinet, poured himself another drink, and took a large swallow.

He stood unsteadily, staring at us, still on a

talking jag. Well, I sure wasn't going to tell him he had a right to be silent. I wanted to know what happened.

"I was so scared I felt sick. And she turned and began walking slowly towards the house. We were at a bend in Uncle Harwood's drive now, not in sight of the windows. I had to take great long strides to catch up to Mother.

"I may have a deformed hand but I'm strong. I do sit-ups and push-ups." Albert crooked his arm to show the muscle. "I took the flashlight and swung it with every bit of my strength and hit her in the back of the head." He hesitated, like he'd like to stop there.

"Go on," I said.

"It made this awful noise, like smashing a coconut. So I pulled her behind a bush. I expected the back door to open. I heard the television even with the door shut. Nobody came. So I waited a minute and felt Ma's pulse. She was still alive. Then I panicked. God knows what she'd do if she came to. I picked her up and carried her down the gravel path around the house to the pond. No matter how I tried to be quiet, the gravel crunched. It sounded so loud, I expected old big-mouth Arabella Horton down the road to hear and call the police. But, of course, she didn't. I put my mother's face down in the pond. I had to. I was desperate." He glared at me defiantly.

Then he sighed. "There was still time to pull her out. She wasn't dead yet." He shook his head, from side to side: No.

"But all I have is beauty." His eyes ran around the room. "My shop of beautiful things. I may be ugly but I have that. But I stood there for at least a minute. Torn. She had that ugly hole in the back of her head. It was too late. I turned and left her."

I shuddered. Albert was convincing himself it was all logical. And logical to kill us. I didn't believe he'd leave his things and run with Ben. And what was it worth to Ben to save us? A little effort in case he was accused of helping to kill us. But how much?

I was sure Albert shouldn't trust Ben, that Ben was only out to save his own skin. But that wasn't my worry, was it?

Ben came back with a cardboard box and began to fill it with the choicer smaller items, beginning with the little portraits and buckles.

"I need your help, Ben," Albert begged him, voice really slurred by now. "I can't run. I need to load these people in my van and get them out of here." Right at that moment all the clocks in the shop began to bong. Not quite in sync. In many voices. Six o'clock. I thought: the clocks are saying it's too late. Too late for Albert? Too late for us?

Ben's eyes went sharp, calculating. He didn't ask Albert to tell him any more about what he intended to do. I realized what he was up to. He didn't want to be involved any more than he could help. But he didn't want Albert to sit there in the shop and drink till he passed out, either. He didn't want us to get loose, somehow, and call the police before he had plenty of time to get away.

"All right," Ben said. "I'll help you get them in your van and you can take them wherever you want to. It's none of my business. Bargain for a ransom if you want to. And in return, I get to load up all the small valuable antiques in my own van and get out of here."

"He's going to kill us," I said. "You'll be an accessory. There's a law against that."

But Ben was not a person who cared about what happened to people. Just money.

He helped Albert move us, chairs and all, into a corner. They removed the contents of the cavity under the floor, and began to pack boxes. Ben went off somewhere and came back with more boxes and stacks of newspapers for extra packing material. This was serious moving. No hurry. The longer it took, the longer we got to stay alive. After skimming the shelves in the back, they went in the front room and left us. They left the small stone angel, evidently not valuable enough to make up for being heavy. It reminded me of a tombstone. For a child. For the child Albert who I'd seen in my mind, long after he'd turned into somebody else.

If I could wobble my chair even slightly, maybe I could wobble my way over to the scissors Albert had left on his worktable. Maybe they were near enough the level of my bound hands so I could get hold of them. And Ted was struggling to shrug his chair along too. If I got hold of those scissors, I could cut Ted's wrist bonds. Or he could cut mine. But, tied as we were, it was incredibly slow and hard to move without tipping the chair over or making a big noise. Agonizingly slow. When an hour and a half had passed, we'd managed to move a few feet.

Before we'd gotten far enough to reach the scissors, Albert and Ben came back for us. Businesslike. As if we were just part of the packing. Why couldn't *somebody* come to help us? I couldn't hear any sound of life out in the street of shops. But I prayed for a passer-by. It was still daylight, but late enough so that the shops were closed. Albert and Ben carried me between them, chair and all. I caught a glimpse of Ben's blue van, just down the street. Albert's white van was parked with two wheels up on the sidewalk, the side door open close to the shop door. Albert pointed the gun at me and said "No noise." They laid me and the chair on my back in the back of the van. I couldn't see out. My head was too low. I could see my legs sticking out of my foreign correspondent's skirt in front of me. I could see my feet in their familiar loafers, so strangely up in the air tied to the chair legs. I could see boxes stacked in the end of the van. I hoped they wouldn't fall on me if we drove around curves. I turned my head toward the door and saw Albert and Ben shoving Ted and his chair into the side of the van. Ted winked at me again: *Don't give up.* I winked back.

Albert kept his gun on us. "No noise. I shoot the first one who screams." Ben wasn't there to tell him he was a fool. Ben was closing up the shop.

One of my legs touched one of Ted's. I was grateful for that. I managed to move my leg slightly against his, meaning, "I love you." He moved his the little bit he could and I knew he meant the same.

I kept thinking there must be *something* we could do. I couldn't think what. Use ingenuity, I told myself desperately. So what tools did I have?

I had the knife around my neck, totally out of reach. Damn. Why hadn't I put it in my pocket. That was at least nearer my bound hands. I had quarters in my pockets, that was all. A lot of quarters. If I hadn't felt so wretched, I might have laughed. Quarters to make phone calls for help: Chapter nine, page five, *How to Survive Without a Memory.*

My quarters had been of no use when my brakes went. Because it didn't happen in reach of a phone booth. And besides, I was trapped. How thoughtless of Albert not to have arranged a phone booth. Those quarters would be no damn use with me tied to this chair in this van, either. I prayed for inspiration. I prayed for the police to show up.

I heard the shop door close. I heard the door of

Ben's van close and the engine start. He was off to save himself. We were beside the point.

Albert slammed the door of his van. I could tell by the jerky way he took off that he was angry. Ben got the best of him, somehow. Good. Then we drove for a long, long time. Unsteadily, in lurches and bursts of speed. Dear God, I thought. Let Albert be stopped for drunk driving. And don't let him run off the road and kill us all first.

I spent my time straining against my bonds, trying to stretch the string. Every tiny bit of mobility might somehow help. And I couldn't think of anything else to do with even the wildest chance of saving my life.

At the same time I raged against Albert. The snake! I thought about the ways I'd been nice to him, like the time I bought him skates for his seventh birthday.

The van lurched wildly, and Albert said "Boy, I almost fell asleep." Great.

"Talk to us," I said. "That'll keep you awake. I don't guess I ever really knew you like I thought I did."

"No," he said. "You never knew what it was like. Like the time my father beat me with his belt for breaking my mother's best terrine, because she told him to beat me. And then we'd go and visit you all, Peaches, and play the perfect family. And when you knocked a glass of milk on the floor with your elbow, my father and mother just laughed. You could be a scatterbrained fool

406

and nobody cared. And when my father ran over my dog, I invited you to a memorial service and you forgot to come."

That was true. I came at the wrong time, which was no help. "I have always felt bad about that, Albert," I said. "Because I could see it made you feel like nobody cared." In fact that's when I began to seriously collect memory devices. And now I could see that Albert never quite forgave me. And I thought how strange, that of all the sins in my lifetime the most hurtful might be that I was late to a dog's memorial service.

And God knows I never suspected Cousin Albert was angry enough inside to go off the deep end and kill. I might die for not suspecting that. I shuddered. So much for trusting my intuition. And because of me, Ted might die too. I kept straining to loosen or stretch my bonds. I could hear Ted doing the same thing. The van lurched wildly.

"Albert," I yelled, "are you falling asleep again?" Of course. He probably had the bottle of whiskey in the front seat with him. Nipping Dutch courage. Oh, brother!

"And so you were angry enough to kill," Ted said. That should get Albert's attention. "And you stole your mother's pocketbook, to make it look like someone had killed her for that."

"Yes," Albert said. And then he laughed, a weak little drunken tinkle. "I looked pretty silly riding back to my car on funny old Arabella's horse, with a big old broken flashlight in one hand, and a white pocketbook in the other. But I got to my car. And I was pretty smart about the airport. There it was. Right on my way. So handy. Inspiration. Dump the pocketbook. I took the money and the portrait out and dumped it there. As if somebody killed fancy Nancy and then flew away."

And then by sheer chance Florence what's-her-name had come along and taken the pocket-book, and thrown it over the cliff at Buzzard's Rock.

The van lurched so sharply to the right, I thought it was going to turn over. We skidded in something loose like dirt or sand. Then Albert drove along like this was all on purpose, on whatever was first bumpy and then flat. And then the van came to a stop. He said, "By God, we're here!"

Wherever here was. With my head so low, all I could see out the windows was sky, and even that was dark now, with a sprinkling of stars. At least if the stars were one of the last things I was ever going to see, they were lovely bright points against a black velvet sky.

CHAPTER
32

LATER, ON THE BEACH

The side of the van opened and Albert pointed the gun right at my head. "No noise," he said. "And shut your mouth or I'll shoot." He climbed into the back of the van slowly and deliberately, and clambered over to me, even though I was farthest from the door. He pulled out a dispenser of that super-sticky package strapping tape and criss-crossed it over my mouth. He did the same with Ted. Then he climbed back down to the ground and began to pull at Ted's chair.

I could see the top of Albert's head and his hands over Ted. Moonlight streamed in and Ted looked as out-of-kilter and helpless as I felt, with his legs up in the air tied to the chair legs and his back and arms and head down flat, tied to the chair back. Certainly when you were about to be killed you deserved at least to be dignified. I hated Albert. For him I welcomed the idea of the eternal fires of hell.

Albert dragged the chair to the edge of the van where the side door was open. He pulled until Ted and chair fell over, making a dull, creaky thud. I felt in my bones how hard he hit. Ted could not even cry out. All I could hear was Albert breathing hard from the effort. He never was very athletic. I heard a rhythmic, whishing sound. Then more dragging noise.

Albert was efficient, right? Why was he moving Ted alive and bound to a clumsy chair? Dead would be easier. Dead men don't need chairs. But thank God for alive, except I knew Albert didn't intend for us to stay that way. The air smelled brackish. I realized I was smelling sea air. The rhythmic sound was waves on a beach. What would Albert do? Drown us? My stomach turned over. Suppose he was dragging Ted into water over his head? And I couldn't even scream. I made what sound I could in my throat.

"You be quiet!" Albert was back. He pulled me to the edge and I bumped down so hard I almost blanked out. I mustn't.

I could tilt my head back far enough so that I could see behind us. Surprise. In the distance was a lighted building with a sign. It took me a minute to figure it out upside down. "The Anchor." It must be across a road from the beach. Far enough so no one would be likely to notice us, in spite of the full moon. But I also began to understand what Albert was doing. He was gambling. Taking a chance. Making Fate take responsibility for whether we died. By leaving a very slight chance that someone might see us. Kidding himself that if we died it would be due to chance, not Albert.

He pulled me by the feet across the sand, the lower part of me riding on the chair like a sleigh, feet up in the air. But my head and shoulders dragged directly in the sand. He was dragging me towards the water, breathing hard. I could move my hands slightly. I remembered Hansel and Gretel who dropped crumbs to make a trail to find their way out of the woods. I wanted somebody to find their way to me. Hey, I did have quarters! I managed to get some out of one pocket, and let them drop to the beach. All together, so somebody might notice. Then I squirmed my hands to the other pocket. My string bindings were not loose enough to escape, but they were squirmable. I began to drop those other quarters, one by one for a trail. Now the beach was bumpy with small stones or shells. From the corner of my eye I saw movement, and turned my head sideways to see sand fiddlers, scuttling away. The sand was wet and flat. Low tide. I ran out of quarters before Albert stopped dragging.

We'd reached a spot where some pilings stood up. The remains of a dock, and there was a chunk of a cement wall, left from some building, not yet entirely battered away by the waves. Albert dragged me to the sea side of the bit of wall, into the shallow edge of the water. I caught a glimpse of Ted and his chair in deeper water.

411

"I am sorry about this, Cousin Peaches," Albert said. He looked so bizarre, his head seen between my feet still lashed to the chair feet. The moon behind him, turning him into a shadow man. "Sometimes you were kind to me." He actually sounded tearful, half-choked. But not tearful enough. He took another piece of rope and tied me, chair and all, to one of the pilings. No wriggling up the beach.

Then I heard Albert's footsteps crunch up the beach. I didn't hear him pause as if he were picking up quarters. Score one point for our side. Maybe we had a one-in-ten-thousand chance of being found before the tide came in and stopped our breath. If someone came walking on the beach, they might just see the quarters leading to us and think further. Maybe. I kept working at my bonds, and also praying.

The wavelets came higher and higher. The tide was coming in. Each wave lap, first out, then in, washing around me, wetting the back of my head against the sand. And Ted was in deeper water. He'd drown first. Because of me. I couldn't see but a hint of him, he was on the chair-bottom side of me. I made the only noise I could make in my throat, like a sick cow. Ted made a sick-bull noise. Which was beautiful to me. He was still alive.

I listened so hard for the least sound of feet on the beach that my ears ached. My nose itched and I couldn't scratch it. I thought how unfair that was. *The condemned woman died without*

412

being able to scratch her nose.

Hansel and Gretel escaped. I clutched at straws.

There was nobody on the beach. And why should there be? It must be eleven-thirty or twelve. If The Anchor was a restaurant, it would be closed. If it was a bar, it probably had a legal closing hour. Midnight? Nobody would be on the beach and nobody would be across the road. An ambitious wave half-covered my face. Was Ted under water?

If I could just work my hands far enough around to get hold of a shell, I might use it to saw through my bonds. I couldn't reach a shell. I could move my hands side to side to reach my pockets, I couldn't move them up to the knife around my neck. I kept trying to work my bonds looser. But now there wouldn't be time. Water lapped over my face again. I held my breath until the water receded. And the waves would wash my Hansel and Gretel quarters away! But they were farther back from the water. By then I'd be dead.

Then I heard laughter mixed with music in the distance. People were walking down the beach. I mooed as loud as I could. Ted joined in. A crazy harmony. Hardly as loud as the ocean waves. The music came closer and drowned us out. That and kids all laughing and talking together. Kids to me. They must have been teens or even young twenties, judging by their voices. The wall hid them. "Hey, look," one yelled. "Here's some quarters." A cloud came over the moon. "I can feel them with my feet!" one yelled. "Walk around — that's the easiest way to find them."

They've got to hear us. They've got to find us. I told myself that. Suppose they came this close and could only hear and see each other. Damn self-centered kids.

They came closer, music louder, there was no way they were going to hear me. Another wave came over my head. I kept hoping the water might loosen the tape on my mouth. No luck. At least the moon was back out from under the clouds. I wouldn't die in the total dark.

"This is all the quarters I can find," a kid said. "Let's go." I mooed as loud as I could. Music blared. They began to move down the beach.

I gave up mooing. My throat hurt from the effort. I had done everything I could think to do and it hadn't worked. A wave came so high so suddenly that I breathed in water. Panic grabbed me. I thought of Ted winking. A wink meant don't give up. Dear God, please let us live.

I had to give my whole effort to grabbing a breath whenever the water was low enough, and holding my breath between. I'd loved the beach, and the beach was going to kill me. I'd always loved the full moon. The moon would watch us die. Ted must be drowning. No sound from him. I was about to drown. Soon only our feet would be above the water. Whoever found us would find us dead. I hated that person for not coming quick.

But then the water pulled way back. I had a short breather — in every sense of the word. I heard a young squeaky voice, very pleased with itself. "But look here, these funny marks down the sand, like somebody pulled something. Go on around that junk." Somebody had lagged behind, a girl.

A boy's voice: "You expect a pot of gold at the end of the marks?" The girl laughed. "No. But let's look."

He said, "I didn't come here to *look*."

"But there is kind of a noise. Don't I hear something?" she asked.

"An ocean ghost. Run!" he teased. I mooed loud as I could and prayed with all my being: *Don't run.* If they ran and I died, I'd haunt him silly.

But then they were both near me, gasping to see me tied up, and screaming for the others to come back.

Kids were pulling me back, pulling the tape off my mouth. I heard someone say, "Here's another one. This is bad! He's dead!" Ted. I wouldn't let him be dead.

The tape was off my mouth. I gasped, "CPR! Get me loose. I can do it."

The tallest boy said, "I can do that. I'm a lifeguard," like he deserved a prize. Then he began wrestling with Ted and his chair. He called out, "I can't get him untied from this chair. It's gonna be too late."

There was less of that awful strapping tape

around me, they nearly had me loose. Except for the handcuffs. But I could move my manacled hands up to my neck. I pulled out my pocket knife.

Life Guard grabbed it, struggled to open it quick, and cut Ted free fast. They lay him down on the beach, and the next minute Life Guard was blowing air into Ted's mouth, then pushing his chest with stiff arms in a quick rhythm. I wished I was the one that close to him, but I didn't have the strength. I tried to stand up, and was so dizzy I sat back down on the sand again. All the kids gathered round Ted, almost as anxious as I was. I wanted to hug them all. I also wanted to tell them to get out of the way.

The kids crowded around and then Life Guard told them "Hey, get back!" Then they crowded round again. This was taking too long. I sat on the beach about three feet from Ted, and prayed. In that cold moonlight, he looked dead. Even his hair was plastered to his head, wet, no longer standing up. His body moved with Life Guard's movements, not with his own.

"Please don't leave me, Ted," I said. "Please."

And one of the kids gasped out to another: "Gee. I never saw a dead man, did you?" And I began to cry.

And then there was a ripple of noise in the group that had pulled back closer around Ted, and Life Guard puffed, "Get back! Give him air!"

And I thought: If he needs air, he's alive. He's

started breathing! I threw myself towards him, but someone took hold of my arm and pulled me back. It was a man in a uniform. A state trooper? Where did he come from? He said: "Are you Peaches? And if you're not, who is? We have to find someone named Peaches quick. Or she'll be dead."

Another siren sounded. Another car arrived. A man and a woman in uniform got out and ran over to State Trooper and me. With them was a big man not in uniform. He had a deep, gruff voice. "Yeah. This crazy man in the bar said there were two people left on the beach to drown, and one was named Peaches. I swear."

"I'm Peaches," I said. I wanted to get them over with. Ted was breathing.

I ran over and put my arms around Ted. "You're alive!" He was wet and cold as a fish. "You make a good blanket," he whispered. But I was replaced. Someone brought a real blanket and put it around him. From the police car, no doubt. Someone said an ambulance was coming. The policewoman took me in tow.

One of the kids was saying, "We followed the quarters on the beach, and there they were, tied up and almost drowned. Say," he said. "I guess we were smart. We saved 'em!" I was pretty sure he was the same one who said I might be a ghost. Smart. Ha ha. A policeman led him off.

The big man with the gruff voice kept talking. "This guy came in the bar, and had a couple of drinks, and I was about to tell him that was all. He was sitting there crying, must have had a snootful before he arrived."

Albert, I thought. Policewoman was trying to ask me something, but my ears were glued to Gruff. "And then this guy came over and pointed a gun at me, and I thought, Good God, a stickup. And he said, 'There are two people tied up waiting to drown on the beach. And I can't do it. Tell my Cousin Peaches she wins.' And then he turned that gun around and shot himself right in the mouth."

And I surprised myself. I began to cry again. Policewoman handed me a tissue out of her pocket. She was patient.

I could still hear Gruff. "I was stunned," he said, "that a man would shoot himself in *my* bar. That part about two people drowning on the beach, why, that just didn't sink in, and I called the law about this dead man in the bar" — he nodded to the police types — "and then Marsha here kept pulling my arm and saying, 'We have to see about those people on the beach,' and I said 'By God we do, because sometimes even crazy men tell the truth.' And I kept thinking: his Cousin *Peaches*. There was this transvestite bar with a dancer named Peaches. Was that the Peaches on the beach?"

I have certainly never been a transvestite. I would've remembered that.

So, I thought, Albert made a choice to kill himself instead of Ted and me. Since we were both alive, I partly forgave him for nearly drowning us. Albert didn't have the ingenuity to avoid extremes. To bend instead of break. And worse yet, he hadn't been able to make up his mind as fast as the tide came in. He'd almost killed me and Ted as well as himself.

CHAPTER
33

A WEEK LATER, BACK IN ASHEVILLE

I felt all lighted up with Christmas-tree lights, the blinking ones in many colors. I held Ted's hand as we drove over to Pop's house. So Ted was driving too fast with only one hand on the wheel — I wasn't going to worry. How could he be perfect? His hand, which I'd been forced by Albert to tie up, was free and solid and warm. He was sitting in the car in the proper, approved position — head up, feet down. Of all the things in my life that I'd expected to be grateful for, sitting head-up wasn't one. But I was profoundly grateful.

And so glad that we didn't have to worry who might be following us or trying to kill me. Maybe I was even a little thankful that I'd almost died. And that made me know how I loved Ted. And that Roger wouldn't mind. Roger would be glad. Of course he would.

Roger would even have approved of the way Ted asked me to marry him the final and official time. He'd come by my house at eight o'clock the night after we got back from our "trip to the beach." Looking pretty good for somebody just twenty-four hours from almost drowning. His hair had entirely recovered and was sticking out cheerfully. Nothing dampens that twinkle in his eyes. In one hand he had a quart of chocolate frozen yogurt. That's my favorite dessert and his, too. In the other hand he had a large bunch of red roses with an extremely realistic artificial bee sticking to the top rose. "This is what marriage is like," he said. "A beautiful bunch of roses, but not without an occasional bee sting. We could make the most of both together. We've proved it.

"That proof is not," he said, "to be confused with the birds and the bees and the flowers your mother told you about. Which are important, too."

The yogurt melted because we forgot about it. There are times when I recommend forgetting. Pop would have been deeply shocked, or pretended to be, because Ted never went home that night. In fact he'd more or less moved into my house. And now, a week later, I could hardly imagine what the house was like without him. Empty. That's what.

Now we were on our way to Pop's.

"I'm so curious about Pop," I said. "He said he had something important to tell me, and specially wanted you to come, since we're engaged, and since we're both still alive. That's how he put it. But he wouldn't say what it was."

"He appreciates the dramatic value of suspense. Perhaps he wants to give us an engagement present," Ted said.

"But he acted so strange. Almost belligerent. Almost bullying. 'If you expect me to leave you anything in my will, be here by two o'clock.' Back to that old canard.

"Of course, he's been upset about Albert," I sighed. I felt a pang of sadness. For the little Albert who made a bunny that looked like a leopard, and was almost like my own child. "At least my intuition was partly right about Albert. In the end he couldn't kill me."

"Just almost."

"He killed himself really the night he killed his mother," I said. "Because whatever else she was, she was his mother. And people mattered to Albert. Even while he gambled with killing."

"What I have never understood," Ted said, "is why Albert called and suggested we put that miniature and the belt plate in the safe-deposit box. That meant we were bound to notice they were missing. Why would he want us to do that?"

I shook my head. "I don't know. Maybe deep down he wanted to be caught. Or maybe he figured that if he was the one who insisted we take care of those things, we would never suspect that he stole them. Once I thought I knew Albert. Now I know I didn't. And boy, was that dangerous!"

I looked in the rearview mirror. At quite a distance behind us I saw the black car I'd seen shortly after we left my house. Appearing, disappearing, on the windy road. Were we being followed? I remembered the car that seemed to follow me just before I went over the mountainside. Afterwards I assumed it had just been a car traveling the same way. Was that wrong? Oh, come on! All that stuff had to be over. But why would the car go as exactly too fast as Ted did? Very odd. Unsettling.

"Pop was back to being afraid, yesterday," I said. "The excitement of all the real danger we were in seemed to help keep his mind clear. How strange. Now he's in and out of reality again. Yesterday he told me Hannibal's army was about to attack. He's been reading a biography of Hannibal — or getting Elsie to read it to him. So I reminded him Hannibal died a long, long time ago, and his conquering had to end when he couldn't cross the Alps with elephants."

"Did that calm him down?"

"Mostly," I said. "I wheeled him around to look out every window and see that nobody was in sight."

"Good."

"But then he said, O.K., he wouldn't worry if I would absolutely promise to tell him if I saw an elephant."

Ted laughed. "I'll help look."

"Is that black car following us?" I asked.

"I can't think why anybody would follow us," he said. "Nobody has a reason to kill you anymore. Since the police even picked up Ben in Prosperity." Imagine — Ben being picked up in *Prosperity*, South Carolina.

The car turned after us as we turned into Town Mountain Road. We turned into Pop's driveway and parked. The black car caught up with us, and turned in and stopped, too. Homer Sawyer, Pop's lawyer, stepped out. He lives down the road beyond me.

I should have remembered Homer has a black car. He has a formal black-car kind of personality. He wears white shirts, a fountain pen in his jacket pocket, and a poker face at all times. As far as I can make out, he has no sense of humor, but he's absolutely thorough, and kind to Pop. I like him. I think he likes me. I don't think he ever knew that Pop considered him a suspect. He would not have cared for that.

Homer congratulated us, first on our rescue at the beach, and then on our engagement. We all went in together. Pop was sitting in his wheelchair, looking out the window at the garden. He whirled that chair around so fast I knew he thought we might be burglars. "Homer," he said in a greatly relieved voice. "You're just in time for a piece of chocolate cake my cousin Gloria brought me. She's the best cook in North Carolina."

"Then Gloria's not mad at us any more?" I was glad.

He turned and examined me. "I'm often right, you know, Peaches," he said, as if I'd said he wasn't. "You remember how you were sure that Nancy was killed in a dress just like yours for some reason that had to do with you?"

Well, thank goodness that had been by pure chance. What did it have to do with chocolate cake? Anything?

"And I said that if she got a dress like yours at a sale it was because she was as broke as she said she was."

Why was he remembering that?

"When Nancy was broke, it brought out the worst in her," he said, nodding to himself. "Always did since she was a kid and robbed the pennies from my pants pockets. The worst in her came out, so Albert killed her. And that brought out the worst in Albert. I could have solved the whole thing."

Then he turned to Homer. "I'm glad you're here. I want to speak to you alone."

So Ted and I went into the kitchen. Elsie was out there making custard. Pop always wants custard when he feels in need of comfort. Elsie was stirring it in a double boiler at the stove. She saw us and flushed. Her eyes were red, almost matching her red hair.

"I'm sorry," she stammered. "I don't mean to keep crying. But when I think I'm going to be alone, and no one will see, I let myself cry."

"You have a right," I said. I went over and hugged her, smelling the sweetness of the custard, the saltiness of her tears. Feeling her tremble.

She pulled the custard off the burner, and sobbed. "I should have known that whoever I picked to love would be loused up. That's the way I am. Albert was like that. My husband is like that. I don't know why."

I said, "You're the kind of person who wants to help."

"Well, now I'm going to help *me*," she said. "I'm going back home and face the charges. I'm going to prove that I shot my husband in self-defense. Your father says he'll pay for F. Lee Bailey to defend me." I was amazed. What had come over Pop? But then he gave my mother that splendid diamond ring. And he was deeply fond of Elsie.

Elsie wiped her eyes on her hand. "Oh, by the way," she said, "your cousin Gloria left a message for you. I bet your father forgot it."

"You win the bet."

"She said to tell you never to believe a word she said when she was angry, and she'd be by to bring you an angel food cake." Elsie looked confused at that. I didn't enlighten her.

"Peaches!" Pop was bawling for me.

I gave Elsie one last squeeze and went back out into the living room. Pop was at his table, with Homer next to him. In front of Homer were some documents. What on earth?

Pop waved his hand in his grandest manner and indicated we should all sit around the table.

426

He got right down to business. "I intend to leave my money to charity so no one will kill me," he said, pointing at the documents. His last will and testament? "I believe I have been the target all along. After Albert killed Peaches, all he had to do was kill Eve and Mary and me. And he almost succeeded in killing Peaches. So I won't tempt anybody." He sounded like I'd threatened him.

"But Homer here says I have to leave you enough to be comfortable in your old age or you can break the will. If I leave you enough to be comfortable in your old age, will you promise not to kill me?"

"It would be nice," I said dryly, "if you also left something to Eve and Mary."

"Yes," he said, "or they might break the will. I'd better leave something to them both." He nodded at Homer. "Or you'll all gang up on me.

"Of course," Pop added, "If Mary is in my will, that John Q. Denton may marry her for her money. He's taking her out, you know. Arabella is jealous." He chuckled at that.

Homer coughed. "I have persuaded your father that if he wishes to leave money to charity, he leave it to the Community Foundation in a donor-directed account, with the provision that you may have a say in how the money is to be given after he is gone, and Eve may have a say after you are gone."

Well, good old Homer. I'd enjoy that. And Homer pointed to the documents. "This will sees that you are well provided for. And also Mary and also Eve "

Pop was trembling and frowning. Did he think I was going to raise hell about the will? Or had he seen an elephant?

I prayed that when I was old and sick I wouldn't be paranoid.

I kissed Pop. "Luckily," I said, "I'm not the type who likes to play the stock market." I saw he found it hard to believe that. Because he liked to play the stock market so much.

I asked him if he remembered a song he used to sing me when I was a kid, about a place where money grew on trees. We sang it. Ted joined in on the chorus. Even Homer joined in on the chorus without ever changing his poker face. Pop began to relax. We sang the song about the Big Rock Candy Mountain where the cops have wooden legs, the bulldogs all have rubber teeth, and the hens lay hard-boiled eggs.

"Do you remember the poem you used to recite to me about Old Aunt Dinah?" I asked. And he recited it perfectly:

Old Aunt Dinah was so fat,
She couldn't wear nothin' but a beaver hat.
By and by she grew so tall,
She couldn't wear anything at all.

"I'm glad you remembered that poem," Pop said. He smiled at me, doing one of those sudden turnarounds. "Peaches," he said, "I like the way

428

you remember the things that really matter."

"She did more than that," Ted said, "and don't you forget it. She outwitted the killer like she said she would. She saved my life. And maybe yours."

Pop inclined his head graciously. He reached out his hand as if he might be King Arthur ready to knight me. "We're going to dub you the Absent-Minded Detective," he said.

I thanked him. "As Mary would say, I have solved both cases: my first and my last."

Pop shook his head. "Oh, I hope not. You haven't done a damn thing about the burglars on the roof."